ALSO BY STEPHEN FREY

The Takeover
The Vulture Fund
The Inner Sanctum
The Legacy
The Insider
Trust Fund
The Day Trader
Silent Partner
Shadow Account
The Chairman
The Protégé

THE POWER BROKER

BALLANTINE BOOKS

NEW YORK

THE POWER BROKER

A NOVEL

STEPHEN FREY

The Power Broker is a work of fiction. Names, characters, places, and incidents are the products of the author's imagination or are used fictitiously. Any resemblance to actual events, locales, or persons, living or dead, is entirely coincidental.

Published in the United States by Ballantine Books, an imprint of The Random House Publishing Group, a division of Random House, Inc., New York.

BALLANTINE and colophon are registered trademarks of Random House, Inc.

ISBN 0-345-48060-0

Printed in the United States of America on acid-free paper

www.ballantinebooks.com

9 8 7 6 5 4 3 2 1

FIRST EDITION

For Diana and our new daughter, Elle—
I love you both so much.

ACKNOWLEDGMENTS

Special thanks to Cynthia Manson, my agent; and Mark Tavani, my editor.

Thanks also to Jim and Anmarie Galowski, Gina Centrello, Kevin "Big Sky" Erdman, Dr. Teo Forcht Dagi, Stephen Watson, Matt Malone, Chris Tesoriero, Andy Brusman, Gerry Barton, Baron Stewart, Jack Wallace, Gordon Eadon, Marvin Bush, Bart Begley, Barbara Fertig, Bob Wieczorek, Scott Andrews, Jeff Faville, Jamie Faville, John Piazza, Bob Carpenter, Pat and Terry Lynch, and Mike Pocalyko.

PROLOGUE

TWO YOUNG MEN knelt side by side in front of a crude altar—a wooden crate they'd found in a cobblestoned alley off Nassau Street—covered with an azure cloth. On the altar was a human skull flanked by two candles. Before the skull lay a polished saber, a Bible open to a favorite passage, and a rolled parchment. Several dark drops stained the Bible and the parchment. Blood from cuts the young men had slashed in their palms.

When the clock on the wall chimed midnight, one of the young men stood and moved behind the altar, pulling the hood of his black robe over his head until only his face was visible in the dim light cast by the flickering candles. With trembling hands he picked up the parchment and untied its scarlet ribbon. Then he solemnly read the flowing script aloud, pausing at the end of a sentence or a long phrase so the other man could repeat after him. When he was finished, they changed positions and repeated the sacrament.

After they had both taken the oath, they shook hands and moved to a desk in one corner of the dormitory room. There they signed a confession, each of them inhaling deeply, thinking long and hard before finally picking up the quill and scratching their names at the bottom of the page. Admitting in detail to the recent rape of a sixteen-year-old girl from town who hadn't gone to the police because they'd threatened to kill her if she did. They were both from prominent Northeastern families. They could deal with the jail sentences—maybe—but not with the shame they'd cast on their families if the crime ever came to light.

Ink dry, they stored the confession, the parchment, the skull, and the Bible in a combination safe in the closet. Then they wrapped the saber in a blanket and slid it under one of the beds in the room.

There were two of them now. They needed seven more.

PART ONE

1

CHRISTIAN GILLETTE sat on the balcony of his suite at Caesar's Palace in Las Vegas, watching first light scale the craggy peaks in the distance. In a few hours tourists would be mobbing the casino on the ground floor. He hoped soon it would be *his* casino they'd be mobbing.

Christian ran Everest Capital, a Manhattan-based investment firm that owned thirty companies in a wide range of industries—smokestack to high-tech. The companies were all large, at least a billion in sales, and Christian chaired eighteen of them. He also chaired Central States Telecom and Satellite, a communications company in Chicago that Everest had taken public six months ago—after owning for three years. Everest had made four hundred million on the CST initial public offering—Christian had gotten twenty of that. Forty years old, he'd already made fifty times more than most people did in a lifetime, but it hadn't gone to his head. Money was just money, and success could be fleeting.

He dialed Nigel Faraday's cell number. Nigel was one of Everest's five managing partners. There were sixty-four people at the firm, but, other than his assistant, Debbie, the five partners were Christian's only direct reports. Beneath the partners was a burgeoning pyramid of managing directors, vice presidents, and associates, but he rarely dealt with them. Five years ago, he'd known everyone at Everest by name. He missed those days.

Nigel answered on the third ring. "Well, well, you gambling, Chris?"

Nigel had lived in the United States for almost twenty years, but his British accent remained heavy. "Sitting in front of some one-armed bandit with your bucket of quarters?" He laughed. "Ah, the *slot machine*. Another wonderful contribution to mankind from you Americans. Right up there with rap music and the Big Mac."

Playing the slots actually sounded like fun to Christian, if only for its pure simplicity, but there wasn't time. It seemed like there never was anymore for things like that. "Hey, I don't mind rap once in a while, and I don't know why you, of all people, would bash the Big Mac. You've eaten your share."

"Hey, chap, what I eat is my business."

"Relax, *chap,* I'm just kidding." Christian heard traffic in the background at the other end of the line—horns blaring, engines revving, tires skidding. "Where are you?"

"Walking down Park. Bit of a late start to the office this morning, I'm afraid."

Nigel was huffing as he strode toward Everest's Park Avenue headquarters. The Brit was thirty pounds overweight thanks to a steady diet of rocky road ice cream and those Big Macs. "Up late last night?" Christian asked. Nigel was fresh into a new relationship with a pretty brunette he'd met a few weeks ago. They were in the infatuation stage, calling each other five times a day and staying out late every night. "I don't want that woman distracting you, no matter how wonderful she is."

"Look, I—"

"No, no, I'm glad you're finally enjoying yourself," Christian broke in. Nigel had put in a lot of long days the last few years, taking care of administrative details so Christian could focus on the big picture. Nigel had been Mr. Inside so Christian could be Mr. Outside, and the formula worked. Both *Forbes* and *Fortune* had tabbed Everest Capital as one of the top investment firms. "Now, any updates?"

Dead air.

"Nigel?"

"Just one."

Christian picked up something in Nigel's tone, and a tiny alarm went off in his head. "What?"

"After you left for Vegas last night, I got an e-mail from Bob Galloway."

Bob Galloway was the chief financial officer of CST. Despite being chairman of CST, Christian didn't know Galloway well, just saw him for a few hours at quarterly board meetings. Nigel, on the other hand, knew Galloway very well. Though Nigel wasn't technically a CST officer like Christian, he was Everest's day-to-day person on the investment. The one at Everest who constantly kept up with how CST was doing. The one who knew CST's financial staff and had been in charge of dealing directly with the lawyers and investment bankers during the IPO.

"Some woman from the Securities and Exchange Commission called Galloway yesterday," Nigel explained.

Hearing from the SEC was like hearing from the IRS or the Grim Reaper: Safe bet it wasn't good news. "What did she want?" Christian asked.

"She called to demand a meeting. Didn't tell Galloway any more than that."

"Okay, call Galloway as soon as we're finished. Tell him to get back in touch with the SEC right away and find out what's going on. Let me know as soon as you hear anything. And, Nigel?"

"Yeah?"

"Make sure Galloway doesn't mention this to anyone else at CST."

"Sure, sure."

Christian heard a trace of fear in Nigel's tone. "It'll be fine, pal. Don't worry."

"Oh, I'm worried all right," Nigel admitted.

"Being worried doesn't help."

"Sorry I'm human. I'm glad you can stay so cool about it, Chris, but those people scare the hell out of me. They can destroy anybody anytime. Remember that guy who got twenty years for telling his girlfriend he had a stock tip over the phone, when what he really said was he had a sock that was ripped?"

"What guy? I don't remember that."

"And with my accent," Nigel continued, "I could see it happening to me."

"It's not like that."

"Oh yeah? Ask the guys at Enron and MCI."

"They got what they deserved."

"You'll be whistling a different tune when they bust into Everest and lead you and me out in shackles in front of the whole firm."

Sometimes Nigel panicked too quickly. He didn't have many faults, but hitting the eject button prematurely was one of them. "That call Galloway got was probably nothing, probably just some kind of follow-up on the IPO."

"I hope so. Hey, what about the casino license?" Nigel asked, his voice growing stronger as he switched subjects. "Everything all right there? Opening day isn't far off."

Two years ago Everest Capital had won the National Football League's new Las Vegas franchise and named it the Dice. They'd spent over seven hundred million for the team and a new stadium they were building east of the city. As part of the deal with the NFL, Christian had gotten permission to build a casino, also naming it the Dice. The casino was supposed to open the day of the team's home opener, which was just a few months away. On top of the seven hundred million for the team and the stadium, Everest had forked out a billion on construction of the casino—which was almost finished. Now, at the last minute, the Nevada Gaming Commission was holding off on approving the operating license. What seemed like a dream come true a month ago was turning into a nightmare. Christian hadn't told anyone else at the firm how bad the situation was.

"We'll get the license," he assured Nigel. Trying to figure out what was going on with the license was Christian's main reason for coming to Las Vegas. At two o'clock he was meeting with the chairman of the Gaming Commission. "Don't sweat it." Sometimes it seemed like he spent half his life convincing people there wasn't any smoke and the other half putting out fires.

"You think the Mob's involved?" Nigel asked. "Think they're holding the commission up for some last-minute dough?"

"I don't know. That's why I'm here, to find out."

"Didn't we hire somebody in Vegas to take care of those things, to deal with the Mob? Like most people out there do when they're building something big. What's his name?"

"Carmine Torino." Christian had been trying to reach Torino for a week, but suddenly no one could find him. Until now the guy had never taken more than fifteen minutes to return his call. Torino had vanished into thin air.

"Yeah, right, Carmine Torino."

"I've gotta go, Nigel. Ray Lancaster's going to be here in a few minutes."

Ray Lancaster was the Dice's head coach and general manager. Christian had hired him away from the Tampa Bay Buccaneers last February. Nigel had gone to Florida to do the negotiating on the contract, so this was going to be Christian's first face-to-face meeting with Lancaster.

"Ray's tough," Nigel warned.

"He better be. I want the Dice in the play-offs this season so we get all that extra publicity for the casino. Call me back when—"

"What about Laurel Energy?" Nigel interrupted. "Anything on that? Are we close to selling it?"

Christian let out a ten-ton sigh. "Let's talk about it later." Laurel Energy was a Canadian oil and gas company—and another Everest problem child. Christian—and everyone else at Everest—had been anticipating a huge profit on the sale of Laurel, but it had been on the market for a while and there weren't any takers. Just a few nibbles from bottom feeders, and no one could figure out what was wrong because it was reserve-rich. "I've got to go," he said firmly. "Call me back when Galloway knows why the SEC's snooping around CST so I can—"

"Where's Allison?"

Another of Nigel's annoying habits. Sometimes it was impossible to get him off the phone. "What?"

"Where's Allison? I've been trying to get her for days. She's been out of the office and hasn't returned my calls."

Allison Wallace was another of Everest's five managing partners. "She's on the West Coast working on that deal, you know, that company she's been trying to buy for a month. Aero Systems. I talked to her last night. It's going pretty well. She thinks the sellers are about to agree to terms."

Nigel snorted. "I guess the bitch doesn't think I'm important enough to call back."

"Hey, Nigel, none of that. She's just—" There was a loud rap on the suite door. "Talk to you later, Nigel." Christian slipped the phone in his pocket as the person in the hallway knocked again, louder this time. "Who is it?"

"Ray Lancaster."

"Hi, Ray," Christian said, extending his hand when he'd opened the door.

Lancaster had played defensive back for the Lions in the early eighties, but age and the stress of coaching had clearly caught up with him.

His curly black hair was thinning and streaked with gray, his cheeks were pudgy, and there was a bulging spare tire beneath his shirt. Like Nigel, Ray probably ate a lot of his frustration.

"Christian Gillette. Thanks for coming so early."

"No problem, been looking at tapes since five this morning. First game's closing in. Cleveland Browns. We're gonna kick some ass. At least on defense."

"Good. I want to make the play-offs this season."

Lancaster stopped short. "Well, I don't know if we're—"

"Let's go out on the balcony," Christian suggested, motioning toward the back of the suite. "I like it." Christian pointed at the Dice logo on Lancaster's aqua golf shirt as they sat down. Two tumbling die—one showing a single dot, the other six—with a sharp orange flame trailing behind them.

"Yeah, it's way cool."

"How's your family doing?" Lancaster and his second wife had two boys—one thirteen, one eleven. Whenever Christian relocated an executive he always worried about the family adapting to the new city. If the family wasn't happy, neither was the executive. "Las Vegas is a big change from Tampa."

"They're fine. Thanks for asking."

Lancaster seemed anxious, like something was on his mind. "Everything all right, Ray?"

"I should have called you after we inked my contract, but, well, better late than never." Lancaster looked directly into Christian's eyes. "Thanks for giving me this chance. I owe you."

Lancaster hadn't been the Buccaneers general manager in Tampa, just head coach, so this was a big promotion. "Win me a Super Bowl and we'll call it even."

Lancaster laughed nervously. *"Yeah, right."* He tugged at the front of his shirt like it had suddenly gotten tight. "I didn't think I'd ever get a shot to be a GM in this league," he continued, skirting Christian's Super Bowl demand. "Hardly any black men get to be head coach in the NFL, let alone GM."

"You've won a lot of football games. You got the Bucs to the NFC championship last year without a lot of talent. You deserve this."

"And I really didn't think I'd get a shot from a *white* man," Lancaster went on. "I thought I might eventually get it from a black owner, but not a guy like you."

Christian could tell it had been tough for Lancaster to admit that. "I don't judge a person by his skin, Ray, I really don't. I look at track record and work ethic, and I listen to what people close to him say." Christian understood the value of letting a camel get his nose into the tent every once in a while, the value of giving someone a brief window into his life, even if it was just momentary. "I grew up in a big house in LA, Ray. We had a couple of Hispanic maids, and my stepmother treated them like dirt. Not because they were maids, because they were Hispanic. I hated that."

Lancaster thought on that, then nodded.

"Now," Christian said emphatically, "how many games are we going to win this season?"

Lancaster gazed out over Las Vegas, his eyes finally focusing on the tower of the Stratosphere Hotel in the distance. It was easily the tallest structure in Las Vegas, over eleven hundred feet, with several terrifying rides at the top. "It's gonna be a wild year. We'll have a lot of close games."

"Why?"

"We got a good defense but no quarterback worth a damn. We're not going to score many points. It'll come down to the last possession in a lot of games."

"You going to start Ricky Poe at quarterback?"

"He's the only game in town. We picked him up in the expansion draft from the Cowboys, but he's—"

"Not taking anybody to the promised land," Christian broke in. "Yeah, I know. So make a trade. We've got a couple of all-pro linebackers you can use as bait. If I have to choose, I'll take a top quarterback over a top linebacker any day."

Lancaster nodded, impressed. "Did you play something at Princeton?"

"Rugby."

"Man, that's tough. Basically football with no pads."

Christian turned his head so Lancaster had a profile. "Broke my nose twice. The second time it was almost in my left ear when I came to."

Lancaster made a grim face.

"Thank God for plastic surgeons."

"Uh-huh, well, look, I've been trying to make a trade for weeks and won't nobody talk to me."

"What do you mean?" For the second time in a few minutes that tiny alarm went off in Christian's head.

"I've been calling other coaches around the league, guys I'm close to. Guys who need linebackers and have a good backup quarterback. Guys who would be real likely to trade, but they ain't calling me back. Christian, these are guys I was on staff with at other teams, guys I go way back with. I even played with a couple of them. But it's like somebody got to them, like somebody told them not to talk to me."

"That's ridiculous."

"I know how it sounds, but I don't know how else to explain it."

Christian's cell phone rang. "Excuse me, Ray."

"Sure."

"What's up, Nigel?" he asked, turning away from Lancaster.

"Galloway talked to the gal at the SEC."

"And?"

"She wouldn't say much, but it sounds like they're going to start an investigation of CST. Accounting irregularities, she claimed. It sounded serious."

"*What?* That's impossible. We run things squeaky clean at all our portfolio companies."

"Hey, don't shoot the messenger," Nigel complained. "I'm just telling you what Galloway told me."

Christian closed his eyes. There were a lot of strange things going on lately. Too many.

THE THREE MEN hustled Alan Agee out of a limousine and into a freight elevator of the Stratosphere Hotel. Agee's hands were bound behind his back, his mouth was gagged with a greasy rag, and a gray hood was drawn tightly over his head. As the elevator doors closed, the men picked Agee up and tossed him roughly into a garbage cart, then slammed the lid shut. His muffled screams were barely audible now.

When the men reached the lobby, they wheeled Agee across it, straight past reception and a sleepy-eyed concierge. It was before seven and the lobby was still quiet, so only a few people saw them push the garbage cart into the tower elevator. Normally this elevator wouldn't have been running until later, but today was different. Things had been arranged.

Moments later the elevator doors opened and they were eleven hundred feet up, looking out over a crystal-clear Las Vegas morning. The wind was stiff, and the men had to lean into it to keep their balance. They hauled Agee from the cart, cut off the hood and removed the gag, then untied his hands. He wouldn't try to run. There was nowhere to go.

Agee squinted against the bright sun as the hood came off, then glanced toward the railing, terrified. "What do you want?" he asked the man standing closest to him, the leader of the crew.

"I want you to call Christian Gillette and tell him you won't meet with him. Not today, anyway. From now on, you're mine. You do what I say. *Exactly* what I say."

Agee shook his head. "No," he whispered. "You're not gonna scare me like that. This is America."

The men chuckled callously. They'd heard that one before.

The leader nodded and the other two men grabbed Agee. They dragged him to the edge of the deck kicking and shouting, then picked him up and dangled him over the railing by his ankles.

"Please don't drop me!" Agee screamed back up at them bug-eyed, his arms flailing wildly. "I'll do anything you want! *Anything!*"

PATTY ROTH knelt behind the base of a pine tree as the chopper landed, whipping needles, twigs, and dirt into a tornadic frenzy. She was a hundred feet from the helipad, well hidden in the underbrush, protected from the flying debris. Through the telephoto lens she watched the passenger shake the pilot's hand, then hop out and run toward the lodge, bent over at the waist, an arm in front of his face. She hated these men for what they were doing to her husband. Treating him like he was nothing because he'd taken the fall for someone else.

She had to help him. He wasn't going to help himself.

CHRISTIAN AND LANCASTER had been talking strategy. An intense investor, Christian was active in all of Everest's portfolio companies, even the ones he wasn't chairman of. And he loved football. He and his father had watched football and golf together on television when he was young. His father had been away a lot, so Christian had precious little time with him, and he'd coveted those Sunday afternoons in the big study watching a big game or a final round. But memories were all he had now. His father had died in a plane crash nearly twenty years ago.

"Let me ask you something," Ray Lancaster spoke up.

"Shoot."

"I read on the Web site that you guys at Everest Capital own thirty companies. You're chairman of Everest, chairman of eighteen of those thirty companies, including the one you created to buy the football team and build the casino, and you're chairman of some public company in Chicago named, um, Central Satellite Telecom or something like that."

"Central States Telecom and Satellite," Christian corrected, instantly reminded of the SEC's sudden interest in the company. God, it irritated him to have to deal with the SEC. He was constantly on people's asses to get them to go the extra mile to make sure something like this *never* happened. "We call it CST." Christian had been wondering if there was something he'd missed, something he should have seen. Wondering if he should have been more personally involved in the IPO instead of letting Nigel handle everything. Wondering if he hadn't gotten as involved in the IPO as he normally would have because the truth was he couldn't take dealing with the minutiae anymore. If, after ten years of constant pressure, he was burning out. "I'm chairman of that company because we owned it before we took it public, and the public shareholders voted to keep me on."

"How the hell do you have time to be chairman of all of those companies?"

"I've got good people working for me who run the businesses day to day. People like you."

"I hope you're still saying that in a couple of years," Lancaster muttered. "Is it all yours and Nigel's money?"

Christian grinned. "I wish. No, the way it works is that big investors front us the money. Insurance companies, banks, pension funds, wealthy individuals. We buy the companies with the money the investors commit to us, operate them for a few years, then sell them, hopefully for a lot more than we paid."

Lancaster looked puzzled. "But I read in *Forbes* magazine that you're worth like five hundred million bucks. If it's not your money, how can you be worth so much? Do they pay you *that much* in salary?" He hesitated. "Or did you inherit it?"

Christian hadn't inherited a cent. After his father's death—right after Christian had graduated from Princeton—his stepmother had cut him off from the family. From the money, from everything. For a while he'd been forced to beg, borrow, and steal—sometimes literally. "Neither," he answered. "When we sell companies, we keep twenty percent of the profits. When we sold CST to the public we made four hundred million dollars more than we put in. Our investors got their investment back and three hundred twenty million of the profit. We kept eighty of the profit. One of my jobs as chairman is to spread that eighty around the firm."

Lancaster shook his head. "Jesus, no wonder you're worth so much."

"It isn't as easy as it sounds. Selling a company for more than you paid takes a lot of work, and almost as much luck."

Lancaster was looking off at the Stratosphere tower again, a strange expression spreading across his face. Like he had another important question on his mind, but he really didn't want to ask it.

"What's wrong?" Christian pushed.

"What happened a couple of years ago?"

"What do you mean?" But Christian was pretty sure he knew what Lancaster was getting at.

"There were all these articles on the Internet about you killing the mayor of some little town in Maryland," Lancaster answered, "and being hunted by the cops. The feds even got into it. You were public enemy number one for a few days. Then, bam, you go from desperado to hero. The later articles didn't really explain *why* you were suddenly a hero, but a bunch of senior government people were singing your praises."

"I didn't kill that woman," Christian said sharply. "The mayor of that town, I mean."

"What *did* you do?"

"It's a long story. Some people were trying to frame me for her murder, but, in the end, the truth came out. They were the ones that killed her."

Lancaster nodded. "I know, I read all that. I was just wondering what it was all about."

Christian took a breath. "Here's the thing, I—" His cell phone went off. It was a Las Vegas number he vaguely recognized. "Hello."

"Christian Gillette?" The voice at the other end of the line was faint.

"Yes."

"This is Alan Agee. I'm chairman of the—"

"The Nevada Gaming Commission," Christian interrupted. "Of course." The guy sounded awful, like he was about to puke. "I'll see you at two o'clock, right?"

"Can't do it," Agee said. "Got to put it off. Maybe tomorrow. I'll call you back."

The line went dead before Christian could say anything, and he closed the phone slowly. Things were going from strange to bad. And he got the awful sensation that *worse* was lurking just around the corner.

2

CHAMPAGNE ISLAND lies southeast of Acadia National Park in the frigid North Atlantic, nine miles off Maine's rocky coast. The island is far enough offshore to discourage unwanted intrusions from weekend pleasure boaters but close enough to make helicopter flights from the mainland convenient.

Champagne is small—seven hundred yards long, three hundred wide—and densely covered by towering pines. There are only two structures on the island: a lighthouse built atop a windswept rocky ridge on the northern tip and a large, rustic lodge. The lodge, made of logs cut from trees growing on the island, was built in 1901 in a natural depression near the middle of the island so it would be hidden from the ocean by berms and thick foliage. There's a helipad beside the lodge, but it doesn't bear the brightly colored X most helipads do.

Local lore goes that Champagne Island was a Native American burial ground before whites settled the Northeast, and that it's owned by some state or federal agency now. But local lore has it wrong. The island is owned by a private entity called the Molay Trust. A trust that hasn't made any of the standard state and federal declaratory filings trusts usually file since 1900. Local lore also goes that the island is haunted by the Native Americans buried in its rocky soil and by the pirates who used it as a haven from nor'easters and the law between raids on clipper ships in the late eighteenth century. Lore the Molay trustee does nothing to dispel.

In the great room of the lodge, eight men sat around a long table as the brilliant rays of a late spring sunset shimmered on the western horizon. Normally, they were nine, but one of the men hadn't made it. The blinds and curtains of the room were drawn and the room was lighted only by candles. The small flames cast a feeble glow about the place.

The men had flown in from Portland and Augusta that morning and had just finished a late lunch prepared by Champagne's caretakers—a married couple in their late thirties. The couple had been told when they were hired that the group was a charitable organization of senior executives who maintained the island as a retreat from cell phones, e-mail, and pushy executive assistants. There was excellent fishing off the island and they regularly took advantage of it during their visits.

The men around the table had a great deal in common. They were all white, wealthy, socially prominent, Protestant, senior leaders or ex-senior leaders of their organizations, long married with children—in most cases, grandchildren—graduates of Harvard or Princeton. And all of them were guilty of extramarital affairs—which was critically important.

Before a man could be initiated into the group, his affairs had to be videoed. The sexual trysts were recorded with the man's permission but without the woman's knowledge. The men were required to have at least two affairs with different women videoed prior to initiation; had to have a tryst videoed every three years to maintain membership; and regularly had to admit to recent sexual thoughts and fantasies in front of the others. Called "confessions," these admissions were audiotaped. The video- and audiotapes were the group's bond, insurance against a member conveying the intimate secrets of their society to anyone outside the circle.

Down through the years the "infidelity requirement" had scared off several promising candidates. Which was something that inspired pride in the members. It was a huge leap of faith for men like these to allow such damning evidence to exist, but it worked. Not once in the history of the Order had anyone disclosed anything about the group to an outsider.

Samuel Prescott Hewitt, master of the Order for the last seven years, sat at the head of the table, his trademark black Stetson lying in front of him. Chairman of U.S. Oil, the largest industrial company in the world, Hewitt was a tough Texan from a long line of wildcatters. He was a man who always played to win. Whether it was the world energy markets or a game of poker with acquaintances at his sprawling ranch outside Dallas, he was as competitive as they came. He called most people acquaintances because he didn't feel he had friends, not as other men defined the term. Which was fine with him. He'd always been a loner, and he'd always liked working that way because then it was easier to lead—there weren't any emotions holding you back. He wasn't even that close to his wife and children. In fact, the only person in the world who really mattered to Hewitt was his fourteen-year-old grandson, Samuel Prescott Hewitt III—Three Sticks, as Hewitt affectionately called the boy. If Hewitt's confession tapes ever got out, it would destroy the boy—and him.

"The Order will now come into session," announced Hewitt in a voice that silenced the room, a sharp edge wrapped in a Texas drawl. A natural tone that silenced an auditorium full of ten thousand shareholders as effortlessly as it did a small group of important men. "Proceed."

The men bowed their heads and in unison recited a brief prayer in Latin, then picked up their glasses of port.

Hewitt stared each man straight in the eyes, thinking of how similar they all were, how they even looked alike. White, male, tall, silver haired, strong chinned, handsome. Like most of the United States Senate, he thought to himself—at least, as long as the Order maintained its influence. He leaned forward and thrust his glass higher into the air. "To Hugues de Payens," he said fiercely.

"Hugues de Payens," the other seven echoed solemnly, then drank.

When Hewitt finished his glass, he pointed at Mace Kohler, then at Franklin Laird. Kohler was CEO of Networks Systems International, a large telecom company, and Laird was an ex-chairman of the Federal Reserve. "Please, Mr. Kohler." The men addressed each other formally once meetings began. "If you would."

Kohler rose and moved deliberately to a sideboard centered beneath the large, antlered elk head. He picked up a glass and a bottle of Chivas Regal from atop the sideboard, returned to the table, placed the glass and the Scotch down in front of Laird, then retook his seat. Since Laird had missed the last meeting he was in the hot seat tonight, the one who had to confess. Generally, when a member missed a meeting he was the confessor at the next meeting. It was a tradition that kept attendance very high.

After staring at the honey-hued liquid for a few moments, Laird set his thin lips, poured, and swallowed, gasping as he threw back the first gulp.

The other men remained silent while Laird continued to drink straight Scotch. The confessor wasn't allowed ice.

When he was satisfied that Laird had swallowed enough, Hewitt nodded. "That's enough, Franklin."

"Thank you," Laird answered hoarsely, wiping his mouth with a linen napkin as he put the glass down.

"It's your turn tonight, Mr. Laird. You know how it works."

"Yes."

Hewitt gestured toward Richard Dahl, an active five-star Army general who was with the Joint Chiefs. "Please, General Dahl."

Dahl reached for a tape recorder on the table in front of him and switched it on. "This is Mr. Laird's confession," he began, "as documented during meeting forty-seven of the twenty-ninth Order."

"Twenty-ninth" referred to this being the twenty-ninth distinct group of nine men to comprise the Order. One of the members had died four years ago, ending the twenty-eighth Order. That individual had been replaced by Kohler, marking the beginning of the twenty-ninth.

"Proceed, Mr. Laird," said Hewitt.

Laird hesitated, allowing the alcohol a few more moments to sink in, trying to find his courage. "On the plane up from D.C. this morning," he began in a low voice, "there was a very pretty flight attendant. I—I was attracted to her."

"Did you fly first class?" asked Trenton Fleming. Fleming was chairman of Black Brothers Allen, the last of Wall Street's great private partnerships. An investment firm outsiders knew little about. "Well, Mr. Laird?"

"No, I flew commercial. Middle seat, too," he added, clearly annoyed.

"Good," Hewitt commended. He knew how much Laird hated dealing with the "great unwashed," as he called anyone who he felt wasn't of his ilk. But it was good for him to live in the real world once in a while. More important, by flying commercial he was less likely to be recognized on his way to Maine. "Go on. Describe the woman."

"She was tall with long auburn hair."

"Big breasts?" Fleming asked. Laird's fixation with breasts was well documented on both the video- and audiotapes.

"What do *you* think?" Laird snapped.

The other men nodded. They knew one another so well.

"Anyway," Laird continued, "I fantasized about her."

"Details, brother."

"I undressed her in my mind."

"What did you have her do?"

"I—I—" Laird's voice faltered.

"Come on," Hewitt pushed. Laird still had a problem with the ritual—even though he'd been a member of the Order for sixteen years. Of course, Laird wasn't the only one. They all did—when it came to being the one in the hot seat. All of them except Hewitt. He actually enjoyed it. Each time it reminded him of the ritual's simple beauty, its incredible tradition. "We're brothers here, blood brothers. No one will ever tell your secrets as long as you don't tell the Order's. You believe that, don't you, Mr. Laird?"

"Yes, of course."

"So?"

Laird took another gulp of Scotch. "I watched her have sex with the pilots."

Laird's fantasies didn't usually involve him having sex. He liked being a voyeur, confessing to the others a few years ago that he had kept an extensive collection of pornography in his office at the Federal Reserve so he could watch it whenever he wanted to. Even more startling, he'd admitted to paying an aide to have sex with a woman in a private bathroom connected to his office at the Fed—and secretly videotaped the act.

"What was her name?" demanded Blanton McDonnell. McDonnell was CEO of Jamison & Jamison Pharmaceutical, the largest medical device manufacturer in North America.

"Carolyn."

"Did you get her number?"

"No."

"Did you try?"

"Yes."

Hewitt motioned for the others to refrain from asking any more questions on this subject. "Anything you want to tell us about your personal life?"

Laird glanced toward the head of the table, fear in his eyes. "Yes."

"Go on."

"A few weeks ago I hired a personal assistant. A twenty-seven-year-old blond woman," Laird continued, his voice trembling. "She's very capable."

"And beautiful," someone assumed.

"Yes," Laird agreed quietly. "*Very* beautiful."

"Have you had sex with her?"

Laird drew tiny circles on the table with his index finger. "Yes," he whispered.

"Have you videoed that for us yet, Mr. Laird?" asked Stewart Massey. Massey was a grizzled ex–United States senator from Texas. He'd been a prosecutor before going into politics.

"No," Laird admitted.

"Do," Hewitt instructed. "Within the next thirty days."

"All right."

"Does she have any fetishes?" Massey wanted to know.

Hewitt watched Laird struggle. He was so obviously uncomfortable, which was exactly how it was supposed to be. The founders of the Order were brilliant, Hewitt thought to himself. It was a beautifully conceived ritual—with a little modern technology baked in over the years.

Laird took a deep breath. "She likes to be tied up."

"Make certain you get *that* on tape," Hewitt ordered, glancing around the table at the others. "I think that's enough. Thank you, Mr. Laird."

Laird eased back from the table into his chair, smiling like a man who'd won a reprieve from the electric chair.

It was *such* a beautifully conceived ritual, Hewitt thought to himself. Such a beautifully conceived Order.

ELIJAH FORTE was one of the wealthiest black men in America, one of the wealthiest *men* in America. And he hadn't achieved his success by wasting time on indecisive people. But this was important, critically important, so he was forcing himself to be patient. "You okay?"

"Yes."

"Tell me what happened."

"I was approached."

"By who?" Forte asked.

The other person hesitated.

"Who approached you?" Forte asked again, dialing up the pressure in his voice.

"Someone who wanted to know about Jesse Wood."

Forte glanced over at Heath Johnson, his executive vice president.

Johnson raised one eyebrow and nodded. "What did this person want to know?" Forte asked.

"Whatever I was willing to say."

"What did you say?"

"That I had to think about the offer."

"What was the offer?"

"Money."

Forte's eyes narrowed, anticipating the shakedown. "Is that what you want from me? Money?"

"No."

Forte looked up from an old ballpoint pen he'd pulled out of his shirt pocket, surprised by the response. "Then what *do* you want?"

"I want you to protect Jesse Wood. I want the dream to come true. I don't want this person to hurt Jesse or keep Jesse from getting what we all want him to get. What we've all worked so hard for him to get."

Forte rarely felt deep sentiment. He'd endured a brutally hard childhood and his emotions were buried deep, but this was an amazing display of loyalty. He felt a warm moistness coming to his eyes. He coughed and looked away for a moment. "Do you think this person would hurt Jesse?"

"If that were the only alternative, the only way left to stop Jesse, I think this person would have Jesse killed."

Forte let out a long, concerned breath. "I'll protect Jesse," he promised, "but I'll need your help."

"I'm willing to do anything."

"Good." Forte leaned forward in his seat. "Tell me the name of the person who approached you."

3

QUENTIN STILES was an Everest Capital managing partner and Christian Gillette's best friend. Christian's father, Clayton, had been a wealthy California investment banker turned United States senator, and Christian had grown up wanting for nothing material. At the other end of the economic and social spectrums, Quentin had grown up dirt-poor in Harlem. He had never known his father, and his mother had died of an overdose when he was still a kid. But they were both self-made men who'd overcome mountains to get where they were—Christian because his stepmother had left him penniless the day his father died, Quentin because he'd had nothing to begin with.

Christian wanted Quentin in Las Vegas with him to help figure out what was going on with the casino license. If there was one guy in the world he trusted with a job like this, it was Quentin. The guy was a bloodhound, and fearless.

He glanced across the table as they sat on the suite's balcony, watching Quentin munch on an apple. Quentin was tall, broad-shouldered, and cut, a handsome African-American man with a smooth way about him, like he was totally in control of himself and his surroundings at all times. He loved cars and guns and he rarely wore any color but black.

To get him out of Harlem and away from a tough street gang he'd hooked up with, Quentin's grandmother had sent him off to the Army at eighteen. It had been the turning point of his life, he often told people.

He'd become one of the youngest Army Rangers ever—a legend in that elite force now—was later recruited into several highly classified clandestine military and domestic anticrime operations, and ended up on President Clinton's Secret Service detail. After a few years serving the White House, he'd resigned from government to start his own security company, quickly picking up a solid list of high-profile clients, including Christian.

A couple of years ago, Christian had bought Quentin's firm, QS Security, using a much larger Everest portfolio company to make the acquisition. Christian had paid five million dollars for QS, then made Quentin a managing partner at Everest. Some, including a few inside Everest, had questioned the deal. Quentin had saved Christian's life a year before, taking a bullet to the chest, and there were whispers that five million bucks and a senior executive position at Everest were payback for the pain and suffering. That QS wasn't really worth the price and Quentin didn't deserve the position. But it had been two years since the transaction and QS was now worth at least twenty million. The critics had gone silent.

"Better not make a habit of that, robo-chairman." Quentin pointed at a plate of half-eaten blueberry pancakes. Christian had ordered the pancakes after Ray Lancaster left. "Not if you want to keep your cover-boy status."

"First of all, I don't care about being a cover boy." Which was absolutely true; Christian hated publicity. But, as chairman of the largest private equity firm in the world and chairman of so many portfolio companies, he couldn't avoid the spotlight. In the last two months he'd been on the covers of both *Fortune* and *Forbes.* "Second of all, looks don't matter when it comes to *Fortune* and *Forbes.* They're business rags."

"*Forbes* and *Fortune* today, *GQ* and *People* tomorrow. Maybe even *Time,*" Quentin muttered. "And I bet if you talked to the editors at those business rags and they were being completely honest, they'd tell you one of the reasons they put you on the covers is that you got a mug women don't mind looking at."

Christian had sharp facial features—a thin, still slightly bent nose despite the plastic surgery; strong jaw; prominent chin; high, defined cheekbones; and intense gray eyes. His hair was black—parted on one side and combed back over his ears—and flecks of silver were starting to appear at the temples. Forty years old, he kept himself in good shape. Six two, one ninety-five, he regularly won his age group in competitive

10Ks. More and more, he was appearing on high-profile most-eligible-bachelor lists.

"Pretty soon you're gonna have rock-star status," Quentin observed, "just like your better half."

Christian groaned. "I hope not."

"Me personally? Hey, I don't know what women see in you."

"Give me a—"

"Speaking of your better half," Quentin cut in, "how's Faith doing?"

Faith Cassidy was Christian's girlfriend, though they hadn't seen much of each other lately. A pop star, Faith was petite, blond, and vivacious with a tremendous voice and dance moves to match. She'd released three albums, all of which had gone platinum. Right now she was in Europe on a concert tour. Sixteen cities in five weeks.

"She's fine," Christian answered, pulling out his BlackBerry to check e-mails. "I talked to her before I left New York yesterday. She's in Paris for a few nights."

"Those tours must be a grind. You guys doing okay?"

Christian hesitated. "I guess. It's tough when we both travel so much, but it'll work out."

"When's she back?"

"Two weeks."

"You miss her?"

Christian looked up from the device. "Why the third degree, big guy?"

Quentin put on his sunglasses as he looked out over Las Vegas. The city was bathed in sunshine.

A stall tactic. Christian knew him so well. "What's the matter, pal?"

"I swore I wouldn't tell you."

"Quentin."

"All right, all right. Faith called last night."

Christian recoiled slightly. Faith and Quentin knew each other pretty well. Still, it was surprising that she'd call him. "Why?"

"She was checking up on you. She's worried."

"About what?"

"Allison."

Christian rolled his eyes. "Jesus."

Allison Wallace had joined Everest a few years ago when Christian and Nigel were raising the firm's latest corporate buyout fund. A twenty-billion-dollar megafund, the largest of its kind ever raised. Out of Chicago, Allison's family was one of the richest in the country. They'd committed five billion to the new fund, but, of course, there'd been a catch to the huge commitment. Gordon Meade, an outsider who ran all the Wallace investments, had demanded that Christian allow the family to put at least one of their own people on the ground at Everest Capital. To watch over their money—and to learn. Christian wasn't happy about the demand—it wasn't a good idea to have your investors so close to you because then they could second-guess all your decisions—but he'd relented. After all, five billion dollars was five billion dollars.

Allison had moved to Manhattan and joined Everest full-time. In her early thirties, she was very pretty; very well connected; and, when she wasn't working, very into having a good time.

"I can understand why Faith worries about her, Chris," Quentin said. "Allison's beautiful; you see her a lot more than you see Faith; and, well, Allison seems to like you." He paused. *"A lot."*

"No more than she likes you."

Quentin spread his hands. "Hey, man, it's me. No need to bullshit. You *know* what I'm talking about."

Quentin was right. There'd been a spark between them the first time he and Allison had dinner—in Manhattan, just the two of them—but they'd never acted on it. They'd always kept it professional. "I'll call Faith later," Christian promised. "And I won't let on that you told me about her calling you."

"Good. So, how'd it go with Ray Lancaster, robo-chairman?"

Christian gritted his teeth. "Cut the robo tag, will you?"

Quentin put his head back and laughed loudly. "You know, they should have an action figure named after you. A little guy dressed up in a pin-striped business suit and a black cape with a big C on it. I'm going to call one of the toy companies and suggest that."

"And they should have one of you wearing anything *but* black. Look, it's been a while since all that happened. I mean, are you really still jealous?" It had been two years, but there wasn't a week that went by that Quentin hadn't made some kind of joke about it.

"Damn right," Quentin said. "You keep saying you told the reporters about me, but I bet you didn't. You wanted the spotlight all to yourself."

"Oh, sure. You know how much I crave atten—"

"Glory hound."

Christian was about to fire back, but he caught himself. Quentin loved ribbing him, loved getting a reaction. No point giving it to him.

"Did Ray Lancaster ask about it?" Quentin wanted to know.

"Oh, yeah. Found the articles on the Internet."

"What'd you tell him?"

"The truth. That a couple of high ups inside the federal government were using one of our companies to hide some big developments their people had made in nanotechnology. That we figured out they were also trying to cut the technology out of the government for themselves. That they did everything they could to set me up when they realized what we knew, including murdering that woman in Maryland and trying to hang it on me."

Quentin shook his head. "You were quite a story there for a few weeks." He snapped his fingers. "Hey, I forgot to ask you on the way out here. You ever get in touch with Carmine Torino about the Dice license?"

"Nope. Pisses me off, too. We've paid that guy a lot of money."

"Yeah, I know," Quentin agreed. "Carmine was supposed to take care of this kind of red-tape crap. I'll check around the city while you're meeting with the Gaming Commission today. See if I can scare him out from beneath whatever rock he crawled under."

"I'm not meeting with the commission today."

Quentin looked over. "Huh? I thought you were sitting down with the chairman, with Alan Agee."

"I was, but he canceled on me this morning. Said he'd call later to let me know if he could do it tomorrow." Christian grimaced. "He didn't sound very good when I talked to him."

"What do you mean?"

"He sounded scared." Christian pursed his lips. "We've put almost a billion dollars into the Dice Casino. It'll be over a billion one by the time everything's all said and done. It's going to be hard to make any money on it if I can't open the craps tables."

"Who do you think got to Agee? The Mob?"

"Who else would it have been?" Christian had been afraid the Mafia might pull something like this ever since they'd made the final decision to build the casino. But if they were the ones who'd gotten to Agee, they ought to be making contact. Their angles were always money or revenge, and there wasn't anything they needed to take revenge for in this situation. Not that he knew of anyway. "We've had a great track record at Everest. Writing off a billion dollars would *suck*. To put it mildly."

"Well, the investors would have to understand something like this. There's no way you can control the Mob. Besides, you've made our investors a lot more than a billion dollars over the last five years."

"They won't understand, Quentin. They'll say I should have known what the Mob would do. In this business, you're only as good as your last deal. Remember that."

"I'll find Torino," Quentin promised. "We'll figure out what's going on. Don't worry."

"I'm not worried." He *was* worried, of course—deeply worried—but there was no upside to letting anyone in on that. Even Quentin. He was the chairman, the man who stayed calm in every situation, no matter how grim things looked. "It'll work out."

"What are you going to do about Chicago?"

Christian banged the arm of the chair. "Chicago, that's right." He was supposed to be in Chicago tonight for dinner with Gordon Meade, the man who ran the Wallace Family money. Meade had asked for an update on how the fund was doing—the answer was: great if you assumed they got the casino license, terrible if you assumed they didn't. Allison was supposed to be flying in from San Francisco to join Christian and Meade for dinner. "I've got to call Gordon and move dinner to tomorrow night."

"You really going to screw around out here for another day? That's a lot of wasted time."

"I don't have any choice. Getting the casino license is number one on my Christmas list right now."

"What if Agee never calls and you can't reach him? What if he disappears like Torino?"

"I'll put you on his trail, too." Christian pulled out a notepad that contained all his to-do lists. "I need you to get me information on someone," he said, eyeing the first item on one of the pages.

"Who's the mark?"

"A guy named Samuel Hewitt. He's—"

"Chairman of U.S. Oil. I know who he is. He's a damn important guy. What do you need to know about him?"

"Anything you can find out."

"Why?"

"I'm meeting with him," Christian explained. "He graduated from

Princeton, too. There's a bunch of alumni stuff going on in a few days at the campus, and he wants to get together with me then. Called me about it yesterday."

"Did he say *why* he wants to meet?"

"No."

"Hopefully it's about Laurel Energy."

Christian shut his eyes tightly. Everybody at Everest Capital was focused on the sale of Laurel Energy, especially the managing partners. If the sale went down, the payout was going to be huge, the biggest in Everest history.

They'd acquired Laurel several years ago for three hundred million, then, after the purchase, discovered a vast new reserve field on an option property that had come along with the company. It had been a bonanza. Everest's investment bankers—Morgan Stanley—had told Christian that one of the big boys—U.S. Oil, Exxon, or Shell—should pay at least five billion for Laurel, meaning that Everest would make nine hundred and forty million—20 percent of the $4.7 billion profit. *Nine hundred and forty million dollars,* and a lot of that would go to the top people: Christian and his five managing partners. Which was why they were constantly asking about it.

But in all the time Laurel had been for sale, Everest had gotten just two offers, both from bottom feeders, neither anywhere near five billion. The big boys hadn't even sniffed at it, and Morgan Stanley couldn't figure out why. Laurel was a great company; the reserves were proven. The fact that it hadn't sold made no sense. But then that was how business went sometimes, Christian knew. How life could go. Sure things turned into train wrecks, and train wrecks became sure things. But Laurel had been a sure, *sure* thing.

"Yeah, *hopefully,*" Christian echoed.

"Have you ever met Hewitt?" Quentin asked.

"No. Always wanted to. Like you said, he's an important guy, but he's supposed to be a character, too, big into poker. That's one of the things I want you to find out. If he is, I'm going to try to get a game with him. Maybe I can convince him to buy Laurel from us during the game. Dump a big pot to him or something, you know? Then ask for the offer."

Quentin jotted Hewitt's name down in his notepad. "I'll find what I can."

There was a knock on the door.

"I'll get it," Quentin volunteered, rising quickly from his chair.

"Thanks."

Christian picked up a copy of the *Journal* and started reading an article about Jesse Wood, one of the Democratic hopefuls in the November presidential election.

A moment later Quentin was back. "Look who showed up."

Christian glanced up. Allison was standing next to Quentin. "What are you doing here?"

"You know me—I never miss a party." She gave him a sparkling smile. "You been up all night gambling?"

Christian laughed. "I thought you were in San Francisco working on the Aero Systems deal."

"I finished up late last night so I figured I'd meet you here and go with you to Chicago. Figured that would be more fun than flying there by myself. And," she continued, "I was hoping we could get a little gambling in. You know how much I love poker."

Unfortunately, Christian did. Last month he'd taken her to a weekly game a couple of his friends in Manhattan ran. She'd cleaned them out.

"I'll be right back," Quentin spoke up. "I'm going to start running some lines on that guy we talked about."

"Thanks," Christian called as Quentin disappeared into the suite.

Allison sat down and picked up a strawberry from the same bowl Quentin had gotten his apple. "You know, we should call Gordon and tell him to put off dinner until tomorrow. That way we can stay here tonight and have some real fun."

She was going to love this, he knew. "Actually, I'd like you to call and ask him if we could do just that."

Her eyes flew open. *"Really?"*

He nodded. "Yeah. My meeting was put off until tomorrow. I've got to stay here again tonight."

She clapped her hands twice. "Awesome. I can't wait to get you into the casino." She took a bite of the strawberry and gave him a coy smile. "You know what they say, right?"

"What?"

"What happens in Vegas stays in Vegas."

PATTY ROTH held a magnifying glass in her left hand and a pair of tweezers in her right, slowly moving the tweezers toward the paper beneath the glass. Then she heard Don's heavy footsteps coming down the hall. She managed to get everything stuffed into the top drawer of the desk just in time and spun around to face him.

"What are you doing in here?" he asked, leaning into the small room she used as an office.

"Working on the computer."

"It's dark," he said, pointing at the monitor. "Screen saver isn't even up."

"I was *about* to start working on it," she said, rising from the chair and moving to where he stood. "I'm going to write a letter to Mom, and I was thinking about what I wanted to say before I started." She gave him a quick peck on the cheek. "Need me for something?"

He eyed the screen suspiciously for a few moments, then glanced down at her. "Yeah, they're just about ready for dinner. I need you to help me serve it."

4

THE ORDER OF the Ivy was established at exactly midnight on October 11, 1839, in a candlelit dormitory room of Princeton University by two third-year students, Prescott Avery Fleming and George Ellis Black. The Order's official reason for being was to forever protect the United States; its Constitution; and "those certain perfect ways, laws, and customs not specifically set forth in the Constitution or other official documents of the United States government but understood, interpreted, or desired to exist by the Order." Those initiated into the Order vowed to protect the country and its perfect ways, laws, and customs "using any and all means available, existing, or imagined." They took the oath with their left hand on a human skull and their right holding a saber carried by George Washington during the Revolution. Since 1877 the skull used in the initiation ceremony has been that of Man Bear, one of the nineteenth century's fiercest Sioux chiefs.

The Order's rituals and bylaws were based on those of the Knights Templar, who in 1118 took a perpetual vow to defend the Christian kingdom. Specifically, to protect pilgrims along the path from Europe to the Holy Land. The Order's bylaws limited membership at any one time to a maximum of nine individuals—the original number of Templars, who were led by Hugues de Payens, a prominent knight of the province of Champagne. The bylaws also strictly limited membership to those attending or graduated from Princeton or Harvard. Even at the beginning, it was clear to Fleming and Black that, if the Order was to have the breadth of influence upon the country they envisioned, it would ultimately make more sense to have members of great power, members who were established.

During the rest of 1839 and the spring of 1840, Fleming and Black recruited seven more members into the Order: five classmates from Princeton and two family members from Harvard—Fleming's cousin Elias Holmes, and Black's brother, Charles. By April 1840, the Order—the name was shortened in 1861 from the original the Order of the Ivy for reasons undocumented—was meeting every few weeks in a New York City hotel room. They didn't build a mausoleum like the Skull and Bonesmen of Yale, nor did they ever reveal membership, even at death, the way The Sevens of the University of Virginia did with a 7 printed at the end of the member's official obituary in *The New York Times.* The Order's was a vow of *complete* and *perpetual* secrecy.

Though Fleming's and Black's families were wealthy and powerful, the Order wasn't involved in anything of real importance until Prescott and George themselves achieved positions of influence. Since they couldn't disclose the society's existence to anyone outside the Order—even family members—they weren't able to use their families' connections for the Order's purposes until they personally had the ties. Fleming took over his family's sprawling New Jersey steel operation in 1859. Black and his brother teamed with William Allen—also one of the original nine Ordermen—and borrowed a million dollars from their fathers to found the investment banking firm of Black Brothers Allen in 1860. It remains a Wall Street powerhouse to this day.

The Order began its activities benignly enough, establishing several anonymous scholarships at Princeton and Harvard in the mid-1840s for students of limited means. The amount of the gift and the recipient were announced mysteriously, yet with great fanfare: an envelope suddenly fluttering down from an overhead scaffold to the podium in the middle of the valedictorian's speech at graduation; a note handed to the public address announcer who read the instructions printed on it at halftime of the Princeton–Harvard football game; the groundskeepers digging at the middle of the fifty-yard line to find a box with the particulars of the Order's gift inside and the letter inside the box quickly taken to the announcer who read the name of the recipient and the amount of the gift to the roar of the crowd.

As the members' wealth increased, so did their anonymous donations—mostly to churches and orphanages on behalf of the Order. So did their desire to be more active, for the Order to do more than just give away money.

In 1865 they did a great deal more than donate money. Staunch Unionists irate at President Lincoln's compassionate reconstruction attitude toward the rebellious South, the Order changed the course of history for the first time. Through David Blake, another original member of the Order, they assisted John Wilkes Booth with his assassination plot. Blake, a fishing magnate from New England, was a distant relative of Lincoln's Secretary of War Edwin Stanton. Though Stanton was later accused of participating in the conspiracy to kill the president, the Order's involvement in the assassination was never exposed.

In 1876 the Order secretly helped sculpt the nation's landscape once more, this time in a less immediate though no less powerful way. In June of that year Rebecca Black, Charles's youngest daughter, was traveling west by railroad to San Francisco in a private Pullman car coupled to the end of a Union Pacific passenger train. On a lonely stretch of track in central Nebraska the train was attacked by Sioux warriors. Another treaty with the Sioux had just been broken and the raiding party was hell-bent on revenge for a U.S. cavalry ambush on a Sioux village, during which seventy-two women and children had been murdered. The Sioux warriors stole several thousand dollars from passengers, shot and killed eleven men aboard the train, and kidnapped three women—one of whom was Rebecca Black. She was found a week later in a dry streambed thirty miles away. She'd been scalped, gutted, and left to die.

The Black brothers vowed revenge on the Sioux for Rebecca's murder, specifically against the chief of the region, Man Bear—who, it was rumored, had ordered the attack on the train. Thanks to the Order's growing connections in Washington, several U.S. Army columns were quickly and quietly dispatched to Nebraska and what would later become South Dakota, to find and kill Man Bear. The mission was carried out in forty-two days with little fanfare.

A week after Man Bear's execution, the Blacks were presented with the Sioux chief's cleansed skull by the ranking field general in a clandestine ceremony at the Wall Street headquarters of Black Brothers Allen. Later that year, several senior federal officials and Army generals, including the field general directly responsible for Man Bear's capture and hanging, were quietly allocated shares in three new equity offerings brought public on the New York Stock Exchange by Black Brothers Allen. The men all made millions.

But the Order didn't stop with Man Bear. So enraged were George and Charles by Rebecca's death that they organized death squads: three-man teams funded through a maze of trusts and corporations secretly established by Black Brothers Allen. The teams were charged with murdering any Indian chief, Sioux or other, who whispered the words "peaceful settlement with whites." They were to use any means available, existing or imagined, to carry out their orders. The fate of the Native American has been well documented.

The Order began assembling in secret at the estates of its members in the late 1850s and continued to do so until 1899. During the fall of that year a meeting of the Order was nearly discovered by a group of Yale's Skull and Bonesmen who had followed a friend they felt was acting suspiciously—a man of the Order. The men escaped from the house without being recognized, but the Molay Trust was formed the next day to purchase what was renamed Champagne Island from the federal government so the Order could meet with no fear of detection. The trust was named for Jacques de Molay, the last grand master of the Knights Templar. Molay was burned at the stake in 1314 when the Templars were crushed by the Inquisition after falling into disfavor with the Catholic Church.

Even in 1899 the federal government didn't make a habit of selling land to the private sector. However, a member of the Order was married to a sister of Maine's ranking United States senator at the time, and a deal was struck. The Molay Trust purchased Champagne for five hundred dollars—paid directly to the senator—and there were never any records of the transaction. In 1900 the Maine legislature and the full United States Congress forever exempted Molay from any filings and the veil was permanently drawn.

Construction of the lodge was completed in 1901. From then on the Order officially met only on Champagne Island.

AS THE SUN SANK toward the horizon, the members of the Order were discussing July's Democratic national convention. One of the prime candidates was a black man named Jesse Wood, a former professional tennis player who in the mid-1980s had won the U.S. Open and

Wimbledon—twice each—and the hearts and respect of millions of Americans. Wood was handsome, smart, charismatic, and being mentioned increasingly often in the press as someone who could unite a twenty-first century America growing more, not less, racially and economically divided. He appealed to whites because he'd never made race an issue during his tennis days, never used his victories as a platform to preach about the crimes White America had committed against Black America. And he appealed to blacks because he was a stellar example of what a man could do if he set his sights on something. As a teenager, Wood had pulled himself out of a Bronx ghetto by his bootstraps up into a bastion of the establishment—the professional tennis world. Once his competitive days were over, he'd become a senior partner at one of the most prestigious law firms in Manhattan, then won a United States Senate seat with over sixty-five percent of the vote.

"What's your point, Senator Massey?" Hewitt asked, taking control of the conversation. They'd been at the table for almost three hours but still hadn't gotten to the most important agenda item.

"My *point*," Massey responded in his nasal drawl, "is that Jesse Wood is a wolf in sheep's clothing. His backers include some of the old Black Panthers who we know have no intention of ever coexisting peacefully with us. A shadowy group of sinister figures bent on wresting control of our great country away from whites." Massey always spoke like he was giving a speech, even in casual conversation. It had been a year since he'd retired from the Senate, but he couldn't seem to make it off the floor. "Wood's association with the group has been kept quiet, but I confirmed it yesterday. If he won the election he'd be a formidable opponent. He might be the disaster scenario we've been fearing."

"You're jumping to conclusions, Senator Massey," Mace Kohler retorted. Kohler was the youngest of the Order, just fifty-three. Before founding Network Systems he'd been a Green Beret, and, like Hewitt, he didn't take any crap. "It's ridiculous to call Wood a wolf in sheep's clothing, and the idea that some 'shadowy group of sinister figures,' " said Kohler, curling his fingers to form quotation marks, "of old Black Panthers is trying to take control of the country is ludicrous, too. I seriously doubt a group like that even exists."

Kohler was always outspoken in these meetings. Sometimes that was good, sometimes it wasn't. "*We* exist," Hewitt pointed out.

Kohler shrugged, silently conceding the point to the master.

"You're naïve, Mr. Kohler," Massey added. "Young and naïve."

"And you're paranoid," Kohler snapped, returning fire. "Old and paranoid."

"And *you're* out of order, Mr. Kohler," Hewitt broke in sharply. "Calm down."

But Kohler kept going. "Look, I've met Wood several times. He's a sincere man."

"No, no," Franklin Laird spoke up, still a little intoxicated from his confession, "I agree with Senator Massey. I've met Wood, too. He'll make you think he's a moderate, but, once this population thing turns on us and the other side gets momentum, you'll see a different man."

Kohler laughed heartily. "What do you mean? You think Wood is going to get his Black Panther buddies to scare all Congress into voting for a referendum that would force every white American to give every black American a hundred thousand bucks?"

"That lawsuit still has legs," Laird retorted. "It's still on the active docket in Manhattan. It could be—"

"That suit isn't going anywhere," Blanton McDonnell cut in. "There's nothing to it. It's pure bullshit. It's just a way for a couple of whacko blackos we all know and hate to get some publicity. Like that jive minister from Philadelphia who's always trying to rile up the blacks." McDonnell looked around. "What's that guy's name? I can't remember."

"Jefferson Roundtree," Kohler answered.

"Right, right, Roundtree. That lawsuit's just a platform for guys like him to scream and yell." McDonnell pointed at Laird. "Really, Franklin, Mace is right on target here," he said, motioning toward Kohler. "Let's be real. Let's not waste everybody's time on something that's way out there."

Hewitt's eyes narrowed. Kohler had shown compassionate tendencies before for minorities, but McDonnell never had. "Mr. McDonnell, please remember that we address each other formally in these meetings. No first names."

"Sorry."

"And no matter what you think of Senator Massey's assertion about a wolf in sheep's clothing," Hewitt continued, "Mr. Wood is meeting with Christian Gillette in the next few weeks."

The room fell silent. The men around the table were familiar with Christian Gillette.

"How do you know Gillette and Wood are meeting?" Trenton Fleming asked. Fleming had been jotting down a note, reminding himself to talk to Hewitt after the meeting about a deal they were working on together. "Our investment bankers talk to the Everest people all the time. I haven't heard anything about that."

A nice touch, Hewitt thought to himself. Fleming making it seem like he was in the dark about it. In reality, Fleming was as savvy and calculating as they came—and a wonderful actor. "You wouldn't have. The arrangements are being kept hush-hush," Hewitt explained. "But we have help from inside Everest." He had help from inside Jesse Wood's camp, too, but that had to be kept secret. The individual's life would be at stake if the connection were ever exposed. "A very credible source."

"Who?" Kohler demanded.

"I can't say, not even here."

"When are they meeting?" Kohler asked.

"Soon."

"Where?"

"It hasn't been decided yet." Hewitt knew, but he wasn't going to tell Kohler. He wasn't going to tell Kohler about the meeting he was having with Gillette, either. He didn't like the way Kohler was acting, or how he seemed to be influencing McDonnell. He was starting to think Kohler might be the cancer.

"Why does Wood want to meet with Gillette?" Laird asked.

"Financial support and the support of Gillette's investors," Hewitt explained. "Gillette can bring the heat when it comes to money. According to my sources, *Forbes* and *Fortune* didn't even come close when they tried to rate Gillette's ability to raise dollars." Hewitt grimaced. With Gillette's backing, Wood could become unstoppable.

"Will Wood get Gillette's support?"

Hewitt shrugged. "We can't get a clear read on where Gillette is politically. There's no pattern to his voting record. He's an enigma as far as that goes. As far as a lot of things go, really. His investors at Everest Capital are mostly WASPs, and they love him for how much money he's made them, but his best friend is a black guy who's a managing partner at the firm. And he just hired a black guy to be head coach and general manager of that new NFL franchise Everest controls. He supports a lot of minority causes, but he's also a member of places like the Manhattan Lawn and Tennis Club. The only minorities who've ever walked through those doors are employees."

"Sounds like a nigger lover to me," Massey spoke up. "Probably one of those idiots who donated a lot of money to help all those hoodlums in New Orleans after the hurricane hit." He chuckled. "I swear, every looter you saw on CNN was a fucking nigger."

"Maybe that's because they were the ones who couldn't afford to get out," McDonnell spoke up. "And I'd appreciate it if you wouldn't use the term 'nigger.' "

"Agreed," Hewitt said firmly. "Let's get back on point."

Dahl shook his head. "It doesn't make any sense for Gillette to support a Democrat like that. What about his father? What about Clayton?"

Hewitt flashed Dahl a reproachful glare. "I can't answer your question, General Dahl, but this I do know: Gillette and Wood are meeting. Which isn't good."

"It makes sense for Gillette to meet with Wood if he thinks Wood has a chance of being president," Laird observed. "It's always a good idea to have the next chief executive of the country on your side, even if you don't agree with his politics. And it sure looks like Wood has a chance of at least winning the Democratic nomination."

"It's a *lock* he'll win the donkey nomination," Hewitt agreed. "Look at the primaries he's already won."

"He's the clear choice for the Democrats," Fleming seconded. "The other two candidates got crushed by the man in charge four years ago. Their stories are old—so are they. People under forty can't stand either of them."

"And they've both got baggage," Massey added. "I talked to people who know, and there's a couple of things Jesse Wood's handlers could leak to the press that would have each of the other guys running for cover. No, Mr. Hewitt's right on target here. Jesse Wood will be the Democratic nominee."

"Our problem is that Jesse might win in November, too," said Hewitt. "It's looking more and more like that every day. Which," he continued quickly before anyone could say anything, "brings me to our most important agenda item. I have the new population projections," he announced, opening a manila folder and passing papers down both sides of the table. "The figures are startling, and make our discussions about Jesse Wood even more relevant." Several of the men pulled out reading glasses and donned them as Hewitt kept going. "The Census Bureau now projects that by 2030, whites will be less than fifty percent of the United States population. *We* will be the minority at that point."

"Jesus," Fleming whispered, gazing at the page Hewitt had passed around, a stunned look on his face. "My children's lifetimes, maybe even *mine.*"

"Definitely yours," Hewitt agreed, "if the trend continues."

"I thought it was *2040,*" McDonnell said. "That's what I have in my notes from last time."

"It was," Hewitt confirmed, "but the numbers have changed." He pointed at the second line on the page. "And the acceleration of the decline in the white percentage is what's most alarming. In 1990 we were seventy-six percent of the population; in 2000 sixty-nine percent; today we're only sixty-four percent. *And,*" he said, his voice rising as his fingertip moved across the page, "by 2030 the numbers say we'll make up less than half the projected four hundred million people in this country."

"We don't need to worry," Dahl growled. "The people at the Census Bureau don't know what they're doing. The projections keep changing so much they can't be accurate."

"I think they know *exactly* what they're doing at Census," Hewitt argued. "I think they're sandbagging us."

"Huh?"

"The top statistics guy at Census is a man named Raul Rodriguez. Someone we know there says Rodriguez is putting out conservative numbers on purpose."

"Why would he do that?"

"He knows that whites will become the minority *sooner* than 2030. He's hiding that data so when the numbers actually flip, it'll take us by surprise and we won't be able to do anything."

"Christ."

"It's the Hispanics," Laird hissed, analyzing the data. "This thing shows they'll be twenty-seven percent of the population by 2030, up from thirteen percent in 2000. Are they really screwing that much more than us?"

"They fuck like rabbits on Viagra," Massey said loudly, "and they never use birth control, for Christ sake, because they know we'll take care of them."

"They do tend to have larger immediate families," Hewitt agreed, "but a lot of the growth in that number is due to immigration."

"Yeah," Fleming spoke up. "I read the other day that there's something like thirty-five million foreign-born people in this country, mostly

Latin Americans. That's about twelve percent of the population. And the number's up from twenty-six million in 2000."

"You're lucky you *could* read it," Laird snapped. "Pretty soon everything in this country is going to be printed in Spanish. I think more people speak Spanish in America now than English. I got on a plane a few weeks ago and the flight attendants did the preflight blah-blah babble in Spanish *first*. Can you believe that?"

"People shouldn't be allowed to be citizens of this country until they can at least *speak* English," said Fleming.

"We ought to build walls around our perimeters to keep these bastards out," Dahl muttered. "With machine-gun nests every five hundred feet. Then we won't have to worry about people speaking Spanish anymore."

"Or, more realistically, make the naturalization process tougher," suggested Laird. "Five years here without a felony and you can put Jesse Wood into office. That's basically all it comes down to now."

Fleming shook his head. "Do you all know that there are four million people in all of Puerto Rico, and two million Ricans in the United States?"

"Which," said Hewitt, "brings up another alarming fact involving our friend Senator Wood. Two weeks ago he met with the Puerto Rican governor and the island's congressional representative. The men flew to New York secretly and met with Wood somewhere in Brooklyn—we believe it was East New York. Our information is that the discussions centered around full statehood for Puerto Rico if Wood is elected." Hewitt gestured toward Massey. "That gets to Senator Massey's point about him being a wolf in sheep's clothing. Granting PR full statehood would give the left another one and a half percent of the population."

"Most Puerto Ricans vote Republican," Kohler objected loudly. "That's documented. Hell, they probably wouldn't take full statehood if we offered it to them on a silver platter anyway. Too much national pride, and, besides, what do they get for it? Just higher taxes."

"They'd accept statehood if they knew they'd be with the majority coming in, my friend," Massey retorted. "Then everything would change."

"So, if I'm hearing you right, Senator Massey," Kohler replied, "you're saying we have a whole *nationality* acting like a wolf in sheep's clothing. You're saying there's some big conspiracy going on here *and* in Puerto Rico. That all of them in this country are trying to fool us by voting Republican now so we'll never expect it when the secret signal goes out and they flip on us. Right?"

"What's so far-fetched about that?"

"Oh, come on," Kohler groaned, making clear that he thought the entire discussion was absurd.

"But, look," McDonnell spoke up, "the president can't just grant Puerto Rico statehood. Congress would have to vote on it."

"He can sure make it one hell of an issue," Massey replied. "Believe me, I know. A man like Wood could turn the screws on congressmen who didn't come into line with him. Get the minorities and special interest groups fired up to rain hell down on them if they didn't vote like he wanted them to. Most of them would probably vote for it to avoid the bad publicity. They'd figure it was no big deal, that most people already think of Puerto Rico as part of the United States anyway. Why should I risk getting a big part of my constituents all pissed off at me for the next election? That's what they'd say to themselves."

"We've got to put our plans into full effect," Dahl spoke up. "Immediately. We've got to—"

"What you need to do is get to Christian Gillette." The speaker was James Benson, the oldest member of the Order. It was the first time since the toast to Hugues de Payens that Benson had said anything. Like Dahl, Benson was a military man—ex in Benson's case. His last post had been director of the Defense Intelligence Agency. "Gillette could be the key," he said quietly. "We should try to recruit him as soon as possible. At a minimum, we have to keep him away from Jesse Wood."

CARMINE TORINO eased his Cadillac inside an old wooden shack beside a run-down house as long shadows reached the steep peaks to the east. The abandoned ranch was forty miles outside Las Vegas, way up Del Costa Canyon. The closest house was ten miles away, so there shouldn't have been anyone else out there.

Torino climbed out of the car, moved quickly to the trunk, grabbed a shotgun and shells from inside, then pulled the shack's door along the rusty track in the gravel until it was closed—hiding the presence of the car. As he hurried toward the house, he glanced around warily at the dusty landscape—mostly just broken fences, scrub, and sage, framed by the steep rocky mountains on all sides. Thank God he still had friends inside the family.

"**I APPRECIATE** your advice on Christian Gillette," Hewitt said. He and Benson stood beside each other on the lodge's wide front porch, staring into the darkness of the moonless night. The rest of the Order had gone to bed. "I think you're right, Jim." They addressed each other informally now that the meeting was over. "I think we should try to recruit him, though we don't have a place for him right now."

"You should try to meet with him is what you should try to do," Benson suggested, "as soon as possible. And don't worry about a spot for him. We'll deal with that when the time comes."

Hewitt wasn't going to tell anyone about his meeting with Gillette, not even Benson. "I'll try to set up a meeting with him."

"Gillette's a powerful man," Benson muttered, his voice feeble. He pulled his jacket tight. It was chilly out here with the sun down. "He's worth over five hundred million and very connected."

"He'd be worth a lot more if we'd let him sell Laurel Energy," said Hewitt, a sparkle in his eye. "He thought he was going to get five billion for that thing. So did the Wall Street analysts."

Benson looked over at Hewitt. "What's that supposed to mean, Samuel? What are you telling me?" He grinned. "Or what *aren't* you telling me?"

"Gillette's been trying to sell Laurel for a while, but for some reason he hasn't gotten any takers. Not any *real* takers."

"I assume that 'for some reason' means you put the word out in the industry for people to stay away from it."

"I did," Hewitt admitted. "I figured we might need an ace in the hole with Christian someday. I figured it might help our cause if he experienced firsthand what we can do. If he felt some pain, then some pleasure."

"How did you figure all that?"

"I have my ways."

Benson shivered. "We can't let Jesse Wood get to Gillette's money and connections. Wood might actually win if he does."

"That *will not* happen," Hewitt said forcefully. "Jesse Wood will *never* be president of the United States. I can assure you of that."

"He's going to win the Democratic nomination, Samuel, I feel it. You do, too. You'll have to take drastic action if you really mean what you say about him never being president."

"I know."

"Are you prepared to take that action?"

Hewitt nodded. "I am."

"Good man."

"And, like I said, I'm going to turn the tables on the Democrats," Hewitt spoke up. "I'm going to get Gillette to join us, instead. He belongs with us, not them. I'm going to make him see that. If he needs a push, so be it."

"Good, good." Benson shook his head. "You know, the power and the connections we have always amaze me—and I've been a member a long time. By the way, when are you going to let OPEC start ramping up production again? I'm tired of paying five bucks a gallon."

The two men shared a chuckle.

"Other than Laurel Energy, what can you use to influence Gillette if he agrees to join us?" Benson asked.

"What do you mean?"

"He isn't married, he doesn't have children. The usual influences won't work. I'm sure he wouldn't want clips of himself having sex with a woman zipping around the Internet, but it wouldn't destroy his family or his career like it would ours."

"I've got a couple of other things in mind."

"There's always got to be a big stick, Samuel. Laurel might not be enough."

"I hear you," Hewitt assured the older man. They'd need the things he was putting into motion if Gillette *didn't* agree to join them, too.

"Always a big stick." Benson began to cough.

"You okay, Jim?"

Benson waved his hand and nodded, unable to speak.

"There's something else I want to tell you about Jesse Wood," Hewitt spoke up when Benson had finally cleared his throat. "I didn't want to mention this in front of the others because I didn't want Dick Dahl to have a total meltdown."

"What is it?"

"A few weeks ago a man who's close to Senator Wood met with several high-ranking Mexican officials in a villa south of Mexico City. A man who's a member of that 'shadowy group' Senator Massey referred to in the meeting."

"The one Mace Kohler thinks doesn't exist?"

"Right."

"What was the meeting about?"

"Statehood for Mexico. Wood's people are having discussions with Puerto Rico *and* Mexico."

Benson was quiet for a few moments, processing this new, disturbing revelation. "What's Mexico's population?" he finally asked. "A hundred million?"

"A hundred *and ten,*" Hewitt answered, gazing at the old man, satisfied because it appeared that Benson had bought it. Hewitt had no information about Wood's people meeting with Mexican officials—it was all bullshit—but he knew Benson would go straight to Massey and Laird right after this and tell them. Then the news would spread quickly through the entire group, but it wouldn't be like he'd made an official announcement about it at a meeting. Kohler wouldn't be able to grill him on details in front of the others. It would just scare the crap out of all of them, make them all more likely to back his plans without question. And Hewitt wanted them all in, Kohler and McDonnell included. He didn't want to risk the possibility of someone going off the reservation. "That's a lot of fucking Democrats."

"Jesus Christ," Benson whispered.

"If that were to happen," said Hewitt, "if Mexico became part of the United States, the landscape of the world would change forever, drastically and suddenly. And not just here, everywhere. There'd be a mad scramble for control all over the world because of the social and, more important, the economic implications of a United States controlled by a black-Hispanic coalition. I'm not saying we need to worry about Mexico coming in right away—it'll be a while—but Wood can put the process in motion with Puerto Rico. He's the starting pitcher. He can set it up for the closer in ten or fifteen years, maybe sooner."

Benson's gaze dropped to the porch's pine planks. "Getting Canada in wouldn't matter at that point." Benson had been quietly working with several high-ranking Canadian officials for a year. Working with intelligence people he'd gotten close to during his years at the DIA. People who felt the world would be safer with an officially unified Canadian–United States coalition. "Canada only has thirty-five million people."

"We aren't going to get Canada," Hewitt growled. "You and I both know that, Jim. Besides, even if by some wild stroke of luck we did, they might end up voting with the blacks and the Hispanics anyway. That's the risk with the Canucks, very socialist up there. But we *know* how Mexico would vote. There's no doubt about it."

"Yeah," Benson agreed, his tone subdued. "I hear you."

They were quiet for a while.

"Look, I know Dick Dahl's a bit of a hothead," Benson spoke up, "but he was right about what he said at the end of the meeting. The Order has got to start putting things in motion, all the things we've talked about. I don't say that because I dislike minorities in any way," Benson added quickly, holding up a hand. "I have only the deepest respect and admiration for the many black and Hispanic men and women I've worked with over the years." He took a measured breath. "I know it's horrible to actually do some of the things we've talked about, but the world would change so dramatically if there was a shift in power of the magnitude we're talking. There's so much hate on that side of the fence. And rightfully so," he muttered. "When they realize what they can do, when they understand the power they have, they'll take advantage of it. The poor segments of their population will demand it and their politicians will have no choice. The majority will rule."

Hewitt smiled to himself. His plan was working perfectly. Benson was going to go straight to Laird and Massey. "Downside of a democracy, huh? Majority ruling and all that."

"Yeah." An owl hooted in the distance as they gazed into the darkness of the trees. "Samuel, there's something I need to talk to you about," said Benson quietly. "It's got to do with our caretaker here on Champagne. He was spotted talking to someone in Southport a few weeks ago."

Hewitt raised both eyebrows. "*What?*"

"I'm not sure it's something to worry about yet, but the guy wasn't anyone the caretaker's been seen with before. It was strange." Benson began coughing again. "How long have he and his wife been the caretakers?"

"Three years."

"That's a long time."

Hewitt knew exactly what Benson was saying, and it was good counsel. You could never let yourself get too comfortable with people. "You're right. I'll look into it."

"What did you think about Mace Kohler tonight?" Benson asked.

"The same thing you thought. He isn't a hundred percent with us."

"McDonnell isn't either."

"I know."

"We've changed the course of history before," Benson pointed out.

"Lincoln, the campaign against the Indians, Martin Luther King, Bobby Hutton, taking down the Enron boys because they wouldn't play ball. And we would have taken care of Jack and Bobby ourselves if the others hadn't. But this is the first time in a while that we've gotten involved in anything of this magnitude. I mean, we're always influencing things—a judge here, an election there—but this is different. This is the biggest thing we've ever taken on."

"I know."

"And, damn it, I don't want to see Mace Kohler—" Benson couldn't finish. Another coughing spell set in.

"That sounds awful, Jim. You better see someone."

"I'm fine," Benson wheezed. "Really."

Hewitt put a hand on Benson's shoulder, catching a quick glance of a pearl-handled Colt revolver hanging inside the older man's jacket. A sudden wave of sadness overtook Hewitt. Something must be very wrong, probably cancer.

"Will you personally take care of my tapes when I'm gone?" Benson asked after a few moments, his voice barely audible. "I wouldn't want Claire or the children to ever see or hear them. You know, if somehow the tapes got into the wrong hands, it would be . . ." His voice drifted off.

"Of course I'll take care of them."

They stood on the porch for several more moments, listening to the trees rustle in the night breeze coming in off the ocean.

"You should get inside, Jim," Hewitt finally suggested. "It's cold out here. That won't help the cough."

Benson turned to the side, revealing the revolver. "I think I'm going to take a walk, Samuel."

Hewitt looked away. The old soldier didn't want any part of a hospital bed, tubes, or morphine. "Just come inside." The old man was going to end it here, on the island he loved. "Please don't do this, Jim."

Benson glanced back at Hewitt. "Why not?"

"Because . . ." Hewitt didn't know how to say it. Finally he reached out and touched the gun beneath Benson's jacket. "That's why."

A curious expression came to Benson's face, then he broke into a wan smile. "Oh my God." He pointed at the gun. "You mean you thought . . . ?"

"Well, yeah. I mean, why else would you be carrying the gun?"

Benson chuckled. "I always carry it when I take a walk at night. I like the way it feels, and, hey, you never know. Even out here." He shook Hewitt's hand. "Thanks for caring," he said, turning to go, "but you know me, I'll fight to the bitter end. See you in the morning."

Hewitt watched the old man descend the lodge's front steps, then fade into the darkness. To the bitter end, Hewitt thought to himself, heading for the door. To the bitter end.

Fifteen minutes later a single gunshot shattered the stillness of the night.

5

WHEN CHRISTIAN ARRIVED at the Las Vegas office of the Nevada Gaming Commission on East Washington Avenue, he'd gotten a polite smile and a sealed envelope from the receptionist—not the invitation to follow her into Alan Agee's office he'd been expecting. Inside the envelope were printed instructions to go to another address for the meeting with Agee, this time in an industrial section of the city.

"That was quick." Quentin moved over as Christian climbed into the limousine and sat down beside him. "How'd it go?"

"It didn't." Christian pushed the intercom button and called out the new address to the driver. "Agee wasn't there." Agee had called late yesterday afternoon to say he could meet today at the Gaming Commission's headquarters. "The receptionist gave me this."

"Let me see." Quentin reached for the envelope. "I don't know," he muttered after scanning the note and seeing that Christian had had to tear open the envelope. "I've got a bad feeling about this."

"Why? I mean, it sucks that Agee's making me drive all over the city to meet him, but I don't think there's any more to it than that."

"You should let me check the place out before you head over there."

"It's probably just his business address. All these guys have real jobs because they don't get paid much to be on the commission, not even the chairman."

"Then why do they do it?"

"Personal publicity. They're appointed to the commission by the governor." Christian took the envelope back from Quentin and slipped it in his jacket pocket. "Agee probably had something come up at work and couldn't make it downtown in time. Maybe he's doing everything he can to help me."

"Maybe, maybe not. Do you have his cell number?"

"No."

"Does he have yours?"

"His secretary does. Debbie sent my e-card to her last week."

"Then why wouldn't he just call you? Why printed directions inside a sealed envelope without a signature?"

"Procedure—I don't know." Quentin wasn't convinced they should be speeding off to the address on the page, and he was probably right. They probably should be more cautious. But, the way Christian figured it, he didn't have any choice. He had to get the casino license, and he had to get it fast. If that meant seeing more of Las Vegas than he wanted to, so be it.

"Well," Quentin spoke up, "I've got some preliminary stuff on Samuel Hewitt."

"Already?"

"Like I said, it's preliminary. I'll have more before your meeting with him." An expectant expression spread across Quentin's face. "You know, I was thinking Hewitt might be able to help us with the Laurel thing. Maybe he's so far up the ladder at U.S. Oil he hasn't heard that Laurel's for sale. When he does, when you tell him, maybe he can get his people to take a close look."

Christian had assumed Samuel Hewitt knew Laurel Energy was for sale. Hewitt was the savviest energy executive around, maybe the savviest executive around period. But if somehow Hewitt didn't know about Laurel, Quentin was right: There might be an opportunity. And if Hewitt did know about it, Christian could get some good market intelligence about why the big guys weren't biting.

The more Christian thought about Laurel Energy not selling, the more it frustrated him. An investment banker from Black Brothers Allen had called a few days ago asking if he could replace Morgan Stanley and "get the Laurel Energy deal done" for Everest. Christian hadn't called back yet. Morgan Stanley had done a lot of good work for Everest Capital in the past, and he was loyal to them. But Laurel had been on the block for a long time, too long, and Black Brothers Allen had a reputation for finishing assignments other investment banks couldn't. Plus it was starting to get out that the Laurel deal was going stale, that Everest had a bomb on its hands. Which was the kind of publicity that really stung in the financial world, no matter how good your track record was.

"I'll mention it to Hewitt." Christian noticed they were getting into a warehouse district. "So, what did you find out about him?"

"He's Texas all the way. Into promoting the state as a great place to do business, travel to, all that kind of stuff. He's tight with the whole political crew down there, too, particularly to ex-senator Massey. They try to keep their relationship low-key, but my source tells me they're close."

"Why do they try to low-key it?"

Quentin shrugged. "I don't know. My source didn't either. I told him to dig into that one."

"Just so no one figures out it's me behind the digging."

"Of course." Quentin flipped back and forth in his notepad for a few moments. "As you know, he's chairman of U.S. Oil."

"Right."

"Runs the ship with an iron fist, and his shareholders love him. Been in charge for almost two decades and the company's reported profit increases every year."

"Background?"

"Blood runs black, as in oil. Granddaddy was a wildcatter who went boom and bust more times than a Vegas showgirl. Sent Hewitt to Princeton while he was on top of one of those waves, then lost it all a few years later so Hewitt had to get a real job after graduation. Started with U.S. Oil as a grunt in the finance department, but it was a rocket ride to the top from there. He was head of the North American division at thirty-eight, head of worldwide exploration at forty-six, and head of everything at forty-nine. Handed the CEO job over to a younger guy a few years ago, but he still runs the place. The CEO move was just for Wall Street, to show investors that there was a succession plan in place."

"Family?"

"Wife, three children, and seven grandchildren, one he's very close to."

"Let me guess. The one named after him. As in Samuel Hewitt the third."

Quentin nodded. "He calls the kid Three Sticks. How the hell—"

"Only makes sense. Hewitt wants his namesake to be the smartest one of the crew, so he spends the most time with him, tries to pass on his experience and knowledge." Christian had seen that trait before in successful older executives: the desire to pass on what they knew. He'd had a few mentors along the way. "What's Hewitt like?"

"He knows when to use the hatchet and when to turn on the charm. He was a political animal during his younger days at U.S. Oil—did whatever it took to move up the food chain and didn't care who he screwed on the way. There's a rumor he secretly videotaped one of his bosses having sex with a secretary, then anonymously dropped the tape off at the personnel department so the guy would get fired and he could get the guy's job. Never substantiated, but the guy resigned under a cloud and Hewitt ended up getting his job."

"I'm surprised he hasn't gone into politics," Christian said, "especially with all those connections."

"Sounds like he has for all intents and purposes. Just hasn't bothered to run."

"What do you mean?"

"My source says Hewitt pulls a ton of strings," Quentin explained. "In return he gets a ton of favors."

"Plenty of people do that."

Quentin shook his head. "Not like this, robo, not on this scale. I'll give you an example. A couple of years ago one of U.S. Oil's big tankers ran aground off Alaska. Spilled millions of gallons of crude, wiped out wildlife up and down the coast for miles—it was as bad as the *Valdez*. They'll be feeling the effects of that accident way after we're dead and gone."

"I never heard about it."

"Not many people did. It was kept *very* quiet. Alaska's politicians didn't say a word, the Coast Guard never said anything, the media never got hold of it. Hewitt had everybody in his pocket." Quentin paused. "One local reporter tried to do a story on it. He's been missing since two weeks after the accident and nobody knows what happened to him."

Christian wagged a finger. "You can't assume Samuel Hewitt had anything to do with that guy's disappearance."

"I'm not assuming anything," Quentin spoke up quickly. "I just thought you should hear about it."

"Uh-huh." Christian wasn't buying into that kind of speculation. He'd called some friends who'd gone to Princeton, and everything they had to say pointed to Hewitt's being a model citizen: a man who gave lots of money to the school as well as to a number of charities. "Anything else?"

"You were right about poker. It's Hewitt's passion. Plays as much as he can and plays for big stakes."

"Good." Christian pulled out his cell phone when it started to ring. "Hello."

"Christian, it's Ray Lancaster. Remember that quarterback I told you I wanted?"

Lancaster had called earlier to tell Christian he was targeting Buffalo's second-string quarterback as a replacement for Ricky Poe. "Yeah."

"In return they want one of our all-pro linebackers, our placekicker, *and* five million bucks in cash."

"You've got to be kidding," Christian said angrily. "A second-string quarterback can't be worth that much."

"He isn't," Lancaster agreed. "Problem is, he's the only decent guy available in the whole league. We know it, they know it, and you said you wanted a quarterback."

Christian went through the options. Give away the farm to get a good quarterback, or give up on the play-offs this season, go with Ricky Poe, hope for 0 and 16, then take the top quarterback with the first pick in next year's college draft. "Wait a few days, then try one more time if you don't hear from them first," he instructed. "Call me after you talk to them."

"Got it."

"So, what did you and Allison do last night?" Quentin asked as Christian hung up.

Allison had convinced Christian to go to the casino after dinner. Quentin hadn't gone—he was tired—but Christian had been wide awake and hadn't felt like heading back to his suite to work. Odd, too, now that he thought about it. Normally he would have felt guilty doing something fun like that on a business trip, something that wasn't in any way related to creating value for his investors. But the entire time he and Allison had been in the casino he hadn't thought about Everest once. Maybe he really was burning out. Or maybe he'd just enjoyed his time with Allison so much that he'd been able to block work out. No woman had been able to make him do that for a long time, and it wasn't because the women weren't interesting. He'd just been too obsessed with Everest.

"I watched her play the craps tables," Christian said slowly, bothered by both answers to the question that was eating at him. "Turns out she's good at that, too. She won a bundle."

"Figures. The rich always get richer."

"Hey, pal, you're not doing too bad yourself these days."

Quentin tapped the leather seat. "You didn't have a copilot last night, did you?"

Christian glanced over. "*What?*"

"Did you sleep with her?"

Allison had looked incredible last night in a tight top with a plunging neckline, short skirt, and spike heels. Every guy in the place had stopped to stare. She kept grabbing his arm every time the dice came up right, throwing her fists up in the air and shouting when she won a few grand on a single roll.

Quentin rolled his eyes and groaned when Christian didn't answer right away. "Oh, no."

"She looked good last night, pal. I saw a couple of guys actually drooling in their drinks."

"Jesus, Chris, the investors'll go nuts if they think the chairman of Everest is having an affair with one of his managing partners. Especially when it's the managing partner who represents the single biggest investment in the fund. Not to mention how Faith will feel," he added.

"Everybody's going to feel fine," said Christian. "I didn't sleep with her."

Which was the truth. But it was also true that he was finding himself more and more attracted to her. They had so much in common, and he liked her wild streak. Plus, it seemed like he and Faith never saw each other anymore anyway. Faith was always off on concert tours and he was always on the other side of the globe on business. At least he saw Allison. But Quentin was right. A romantic relationship with Allison was probably out of the question.

"It's almost a pain in the ass to be out with a girl like Allison," Quentin remarked. "Every guy in the place is trying to snake you. She's so damn hot."

Christian patted Quentin's shoulder. "That's why you're around," he kidded. "To keep them away."

"Well, one reason anyway." A curious smile moved Quentin's lips.

"Tell me something, Chris. You think Allison had a boob job? That top she was wearing last night wasn't covering much, and, I mean . . . well, you know. Wow. Has she ever told you anything about that?"

It was one of the first things she'd told him on the way to that first dinner, how she'd had her breasts enhanced, and how she'd felt completely different afterward—so much better about herself. He'd been speechless for a few seconds when she told him, taken completely by surprise—which rarely happened to him. "I have no idea."

"Oh, come on," Quentin complained, "you do, too. You're just not saying."

"I'm being the same way I'd be if anyone asked me something personal about you."

"Okay, okay." Quentin snapped his fingers. "Hey, did you talk to Faith yesterday?"

He'd been about to call twice, but someone had called him each time he was dialing her number. "No," Christian admitted. "I will today." He thought about a call he needed to make and started to reach for his cell phone, then stopped. "Quentin?" he asked quietly.

"Yeah?"

"You've always told me you think I'm too intense, that I work too hard."

"Absolutely. You've been killing yourself the last few years. Can't keep doing that."

Christian hesitated. He couldn't ask this of anyone but Quentin because it would show weakness. But Quentin wouldn't take it that way. He'd take it just for what it was: a friend asking another friend for advice. "Do you think I'm slowing down at all?"

Quentin didn't answer right away. "No," he finally said. "But you seem tense lately. Mmm, maybe impatient is a better way to describe it. Like when you snapped at that associate last week in the meeting. Never seen you do that before."

Christian nodded grimly. He had snapped at the kid, bad.

"I mean, the guy royally screwed up the numbers he was working on for that deal," Quentin continued. "And what do we pay him? Two hundred grand a year, I think. For two hundred grand a year a guy shouldn't screw up, even if he's only twenty-six. It's just that I've never seen you do that before."

"Yeah, I know." Christian wanted to keep talking, but he saw that they were closing in on the address Agee had given.

A few moments later the driver swung the limousine slowly past a large metal gate, picking his way carefully around trash that was strewn about the potholed lot, then pulled to the right quickly to avoid a truck bearing down on them.

"What is this place?" Quentin asked.

"Looks like a transfer station."

"A what?"

"It's where garbage trucks that go through neighborhoods bring trash." Christian pointed to a large building off to the right. "They dump it on the floor in there, then a front-end loader puts it into an eighteen-wheeler that takes it to a landfill. It's not usually efficient for the route trucks to go all the way to the dump."

"How do you know all that?"

"We owned a waste management company a while back at Everest, before you joined the firm."

"Oh yeah, a couple of funds ago."

"The company we owned had about fifty of these stations in the system. Made some money when we sold it, but I was just glad to be rid of the headaches. The NIMBYS are constantly on your ass."

"Nimbys?"

"Not-in-my-back-yarders. People who live around transfer stations and landfills and don't want them there."

"Uh-huh." Quentin gestured toward the building. "Still think it was a good idea to come here? It really would be better if we found out who owns this place before we talk to anybody."

Christian knew exactly what Quentin was implying. It wasn't a stretch to think the Mob might be involved in their being steered here. "Look, I've already lost a day in this city, and, like I told you, we've spent a billion dollars on the Dice Casino so far. It's got to be ready to go for the team's home opener. I'm running out of time. I've got no choice."

The limo driver pulled to a stop in front of what looked like the office. Before Quentin could get out, a young man wearing jeans and a T-shirt emerged from the building and swaggered up to the limo.

Quentin put his window down.

"You Christian Gillette?" the young man asked, smacking gum as he leaned down and peered inside.

"Nope."

"He in there?"

"Who wants to know?"

The young man smiled smugly. "The guy who left him the envelope at the Gaming Commission. Who the hell are you?"

"Michael Jordan."

"Fuck off, nigger."

Quentin reached for the door handle. "You little piece of—"

Christian grabbed Quentin's arm. "Easy," he urged. "He's scum. He's not worth it." Christian leaned forward so the young man could see him. "I'm Christian Gillette and this is Quentin Stiles," he said, pointing. "I want Mr. Stiles to search you. If you don't let him, I'm outta here."

The young man backed off a step and spread his arms wide. "Hey, why not? Long as you don't get too personal, boy."

Quentin got out and patted him down. "He's clean, Chris."

A moment later the young man climbed into the limousine and shut the door. "I'll make this quick, Mr. Gillette," he said after he was sure the intercom to the front seat was shut off. "You pay me a million in cash and you get your casino license. Otherwise the license will be tied up in red tape for years." He made a face like he was actually feeling physical pain. "I hurt for you, man, I really do because it would be awful if you had to go through that. You know, the endless code violations, things breaking down all the time, dirty money rumors. I've seen it happen before, and it just gets worse and worse. I don't know if you'd *ever* get the license. You'd probably have to sell the casino to someone else at a big discount if you wanted to get any money back at all." He pointed at Christian. "But if you pay me a million bucks in cash by next Friday, you'll have your license on Monday." He reached for the door handle, then hesitated. "And it's got to be *you* giving me the cash. It's got to be you, and it's got to be cash. Got it?" He opened the door and got out, then leaned back in. "Have a nice day, Mr. Gillette. And remember, what happens in Vegas stays in Vegas."

Christian watched the young man go back into the office. He was starting to hate that saying.

JESSE WOOD glanced up at Clarence Osgood and Stephanie Childress, smiling his trademark photogenic smile—full lips; deep dimples; and a mouthful of straight, white teeth. His dark brown eyes glistened beneath his wide forehead and he clapped his hands once. "These numbers are fantastic," he said, checking the report on his desk one more time, unable to control his excitement. "Better than I could have hoped for. If the Democratic convention was held today, I'd get sixty-two percent of the vote, Clarence."

Osgood nodded. He was chief of staff, had been since Jesse's successful Senate campaign. Like Jesse and Stephanie, Osgood was African-American, but, unlike them, he was very dark. Short and heavyset, he wore large, thick glasses. Like Jesse, he was a lawyer by training. "I agree, but don't get too happy about it, Senator." His smile was almost as wide as Jesse's. "We don't want to get cocky. Not now, not so close."

"Let Jesse enjoy himself for a few minutes," Stephanie chided. She was his PR person. Forty-seven, she was still pretty, though not the beauty queen she'd once been. She was statuesque with long arms and legs, straight black hair, and striking facial features. But her jowls were starting to puff, and wrinkles were appearing at the corners of her eyes and mouth. "He deserves it." She beamed at him. "He's worked so hard."

"Thanks, Steph." Jesse gazed back at her for a few moments. She'd been with him for a long time, too, longer than Osgood. She was a wonderful woman. They'd had a brief affair near the end of his tennis career, before he'd gotten married. When the young groupies had started ignoring him because he wasn't winning anymore. "I love you."

She folded her arms over her chest and looked away. "You love everyone," she said, "as long as they vote for you."

Jesse winked at Osgood, then looked back at Stephanie. "Don't be so hard on me, sweetheart."

"You better stop calling me sweetheart, or I'll tell your wife."

Jesse shook his head. "No, you won't."

She sighed. "No, I won't, and that's my problem. I'm too loyal."

Osgood laughed heartily. "*I'll* tell your wife." He paused. "Unless you pay me."

"You always were the opportunistic one, Clarence."

Osgood grabbed both lapels of his jacket—a habit when he went into sarcastic mode. "That's me," he said in a loud voice. "Mr. Opportunity, and a heck of a one this is. Yes, sir, with the salary you pay me, I'll be a rich man someday. I might be able to retire by the time I'm eighty."

"If you get me elected president," Jesse shot back, "you'll end up being a very rich man, richer than you ever dreamed." Stephanie was his cheerleader, the one he turned to when he was down. But Osgood was his money player, the one he wanted on the foul line for the last shot with the game's outcome hanging in the balance. Jesse's expression turned serious. "Will you get me elected, Clarence?"

Osgood nodded, his expression growing grave, too. "Yes, I will. And you can take that to the bank, Senator."

6

DON ROTH sat in a booth near the back of the Southport Harbor Diner, sipping black coffee and pulling apart a stale bran muffin—not really eating it so much as entertaining himself while he waited. He'd taken the Boston Whaler in from Champagne Island this morning, leaving Patty at the lodge by herself. She didn't like being alone out there, but she'd be fine. She carried a .357 Magnum on her at all times when he was gone, and she knew how to use it. She'd been a Miami cop for twelve years before coming north with him.

The trip into Southport had been rough, right up until he'd reached the mouth of the harbor. It had taken almost two hours to get in, forty-five minutes longer than normal. The late-spring sky was cloudless, but there'd been a stiff northeast breeze. Tall waves had rocked the small boat all the way in, forcing Roth to don a bright yellow slicker to protect himself against the cold salty spray constantly pelting him from over the gunnels. He rose up slightly off the restaurant's brown vinyl seat to check the boat, which was moored to a dock right outside the window. It seemed fine, swaying gently with the slight chop of the harbor. He was wary about it being tampered with today. He'd never worried about that before.

Roth had told Patty he needed supplies. Specifically, bulbs for the lighthouse and some plywood and tar paper to fix a leak in the toolshed roof. He needed those things, but he could have waited. There was something else much more important drawing him to Southport today.

When Roth saw Todd Harrison come through the diner's revolving door he put down the muffin. Harrison was the stranger who'd tapped him on the shoulder at the hardware store down the block three weeks ago, begging to ask a few questions about the island. Harrison was the reason Roth had come to the mainland today. He watched the young man glance around the restaurant and waved when their eyes met.

"Thanks for coming, Don," Harrison said, shaking hands as he eased into the other side of the booth, setting an old backpack down beside him and pulling out a spiral notepad from one of its pockets. "You're really helping me out."

Harrison was in his late twenties, Roth figured. Short and stocky with long, curly hair flowing from beneath his Yankees baseball cap. He had that hungry look all young investigative reporters wore like a badge of honor. Here, Miami, it didn't matter. "Sure."

"Sorry I'm late, but I took the long way getting here. I was worried about being followed."

"Why were you worried about *that*?"

A dark-haired waitress wearing a checkered apron ambled up to the table before Harrison could answer. She reminded Roth of a spare tire—worn down at the edges.

"Whatcha want, honey?" she asked, pulling out a pencil from behind her ear.

"A large fountain Coke," Harrison said, "with lots of crushed ice."

"We only got Pepsi."

"Fine. Just make sure you put lots of—"

"Yeah, yeah, the crushed ice. I got it."

As the waitress walked away, Roth noticed a run in her panty hose stretching from the back of her knee to her ankle. She probably knew it was there when she put the stockings on this morning, but she'd worn them anyway. Most folks in Southport eked out a living, and you didn't throw away a pair of stockings because of one run. "Why were you worried about being followed?" Roth asked again.

Harrison put his notebook down on the Formica tabletop, then took off his cap and wiped perspiration from his forehead. "What's the deal with Champagne Island?"

Roth didn't appreciate the guy ignoring his question. "What do you mean?"

"Do you own it?"

"No. Me and my wife just live there. We're the caretakers, have been for the last three years."

"Who does own it?"

Roth shrugged. "I don't know."

Harrison's eyes got big. "You wanna know?"

"Why the hell did you ask me if you knew?"

"Because the official owner of record isn't a person, it's an entity. Something called the Molay Trust. I figured maybe you were the trustee."

Roth had been a Dade County police officer until retiring from the force thirty-nine months ago. Words like *trustee* didn't mean much to him. "I don't know what you're talking about."

"Forget it."

"No, no, what's the Molay Trust?" Roth pushed.

"That's what I'm trying to figure out. That's why I asked you. I want to know who's behind the trust."

"How'd you find the name of it?"

The waitress returned to the booth carrying Harrison's Pepsi on a small tray. She put it down, then dropped a long straw encased in a white paper wrapper beside the glass. "There you go."

"Thanks." Harrison peeled back the straw's wrapper and scrunched it up like an accordion, casing the diner as he stuck the straw down through the crushed ice. He smiled. "I love going to old Maine seacoast towns. It's like going back into the fifties, like being in a Norman Rockwell painting. You get a fountain soda with crushed ice and a red-striped straw with that kink in it so you can bend it." He held his index finger over the top end of the straw, creating a vacuum, then pulled it out of the glass and let a drop of Pepsi fall onto the scrunched-up wrapper. His smile grew wider as the moisture worked its way through the paper and the wrapper uncoiled like a caterpillar undulating along a twig. "My grandmother showed me how to do that when I was a little kid."

"Look, Harrison, I don't have time to—"

"I'm not a local," Harrison interrupted. "I'm not even from Maine."

"Where are you from?" Roth asked, assuming this information was somehow important.

"New York. Only been in this area since Christmas."

"So?"

Harrison gazed out the window across the harbor. "So one night a few months ago, I'm at this hole-in-the-wall restaurant up the coast in

Rockland chasing down a story about a lobster boat that's missing. Everybody thinks drugs are involved. Anyway, it's around ten and I'm sitting at the bar eating fried clams and drinking a beer wondering what the hell I'm doing with my life when this old guy sits down on the stool next to me and starts belting down straight Scotch. After he's polished off a couple of drinks, he goes into this story about something called Champagne Island. He must have been seventy, maybe older, I don't know, and I didn't pay much attention to him at first. Figured he was just the bar's crazy old fishing captain who didn't have anyone else to talk to. Seems like every bar up here's got one of those guys and he was dressed like it, too—ratty jeans, red-checked wool jacket, and a shitty orange rain hat. I'm only halfway listening, just being polite, you know?

"But then the story gets interesting. He tells me how his grandfather and three pals had this secret club a long time ago, when they were teenagers. You know, like a lot of teenage boys do. How they had meetings on this island way offshore. How they paddled all the way out there in canoes to get to it. This was way back in the late eighteen hundreds and the island wasn't named Champagne then. It was called Albany Rock. Nobody from town ever went out to Albany Rock because people swore it was haunted, but the old man at the bar says his grandfather and his buddies never saw anything weird out there. That is, until one summer day when they got chased off by two guys carrying shotguns who told them if they ever came back, they wouldn't leave alive."

Harrison took a sip of soda.

"That old man got me thinking. So for the next few days I drove up and down the coast, checking for records of the island. Finally, in a dusty file room of a courthouse in this tiny town called Blue Hill Falls, I find something."

"What?"

"A property identification form naming the owner of Champagne Island as the Molay Trust. I don't think it's really even a deed. The form was filed in 1899 but not the following year. In fact, I couldn't find any other records about Champagne anywhere, old or current."

"Huh."

"Guess what year the boys were chased off the island."

Roth didn't hesitate. "1899."

"Exactly."

"Wow," Roth said, trying to act interested. "You're right. Quite a story."

"Yeah, it is." Harrison looked around the restaurant again. "So, who comes out there to Champagne Island? Who do you take care of it for?"

"Just a group of guys, older business executives. As far as I can tell, they use it as a vacation place, as a fishing club. They fish a lot while they're on the island."

"How often do they come out there?"

Roth pushed out his lower lip, thinking. "Once or twice a month."

"Even in the winter?"

"Yeah, why?"

"Can't be real good fishing out there in the winter. Even if it is, it wouldn't be very much fun. God, it'd be cold as hell. Seems like people would rather be fishing in Florida during the winter, older men especially."

Roth shrugged. "I don't ask, they don't say."

"Who hired you?"

"One of the men in the club."

"Do they come with their wives? Do they come together? Separately? What's the deal?" Harrison asked the questions rapid fire, jotting down notes in his pad as he talked.

"Never really thought about it. But, now that you ask, it seems like they always come as a group, never by themselves. I mean, they fly in separately on choppers, but they all come at the same time. Never one or two. As far as I know, they've never brought wives, although I think I remember seeing wedding bands on their fingers. In fact, my impression is they're actually trying to get *away* from their wives." He straightened up in his chair. "Why are you so interested?"

Harrison took a deep breath. "Remember I told you I wasn't from around here?"

"Yeah."

"I never would have known Champagne Island even existed if the old guy hadn't sat down next to me at the bar that night and started blathering."

"So?"

"So there wasn't anyone else sitting at the bar. Everybody else in the place was sitting at tables. All the other stools at the bar were empty, but he sat down on the one right next to me and started talking. No intro, no nothing. He just started going on, like he couldn't wait to spill his guts."

"So?"

Harrison rolled his eyes, frustrated. "So after he finishes his story, he tells me I gotta go check out the island. That he's heard something strange is going on out there. He's pretty drunk at this point, and he keeps slurring to me over and over to take up the cause. Which is why I went looking for records the next day. I chartered a helicopter a week later and flew out there, too. Saw the lodge and the helipad, but I haven't been able to find out anything else. Which is why I wanted to talk to you."

"How did you know I lived on the island?" Roth wanted to know.

"I asked around at the local stores. Figured whoever lived at the lodge would have to come to the mainland for supplies, and this was the closest town to the island. A clerk at the hardware store up the block called me on my cell when you came in there three weeks ago, and I rushed right over. I'd given him fifty bucks to let me know when he spotted you. Had the same deal with one of the checkout girls at the grocery store over on Stafford Street." They were quiet for a few moments, then Harrison spoke up again. "Nobody at the bar had ever seen that old man before. In fact, nobody in the *whole town* had ever seen him before."

Roth made a face. "How could you know that?"

"I showed just about everybody in town the old man's picture," Harrison claimed, "and nobody recognized him."

Roth looked up from his bran muffin. He'd been picking at it again. "You took his picture?"

"Yeah, but he didn't know it. I was coming back from taking a leak, and I snapped his mug from across the room. I'm kind of a camera nut."

Some kind of a nut anyway, Roth thought. "And you showed people in town the picture, but they didn't recognize him?"

"Neither did anybody in any of the towns where I went looking for records of the island, including Blue Hill Falls."

"What are you saying?"

"Come on, you know what I'm saying. You're an ex-cop."

Roth's eyes shot to Harrison's. "How'd you know that?"

Harrison put his hands on the table and pretended to be typing on a keyboard. "The Internet, man. There were a bunch of stories about you on there. You retired from the Dade County force a few years ago under a lot of pressure. The rumor was you were involved in protection for a big Cuban drug gang operating in Miami."

"That was bullshit!" Roth shouted, slamming his big fist on the tabletop. He looked out the window, away from the stares of the other customers who'd stopped eating to see what the noise was. "I was framed," he whispered.

"By who?"

"I don't know." Roth let out a long breath. It had been the worst time of his life. The only good thing that had happened was meeting Patty, who had always believed he was innocent—still did. He hated lying to her like that, but it was the only way. She never would have come north with him to Maine if she'd known the truth. "You think the old man found you, right? You don't think it was just a coincidence that he walked in there that night."

"Exactly."

"You think he followed you to the bar," Roth continued, his words spilling out faster and faster. "Sat down next to you, told you the story, and pumped you up so you'd try to find out about the island."

"Now you're getting it," Harrison said.

"Nobody knew him because he's not from around here. He's part of some group trying to figure out what's really going on out at Champagne Island, and he wants you to do the dirty work for him. It's a fair trade. He finds out what's going on, and you get your big career break. If you unlock the secret of Champagne Island, you figure you'll be the next Mike Wallace, Geraldo Rivera, whatever."

"Well, yeah."

Roth slid out of the bench seat. "I can't help. There's nothing strange going on out there, Harrison. It's just a fishing club. I know you want it to be more than that, but it isn't."

Harrison's chin dropped to his chest. "But, I—"

"There's no fire here, Harrison." Roth could see he'd taken the guy down a peg—or ten. "Not even any smoke."

"Well, there's one thing you could do."

Roth pulled out his wallet and dropped a five on the table. "What?"

"Let me look around out there a little."

"No way."

"Why not? Especially if there's nothing going on."

"No."

"But it's just a fishing club. What's the big deal?"

Roth hesitated, then sat back down and picked up a toothpick that had been impaled in the bran muffin. "You still have the picture of that old man who told you the story?" he asked, sliding the toothpick into his mouth.

"Yeah."

"Let me see it."

"I don't have it with me."

"Where is it?"

"In a safe place, along with a copy of that old property ID form I found."

"Anybody else know about this stuff?"

"Yup. I scanned the guy's picture and the form and e-mailed it to a friend of mine."

Roth winced.

"Why?"

Roth took a deep breath and checked the boat again. It seemed fine. His eyes flickered around the restaurant.

"Come on," Harrison pushed, "what is it?"

Roth leaned forward. "You might be onto something," he admitted quietly.

"I knew it," Harrison exclaimed, pumping his fists.

"Shut the hell up, you idiot!" Roth hissed. *"Jesus Christ."*

"Sorry, sorry."

Roth's eyes shot to the door as two older men dressed in preppy clothes moved into the place. He could have sworn they'd both glanced in his direction longer than they should have. "Look," he said, leaning farther across the table, watching the two men sit down at a table on the other side of the restaurant, "my wife says she's seen some strange things out there, and she's not the type to say something like that unless she really did. She was a cop, a damn good one, too." He hesitated. "And . . . well . . . when the guys out there hired me they knew about what had happened in Miami. They knew about the rumors. Actually, they knew a *lot* about them, and they didn't care. In fact, I got the feeling they liked that I'd had a problem."

"So they could use it against you if they needed to," Harrison said. "So you'd stay quiet if you ever found something." He picked up a pen and began scribbling on his pad again. "What kind of strange things has your wife seen?"

Roth was still watching the two men—and they seemed to be watching him. "Not now, not here."

"When?"

"You got a number where I can reach you?"

AS THE PLANE swung around and taxied toward the runway, Christian's cell phone went off. "Nigel."

"Hey, Chris, how are you?"

Christian glanced over his shoulder toward the back of the plane. Allison and Quentin were further back, playing gin rummy. Allison loved games, any kind, as long as she could bet. She was always trying to get him to play real-money Monopoly with a group of her friends. "Been better," he admitted.

"What's wrong?"

"Long story." He had to decide if he was going to pay some greasy guy he'd met once for five minutes a million bucks to get a casino license so he could justify laying out over a billion dollars. Nothing was ever easy. "We'll talk about it when I get back."

"What about Ray Lancaster?" Nigel asked. "He find you a quarterback yet?"

"Yeah, some guy on the Bills, but they want our whole team in return."

"What?"

"They want *a lot,* Nigel. The placekicker and one of our linebackers to start with."

"The all-pro?"

"Of course."

"Which one of the Bills' quarterbacks does Lancaster want?"

"I don't know." Christian could see that they were nearing the runway, almost ready to take off. "I'm going to have to turn off the phone in a second, Nigel. Did you have something specific you wanted to talk about?"

Nigel took a deep breath. "The SEC wants to meet with you about CST. Just you."

Christian set his jaw tightly. They were ramping up the pressure. Time to call the lawyers.

PATTY ROTH climbed the wide staircase to the lodge's third floor, right hand resting on the handle of her revolver, left hand gliding along the polished banister. She glanced back over her shoulder time after time as she moved up the stairs. An ex–highway patrol cop, she'd seen and dealt with a lot of bad things, so she didn't scare easily. But this place gave her the creeps when Don wasn't around—sometimes even when he was. It irritated her that he'd left her out here alone when it didn't seem like he really needed to go to Southport. She'd checked and there were still four spare bulbs for the lighthouse in the toolshed. And the hole in the shed's roof he'd griped about had to be pretty small, because she couldn't find it.

A chill ran up her spine as she reached the third-floor hallway. It seemed cold up here, and this floor had a different smell to it. Like mildew, which made more sense now that she thought about it. She groaned quietly. Three years here and it was just dawning on her. Maybe that was why she'd never made detective down in Miami. That or the fact that everyone knew she and Don were having an affair.

Patty walked the length of the hallway to the room Don had told her never to enter—without any explanation. He'd be furious at her for doing this, but too bad. She'd sacrificed a lot to come here, basically exiling herself on this island for him because she was petrified of boats. But she loved him more than she hated the ocean.

She pulled out her master key, slipped it in the lock, turned, and pushed. The door creaked slowly back on its hinges revealing a room stacked with boxes. There was a large steel door on the far wall with two combination locks hanging from latches near the top and bottom.

Patty took a deep breath. The smell of mildew was even stronger in here than in the hallway, and she could feel her heart beating hard as she gazed at the door, suddenly clear on why the smell was stronger here. She walked slowly toward it, her sneakers making no sound as she moved across the hardwood floor.

Halfway across the room she thought she heard something outside. A snap and a thud.

There were no windows in the room, so she raced to the window at the end of the hall. She froze, paralyzed by what she thought she'd seen far below her—a figure running into the woods outside the lodge. She pressed her face to the glass, eyes darting around the grounds below. She was breathing hard and the vapor fogged the glass. She wiped it quickly away with her sleeve and looked out again, holding her face slightly back from the pane this time, but there was nothing. Nothing except the trees swaying back and forth in the strong breeze coming off the ocean.

Her imagination, she thought to herself, squeezing the handle of the gun. Had to be. It wasn't the first time she'd thought she'd seen something strange out here. And she had a feeling it wouldn't be the last.

7

ELIJAH FORTE was born poor in Oakland, California, in 1949. His father made a few dollars a day shining shoes on a busy corner of the business district, and his mother made only a little more than that as a maid for a white family in San Francisco. Forte had five brothers, and they all lived in one bedroom of their tiny tenement, narrow bunks stacked three high. His parents had come west from Alabama in 1945, fled really, after his father's brother had been lynched for necking with a white girl in the backseat of a Chrysler. They'd been looking for a better way, settling in Oakland after short, unhappy stints in Dallas and Los Angeles.

But the better way hadn't happened. Things had gone the *other* way, backward. They'd grown poorer and poorer, eating only two meager meals a day and wearing clothes until they disintegrated. Finally his father couldn't take it anymore and tried robbing a bank in a rich neighborhood. But he didn't know what he was doing, and the cops surrounded the branch before he could make it out of the building. So he'd hustled several people inside the vault and holed up, trying to negotiate his way out. He'd been killed in there after finally falling asleep. Shot four times in the back—which Oakland police officials had never bothered to explain.

At that point, the task of caring for the family had fallen solely on the slender shoulders of Elijah's mother, a caramel-skinned West Indian woman whose great-grandmother had been white. One of Forte's most vivid childhood memories was of realizing how she made ends meet after his father was murdered.

When Forte was little, his mother often took him with her to the white family's house—a sprawling place on the cliffs overlooking the Pacific Ocean—and he played in a room in the basement while she cleaned and washed clothes. Bored nearly to tears one day, he'd gone looking for her—and found her naked in the man's bedroom. They hadn't noticed him for a few moments, and he'd watched her do as she was ordered. Terrible things he couldn't understand.

When his mother finally saw him standing by the door, she'd screamed at him to leave. He'd raced back to the basement and hidden in a dark corner. She'd never taken him with her again, never spoken of the incident, though she kept working for the family another seven years.

In 1966, Forte had killed the man he'd seen with his mother. Killed the man with his bare hands, their faces just inches apart as the man gasped his last pitiful breath. Then Forte had dumped the body in San Francisco Bay and no one had ever figured out what had happened. Maybe it was just that the man's wife had known all along what a scumbag he was and she'd been glad when he went missing. Maybe she hadn't helped the cops at all, only too glad to collect the insurance after the required waiting period.

At seventeen, Forte had joined the Black Panthers, a group of young black men who followed a victory-by-any-means-necessary credo as they sought a better way for African Americans. During his time with the Panthers, Forte had learned valuable organizational skills—and that you couldn't fight The Man. Not back then, not if you wanted to live. He'd learned that overt, chest-pounding, in-your-face protests didn't accomplish anything except getting you killed, like Bobby Hutton in Oakland and Fred Hampton in Chicago. That black athletes standing on summer Olympic podiums with their gloved, clasped fists held high in the air and their heads bowed did nothing but scare the hell out of whites, making them even warier. Making white police officers more likely to beat you until you had so many broken bones in your body that you couldn't move and there was so much pain that suddenly it didn't hurt anymore because the body had shut down its ability to feel. He'd learned that if you really wanted to make a difference, you didn't advertise your existence, you moved in the shadows. And that money—economic power—was what really made a difference. With it, you could do almost anything you wanted, whether you were black, brown, red, or yellow.

With a brutal work ethic and guile learned on tough streets, Forte had become one of the wealthiest men in America, building an empire that controlled music labels; a cable company; television and film studios; commercial real estate properties in New York, Los Angeles, London, and Tokyo; and several technology companies. He was worth over two billion dollars but his name never appeared on the *Forbes* annual list of the world's wealthiest people because his ownership was concealed behind a maze of corporations and partnerships. His time in the Black Panthers had made him very careful. He'd seen what a government could do to people it hated, and he'd taken the lesson to heart. Even the IRS would have a hard time figuring out what he was worth. At least until they did an enema audit—or he died.

So he'd ordered his accountants to always pay more than what he owed by not taking all the deductions he was allowed. That way, he hoped, the Treasury would never come sniffing around.

There wasn't much he could do about dying—except continue to be careful.

Forte looked out over Los Angeles from his twentieth-floor Santa Monica office. He had a beautiful view of downtown and the sun sinking into the Pacific Ocean out the wide floor-to-ceiling windows that spanned the width of the room. He'd driven down here from Oakland in 1975 in a beat-up Chevy Vega with nothing but one small suitcase of belongings. From scratch, he'd built what was now one of the biggest hip-hop labels in the music industry. He'd used that company as a springboard, pouring the cash it generated into his other ventures, all of which—in musicspeak—had gone platinum, too. He'd never married or had children, never had time for those things because he'd stayed focused on building his empire, on amassing wealth, on the ultimate goal. Everything he'd done he'd done in anticipation of this time. Now it was finally here.

There was a knock on the office door.

"Come in," Forte called. He knew who it was by the knock. Two loud, distinctive raps.

The door swung back and Heath Johnson appeared. Johnson was the executive vice president of Ebony Enterprises, the holding company that sat atop all Forte's investments. He was Forte's best friend—and his alter ego. Johnson had a basketball player's build—tall with long, defined muscles—and usually wore fitted clothes that accentuated his body.

Today it was a maroon turtleneck and black designer jeans. He was balding on top, sported a full beard, and had a character-filled face that gave away his many moods. He was an intellectual—with an undergraduate degree from Morgan State, and a master's in sociology from Stanford—and he spoke in a deep, thoughtful voice. In brief, he was everything Forte was not. Which was exactly what Forte wanted in his top lieutenant.

Forte was short and hadn't set foot in a classroom since tenth grade. He had a closet full of conservative suits and expensive ties and *always* wore a starched white shirt—to constantly remind himself of the color he hated. He didn't analyze things for long, usually shot from the hip, liked making a hundred decisions an hour. So Forte had others do the project analysis—always reviewed by Johnson before they reached Forte's desk—so he could make a final decision quickly. His face was plain, devoid of personality, which was the way it had to be. He could never let others know what he was thinking. So, in business meetings, Forte watched Johnson's face to judge his own emotions, to judge when he should be aggressive with the other side and when he should back off. It worked perfectly, and he'd made Johnson a wealthy man as a reward.

Forte and Johnson had met in the Black Panthers. They'd survived a brutal FBI attack in 1969 at the home of another Panther in which seven people in the house had been killed, and they always had that bond. They'd stayed in touch ever since, and, when Ebony Enterprises began to take off, Forte had asked Johnson to join the company—but Johnson declined. The second, third, and fourth times Forte had asked, too. Finally, six years later, Johnson agreed to become the executive vice president. Now he handled all details—and never complained.

"Hello, boss."

Johnson had called Forte "boss" ever since joining Ebony Enterprises. To remind them both of who was in charge. "I thought you'd gone home for the night, Heath."

"Got one more thing for you to sign," Johnson explained, putting a document down on the desk and flipping to the signature pages in the back. "It's the sale agreement for that property in midtown Manhattan."

"How much did we make on that?" Forte asked, leaning forward and picking up an old ballpoint pen.

"Twenty-two million." Johnson flipped several pages further back. "And there," he indicated, pointing to a line at the bottom of the page.

"Sure."

"What's the deal with that pen?" Johnson asked in his melodious voice as he picked up the document. "I've always wanted to ask you about it. I mean, you always carry it with you. It looks like it's fifty years old."

Forte gazed at the pen. Johnson was right: It was almost fifty years old. He'd used it to gouge out the man's eyes before he'd strangled him. Gouged them out and listened to the man scream—music to Forte's ears—while he was tied up. Tied up exactly the same way the bastard had tied up his mother that day Forte had found them. "I don't know where I got it," Forte answered. From the man's desk, that's where he'd gotten it. He'd kept it all these years as a brutal reminder of how far he'd gone that night—and signed every important Ebony Enterprises document with it. There was still a tiny bit of dried blood inside it.

"You want me to order you a nice Cross pen, boss?"

"No. Sit down," Forte ordered impatiently. "We need to talk."

Johnson relaxed into the leather chair in front of the desk. "You want to talk about Jesse—"

Forte ran his finger across his lips.

"What's wrong?" Johnson whispered.

"When did you have the place swept last?"

"This morning before you got here," Johnson answered, his voice becoming normal again when he understood why Forte was worried. "It's clean."

Forte had become obsessed with making certain no one bugged him or listened to his calls. They'd found a listening device a couple of years ago in this office, and ever since he'd made certain that his offices, homes, and limousines were regularly swept. "Good." He couldn't have anyone finding out what he was doing. "Yeah, I want to talk about Jesse Wood. When's that meeting?"

"Next week."

"Where?"

"In New York at the Waldorf."

"Is Wood going to ask then?"

Johnson nodded. "Yeah."

"Good." Forte eased back in his chair and stretched. He hadn't gotten his workout in today, and he missed it. He'd thought about putting a small gym into one of the office rooms for days like today—crammed so full of meetings and calls he couldn't leave—but he liked getting out of the building. If he put in a gym in here, he'd never step outside. "Jesse's starting to be a pain in the ass."

Johnson glanced up. "What do you mean, boss?"

"Last weekend when we were talking about statehood for Puerto Rico, I could tell he was having second thoughts about it. I mean, it's not like he was jumping up and down and screaming that he wouldn't support it, but I could tell by his body language he was getting uncomfortable. He sure wasn't embracing it anymore." Forte looked up from the pen. "He's been pushing back on Osgood and Stephanie, too."

"You mean about replacing them?"

"Yep."

"Well, that's just not acceptable, boss. You're running the show. I say you lower the boom on Jesse right away. You're his angel, and he ought to act like it. He ought to kiss your feet every time he sees you. He'd be nothing without you."

Eight years ago Forte and Johnson had done a painstaking review of potential black presidential candidates. It was the dream, what they'd talked about so long ago, from the first time they'd met at a Black Panther meeting. Talked about it until four in the morning, until they couldn't keep their eyes open any longer. And they'd talked about it constantly since. A black man in the White House—even joking about calling it the Black House when they got their man in.

Forte, Johnson, and three other prominent African Americans that Forte was close to had secretly compiled a list of twenty names, calling the effort Project Shadow: twenty black men who could potentially win a presidential election someday and make history. From the list they had discarded any prominent black Republican immediately: an Oklahoma senator, a well-known entertainment executive, an ex–secretary of state. The message was too garbled coming from the right, and ultimately they felt the GOP would never nominate a black man for the party's top job, to be the most powerful man in the world. Second, they had discarded any black Democrat from the list who was *already in* politics: a northeastern governor, a senator who was also a minister. Too many enemies, too many preconceived notions, too many biases.

That left three names on the list, one of which had jumped out at the five men behind Project Shadow right away: Jesse Wood. Wood had the recognition factor and the look, and whites loved him. At least on a patriotic level. He'd beaten a Russian in the finals of the U.S. Open at a time when the Cold War was still on, endearing him to everyone.

The downside to backing Wood was that at that point he'd never been in politics, so he'd needed a lot of coaching. And though he was a partner at a big Manhattan law firm and had won a lot of tournaments during his tennis days, he wasn't as wealthy as they'd hoped. He'd need help putting together a war chest to give him a realistic shot at winning. In the eighties, tennis tournaments didn't offer million-dollar purses; and, while he'd been successful in his law practice, he had five children. There were bills to pay, college tuitions to fund, appearances to keep up, and not much left over for a serious political career. Forte had stroked some significant checks to get Jesse Wood where he was today. Jesse owed him big in a lot of ways.

Heath Johnson had approached Wood under the guise of taking on Ebony Enterprises as a client, but the meeting in Wood's Manhattan law office had lasted just fifteen minutes when Wood realized there was another agenda to Johnson's visit. Wood had declined Johnson's invitation to sit down with all five Shadows, even scolded him for misrepresenting his intentions, for wasting his time. Then he politely but firmly showed Johnson the door.

Two days later Johnson had gotten a sheepish call. Wood had thought about it more and had interest after all. A week later Wood met with the Shadows.

The meeting took place in Memphis, Tennessee, because it was central for all of them and it was historic, the site of Martin Luther King's assassination. At it, the Shadows made it clear to Wood that he was never to let on to anyone that the meeting had occurred or who his backers were. They all had business careers and had consciously stayed away from politics because it could have hindered their ability to make money. More important, any hint of their association with him would hurt his chances to win, probably destroy them. They'd all been associated with militant black groups earlier in their lives. If a black man was going to have any chance of taking the White House in the next thirty years—while whites remained the majority—he was going to have to get some of them to vote for him. But even whites on the far left remembered groups like the Black Panthers, and those memories still scared them. Any inkling that Wood was associated with that kind of thinking would torpedo his campaign.

The plan for Wood's road to the White House had developed over several months. He would run for a U.S. Senate seat in New York, then six years later for president. Everything had gone perfectly so far. Wood was smooth as silk; everyone loved him.

"Have you mentioned the video clip to Jesse?" Forte asked.

"No. As far as I can tell, he doesn't know about it."

"Good. That way it'll have more of an effect on him when he sees it."

Johnson chuckled. "Like a sledgehammer hitting him in the stomach, boss. That's what the effect will be."

"Jesse brought it on himself," Forte snapped. "I didn't put this much time and money into him to have him think he can do this without us at the last minute. He's like a kid. All of the sudden he can taste it, and he doesn't want anyone telling him what to do or how to think and act. Doesn't want to have to come through on his promises to me because he knows some of these things will be tough. Unpopular with a lot of folks."

"Too bad," Johnson growled, shaking his head. "It's not about him. It's about something much bigger, an agenda we've been focused on for decades. It's about breaking new ground for our people. You've made it possible for him to be one of the most important individuals in the history of this planet, and he owes you. I say you show him the clip as soon as possible."

Forte gazed out the window as the sun dipped below the horizon. A good idea, and probably something he'd do in the next couple of weeks.

"How about the number-two slot?" Johnson asked. "Any pushback from Wood there, boss?"

"Same thing," Forte answered. "He didn't say anything, but I don't think he likes being told who to run with. I think he wants to make that decision on his own."

"He would have chosen a black from the South, probably Malcolm Thomas," said Johnson, referring to the Florida congressman. "Wood doesn't get it on this one. Thomas wouldn't help us with the bigger picture."

"Exactly."

"The only problem I have with this VP thing," Johnson continued, "is that eight years from now we'll be right back where we started. With a white president."

Forte had already thought that one through. "Don't worry about that."

Johnson looked over, recognizing Forte's ominous tone. "What do you mean, boss? Is there something I don't know?"

"It's better that you don't," Forte answered quietly, understanding that his response had hurt Johnson's feelings. He rarely held anything back from Johnson. "At least, not yet." He looked up. "You haven't seen the clip, have you?"

Johnson shook his head. "No, but I'd like to."

Forte nodded. "Yeah, you should. It's amazing."

JESSE WOOD sat in his office, humming, charged up about the way things were going, more and more convinced he had a legitimate shot to be the next president of the United States. Two more primaries and he'd lock up the Democratic nomination, then it would be on to the big show. On to November and everything he'd dreamed of.

He glanced up. Osgood and Stephanie were hard at work at a table in a corner of the office, comparing notes. Such loyal soldiers. They'd all grown up in politics together, and it had been a fantastic ride.

Jesse focused on Stephanie, remembering the first time he'd seen her. It had been during his second-round match at that tournament in Vermont so many years ago. It hadn't been hard to notice her. She'd been one of the most beautiful women in the world at that point—California's representative in the Miss America pageant two years before—and there weren't more than twenty people watching the match. He'd almost lost to a nobody because he couldn't concentrate, couldn't keep his eyes off her.

After the match, he'd gone right up to her and asked her out, not even bothering to go to his chair to put his racquet down, and they'd spent a wonderful week together, culminating with his last win on tour. He could never figure out why he hadn't married her. It was just something he couldn't put his finger on, some small piece of the puzzle that was missing and always would be. He knew there was still a trace of bitterness inside her about that, and it showed every once in a while. She had never gotten married, and he often wondered if that was because she still carried a torch, still held out hope that they might finally get together someday.

Jesse's computer *ping*ed, indicating the arrival of a new e-mail, and he brought it up, instantly wishing he hadn't. It was another missile from Elijah Forte, reminding him that he needed to start interviewing people to replace Osgood and Stephanie. According to Forte, neither of them were national players, neither of them had the right stuff for the Oval Office. Fine for a senator's staff, but not for a president's. It irritated him to no end that Forte thought he had the right to run every detail.

He glanced over at Osgood and Stephanie again. Maybe it was time to find out if Elijah Forte wanted to play hardball. Maybe it was time for a good old game of chicken.

8

CAL SEGAL turned off the desolate country lane onto his gravel driveway. The driveway led up a steep mountain to the Adirondack hideaway his family had owned for more than a hundred years. A cabin deep in the woods beside a crystal-clear lake Segal had so many fond memories of: fishing with his father, camping with his brother, his first kiss to a girl he'd lost touch with ages ago.

Segal could have taken the helicopter and avoided the seven-hour car ride from the city—he knew how to fly it and there was a field a short distance away from the cabin through the woods where he could have landed—but he'd wanted to drive. Spring was finally breaking winter's hold on New England, and it had been a joy to see the leaves and the flowers in full bloom as he made his way through the mountains. The air smelled so good, heavy with all the floral scents beneath a cloudless sky.

Several deer bounded across the driveway in front of him, startled by the SUV, and he slammed on the brakes, barely avoiding a buck who broke from the underbrush right in front of him. He laughed nervously. That would have been a bad way to start his three days alone up here.

Segal was CEO of a mining company his family had owned for five generations, and things had turned stressful in the last few months. A couple of frivolous lawsuits and a pending strike had worn him down. He couldn't wait to pull out a fishing rod from the closet by the back door, paddle the canoe to one of his favorite coves, and see if he could hook a couple of bass before dark. His was the only cabin on the entire lake, so it wasn't as if there'd be other fishermen around. It would be so peaceful out there.

A half mile later Segal eased the SUV to a stop in front of the cabin, hopped out, grabbed one of his bags from the backseat, and headed toward the door. He'd get the rest of his luggage later. There was still an hour of daylight left and he wanted to wet a line. Evening was the best time to fish up here.

Segal stepped inside the cabin and saw a man he didn't recognize sitting in the living room's easy chair. The man had the chair reclined all the way back, and he was drinking a beer and smoking a cigar, like he owned the place.

For a moment, the fact that the man was there didn't really register in Segal's brain. It was such a strange sight, so completely unexpected. Then it sank in with full force and Segal turned to run. But, as he did, he came face-to-face with another man. The only thing separating them was the long dark barrel of a pistol.

"Get in the house," the guy ordered gruffly.

"What do you want?" Segal asked, slowly backing into the cabin. But he knew what they wanted. They figured since he owned a National Football League team, he had to be rich. They were going to kidnap him and demand millions from his family. "You won't get anything from my wife," he said, his voice shaking. "She has standing orders never to negotiate with kidnappers."

"We aren't here to kidnap you, Mr. Segal," said the man, rising from the chair. "Nothing like that. We're just here to kill you."

Segal swallowed hard. "Please, God, I don't want to—"

The man held up his hands, laughing. "I'm kidding, I'm kidding. People just don't get my humor sometimes, Charlie," he said to the man leveling the gun at Segal.

Charlie grunted.

"Then what *do* you want?" Segal demanded, lowering his hands, trying to take control of the situation.

"Oh, no, don't give me attitude because I said I was kidding," the man warned, his voice rising. "If you give me any shit, I *will* kill you. I'll kill your daughter, too. That pretty little brunette who's about to graduate from Cornell and loves her daddy *so much*." He gestured around. "And I'll burn this place to the ground." His eyes flashed back to Segal's. *"Clear?"*

Segal had learned over the years to read people's eyes, and this man's eyes meant business. "Yes."

"Sit down." The man pointed at the couch. "Here's the situation, Mr. Segal. Ray Lancaster called the general manager of your team. Lancaster's coach and GM of the new NFL franchise in Las Vegas. The Dice." The man elongated the end of the word, hissing it. "I like the sound of that, you know? The Dice." He hissed it again. "Did you know Lancaster had called your man?"

"I did."

"So then you know *why* he called, right?"

"He was looking for a trade, I think."

"He wants your backup quarterback. They're struggling at that position. Ricky Poe ain't cutting it."

Segal was familiar with Poe. "He's not very good."

"So you understand their problem?"

"Yes."

"But your guy's being a horse's ass," the man said, coming closer. "To print the trade he's asking for an all-pro linebacker, a former all-pro placekicker, and five million bucks."

Segal nodded. "That does seem like a lot."

"It *is* a lot." The man pulled out his wallet, sat down on the couch beside Segal, reached inside, and pulled out a picture of Segal's daughter walking to class at Cornell. "Just so you know I'm not kidding around."

"I know you're not kidding around," Segal answered as calmly as he could. Suddenly the lawsuits and the pending strike at his mining company didn't seem so important. "What do you want me to do?"

HEWITT AND MASSEY sat on the long, covered back porch of the ranch's main house, looking out over Texas grassland a hundred miles north of Dallas. The huge timber and stone structure was built atop a bluff on the eastern side of the twenty-five-thousand-acre property, and from the porch they had a sweeping view of green pastures stretching into the distance. Other than a couple of burgundy barns trimmed in white, there were no other buildings in sight. The dark red was so pretty against the lush grass, Hewitt thought to himself. Soon, a lot of that grass would turn brown beneath the summer sun.

Hewitt only made it out here a few days a month, but it was a working ranch. Five thousand head of cattle, fifty miles of barbed-wire fences, and eight full-time ranch hands. He'd always kept the number of ranch hands at eight, ever since he'd bought the property a decade ago—two years after he'd been tapped to join the Order. Just as he had eight full-time executive assistants around the globe at U.S. Oil. He didn't need that many executive assistants—probably didn't need eight full-time ranch hands, either—but he liked the symmetry of it all. Eight ranch hands, eight executive assistants—with him as the master.

He and Massey were enjoying a vintage bottle of Scotch, a couple of fine Cuban cigars from the humidor inside the wide double doors behind them, and the serenity of it all as dusk settled over the ranch. They were the only ones staying in the rambling mansion tonight. Hewitt's daughter-in-law was coming up tomorrow and she was bringing Three Sticks. Hewitt hadn't seen his grandson in almost a month, and he was excited—he was going to take the boy white-tailed deer hunting on the ranch. The boy was growing like a weed—he was six three, weighed two hundred pounds, and could run like the wind. He'd been asked to try out for his high school's varsity football team in the fall. Hewitt hoped he'd play for Princeton someday.

They wouldn't be here until late afternoon tomorrow, so he and Massey had the sprawling place to themselves for now. Massey would leave by noon, so there was no chance of Hewitt's daughter-in-law catching them by surprise.

From Maine, Hewitt had taken a direct flight to Dallas. Massey had flown to Houston first, then taken a small plane to Dallas. It was a roundabout route for the former senator, but no two members of the Order were to travel on the same plane, and Hewitt wasn't going to be the one inconvenienced.

Massey took a long drag of the cigar then blew white smoke into the air. The wind was calm this evening and the smoke hung above them like a small cloud. "A shame about Jim Benson's suicide."

"Yeah, but probably for the best," Hewitt said gruffly, putting his boots up on another chair.

"What do you mean?"

"Better he died now than for him and his family to have to go through those last few days. Better for us, too."

"Why?"

"No telling what Benson might have babbled about if they'd juiced him up with morphine at the hospital."

Massey nodded. "I never even thought about that. Guess that's why you're the master, Samuel," he said, grinning. "Have you told the other members?"

"Not yet." After he'd heard the shot, Hewitt had gotten Don Roth to help him locate Benson's body and bring it inside, where they'd stowed it in the large basement freezer. After everyone had left in the morning, Hewitt had arranged for several men who worked for him to come and get the body. They'd taken it back to Naples, Florida, where Benson had retired, and made it appear as though the ex-DIA director had been shot on a quiet street by unknown assailants. After all, the Order couldn't have cops crawling all over Champagne Island trying to confirm Benson's death as a suicide. A robbery gone bad—Benson's wallet had been left open and empty of cash and credit cards on the sidewalk beside him—was how the newspapers explained it. It was helpful to have "friends," Hewitt thought to himself. "I'll tell everyone at the next meeting."

"You mean that he was shot in Naples, right?"

"Of course. No reason to let the truth go any farther than you and me."

"Exactly. Besides, it doesn't make any difference to the other guys. All they care about is that Jim's gone. Better they think he was killed down there, too. Better to keep the circle as small as possible on this one."

"Right."

"When's the next meeting?" Massey asked.

"Probably next week."

"So soon? Why?"

"I'm worried about Jesse Wood. I want to accelerate our plans."

"Believe me, I'm with you. Can you imagine a nigger running this country?" Massey shook his head and took a long swig of Scotch. "And could you believe Kohler and McDonnell at the meeting?" he asked, teeth gritted. "We don't need that kind of dissension."

Hewitt gazed out over his ranch. He loved it here, loved his life, loved his *way* of life. But he knew it was in danger. He was more convinced than ever that if Jesse Wood were elected president, everything the population swings could eventually bring on would be accelerated by decades. He wanted his grandson to have this ranch. And *his* grandson after him, and so on, forever. He couldn't bear to think of this place being arbitrarily turned over to some black or Mexican family in thirty or forty years. But that's what happened when you lost a war—to the victor went the spoils. There were examples of it happening many times through the course of history. And no matter what anyone else said, no matter how they tried to characterize it, this was war.

"No, we don't need it," Hewitt agreed firmly. "And we won't let it happen. I won't ever let it happen to my Order. Kohler and McDonnell can get in line or else."

Massey settled farther back into his chair. "Or else *what*?"

Hewitt could feel the Scotch. "You know what," he said quietly.

"Think there's any chance any of the others feel the same way Kohler and McDonnell do?" Massey asked. "Think any of them were just siding publicly with us at the meeting because they felt they had to? I mean, there's absolutely no chance Dahl or Laird would ever sympathize with them," he said, partially answering his own question. "Dahl might as well be a Nazi, and Laird would be too scared about his tapes getting out." Massey paused. "But what about the others? Think they might be in that camp? Think they might feel we're going too far this time?"

Hewitt looked out over the ranch again. God, he loved it here. "No chance. It's Kohler and McDonnell, that's it." He puffed on his cigar, then sipped the Scotch. "Just those two sons of bitches."

CHRISTIAN PULLED OUT his BlackBerry as the private jet touched down at O'Hare in Chicago. He watched the messages load up on the display quickly now that they were on the ground. One of them caught his eye. Faith. He brought it up. It read:

Chris, I love you, but I can't do this anymore. We're almost never together, and when we do talk on the phone (rarely!!), I feel like you can't wait to get off. I know you're so busy at Everest, my God, I don't know how you do what you do, how there's enough time in the day for you to talk to all the people who scream for your attention. I just don't want to be one of those people anymore. I want someone who's with me all the time, someone who calls me all the time, who thinks of me all the time. I've finally realized that. Call me needy, I guess, but that's me. You can't do all those things I want. It's not your fault, I know, but it still hurts to be ignored.

This makes me so sad. I'm crying. I'll be back in the United States soon and we can talk about it then. I can't compete with Everest anymore. I love you. Faith.

Christian stared at her name at the end of the message for several moments. The bad thing was that he understood what she was saying. He didn't mean to ignore her, it just happened. Like she said, there simply wasn't enough time in the day. But he didn't have an answer. He was managing billions and billions of dollars for people who expected total commitment. The only solution was to have Faith travel with him, but she couldn't. She had her own career, which he couldn't ask her to give up. Not because he was worried she'd hate him for putting his needs ahead of hers. He was *afraid* to ask her. What if she said yes?

His cell phone rang and he snatched it up off the table in front of him. "Hello."

"Christian?"

"Yeah."

"It's Ray Lancaster."

Christian could hear excitement in Lancaster's voice. "What's up?"

"You're not going to believe this but the Buffalo Bills just called. I swear I was going to ice them like you said, I wasn't going to call them, but they called *me*."

"And?"

"And they're ready to deal, Christian. I don't know what happened. All they want is one defensive tackle and a third-round pick in next year's draft. If we agree to that, we get our quarterback. That's all we have to do. We don't have to give up anything else. It's crazy."

It *was* crazy, Christian realized. "What made them change their minds?"

"I don't know. I didn't ask. I was too excited."

"You think this quarterback you want has some kind of injury we don't know about? Maybe he fell down stairs at home this afternoon or something."

"Maybe, but we'll find out. No trade in the NFL clears until the players involved pass physicals. If he's hurt, the trade's nullified."

Christian remembered hearing that before.

"I don't think they'd offer what they did unless our guy was healthy," Lancaster said.

"Then what do you think *did* happen?"

"I don't know," Lancaster answered, "and I don't really care. All I care is that we've got a quarterback who can win. I might be able to get you to the play-offs this year after all."

Christian looked out the window as the jet pulled up to the general aviation terminal. It would be nice not to have to care about why something good happened, to simply believe that lady luck was on your side. But that was a naïve approach to life. Everything happened for a reason, and it was always best to know what that reason was. Having information, knowing why something happened—whether it was good or bad for you—was the key to success. Being surprised was a much worse outcome. Then you couldn't do anything about it.

What bothered him was that there seemed to be more and more things happening that he couldn't explain, that he needed to investigate. He couldn't decide if that was coincidence—brought on by external forces he couldn't control—or if it was lack of focus. Maybe Faith was right. Maybe it was him, not the situation. With her *and* Everest.

HEWITT STOOD in the darkness by the gate, awestruck by the multitude of stars above him. They called Montana Big Sky Country, but the Texas sky was actually bigger and better. He'd seen both many times and he had no doubt about it.

He watched the headlights of the SUV move slowly along the dirt road toward him. One of his "friends" was driving, bringing him a very important package. As the SUV drew close, he mused on the fact that he thought of these men as more his friends than he did of a man like Stewart Massey. As much as he could have friends, anyway. Of course, maybe that was why he liked them so much. Not just because they were unfailingly loyal and did whatever they were asked without question but also because they knew they could never be close to him. The relationship was steady. Hewitt didn't have to worry about these men ever thinking they might actually get close to him, ever thinking they might get an invitation to Thanksgiving dinner. They knew they wouldn't. They knew the boundaries. Guys like Massey always held out hope for more.

The SUV stopped in front of the gate, and a lone man jumped out. He hurried to where Hewitt stood and handed over the package—a CD case—then turned and jogged back toward the vehicle without a word.

Hewitt smiled. Pay people enough and they were loyal to you forever. As long as someone else didn't pay them more. "Wayne," he called as the man was about to climb into the truck.

"Yes, sir?"

"Come back here for a second."

The man hustled back. "Yes, sir?"

Wayne was an ex–Texas Ranger, with a steadfast belief that the country was going to hell very fast and that something needed to be done. *Ex*-Ranger because Hewitt had offered him triple what the state could pay him. "You're a good man, Wayne. You and the rest of the boys do a great job."

"Thank you, sir." He hesitated. "Is that all?"

"Tell the other guys I appreciate them, too."

"They know that, sir."

Hewitt nodded and smiled. "Okay." Once again he watched Wayne head toward the SUV. Money was the most important thing by far, but sometimes you had to show people a little more to really manipulate them the way you wanted to.

9

GORDON MEADE was in his late fifties. Neatly groomed from his silver hair to his perfectly knotted tie to his shiny shoes. For a man who managed thirty billion dollars, he had a relaxed manner, and when he spoke he did so with a faint smile, as if recalling a secret about a Wallace family member. Something that gave him job security, no matter what. Christian had known Meade now for several years and always wondered about that faint smile—and what it represented.

"I'm glad to hear our investment in your fund is doing so well," Meade said, taking a sip of coffee. They were almost finished with dinner. "You really think it's doubled in value?"

People always heard what they wanted to hear, especially about their investments. Christian had never said that. "Not quite, Gordon. I think your five's worth about eight now." Meade had rounded up, like so many people did about so many things—their salaries, the value of their houses. "That's pretty good, given that we haven't invested all the money yet."

"Remind me again: How big is the fund?"

Meade managed thirty billion himself, most of which was parceled out to other investment managers in much smaller blocks than five billion. So it wasn't surprising that he wouldn't know all the details of his Everest investment. He was a man with a lot on his plate. "Twenty billion."

Meade shook his head. "That's incredible. Any other funds around that large?"

"No. One of the other big buyout shops just raised an eighteen-billion-dollar fund. They were trying for twenty, but they didn't quite get there."

"Are you learning?" Meade asked, turning to Allison. Quentin was at the bar, waiting. Meade had asked that it be just the three of them at dinner. "That's one of the reasons your uncle and I wanted you at Everest, to figure out how this guy does it." He pointed at Christian. "How the master makes his money."

"Hey," Allison spoke up, "I've brought a few deals to the table."

Meade glanced at Christian.

"She has," he confirmed.

In truth, Allison had turned out to be a great addition to the managing-partner team. She'd gone to the right schools, then worked in Goldman Sachs's mergers and acquisitions group after getting her MBA, putting in long hours for a few years as she learned the ropes at one of the most prestigious firms on Wall Street, before coming back to Chicago to help manage the family's enormous wealth. She had the pedigree, the experience; she worked hard; and she was learning how to take full advantage of her long list of connections.

She was learning how to take advantage of her beauty, too. After they got past their egos, men loved working with Allison. She was pretty, she knew sports, and she could drink most men under the table. He'd seen her do it, too, seen her stick around at the bar until the last guy stumbled off to bed. Then be up at seven the next morning, grinding through deal points and tough negotiations while her male counterparts struggled not to lose it on the conference room table as they sucked down cup after cup of black coffee.

Christian smiled as he gazed at her. She was wearing a conservative outfit tonight, a dress that fell below her knees. She would never let on to the family what a party girl she was. She liked the responsibility the elders were giving her, so she tried to act innocent around them and Meade. She knew that Meade told her uncle everything.

"Allison's found two of the eight companies we've bought out of the fund so far," Christian said. "I'm hoping she'll stick around for good, Gordon."

"Oh, no." Meade shook his head. "She's working at Everest so she can bring all that experience back to us when this fund is finished. We all know that."

"*I'll* be the one who decides what I do when the fund is finished, Gordon," Allison said firmly.

Meade gazed at her for a few moments, then turned back to Christian. "How much of the twenty billion have you invested so far?"

"A little over twelve billion, a little over sixty percent of it."

"Are you going to raise another fund?"

"Absolutely."

"When does your operating agreement let you free up to start raising the next one?" Meade asked.

"When we've invested seventy-five percent of it."

Investors wanted Christian and his team focused on their money, so there were restrictions on raising additional funds. But the investors also understood that it took time to raise multibillion-dollar pools of money, often a year or more. Christian needed lead time so the next fund would be ready to go when the current fund was out of money. The agreement he had with his investors was that once he'd invested seventy-five percent of the money in the active fund—fifteen billion out of twenty in this case—he could start raising a new one.

"You going to go for more than twenty next time?"

"Twenty-five." Christian had already started talking to his biggest investors. Based on those discussions, he felt certain he could clear that number.

"Wow." Meade smiled. "And I bet you do it. Unless, of course, there's a hiccup with any of the companies you own now. Then it'll be tough to get to twenty-five billion."

"I don't think that's going to be a problem," Christian answered, picking up his water glass. "Our portfolio companies are doing well."

"Still don't drink, huh?" Meade asked.

Christian hadn't had a drop of alcohol since the night in high school when he'd wrapped his father's Porsche around a tree. When he'd come to in the hospital, his father had been standing over him, tears streaming down his face. That image had stuck with Christian forever. He'd vowed never to disappoint his father like that again, even after his father was gone. "Nope."

Meade motioned across the room to their waiter for the check. "How's the Laurel Energy sale going?"

Everest had bought Laurel using money from the fund that was in place before the current twenty-billion-dollar fund. The Wallace Family had no investment in that fund, so, technically, Meade shouldn't care how the sale was going. "It's taken longer than we expected, but I'm sure everything will be fine. Why do you ask?"

Meade gestured at Allison. "Allison told me it wasn't going well."

Christian's eyes shot to Allison's. You never told the outside world about problems until you absolutely couldn't fix them yourself. Even though Gordon was directly responsible for the Wallace Family investment in the Everest fund, he was still an outsider. The only true insiders were Christian and his five managing partners; even the other employees at the firm weren't real insiders. Allison should never have said anything to Meade about the Laurel Energy sale. He took a frustrated breath. This was one of the big problems with having your single largest investors actually living at the fund with you—they were conflicted in their loyalties.

"I didn't say it wasn't going well, Chris," she said defensively. "I said exactly what you just said, that it's taken longer than you expected." She gave Meade an irritated look. "And it has, that's true."

"It sure would hurt if you couldn't sell it," Meade spoke up. "It'd be a real black eye, wouldn't it? Especially since you thought it was going to be such a grand slam. I think you told me you were going to get five billion for it, didn't you, Christian?"

"Yes," he admitted, ruing the remark. It was almost like Meade wanted Laurel Energy *not* to sell. Like he didn't want Everest to be able to raise another fund, especially not a twenty-five-billion-dollar fund. Like he wanted Everest to do poorly after Allison came back to Chicago so Christian couldn't compete with them.

"Any other problems in the portfolio?" Meade wanted to know. "Or with any of the companies you've taken public?"

Christian felt his eyes begin to narrow, but he tried to keep his expression even. "No, everything's fine."

Meade nodded. "Good. Because, again, something like that, you know, one of those companies you've taken public having problems? That would hurt big-time when you go out and try to raise the next fund. Everything gets so messy with public deals. The SEC gets involved and *boom*. You and your firm are splashed all over the headlines."

"I'm aware of that, Gordon." Christian couldn't remember Meade ever being so passive-aggressive with him. "But thanks for the advice."

The older man leaned back in his chair and patted his stomach. "Well, that was quite a meal, delicious. Thanks for coming all the way out here to Chicago to update me. I like face-to-face so much better than phones and e-mails. Keep up the good work."

"Thanks." Christian glanced over at Allison. She was folding and re-folding her napkin, like she was nervous. Or feeling guilty.

BLANTON MCDONNELL wheeled the shopping cart down the carpeted aisle of a high-end grocery store in Greenwich, Connecticut, toward the canned soup section. He could have had one of the help come to the store for him, but he wasn't actually looking for soup. In fact, he didn't really need anything from the store at all—at least, not any of their products. Of course, he'd thrown a few things in the cart for appearance's sake, like he always did.

As McDonnell neared the soup section, he glanced around furtively. Just a couple of women with kids, one of whom was screaming at the top of his lungs. Good. A distraction.

He quickly found the row of Campbell's Baked Potato with Cheddar and Bacon Bits soup, a flavor that he and Mace Kohler had determined wouldn't cycle quickly. Not like chicken noodle or clam chowder, which probably had to be restocked a couple of times a day. He grabbed the cans two at a time, placing them in the cart until he came to the last one. He pulled it from the back of the shelf and held it up, turning it around. There it was, taped to the back of the can. A note from Kohler. He wanted to get together tomorrow night at the place they'd decided on the last time they'd met.

They never met in the same place twice in a row. It was much too dangerous. You never knew if Hewitt was watching.

TODD HARRISON pulled his rusty Toyota into a narrow parking space at the run-down apartment complex and skidded to a stop, barely missing the fender of a pickup truck that had its left taillight bashed in. He banged off the headlights with his left hand, at the same time twisting the key with his right and yanking it from the ignition. Then he grabbed his backpack off the ripped passenger seat and jumped out, sprinting up the outdoor steps to the third floor. He rapped loudly on the glass storm door when he reached the small landing outside the apartment. "Come on, George, come on," he muttered to himself, looking over his shoulder down into the darkness of the empty lot below.

The door opened and he burst inside, not waiting to be invited in. "Where have you been?" he demanded, tossing the backpack on the sofa beside him as he sat down.

George Bishop shut the door, then moved to a ratty easy chair beside the couch and fell into it, like it had taken all the energy he had left in his body to answer Harrison's knock. "Where *haven't* I been?"

"What do you mean?"

"Well, I—"

"Why'd it take so long to call me? You were supposed to get to me by five. It's almost eleven."

"I'll tell you if—"

"You should have been back hours ago."

"*Hey,* are you going to let me talk?"

"Sorry, yeah, yeah, go ahead."

Bishop played with his scruffy beard for a moment as his gray-and-white cat jumped into his lap. "The wind really sucked coming back in from Champagne Island. I don't know if you could tell from shore, but it blew the surf up something fierce. The waves kept getting bigger and bigger out there. They must have been three or four feet. Never been out in something like that before. I'm a pretty good seaman, but I almost went over a few times."

"Jesus, I had no idea. It was a beautiful day here."

"Yeah, I know—it was weird. Anyway, I'm fighting it, just trying to keep the bow steady, and all of a sudden I barely miss this Boston Whaler coming the other way. I mean, it was that close." Bishop held his hands up a foot apart. "I never even saw it coming because the surf was up so high and I was keeping my head down."

"Roth," Harrison said excitedly. "It must have been Roth going back out to Champagne after he met me."

"Well, I've never seen Roth so I don't know, and I didn't really get a look at the guy in the other boat at that point because it all happened so fast." Bishop chuckled. "But then he started chasing me."

"What?"

"Yeah, the fucker turned around and started hauling ass after me."

"Holy shit."

"Yeah, so I can't come back to Southport, you know? If it's Roth, I don't want him knowing where the hell I live. So I changed course and went up to Logan, and he tailed me all the way there, plowing through the waves right behind me. As I'm tying up at a dock, he comes running over after he's tied up his boat, wanting to know what the hell I was doing out there."

"What did you say?"

"I told him it was a free country, and a free ocean, and I could do whatever the hell I wanted to out there. Then I told him to get the fuck out of my face." Bishop pushed the cat gently off his lap, walked to the refrigerator, and got a beer. "The guy didn't like that very much." He popped the beer open and took several gulps. "Roth. Is he about six feet tall, say one-eighty? Scar over his left eye?"

"That's him," Harrison confirmed.

"He's a mean-looking motherfucker," Bishop said, heading back to the easy chair.

"So, what happened?" Harrison asked. "Did he just leave?"

"Nope. After I told him to fuck off, I went to a place on the waterfront to get something to eat, and he followed me inside. Just stared at me from the other end of the bar while I was eating." Bishop took a deep breath and shook his head. "I had to climb out the men's room window, haul ass to my boat, and get the hell out of there before he knew what was going on."

"Jesus Christ." Harrison glanced at his backpack. "What about Champagne? Did you find anything?"

"I found out Roth leaves his wife alone out there. Glad you told me she might be around."

Harrison winced. "I was afraid he'd do that. I wanted to ask him if he'd brought her with him when we first sat down. I was going to try to call you on your cell and warn you if you still had reception, but I figured it wouldn't be a good thing to ask him. Figured he might get suspicious if I did."

"Wouldn't have mattered if you had," Bishop said. "I lost my antenna halfway out there."

Bishop still seemed shaken. He was already almost done with his beer. "Well, what did you find?" Harrison asked.

"Not much. Landed up by the lighthouse and hoofed it through the woods to the lodge. Tried to make sure no one saw me come ashore. Watched his wife come out of the house and go to a shed, then go back inside." Bishop raised both eyebrows. "She was wearing a holster with a damn big gun. That made me *real* nervous."

"But nothing suspicious."

Bishop relaxed into the chair. "No, not really." His face scrunched up.

"What? What is it?"

"The lodge is built kind of weird."

"What do you mean?"

"It's big, three full stories."

"Yeah, so?"

"And there's lots of windows," Bishop kept going, "like the people who built it loved sunlight or something. Except at one corner. Like that was the vampire's wing or something."

"I don't get it."

"Twenty feet in both directions from one corner of the lodge there's no windows at all. It's weird."

Harrison shook his head. He'd have to see the place for himself. Hopefully Roth would call. "What about the stuff I sent you the other day? The picture of the old guy and that property ID form?"

"Don't worry," Bishop said confidently. "It's safe."

ROTH TAPPED the desk as he listened to the phone ring at the other end of the line.

"Hello?"

"Harry?"

"Yeah."

"Harry, it's Don Roth."

"Hey, Don, how you been?"

"Good, good. Listen, I need a favor."

"Anything. Just name it."

"I need you to run a trace on a boat registration number," Roth explained. "The guy's been circling the island a couple of times, but he takes off when I come out to see what he wants. Last time I used binoculars and got the number off the bow of his boat before I motored out there. I want to find out who he is."

There was dead air at the other end. Then: "What's the number?"

STEPHANIE CHILDRESS gazed at the picture and smiled. She and Jesse together right after he'd won a small tennis tournament in Vermont, still on the court. Jesse had one arm around her shoulders, the other clutching the trophy, and he was kissing her cheek—like he really cared about her. He'd been the only big name in the tournament—the other stars didn't want to hoof it to Vermont—but he was so hungry for a win on the tour at that point. It had been two years since the last championship, and people were starting to forget that he'd won the U.S. Open and Wimbledon. At least, that was how he saw it, and it was sad to see him go through that.

Stephanie glanced into the mirror, then quickly looked away. She was losing her beauty and she hated it. Time was catching up to her. It was so vain to worry about it, she knew, but she couldn't help it. Jesse didn't look at her the same way anymore—no one did. She felt a lump rising in her throat. He was looking at younger, prettier women now. He was forgetting how she had been with him through all these years, how loyal she had been. Soon he was going to be president and women were going to be throwing themselves at him. She'd be forgotten. Completely.

10

IT WAS JUST past two in the morning and Christian and Allison were at an after-hours club in downtown Chicago. The place was officially closed, but there was a jazz band playing in the back room for a hundred people or so. Allison had a connection at the club—one of the managers—who'd gotten them into the private party. They didn't know anyone else here, but it didn't matter. Christian liked jazz, and the band was excellent.

"You okay?" Allison asked as they stood at the raised bar enjoying an unobstructed view of the stage. She was drinking a rum runner, swaying back and forth slightly to the music and the alcohol.

"Yeah. Why?"

"You seem a little depressed."

He glanced over at her. "Depressed?"

"Okay, *distracted*."

"I'm fine."

Truth was, he'd been *completely* distracted, off in his own world, thinking about the SEC's pending investigation of CST, Laurel Energy, and—what was eating at him the most—the guy at the transfer station who'd demanded the million-dollar payoff. Quentin was checking the guy out, but, so far, nothing. Quentin hadn't picked up Carmine Torino's trail, either. There were dead ends everywhere.

Christian had been thinking about Faith, too. He'd explained to her over and over how much time Everest took, how so many people wanted his attention. How he had to give it to a lot of them, even though he'd rather give it to her. He thought he'd gotten through to her but apparently not. If he had, she wouldn't have sent that e-mail.

He picked up his water glass, feeling Allison's gaze. She hadn't been able to take him away from his problems tonight.

"Fine," she repeated. "That's what you always say about everything. Your left arm could be falling off and you'd say you were fine."

Christian checked his BlackBerry one more time, hoping Faith had sent another message saying she was sorry, that she hadn't meant the first one. But nothing. He'd tried calling her several times, but no answer.

"Watched pots never boil," Allison said over the music. "Sounds trite but it's true, if you ask me. What are you waiting for?"

"Nothing. I check this thing constantly. I'm addicted to it. You've been around me long enough to know that."

"I've been around you long enough not to fall for that explanation. I can tell when you're waiting for something. You get this expectant-father look about you, like you've got on your face right now."

Christian managed a half grin. "You're crazy, you know that?"

Uninhibited was probably a better description. She didn't seem to care what people thought about what she said or did, and Christian envied that. He'd tried to be like that when he was younger, but he couldn't let go, not the way she could. Maybe it was the extraordinary wealth she'd been around all her life that made her that way, knowing down deep she could buy anything—or anyone. Maybe it was just her personality, a wild hair stuck in her genes from somewhere.

He snuck a look at her as he picked up his glass again. Tonight's outfit wasn't as revealing as last night's in Vegas, but it still showed plenty. Everywhere they went, he picked up on the hungry looks of the men watching her. Looks that told him they'd do anything to get him out of the way.

Christian glanced over his shoulder. Quentin was sitting on a stool next to him, also sipping water. "You okay?"

"Uh-huh."

"Go back to the hotel and get some sleep."

Quentin shook his head. "Nope. It's my job to make sure you get home all right. I'll stay as late as I have to."

Quentin was being a chaperone. "Get one of your guys to take over."

"It's after two o'clock, Chris. How much longer you going to stay out?"

"As long as I want him to," Allison answered firmly, stepping in front of Christian, then turning and tousling his dark hair. "This is my city and I get to keep him out until the break of dawn if I want to." She smiled suggestively. "Why don't you loosen up a little and have a drink?"

"You know me better than that."

"Come on," she pleaded, "just one."

"I don't need a drink to have fun."

Allison finished what was left of her rum runner and signaled to the bartender that she wanted another. "Is it the Laurel Energy thing that's got you all tensed up?" she asked as the band finished a number and the audience broke into loud applause.

"No, but you didn't have to tell Gordon things weren't going well with it."

"*He* brought it up, Chris." She took the fresh drink from the bartender. "By the way, I got a call the other day from some guy at Black Brothers Allen about Laurel. I meant to tell you that."

"What did he want?"

"He wanted to know if they could help out."

"What was his name?" Christian wondered if it was the same guy who'd called him.

"I don't remember. I saved the message on my answering machine. I'll forward it to you in the morning," she said, raising her voice as the band broke into an up-tempo song.

"It *is* the morning."

"Okay, *later* this morning."

"Why did he call you? You aren't working on that deal."

"Gordon probably had something to do with it."

"What do you mean?"

"My family's done business with Black Brothers for a long time. They raised a lot of money for our railroad back in the day."

Allison's great-great-grandfather had founded the Chicago & Western Railway in the 1850s and ultimately made hundreds of millions selling it to what was now the Burlington Northern. That was how the

Wallace Family had made its first fortune. After that they'd made it big in real estate, then in the cell phone explosion.

"Black Brothers underwrote bonds for us to pay for tracks, engines, cars," Allison continued. "That's when the relationship started. My uncle and his brother still do a lot of business with those guys. Obviously, so does Gordon."

"It's a pretty secretive outfit. You don't hear much about them."

"That's the way they want it, I guess."

"You know people there?" Christian asked.

She shrugged. "Eh. Why?

"Just wondering." Maybe it was time to change horses on the Laurel deal after all. At least time to have a talk with the Black Brothers guy.

"What about the casino?" Allison wanted to know. "You never told me how it went with the Gaming Commission."

She hadn't asked about business last night in Vegas at all. For some reason, tonight was different. "It's going to take a little more massaging than I thought, but it'll be fine."

She put her hand on his shoulder. "You deal with so much."

"Nah." She didn't even know about the SEC dogging CST.

They watched for a few more minutes, then, when the band broke into another fast song, Allison took Christian's hand. "Come on!" she urged, trying to pull him off the bar stool.

But he stayed put, grabbing the seat with his other hand.

"I want to dance."

"No way."

She grabbed his arm with both hands and pulled hard. "Please," she begged.

"Nope."

But she wasn't going to be denied, and before Christian knew it he was on the dance floor, aware that everyone was watching them. He'd made such a production of trying to resist and she looked so damn good. Well, what the hell? If you're going to do something, don't do it half-assed.

When they reached the middle of the polished parquet floor, Christian squeezed Allison's hand and spun her twice, then twirled her around the floor, dodging the other two couples skillfully. He'd learned a thing or two about doing the pretzel while he was at Princeton.

When the song finished, the room broke into loud applause and there were shouts for an encore—even the band waved for them to come back. But one dance was enough. He'd let go enough for the night.

Allison hugged him when they got back to the bar. "That was awesome," she bubbled, breathing hard. "I never would have guessed."

"Hey, I can move a little."

"A *little*? I'm calling you Twinkle Toes around the office from now on."

"You do and I'll kill you."

"No, you won't."

"You're right, I won't. I'll have *Quentin* kill you. That's his gig."

"I'm going to the ladies' room to freshen up," she said, wagging a finger at him. "Just when I think I know Christian Gillette, I find out something else about him. Some little nugget hidden behind that mysterious façade."

As Christian watched her walk away, he felt a tap on his shoulder and turned to face Quentin. "What?"

"Hey, Twinkle Toes."

"Don't you start."

"What the hell are you doing?" Quentin wanted to know, nodding after Allison.

"What do you mean?" But he knew exactly what Quentin was asking. "Look, I'm just having a little fun."

"We talked about this already. She's your business partner, Chris. No dipping the pen in the company ink."

"Believe me, it's innocent."

"All evil springs from innocence."

"Okay, Nietzsche."

Quentin rolled his eyes. "I'm trying to help."

"I know, I know. But, my God, she's fun, beautiful, and I get to see her on a regular basis." Which wasn't true of the other women he'd dated over the last ten years, including Faith. "The way I look at it, that's a damn good start. Maybe I ought to at least get to know her a little bit more outside work."

Quentin hesitated. "Chris, I think it's a mistake."

"It'll be fine," Christian said, checking his BlackBerry one more time.

And there it was. Another e-mail from Faith, this one telling him how wrong she'd been to send the first one. How she'd just opened her eyes in her Paris hotel room and she missed him so much.

He glanced up. Allison was coming back from the ladies' room, staring straight at him, walking that devil-may-care walk, smiling that sly smile.

PATTY ROTH climbed the stairs to the third floor of the lodge quickly, not bothering to look back over her shoulder in the dim light. She had to do this fast. She knew it was so risky, but her curiosity was killing her.

She'd waited until she was certain Don was asleep, lying in bed for two hours staring at the ceiling until he finally settled into the loud, rhythmic snore that had kept her awake during the first few months of their relationship. Then she'd slipped on a pair of jeans and a T-shirt, snatched Don's keys quietly off his dresser, and headed out of the bedroom.

When she reached the third floor, she trotted down the carpeted hallway on her bare feet to that door, to the one she'd finally found the courage to make it to the other day. She cringed as the door swung slowly back on its hinges and creaked loudly. The last thing she wanted to do was wake up Don.

When it was open, she reached inside and found the light switch, a smell of mildew wafting to her nostrils as the room was bathed in light. For a few moments she stared through the room at the steel door with the two latches on the far wall, then she moved across the floor and knelt down to start trying keys in the latch near the floor. Her hands shook terribly as she tried the first one.

"Goddamn it! What the hell are you doing?"

Patty spun around in terror, falling back against the door, cold and hard against her back. "Nothing, sweetheart. I—I—I'm just—" But that was all she got out.

Roth strode to where she was sprawled, grabbed the keys from her hand, tossed them back toward the hallway, clamped her wrist in his big hand, jacked her to her feet, and pushed her against the steel door, hard.

She'd never seen him like this before, never seen him so furious. Instinctively, she put her hands up and turned her head to the side.

"I told you never to come in here! Never, never, never!" he shouted, his eyes glowing. "I meant it, damn it! Don't ever do it again!" He was breathing hard. "Or so help me."

■ ■ ■

"**SAMUEL HEWITT** is certifiable."

They were meeting on the darkened playground of a public elementary school a few towns west of Greenwich, in a grove of trees beside the swings.

"Blanton, some of the things he's talking about are insane," Kohler continued. "I mean, I understand trying to make it harder to immigrate into the United States and making it harder to become a citizen once you're here. And I don't have a problem with that as long as you don't make it *impossible.* It ought to be tough to get in here and stay here. Hell, this is an incredible country. But some of the other stuff he's talking about is crazy." He held up one hand and began to tick off the list. "Getting his buddies at the CIA to help the cartels in South America get their filth past customs. Getting his pals at the FBI to make sure the gangs in the inner cities get their hands on drugs. Funding inner city abortion clinics? Influencing state legislatures to make abortions legal until the end of the second trimester? Assassinating Jesse Wood? How far does it go, Blanton?"

McDonnell tried to break in, but there was no stopping Kohler at this point. He was on a roll.

"And I wouldn't get so worked up about it because it seems so crazy, but . . . I mean, he might actually be able to pull it off." Kohler's voice became hushed. "The guy is more connected than any human being on earth. *He* might as well be president for Christ sake. Of course, then he'd have to actually listen to other people's opinions. No, Samuel Hewitt would be happy only if he could be dictator." Kohler shook his head. "I know he could have Wood killed, and no one would ever figure out he was behind it. And, if you want my opinion, Jesse Wood is exactly what this country needs right now. Someone who can unite us, not tear us apart."

"I agree," said McDonnell, finally able to break in, "but what do we do about our tapes? My wife would . . . She'd take me for everything with that kind of evidence. I'd be ruined. I—I can't deal with that, Mace." His voice was shaking. "I've worked my whole life to get where I am."

Kohler nodded. "I know, I know." This was exactly what the Order's infidelity requirement was supposed to do: terrify you into loyalty. "Did you get the message about the next meeting?"

"Yeah."

"Hewitt's gonna lay the whole thing out for us then," Kohler said. "I can feel it. And we're going to have to do something at that point. We can't let him go after Jesse Wood. If we do, we're as bad as he is."

"So what the hell are we going to do?"

Kohler looked off into the distance, toward the darkened school buildings. There was only one thing he could think of. But it was so damn risky.

11

VIVIAN DAVIS was a senior investigator at the Securities and Exchange Commission, the woman who had called Bob Galloway, the chief financial officer of Central States Telecom and Satellite. African American, Vivian was tall and angular, and her blue chalk-striped suit hung loosely on her lanky frame. She was wearing three-inch heels, so when she and Christian came together in the middle of her office to shake hands, she was at eye level with him. Most tall women he knew wore flats, sometimes even stooped a little to downplay their height, but Vivian was advertising it. No problem with confrontation here, thought Christian. She wasn't going to have any issues going after him, no matter who he was. He was here; he was prey. It was that simple.

Christian noticed that the sleeves of Vivian's suit jacket were a little long. A mid-level government employee, she probably didn't make much, which meant that she wouldn't waste money on alterations because she wouldn't wear the jacket that often. That also meant she wouldn't have much sympathy for a man whose net worth had been estimated at half a billion dollars by *Forbes*. In fact, she'd probably hate him for it.

"Hello, Mr. Gillette."

"Hello, Ms. Davis."

She had a strong grip and an air of forced friendliness about her. He sensed that she didn't want to smile but felt she had to, that she realized he was a man of power and influence, so she was going to give him at least some measure of respect before moving in on him. Like a matador's bow to a bull before the fight.

"This is Nigel Faraday," Christian said, gesturing to his right. "He's the number two person at Everest Capital."

Vivian gave Nigel the same forced smile but no handshake. "Are you an officer of Central States Telecom, too?"

Nigel shook his head.

"I thought it would be a good idea for Nigel to join us," Christian explained. "I travel a lot, and I want you to be able to get in touch with us anytime. Besides, Nigel is more familiar than anyone else at Everest with CST's daily operations as well as with the IPO. We just want to make sure we cooperate with you the best way we can."

"Oh, you'll cooperate," Vivian said confidently.

Too confidently, almost arrogantly. Christian didn't like people who were caught up in their power, but he bit his lip.

"It's nice to meet you, Mr. Faraday," Vivian continued, "but if you're not an officer of CST, then you have no reason to be here." She looked back at Christian. "I didn't ask you to come to my office today in your capacity as the chairman of Everest Capital. I asked you to come here as the chairman of CST. I'm sorry, but Mr. Faraday will have to wait outside."

Christian reached out and grabbed Nigel's arm. He'd been turning to go. "I really think it would be helpful to have another person here, just so there's no misunderstanding later on about what was said." This wasn't starting off well, but he wasn't going to back down. "I hope you understand," he said politely. She couldn't force Faraday to leave. He knew that—so did she. She'd been trying to con him, and it irritated him that she thought he was so naïve. "It's my right to have another person in here with me. You know that."

"Already spoke to your lawyer, did you? Worried about something?"

"I'm careful, Ms. Davis," he said calmly. "Nigel and I manage billions of dollars of other people's money. We have to be careful."

"Then I'm surprised you didn't bring that lawyer of yours along." She moved behind her desk and sat down, motioning for them to sit in the chairs in front of the desk. "Wouldn't that have been the best thing to do if you were worried?"

"I didn't say I was worried," Christian answered sharply. "*You* did." He glanced at the fresh flower in the buttonhole of her lapel. A pink carnation. Her way of telling you she was a friendly person—outside the office. "I said I was careful."

Vivian flipped through a spiral-bound notebook, scanning several pages, then leaned forward, putting her elbows on the desk. "Let me get right to the point, Mr. Gillette. I'm almost certain we're going to initiate an investigation of CST. We've received what we believe is credible information that there may have been some serious misrepresentations in your S-1, in the initial public offering document you and Everest put out six months ago."

"Let me get right to *my* point," Christian said. "The company, its investment bankers, and its attorneys put those documents together. I'm sure you're very familiar with the investment bankers and the attorneys on the deal—top-shelf all the way. It wasn't Everest who put out the S-1, it was the company."

"The company you're chairman of, Mr. Gillette. You're supposed to know *everything* that's going on at a company you're chairman of."

"Oh, come on," Nigel broke in. "That's ridiculous. How can Christian possibly know everything that's going on at a company as large as CST?"

"Let me rephrase," Vivian offered. "Everything *important* that's going on. An initial public offering certainly falls into that category."

"What kind of misrepresentations are you talking about?" Christian asked.

"About your net income, about your earnings per share," Vivian answered. "The key things investors look at when they're trying to decide whether or not to buy your shares. To get to the heart of this whole thing, Mr. Gillette, we believe you significantly overstated revenues at CST during the three years you owned the company before you took it public. We think you're still doing it." She glanced over at Nigel, then back at Christian. "And we all know what overstating revenue means. It means your net income and therefore your earnings per share figures are overstated, as well—*way* overstated. Meaning the stock price is too high because CST isn't doing as well as you'd have us believe it is." Her eyes narrowed. "We think the overstatements were intentional, too, not just an oversight on some clerk's part. Not just a one-time mistaken entry in the books somewhere. We think this is serial fraud and that several senior people at CST knew what was going on." She paused. "Possibly you."

Christian's eyes moved smoothly to hers.

"That's absurd!" Nigel shouted. "Christian's got one of the cleanest reputations in the business world. You can't possibly—"

Christian reached over and touched Nigel's shoulder, silencing him immediately. "Where exactly did you get your information?" he asked.

"Can't tell you."

"I have a right to know who's accusing me."

Vivian leaned back and smiled. "Maybe you should have brought your attorney with you after all."

"Look, I'm not here to admit or deny anything. I can't: I don't have the facts. I don't even really know what you're talking about because overstating revenues can mean lots of different things. But I do know that as long as we were following generally accepted accounting principles, which I believe we were, we weren't overstating anything." He was thinking clearly, not rattled at all by her aggressiveness or the situation. It was a gift to be able to act calmly and think clearly under pressure, a gift from his father. He'd seen Clayton do it under fire several times—on TV and in person. Only once had he seen his father lose his cool, fall completely apart. "What I will say is this. We're extremely diligent at CST—at all our companies—about financial controls. We have an audit committee that works with our independent accounting firm to make certain every measure possible is taken to protect the integrity of our financial statements. That's the only way our public shareholders can really judge how well the company is doing, and we want them to have as much information as they need to make those judgments." He nodded toward Nigel. "As Nigel said, I can't know everything that goes on at CST—it's too big a company. But if you tell me you think there's a problem with the way we account for revenues, I'll do everything I can to find out if you're right. I promise you that."

Vivian clapped slowly several times. "Nice speech, Mr. Gillette. I liked it a lot." She broke into a broad smile. "I think one of the senior executives of MCI Worldcom made almost exactly that same speech the first time we brought him in. Said there was no way he could know everything that was going on, but he'd help us get to the bottom of anything that was." She smiled. "He ended up getting ten years behind bars."

"Christian's the chairman of twenty companies, Ms. Davis," Nigel spoke up. "You know he's not involved in the details at CST. There's no way he could be."

"Maybe not, but maybe he shouldn't be chairman of twenty companies, either." She checked her notebook once more. "How much did Everest make on the CST initial public offering?"

Christian hesitated, knowing how this was going to sound. "Four hundred million."

"And how much of that did you take home, Mr. Gillette?"

He stared at her for a moment, then glanced at her jacket sleeves. "Twenty."

HEWITT WATCHED his grandson raise the rifle and peer through the scope, sighting in a magnificent twelve-point buck. The big deer was grazing in front of a grove of live oaks several hundred yards away. He marveled at how steady his grandson's hand was. They were standing, so Three Sticks had nothing to brace the gun against but his shoulder. Still, Hewitt couldn't detect any motion of the gun tip. It was as though he was looking at a photograph.

Hewitt loved Three Sticks. Loved him more than anything in the world. More than being CEO of U.S. Oil, more than this ranch, more than all his money, even more than being master of the Order. He loved the boy more than life itself. He had sons, but, for whatever reason, they hadn't made much of themselves. For all intents and purposes, his grandson had become his only heir.

He watched the fourteen-year-old take a deep breath, let out half of it, hesitate a moment, then calmly squeeze the trigger. Exactly as Hewitt had taught him to do a couple of years ago in a corral behind one of the big barns on the ranch, using tin cans as targets and a little twenty-two as a weapon.

When the gun exploded, Hewitt's gaze snapped left, just in time to see the buck stagger backward a few feet, then bound away into the trees.

"I got him good!" the boy shouted. "In the lungs. He won't go far."

That was the thing about deer. You could blow their lungs—even their hearts—apart with a thirty-caliber shell and they'd still run, still race off into the underbrush as though they hadn't been hit. Something about them kept the blood pumping even though their hearts were gone. But as long as you hit them in the heart or the lungs, you could follow the blood trail right to the spot where they finally collapsed.

Hewitt and the boy jumped on their horses and galloped toward the grove of trees, quickly finding the spot where the buck had been grazing when he was hit. The grass just inside the shade of the elms was stained red, and, sure enough, there were spatters leading off into the trees. They trotted into the grove, along the blood trail until they reached the buck. Even though it lay spread out on the ground, it was still magnificent.

Hewitt drew a forty-four Magnum from his shoulder holster and put another bullet into the deer's body, chuckling as his grandson hit the deck in shock at the sound of the explosion. The boy had dismounted too quickly, impatient as all young men are to claim a trophy. Hewitt had seen a buck this size—apparently dead—suddenly stand and gore its killer before dropping for the final time.

He dismounted slowly, wincing as his boots hit the hard ground, feeling the arthritis in his joints. He watched the boy kneel down beside the deer, grab the antlers, and lift the head off the ground. There was foam all over the soft black mouth and a trickle of blood running down one nostril. It was a hell of a trophy.

"Awesome," Hewitt said proudly, shaking his grandson's hand, then pushing the brim of his Stetson back. "Awesome," he repeated quietly.

"Thanks, Granddad."

Hewitt smiled, pride welling up inside him, suddenly wishing he could live forever, wishing he could watch this boy all the way through his life. Three Sticks had a brilliant future ahead of him. Already an excellent athlete, he'd scored off the charts on his mental aptitude tests as well. There was nothing this boy couldn't accomplish with the right mentoring—and the world staying the way it was.

THE HEADQUARTERS of Black Brothers Allen was at 9 Wall Street, on the south side of the famous narrow lane just west of Federal Hall—where George Washington had taken the first presidential oath of office. The high-rise building housing the secretive firm was set on almost the same piece of real estate the three founders had chosen in 1860 to start the investment bank. The original building had been replaced twenty years ago by a taller, slicker-looking edifice, but many of the artifacts from that first structure were kept in a museum on the fifty-second floor just off the boardroom. The museum was accessible only to the firm's management committee—the top nine executives.

The artifacts included the headdress worn by Man Bear at his execution. Only Trenton Fleming knew the significance of that. Everyone else on the management committee just assumed it was some trinket one of the founders had brought back from a trip out West long ago. Fleming knew because he was the great-great-grandson of Prescott Avery Fleming and George Ellis Black, the two founding members of the Order. One of Prescott Fleming's sons had married one of George Black's daughters and the families had been inextricably linked forever. Just as they were linked to the Hewitt family—Samuel was his second cousin. And the Laird family—Franklin was his third cousin. There were relationships like that everywhere, but they were kept very quiet. It would have been a challenge if the world knew that the man who ran Black Brothers Allen, one of the most powerful investment banks in the world, was related to the man who ran the Federal Reserve.

Christian and Allison followed a receptionist into an elegantly decorated conference room on the tenth floor—the executive floor. When the woman had poured them both drinks, she smiled and politely bid them good-bye, then closed the door behind her.

"That was strange," Christian observed, taking a sip of chilled water as he pulled out his cell phone. He was still thinking about how badly this morning's meeting with Vivian Davis had gone. How he could tell she was licking her chops at the prospect of going after him. How she probably felt like locking horns with him was her big chance to push her career forward at the SEC. He really shouldn't have expected anything else, and he didn't harbor any ill will against her. The bigger you were, the more of a target you were. She was just doing her job, carrying out her superiors' directives. All he could do was try to avert disaster. "Very strange."

"What was?"

"That woman never asked us what we wanted, just poured."

Allison gave Christian a curious look. "So?"

"She poured you a Diet Coke."

"I love Diet Coke."

"Exactly. And she gave me bottled water, chilled without ice." Christian pressed speed dial for Debbie's number at Everest. "Just the way I like it. But she didn't ask either of us what we wanted. Different drinks, both exactly what we wanted. Strange."

Allison glanced around suspiciously. "You're saying she already knew what we wanted."

Christian held up one hand as Debbie answered his call. "Hey there. Uh-huh. Good. Listen, I know this is a weird question, but did somebody call there this morning asking what I like to drink? Oh, yeah? Allison, too? Okay. Thanks." He clicked off and slipped the phone back in his pocket. "Good news: They aren't mind readers. Just well prepared."

Before Allison could say anything, the door opened and two men entered. Both wore dark suits, starched white shirts, and conservative ties. Christian recognized the taller of the two immediately. It was Trenton Fleming, the firm's chairman. Christian had never met Fleming, but he recognized the face from a sketch in a recent, front-page *Journal* article. The article had appeared a month ago and had gone into detail about how secretive the firm was. Absent from the article were quotes from anyone inside Black Brothers, including Fleming. The only people quoted in the story were investment bankers and lawyers at other firms.

Fleming was tall and slim, with thinning blond hair and round, wire-rimmed glasses. His face was tanned deeply, and Christian remembered that the article had described him as an avid seaman who had sailed around the world by himself several times.

"Hello, Christian. I'm Trenton Fleming. Good to finally meet you. I've read a lot about you."

"Likewise." Christian gestured toward Allison. "This is Allison Wallace."

"We know Allison." Fleming turned toward her. "How's your uncle, honey?"

Christian noticed her give him a quick, sidelong glance. When he'd asked her if she knew anyone here at Black Brothers, she hadn't mentioned that she knew the man who ran the place. Knew him well enough that he called her "honey." Seemed like that would have been a natural thing to say.

"He's fine," she answered quickly. "Thanks."

Fleming nodded at the man to his left. "This is Roy Inkster. He's the lead investment banker in our energy department."

Inkster leaned in to shake hands. "I appreciate you two taking the time to come down here to see us."

When they were all seated, Christian wasted no time getting to the point. "Trenton, why do you think you can sell Laurel Energy for me if Morgan Stanley can't? Morgan Stanley's energy group is excellent."

Fleming removed his glasses and placed them carefully on the shiny tabletop. "They certainly do have a fine group, but, Christian, we're known for our ability to handle . . . *special* situations. To get things done when other firms can't."

"What makes you guys so good?"

"Connections. Simple as that. What makes the world go round. We believe we can get to anyone anywhere. Because of who we know in many different places, we feel we can get to the people who can drive a deal, like in this Laurel situation," he interrupted himself, "with much fewer degrees of separation than any other firm that might represent you. As I'm sure you'd agree, the fewer the degrees of separation, the more likely people are to listen. It's all about connections, which is what you need in this situation. Our ability to get to the CEO of every major energy company in the world, not just to the mid-level guys like I'm sure Morgan Stanley's been contacting. You know, head of business development, head of corporate finance—those kinds of folks. Certainly people that matter, but not the CEO. We'll go directly to the CEOs."

"Have you looked at Laurel Energy yet?" Christian asked.

"I've had a couple of our top analysts all over it the past few days. We're convinced you can get at least four and a half billion for it, based on our assessment of the reserves."

That sounded good. It wasn't five billion, but it was close. Close enough to get him interested. "Who do you think buys it?"

Fleming smiled politely. The same way the receptionist had, Christian thought. Like he knew something you wanted to know—and he knew you wanted to know it—but he wasn't going to tell you, at least not right now. Not until you paid him a big fat fee. Christian looked around. This place had a cult feel to it.

"Well." Fleming chuckled in a way that told everyone in the room he was very sure of himself. "That's where we come in, isn't it?"

Fleming seemed awfully pleased with himself. Like a cat who was about to bag a big canary.

"I suppose," Christian agreed grudgingly, aware of what was coming.

"Let's talk about our fee to do this deal," Fleming suggested. "What our connections will cost you."

One of the main points of the *Wall Street Journal* article was that, while Black Brothers seemed to be able to get things done that other firms couldn't, they charged exorbitant fees to do it. Christian nodded. "Okay."

"We'll get ten million up front just to take on the project, then we'll get a success fee of seven percent of whatever we get for the company on top of that."

Christian gazed steadily at Fleming, trying not to give away his aggravation. He'd been ready for something like one or two percent, maybe three, but seven was ridiculous. If Black Brothers really got four and a half billion for Laurel Energy, their fee would be well over three hundred million, an obscene amount of money. "That seems heavy, Trenton," he said, trying to be diplomatic.

"It's a difficult situation. As you've found."

Christian glanced out the window overlooking Wall Street. Three hundred million to make a few calls. Now *that* was a hell of a phone bill. "Why are you here, Trenton?" he asked.

"Beg your pardon?"

"Why did you come to this meeting? Why didn't you let Roy handle it himself?" Christian motioned toward Inkster. "No offense." He looked back at Fleming. "But candidly, Trenton, I was surprised when you walked in."

"You're an important guy, Christian. *Candidly,* we'd like to do more business with you and Everest Capital. Roy's a talented man, but I figure the chairman of Everest Capital wants to meet the chairman of Black Brothers Allen when he comes to Wall Street."

CARMINE TORINO came to with a start. He'd always been a light sleeper—you had to be to survive in the Mob.

He slipped out of the old bed and instantly hit a creaky floorboard. He winced, then grabbed the shotgun that was propped against the mattress. As he brought the gun to his shoulder, he heard the noise again: something—or someone—in the kitchen.

He stole down the narrow, musty hallway, brushing a cobweb aside, praying he wouldn't hit another creaking board. When he reached the end of the hallway, he stood there for several moments, getting up his nerve to take the next step. He just prayed there weren't more than two of them. He could handle two, but three would be tough. It was an over-and-under shotgun so he had five shots, but to kill three would still be very hard—even with the element of surprise.

Torino counted to five, then swung around the corner and leveled the gun into the kitchen. As he did, a huge object came rushing at him through the air, screeching. He threw his arms up and ducked as a hawk sailed by his head. "Jesus Christ!" he shouted, tumbling to the floor. He glanced up just in time to see the bird sail outside through the open living room window behind him.

After several moments he got up and dusted himself off, still shaking. He'd left a half-eaten cheeseburger on the kitchen counter last night. He wouldn't make that mistake again.

CHRISTIAN LOOKED UP from his computer at the sound of a knock on his office door.

"You wanted to see me?" Nigel asked from the doorway.

"Yeah, come in. Close the door, will you?"

"What is it?"

Christian had called Nigel a few minutes ago on a private intercom connecting their two offices. "I need you to take the lead on this CST thing—with the SEC, I mean. I'm going to be tied up for a while, and I want to try to figure out what's going on at CST *fast.*" He had to focus on the casino license and the sale of Laurel Energy himself, but he couldn't wait to start digging into the CST problem. Couldn't let the SEC get ahead. "By the end of the week at the latest."

Nigel nodded. "I'll do my best."

"Don't do your best, just do it." Christian pointed at Nigel. "First things first. Call Frank Conway over at Tucker Simpson. He's the top lawyer in the city when it comes to this SEC stuff. Fill him in, then ask him what we should and shouldn't be doing."

"I'll call him as soon as we're done here."

"Second, I want you to start poking around at CST itself. Get close to somebody you trust out in Chicago, a low-level controller maybe," Christian suggested. "You know those people pretty well from the IPO. If something's going on, I want to know about it before the SEC raids the place with their storm troopers. And don't mention this to Conway. He'd probably tell you to stay away, but I don't care."

"Shouldn't we follow Conway's—"

"Do it, Nigel."

"But what if—"

"When did you become Mr. Patient, for Christ sake? Usually I'm holding you back."

"I know, but this is different. This is the SEC. I don't want to get sideways with them."

"I hate to tell you," Christian muttered, "but we already are. Did you see the look in Vivian Davis's eyes this morning?"

Nigel nodded glumly. "Yeah, she's out for blood."

"Which is why we've got to act fast. I want to be proactive on this thing, I don't want to play defense."

"All right, all right," Nigel agreed. "The last thing you need, the last thing *any* of us need, is for your name to get dragged through the newspapers because of some kind of scandal at CST. I hate to say this, but you know as well as I do that the reporters will try to connect it to you as fast as they can. You're a big target, being on magazine covers as much as you have been lately and with a girlfriend like Faith Cassidy. You being named in a scandal will sell a lot of copies."

Christian had already thought of that, and Nigel was exactly right. Which was why you did everything you could in life to avoid publicity, so people didn't know who you were and your name wouldn't sell copies. But, as Everest's chairman and with what had happened a couple of years ago, that had turned out to be impossible.

"This whole thing seems so strange to me," Christian said. "I trust Bob Galloway and his staff, and we've never had any cash flow problems. Accounting hocus-pocus only gets you so far. Enron and MCI proved that. Sooner or later there's no cash left, and you gotta pay the piper." He shook his head. "But we're doing fine with cash at CST, right?"

"As far as I know."

"I don't get it."

Nigel shrugged. "I know, it's crazy. And you're right: I trust Bob, too. Besides, the investment bankers, the accountants, and the lawyers were all over CST for months before we took it public. Somebody should have caught something."

"Well, we can't look back at this point. All we can do is play the hand we're dealt." His office phone began to ring. It was Quentin. "Hold on a minute." Christian picked up the phone. "Hi, what do you have?"

"I may have a lead on our friend Carmine Torino."

"Where is he?"

"I'll tell you when I'm sure, but I think he's in hiding somewhere outside Vegas. Somebody must be after him, like you thought."

It had to be somebody important because Torino was still due a big payment from Everest—two million dollars when they got the license. Torino had handled everything beautifully up to this point. There hadn't been any strikes or equipment breakdowns. Everything had gone smoothly because Torino was making certain the right palms were greased. Now, at the eleventh hour, everything was going haywire. Of course, maybe that had been the plan all along, he realized. But if that was what the Mob had been planning, why would they be hunting Torino? He was their friend, the one who made sure they got paid to keep people on the job and machines running smoothly. "Who do you think it is?"

"I don't know. I'm talking to my people, but they aren't sure yet."

"That's strange. Wouldn't you think they'd know exactly who it was?"

"Yeah, I would. It doesn't make any sense."

After his stint with the Rangers, Quentin had been in charge of a very secret government anticrime project. He'd never been completely forthcoming about the project with Christian. He couldn't, he claimed. It had something to do with organized crime, and it was still classified. During the time he'd been on the project, he'd been able to forge deep connections inside several of the big Mob families.

"Maybe it's someone outside the Mob," said Christian.

"Maybe, but who outside the Mob's gonna scare somebody like Carmine Torino?"

Another dead end. At least for now. "What about the guy at the transfer station who wants the million bucks?" Christian asked. "Anything on him?"

"He's definitely Mob. I tracked him to one of the New York families, but . . . it's weird."

"What is?"

"My connect inside that family says that whatever the guy's doing isn't sanctioned by the bosses. Or, if it is, it's way secret. The kind of hush-hush thing that's usually required for hits on the high ups of other families."

"Who owns that transfer station where we met the guy?"

"That's another thing," Quentin said. "It's legit. It's owned by the guy's father who isn't Mob, never has been. That guy we met lives in Brooklyn. He was just out in Vegas for a few days, apparently to meet you."

"Then he can't shut us down if I don't pay him," Christian pointed out.

Quentin didn't say anything.

"Right?" Christian pushed.

"Yeah, well . . ."

"Yeah, well, *what?*"

"There was an electrical inspection today over at the Dice Casino. Did you know about that?"

"No."

"Well, from what I understand, it was a *surprise* inspection."

"And?"

"And it didn't go well. The inspector told the electricians they were going to have to rip out three floors of wiring and start over."

Christian gritted his teeth. A message from the prick at the transfer station, plain and simple. Pay the million bucks or the casino stays dark. "All right, when are you coming back?"

"I need to follow up on this Torino thing. Hopefully tonight."

"Safe travels, pal." Christian hung up the phone.

"Everything all right?" Nigel asked.

"Just another day in private equity," Christian said, forcing a wan smile. "It's—" He was interrupted by Debbie on his intercom. "Yes?"

"Mr. Osgood is here to see you."

"Thanks."

"Who's that?" Nigel asked, standing up to go.

Christian hesitated, not sure he wanted to say anything. But Nigel had been his partner for years. If he should tell anyone . . . "It's Jesse Wood's chief of staff."

"*Senator* Jesse Wood?"

"Yes."

Nigel's eyes widened. "This country's next president?"

"I wouldn't go that far," Christian cautioned.

"Everything I read says he's winning the Democratic nomination in July, then probably winning in November."

"A lot can happen between now and then."

"What does Osgood want?"

Christian shrugged. "I don't know exactly. Senator Wood asked me to sit down with him next week, to get my thoughts on a few things. Osgood probably just wants to go over the agenda for that meeting."

"Senator Wood wants your endorsement," Nigel said, turning to go. "You're getting to be a man in demand, Mr. Gillette, a man in demand. Pretty impressive." He stopped at the door. "I'll get on the CST thing."

A few moments later Debbie showed Clarence Osgood into Christian's office. They sat down in the corner away from his desk, in a comfortable area with two couches positioned around a coffee table.

"I appreciate you coming here," Christian led off, taking a sip from the bottled water Debbie had brought him. "We've got a lot going on at Everest so it's tough for me to get out of the office."

"I understand completely," Osgood said graciously. "No problem."

"I'm looking forward to the meeting with Senator Wood."

Osgood smiled. "No need for formality, Christian. Call him Jesse, just like the rest of us do."

"Okay. Well, when I was growing up, I always admired the way Jesse played tennis. With so much passion. I was a big fan."

Osgood waved his arms. "Oh gawd, don't tell him you admired his tennis when we all get together. We won't be able to pry him off that subject with a crowbar. He'll tell us how he can still beat the young guys out on tour today." Osgood chuckled. "I'm just kidding. Jesse's really a very humble guy."

"That's the way he comes off on camera."

"And that's the way he is," Osgood confirmed. "He's an incredible man, and it's an honor to work for him. I love my job."

"Looks like that job might end up taking you to the White House in November."

Osgood shook his head. "Wouldn't that be something?"

"Sure would," Christian agreed. "It'd be history, like nothing this nation's seen in a long time. So, what are we talking about today, Clarence?"

A gleam came to Osgood's eyes. "Like you said, Christian, history."

"What do you mean?"

"Jesse Wood is going to be the next president of this country." Osgood hesitated. "Jesse wants you to be its next *vice* president."

12

EVER SINCE he could remember, Christian had been around powerful and famous people, so it didn't faze him. His father, Clayton, had started a brokerage firm from scratch and grown it into one of the most prestigious investment banks on the West Coast before selling out to a big Wall Street firm for a hundred million. After that, Clayton had gone into national politics—one term as a congressman from California, then on to the Senate. As he became a high-profile player in Los Angeles, more and more celebrities dropped by the house in Bel Air—sports stars, movie stars, other politicians—and Clayton proudly introduced Christian to all of them. Christian understood powerful and famous people, and he was comfortable around them.

But Samuel Hewitt had something about him that Christian had experienced only once before: an aura that drew you to him so forcefully, that made you want to watch his every move so you could emulate him. It wasn't something Hewitt had to work at making you see, either. It was completely natural, all around him constantly. You felt it even before you shook his hand, when you first laid eyes on him. It was a presidential charisma, a sense of immense power that radiated from him.

The only other person who'd ever exuded that same kind of aura to Christian was his father. Clayton had had that same calm yet intense confidence about him, that same innate ability to make you love to be around him, to learn from him, to emulate him, to want to impress him.

Not only because he made you feel that if you were like him, you'd be successful. Not only because he made you feel he sincerely cared about you. But because you realized he made you feel better about yourself. He quickly identified your talents and made certain to subtly highlight them during your conversation with him. You went away from your interaction with him believing that you did have a lot to offer, that you could make a difference if you really tried.

And it wasn't because Clayton was his father that Christian felt that way; it was obvious to everyone. People told Christian all the time. Only a few months into his Senate term, Clayton had been tabbed by the powers in the Republican party and the press as a favorite to win a presidential nomination. Then he died in the plane crash—along with the dream.

"It's a pleasure to finally meet you, Mr. Hewitt," Christian said as they sat in an anteroom of Princeton's Avery Ellis Hall. It was quiet here, away from the buzz of the alumni function, like being in someone's home—leather chairs, dark wood, bookcases up to the ceiling, an antique globe in one corner, the smell of pipe tobacco. It reminded Christian of his father's den at the Bel Air house. "You're a legend."

Which was no exaggeration. U.S. Oil had been named the most-admired company in America three times in the last decade by several major business magazines—twice more than any other company. Hewitt had been named the most valuable chief executive twice.

"Call me Samuel," Hewitt said, smiling widely. "Okay if I call you Christian?"

"Of course." Hewitt looked the part of a Texas president. Tall, still strapping at sixty-seven, silver haired, rattlesnake boots beneath a crisp charcoal suit, a classy black Stetson lying on the table in front of him. "I was honored that you called."

Hewitt crossed one leg over the other at the knee and settled into the comfortable chair. "And I was honored that you would meet." His smile grew wider. "You're much busier than me. I'm only chairman of *one* company. According to *Forbes*, you're chairman of twenty."

"Private equity," Christian said. "You know the deal. I represent the money, that's why I'm chairman. The CEOs are really in charge at our portfolio companies. Besides, you're chairman of the biggest company in the world."

Hewitt still hadn't stopped smiling.

Christian grinned back. "What?"

"It's eerie."

"What is?"

"How much you remind me of your father."

Christian sat straight up in his chair. "You knew my father?" That possibility had never crossed his mind.

Hewitt's smile faded. "I did, but not well. We had dinner a few times. I thought he was incredible, one of the most dynamic people I've ever met. Good-hearted, too. That plane crash was a terrible thing for him, for your family, and for our country. Clayton Gillette would have been one of the best presidents the United States ever had, I'm convinced of that." He grimaced. "I cried when I heard he was dead."

Usually Christian allowed himself to form only *bad* opinions of people quickly. To earn his respect, you had to do it over time, like Quentin and Nigel had. It seemed like being skeptical about people just came with the turf. But there was something different about Hewitt, and it wasn't just that overwhelming presidential aura. Christian felt an immediate closeness to the man, as if he'd known Hewitt for years. "I appreciate that," he murmured.

"You definitely remind me of your father, Christian," Hewitt spoke up. "Only, and I can't believe I'm saying this," he interrupted himself, "you've got even more charisma than he—"

"No, my father was—"

"Let the son of an old wildcatter talk, son," Hewitt urged, his Texas drawl growing slightly more pronounced.

Christian nodded. "Sorry." It had always been hard for him to take compliments, especially when people were comparing him to his father.

"What is it you young people say?" Hewitt asked quietly, the wide smile reappearing. "Oh, right," he said, snapping his fingers. "You've got it going on, son. You've got the look."

"Thanks."

"Ever thought about going into politics?"

Christian glanced up, wondering for a split second if Hewitt knew something. But that was impossible. "Well, I—"

"Sorry," Hewitt apologized, holding up his hands. "I don't mean to waste your time. Let's get to why I wanted to meet. Princeton needs a new library." A sheepish expression came to Hewitt's face. "Well, I guess *need* is a relative term when it comes to the Ivy League. Anyway, some of the other alums and I decided that we do, and, of course, we want the best money can buy. So we formed a committee to start raising it. I'd really appreciate it if you'd join us."

"Of course, I will." Christian didn't hesitate. "I'll donate a million bucks, too."

"Jesus." Hewitt shook his head. "Now don't I feel like an ass? I only committed *half* a million."

"And I'll raise a lot more from people I know."

"I figured you'd know a lot of—"

"But I'll do it on one condition."

Hewitt looked up. "What's that?"

"Ten percent of what we raise goes to scholarships for kids from the inner city. What's the target raise?" Christian asked without waiting for Hewitt's answer. Suddenly the old man seemed a little miffed. As if he didn't like conditions made by anyone.

"A hundred. We think that'll get us a first-rate facility."

"Then it'll have to be a hundred and *ten*. Do we have a deal?"

Hewitt snickered. "Does everything have to be a negotiation?"

Christian winked. "*You're* asking *me*?"

"Well, I—"

"We should be able to get to that number pretty fast." Christian ran some numbers in his head, thinking about who he could lean on. "I'll call a few Tigers on Wall Street who owe me favors."

Hewitt smirked. "Or who would kill to do business with Everest Capital."

"Exactly."

A young waiter approached the table and waited politely to be acknowledged.

"You want anything, Christian?" Hewitt asked. He'd ordered a soft drink and a sandwich before Christian arrived.

"No, thanks."

Hewitt looked up at the waiter. "Just the check, son. You can put it on my tab."

The waiter reached into his pocket. "Already done, sir," he said, handing it to Hewitt.

"So, you guys own Laurel Energy, right?" Hewitt asked, taking the check and scribbling his initials in large looping letters, then handing it back.

Christian caught his breath. He couldn't have scripted this meeting any better. "We do."

"Yeah, I went on your Web site this morning and checked out your portfolio companies," Hewitt said, watching the waiter head off. "It's an impressive list, but, of course, the one that caught my eye right away was Laurel. I talked to one of my senior engineers up in Calgary. Obviously we have a bunch of assets up there in Canada, too," Hewitt explained. "He said Laurel has some very solid reserves. I guess he'd spoken to some friends of his at the company."

"It's been a good investment for us," Christian agreed, trying to stay low-key, trying not to seem eager.

"What are you guys going to do with Laurel, if you don't mind me asking? You're an investment company. I know how those funds you guys run work. You don't usually hold on to portfolio companies for more than five or six years."

"It's interesting you mention that." Apparently Quentin was right. Hewitt didn't know Laurel was for sale after all, which Christian found surprising. "We're actually in the process of selling Laurel now."

"Really?"

"Honestly, we've had it on the market for a while." It didn't make sense to try to con Hewitt into thinking they'd just started the process. Hewitt would find out very quickly that Morgan Stanley had been peddling it for a while.

"Oh?"

Christian could see the doubts zipping through Hewitt's mind right away, but it was better to hit this head-on. Never dance around an issue, especially with someone as sophisticated as Hewitt. That was just inefficient. "We sent it to your business development people a while ago, but they turned it down. We sent it to all the big companies, but so far no takers."

"What's wrong with it?"

"Nothing."

"Come on."

"Read the engineering reports, Samuel. The reserves are there. Honestly, I don't know what the problem is."

Hewitt tapped his chin for a few moments. "Who's managing the sell process? Who's the investment bank?"

"Morgan Stanley." Christian watched the older man frown, as though that information didn't sit with him very well. "But I'm probably going to change advisers soon. It looks like we're going to hire Black Brothers Allen to take over."

Hewitt rolled his eyes. "Uh-oh. Well, I better move quick if I'm interested. Those guys at Black Brothers will get the deal done for you, but Trenton Fleming's a shark. He'll charge you an arm and a leg, but he'll get it done."

"You know Fleming?"

Hewitt made a face. "A little. They did some work for us a few years ago, but, like I said, their fees are flat ridiculous. I didn't think it was worth it. You've got a selling memorandum that describes Laurel, right?" Hewitt asked. "I assume Morgan Stanley put one together."

"Of course, and it's got everything in it. All the reserve information, all the technical stuff your guys will want. And the engineering firms we retained are excellent."

"Jones and Huff?"

"And Shay, Strong, and Meyers."

Hewitt nodded. "You don't get any better than them."

"Exactly."

"Send the book to me in Dallas, will you?"

"Sure."

"I'll be back down there in a couple of days," Hewitt explained. "My assistant's name in Dallas is Rhonda. Send it to her attention. I'll let her know it's coming."

"I'll have it out tomorrow."

Hewitt smiled. "Don't worry, Christian, we'll get something done. Maybe I'll even stretch on the price, give you a little more than what you deserve so you've got an incentive to help me get this library. Just don't tell my shareholders."

"Believe me, Samuel, if you buy Laurel Energy from me at a decent price, I'll get you your library and I'll never say a word."

"Probably fund it yourself out of what you personally net from the Laurel sale." Hewitt winked, like he figured he was exaggerating.

But actually, he wasn't too far from the truth. "I hear you're a poker player," Christian said.

"That I am," Hewitt answered enthusiastically.

"Well, if you're ever in New York, I know where you can get a good game."

"Oh?"

"Yeah, a friend of mine on the Upper West Side runs it. Pretty high stakes and good players. You'd like it. I'd be more than happy to take you one night."

"Thanks, son. Might take you up on that." Hewitt pointed at Christian and leaned forward in his chair. "What we *should* do is have you come to my ranch outside Dallas. I'll get a couple of the boys from town, and we'll have one of those all-night games. Scotch, good cigars, big pots."

"Love to." He wouldn't drink any Scotch, but he might smoke a cigar. Most important, he'd have that time with Hewitt. Suddenly, the sale of Laurel Energy was looking good. Things changed so fast sometimes.

Hewitt started to get up. "Well, Christian, it's been a pleasure to—"

"Do you have a few more minutes, Samuel?" Christian had been thinking about whether or not to bring this up with Hewitt since they'd first sat down. Since the older man had admitted knowing Clayton. "There's something I'd like to run by you."

Hewitt sank back into his chair. "Of course. What's up?"

Christian took a few moments to collect his thoughts, making certain he wanted to do this. "I need you to keep this quiet." Instantly, he regretted saying that. After all, he was the one who'd brought it up.

Hewitt shut his eyes and nodded, silently mouthing the word "okay." Like it was already understood that everything they discussed was confidential, but if Christian needed to hear it, fine.

"Jesse Wood is going to ask me to be his running mate if he wins the Democratic nomination in July," Christian explained. "He's going to ask me to be his vice president."

Hewitt's mouth fell open. "You're kidding."

Christian grinned. "No, I'm not."

"Jesse Wood is a Democrat," Hewitt snapped, his friendly demeanor souring.

Christian hadn't been ready for so strong a response. "Right."

"Your father was a Republican," Hewitt said, his voice rising. "A damn fine one, too. And he—" He stopped abruptly, holding up one hand and shaking his head. "This isn't fair," he said, his voice dropping back to normal. "I made an assumption, and I shouldn't have. I've got to get used to this new world we live in."

But the party issue was bothering Christian, too. "I've been thinking a lot about that," he admitted, still surprised by the intensity of Hewitt's reaction. "That's one of the reasons I wanted to talk to you about my meeting with Wood. I wanted to get your opinion on me running as a Democrat. People will expect me to run as a Republican, especially people in California."

Hewitt hesitated. "Well, *I'm* a Republican, been one since the day I was born, and I'm proud of it. Of course, you probably already knew that."

Christian nodded.

"Don't hold it against me, but I think people should work for a living."

Christian started to say something, but Hewitt cut him off.

"I'm just kidding, I understand the need for another party."

"Actually, I think there's a need for a *new* party. One that's fiscally responsible but helps people get back on their feet when they're down. But I've got to work within the system right now. Maybe down the road, though."

Hewitt smiled. "Already talking like a politician."

"I've been thinking about the idea of a third party for a long time, Samuel."

Hewitt took a deep breath. "Look, from everything I can tell, you'd make a tremendous contribution to this country, no matter what ticket you run on. You make an incredible first impression, you're a deep thinker, you have great experience running a lot of large entities—in one week you probably deal with more stress than most people do in a lifetime—and, from what I hear, you really care about people."

"Thanks, Samuel." Christian liked the man more and more. He knew that had been a hard thing for a die-hard Republican to say, but Hewitt had sucked it up and said it anyway. "Could I call you from time to time for advice? I'd never let on that you were advising me, I'd never tell anyone because I wouldn't want to embarrass you in front of your Texas GOP friends. But I could really use your counsel."

Hewitt nodded. "Of course, Christian."

"Call me Chris."

Hewitt nodded again. He was silent for a few moments, then he looked up. "So, you going to accept Wood's offer?"

FORTE RECLINED into a comfortable easy chair as Johnson slid an unmarked CD into a DVD player sitting on top of the eighty-inch screen.

He'd always liked the way CDs disappeared smoothly once the machine felt them. Just another modern marvel. "How many more copies of this thing are there, Heath?"

"Three more, boss," Johnson answered, sitting on a sofa in front of the screen. "All stored in safe deposit boxes around Los Angeles. I've got one set of keys to the boxes, you've got another, and there's a third in the safe at your beach house."

"Right." Forte remembered now.

"There's also a list of the banks and box numbers in that safe."

"Good."

They'd come to Johnson's house so he could finally see the clip. It had been a hectic morning and they'd decided they needed a break, but they didn't want to do this at the office. Too risky—someone might come in unexpectedly. Safer at Johnson's house which was only a few miles from the office. Johnson's kids were in school and his wife was out shopping. They wouldn't be discovered.

"You're not going to believe it when you see it," Forte said.

"Where was it shot?" Johnson asked, picking up a drink off the table in front of the sofa, not taking his eyes from the screen.

"Backstage after a press conference in Washington," Forte explained.

"When?"

"Not quite a year ago."

"Good, it's recent."

"Oh, yeah," Forte confirmed. "It's not like Jesse could say it happened years and years ago, and he doesn't feel this way anymore. People will get it."

The screen cleared and images appeared, murky at first, then sharper and sharper as the camera zoomed in.

"There he is." Forte pointed excitedly toward the right side of the screen.

"I see him, boss," Johnson acknowledged. "That's Jesse, no doubt."

The camera focused on Wood, who was standing with Clarence Osgood, Stephanie Childress, and another man.

"Who is that guy?" Johnson asked, taking a sip of soda. He'd known Osgood and Stephanie for a while so they were familiar to him right away. "He looks so damn fa—" Johnson banged the sofa. "Now I remember. That's Jefferson Roundtree, that activist minister from Philly."

"*Nut job* from Philly is more like it," Forte said. "We don't want Jesse anywhere near him now, don't want Jesse seen with him at all because he scares the crap out of whites. But he served his purpose here," Forte added quietly.

"Boy, it's a nice clear shot of Jesse—"

"Shh! Here it is, here it is." Forte picked up the remote and turned up the volume.

The camera panned in on Wood's handsome face as he turned to Roundtree. "Yeah, that Jew from CNN was such a prick," Wood said, smirking, "asking me about my voting record on civil rights."

"You got it, brother," Roundtree agreed heartily. "Like any cracker should have the nerve to ask you about that."

Osgood and Stephanie nodded.

Then there were a few muffled words, but nothing audible.

Johnson looked over at Forte. "If we get this disk to the right people, we might be able to pick up what they just said. I know some people who'd help us and never say a word."

"I wouldn't trust anyone with this, even those people."

"No, these guys are—"

"It won't be necessary, believe me," Forte interrupted again, pointing at the screen. "Keep watching."

There was more muffled chatter, then Wood held his hands up.

He said, "You know, I had to put up with so much crap from Whitey when I was playing tennis back in the day, it was ridiculous. Real bullshit stuff, too. Tennis racquets busted while I was in the shower, no towels, the worst locker, called nigger all the time, even by the help." He looked over at Osgood. "I'm telling you, Clarence, if I get elected president, I'm gonna act the way I'm supposed to act in front of the camera. Smile and dance like a good black man, do what I'm expected to do like a good boy. But behind the scenes, I'll fuck Whitey, and I'll fuck him good, I really will."

"You go, man," Roundtree encouraged. "I'm with you all the way. Every black man will be."

Stephanie held her hand to her mouth to hide a smile.

Wood glanced down at her and touched her thigh. "It's gonna be fun, isn't it, Steph?"

Forte paused the disk. "Did you see that?" he asked sharply.

"See what?"

"Jesse putting his hand on Stephanie's thigh. It was just for a second, but he did it."

Johnson shook his head. "No, I didn't catch it."

Forte played the segment back. "There, see?"

"Oh, yeah, uh-huh."

"Interesting, don't you think?"

"Very."

"Do a little work on that, will you, Heath? I know they had something a long time ago, but I want to know if it's started up again."

"Okay, boss."

"Good. All right, here we go." Forte restarted the clip.

Stephanie looked up at Wood. "Oh, yes, it's going to be incredible. And I'd love to see you do anything you can to put whites in their place."

"I'd use all my powers to do to them what they did to us," Wood promised. "I'd even—"

At that moment Osgood happened to look up, directly into the camera.

Suddenly there was nothing on the screen but the floor tiles bouncing around as the cameraman took off, realizing he'd been seen. Then the screen went dark.

"What do you think?" Forte asked, stopping the disk.

Johnson chuckled. "I think Jesse'd rather sleep in elephant shit every night for a year than have this thing get into the hands of the news networks. It would kill his campaign, probably his marriage, too."

Forte smiled widely. "I couldn't agree more," he said smugly. "When he sees this, the good senator will do whatever I want him to do. He'll be right where I want him: in my back pocket."

CHRISTIAN LEANED BACK in his chair and gazed at the ceiling of his office. His eyes stung and his temples throbbed. This business with the SEC couldn't have come at a worse time. He could just see Jesse Wood announcing him as the vice presidential candidate, then Vivian Davis announcing her investigation of CST the next day. Working his name into the press conference, somehow inferring that he was culpable. That was how she'd get the most mileage out of the announcement. And that would be a nightmare of epic proportions, even when he was ultimately cleared of any wrongdoing. By then, the court of public opinion would have already made its decision: guilty by association.

Nigel was sitting in front of him, holding his tie up, dabbing at a small stain on it. Ice cream, Christian thought to himself, probably rocky road. "There's something I need to tell you."

"What?"

"Remember that guy who was here yesterday."

"Osgood?"

"Yeah."

"What about him?"

"He came to tell me that Jesse Wood is going to ask me to be his running mate."

Nigel's tie fell back to his shirt. "You're fucking shitting me, chap."

Something about the response made Christian want to crack a smile, but he just nodded.

"That's incredible." Nigel stood up and shook Christian's hand. "*Incredible.* Like I said, the man in demand." A curious smile came to his face as he sat back down. "Jeez, I've known you for years, and I just realized I didn't even have a clue that you were a Democrat. Honestly, I thought you were a Republican. I don't know why I assumed that, but I did." Nigel waited for a response, but there wasn't one. "Are you going to accept?"

"I'm not sure yet, but, if I do, obviously there are lots of implications."

"I'll say," Nigel agreed loudly. "We'll need a new chairman here at Everest. That's the biggest implication for me."

"Yup." Christian saw the wheels already spinning a million miles an hour inside Nigel's head.

"You won't have time to groom a protégé. The convention's not that far off."

Christian nodded wearily. He'd tried to groom one a couple of years ago, but it hadn't worked out.

"Are you going to bring someone in from the outside?" Nigel asked hesitantly, fiddling with his tie again.

"No."

The Brit's eyes got big and Christian saw him swallow hard, like he wanted to ask the next logical question, but couldn't bear to do it. The answer might be no. "If Jesse Wood asks me to be vice president, if I accept, and if he wins the Democratic nomination, then I'll name an interim chairman. If Wood and I win in November, then that person will become the permanent Everest chairman." Christian watched the enormity of what he'd just laid out sink in. "The interim chairman is going to be you . . . or Allison."

Nigel looked up, fire in his eyes. "I'd do a good job, better than she would."

"You *both* would do a good job," Christian said firmly. "The reason it's a tough decision for me is that you both have very different skill sets. You're a details guy, Nigel, you make sure things run around here."

"I've had to. It's what you wanted me to do."

"*On the other hand,* Allison's a big-picture thinker. Not that you aren't—she's just been at it longer, basically since she came out of the womb. She's got a hell of a lot of connections, too."

"*And* she's going back to her family in Chicago when this fund is finished. Don't forget that."

"And you could take another job tomorrow and be out of here."

"You know I'm not going to do that, Chris," Nigel snapped. "I'm here for good. I'm as loyal as anybody could be. Allison's the one with other loyalties. Her plan has been to go back to Chicago all along."

Nigel was right: that had been her original plan. Something Gordon Meade had gone out of his way to remind Christian of at dinner. But now Christian wasn't sure Allison really wanted to go back to Chicago as much as she had when she first came to Everest. She'd taken quickly to New York City's nightlife, and he knew that in the back of her mind she was as curious as he was about what might happen between them. Clearly, Meade wasn't sure Allison wanted to come back to Chicago now, either. Christian had seen that in Meade's expression the other night when Allison snapped at him.

Of course, Allison had volunteered to Meade how poorly the Laurel Energy sale was going—bad form if she was going to be loyal to Everest. And she hadn't mentioned that she knew Trenton Fleming—knew him pretty well it turned out. When he'd quizzed her about it after their meeting with Fleming and Inkster, she'd seemed guarded. Just a feeling, but that was enough for him to think twice. And he didn't want to have to think twice about the person he named the next Everest chairman.

"Look, Nigel, a lot of things have to happen before we get to the point of me naming an interim chairman, so don't worry about it yet. I just wanted to let you know it was on the horizon, that's all."

"You're fucking with me, chap, that's what you're doing. What are the odds Jesse Wood will ask you to be his vice president?"

"Seventy-five percent."

"You're always conservative when we do this kind of thing, so we'll bump that to *ninety*-five percent. What are the odds that Wood gets the Democratic nomination?"

Christian thought about that one for a few moments. "Sixty percent. He's got a lot of momentum."

"We'll put that one at eighty, no ninety. Everything I read says he's about to win two more primaries and that'll put him over the top. So, then what we're really saying when we break it down is this: Will you accept the slot when he asks you? If you do, then you'll have to name an interim chairman who would become permanent if you and Wood win in November. It's really under your control." Nigel paused. "So?"

Christian considered his response for a moment. "If this SEC thing spins out of control, I might not even have a chance to accept. Worse, if I do, and *then* it spins out of control, well . . ." He didn't finish. That scenario was too painful to even think about.

"**YOU GET THE CALL?**" Kohler asked, checking the tombstones. This time they were meeting in a church graveyard.

McDonnell nodded. "Yeah, I'm leaving in the morning."

"How you getting there?"

"Driving to Augusta."

"Not flying?"

McDonnell shook his head. "I want some time to think. I think better in the car. How about you?"

Kohler hadn't made any plans yet. "Look, are you going to be with me in the meeting or not?" McDonnell was showing signs of weakness, of backing off on his promise to support. "I need to know."

"I—I'm with you, Mace."

"You can't be half-assed about it, you've got to be strong."

"I will, it's just that . . ."

Kohler felt his fingers curling into fists. "Just *what*?"

"It's just that, well, it's that Hewitt's got me on tape with a woman from the country club. Nancy Grimes. I'm such an idiot, I had to submit my tape, and I knew Nancy would do it with me anytime. She's always all over me at the club. She and my wife hate each other. If my wife saw me—"

Kohler watched McDonnell choke up, and it took everything he had not to slug the guy to snap him out of it.

"If my wife saw that tape," McDonnell continued, "I'd lose everything. She'd hire the biggest pit bull lawyer in Manhattan, and I might as well forget about it."

"We can't let Samuel Hewitt shape the course of history."

"Well he's going to *damn sure* shape the course of *my* history if we try anything," McDonnell retorted angrily, thinking about what it would be like to go from living in a ten-thousand-square-foot mansion with all the amenities to living in a one-bedroom condo in Jersey City with a few pieces of stick furniture. "I like being CEO of Jamison and Jamison, too, you know?"

"Hewitt's going to assassinate Jesse Wood, for Christ sake."

"You don't know that. He's never actually said that."

"He doesn't have to say it. Don't be naïve."

"Why not?" McDonnell asked, leaning back against a tombstone. "It's easier." He took a few nervous breaths. "Mace, I hear what you're saying. You know I'm going to do the right thing."

Kohler nodded approvingly. "Blanton, I've made a decision."

"About what?"

"About Hewitt. About what I'm going to do."

McDonnell rolled his eyes. "What's my part in all this?"

Kohler's expression hardened. "Nothing. I'll take care of everything myself."

"What are you going to—"

"Shh!" Kohler's eyes had flashed to a sudden movement in the shadows.

"What is it?"

"There's something over there," Kohler hissed, pointing at the trees. "We've got to get out of here."

THE INTRUDER moved quickly into George Bishop's tiny apartment—it had taken only a few seconds to pick the flimsy lock—and rummaged through drawers and closets, looking for the photo of the old man and the documents Todd Harrison had mentioned sending to someone. Bishop had to be the guy Harrison was talking about. They'd been seen together several times, and Bishop had been snooping around Champagne Island—the boat registration number had led them to him.

The man searched the apartment twice—it took only a few minutes—but found nothing. Bishop had either hidden the stuff somewhere outside the apartment or it was stored electronically, he thought, standing in front of Bishop's computer.

He took a step toward the computer but stopped when he heard noises outside, someone treading heavily up the stairs. He moved beside the door and listened. Now he heard voices, a man and a woman. Bishop had company.

He watched Bishop and the woman stumble into the apartment, falling against the kitchen counter and giggling as they groped each other, not even bothering to close the door behind them. He could have killed them so easily, but that would have caused unnecessary complications. There would be another time, he realized, slipping out the open door and moving quickly down the steps. Another place.

PATTY ROTH raced up the third-floor staircase, determined to find out what was behind that door. She'd gone up in the lighthouse and watched her husband head off for the mainland, watched the lights of the Boston Whaler until they'd disappeared on the horizon. It was strange for Don to go to town at night. She couldn't ever remember him doing it before. But then he'd been doing a lot of strange things lately.

She pushed open the door, listening to the familiar creak of the hinges as she hurried to the steel door on the far wall. Maybe she was reading too much into it, maybe it really was as he'd explained. That the men hadn't given him the usual week's notice they were coming to Champagne. That he had to get supplies quickly.

She knelt down, her fingers not shaking at all this time as she started trying keys in the locks. She had plenty of time. Don wouldn't be back for hours.

These weren't Don's keys she was trying this time. He'd never leave his set here when he was going into town, especially not after catching her trying to open this door. She'd found these keys completely by accident as she was cleaning the sideboard beneath the elk head. She'd pulled one of the drawers out too quickly and almost dropped it. The silverware inside had crashed to the floor and the bottom of the drawer had come up slightly, revealing a tiny compartment beneath. These keys had been in the compartment.

Patty cried out as the bottom padlock snapped open, then rose and excitedly tried the top one. A moment later it popped, too. She removed the locks and laid them on one of the boxes in the room, staring at the steel door for a few moments. Then she moved to it and pulled it back. It was heavy and it took a strong effort, but she finally got it to swing open. She took two baby steps toward the doorway and peered into the darkness. There was a narrow stairway leading down.

She glanced over her shoulder one last time—and froze, her heart suddenly in her throat, all her husband's warnings racing back to her. In the doorway of the room stood two men she'd never seen before.

Patty went for her gun, but they were on her before she could draw.

One of them grabbed her wrist and slammed it against the wall, the other grabbed her by the neck. The gun flew from her fingers and clattered across the floor. She tried desperately to break the grip on her throat, but it was no use. He was immensely powerful. She couldn't even kick because the second man had gathered her legs together in a paralyzing embrace.

She tried to scream, tried to beg as she beat him about the head with weakening blows, but it was no use. Nothing escaped her lips but a raspy moan.

She felt awful pressure building in her head as she searched the man's face for emotion—hatred, lust, compassion. But there was nothing, just cold, dark eyes. They were the last things she ever saw.

IT HAD TAKEN a lot of digging for Quentin to finally find out where Carmine Torino had holed up. He'd pushed his contact inside the family to the edge, and fortunately he'd come through, whispered that Torino was in a canyon outside Las Vegas. The downside of pushing so hard was it would be a long time until he could ask the guy for another favor like this. Christian would never fully appreciate what this had taken.

Quentin had parked the rented Jeep a mile back down the canyon's dusty, twisting road, not wanting to give Torino any warning that he was coming. There were lots of questions he and Christian needed answers to. Most important: If it wasn't somebody inside the family who'd made Torino run—the family had put him up out here in the canyon so it couldn't be them—who was it? And did his running have anything to do with the Dice Casino? Christian was convinced it did. Christian didn't think it was any coincidence that Torino had dropped out of sight at the same time the prick at the transfer station had appeared. But Quentin couldn't find out anything more about the guy, not even from inside the families. They claimed they didn't know, and he believed them.

It was almost dark as Quentin snuck along a dilapidated fence toward the house, gun drawn. He was taking no chances. There was something very weird going on here. So he was prepared to do whatever he had to do to get answers from Torino. Even if that meant using a couple of things he'd picked up along the way in the Rangers.

The fence ended, and he crouched down by the last post. The house was still fifty yards away across open ground. He probably should have waited until it was completely dark to approach, but he needed to get back to Vegas to catch the red-eye to New York. He had to be with Christian tomorrow evening for something very important, something so important Christian wouldn't discuss it on the phone. There couldn't be any chance of his being delayed—Christian had said that three times on the call.

Quentin took several deep breaths, then dashed toward a rickety-looking shack beside the house. He moved to the corner of the building, then sprinted for the front of the house and burst inside, lunging behind an overturned chair and aiming his pistol at what was hanging from the rafter.

Quentin rose from his knees slowly. Carmine Torino was hanging from the rafter. Quite dead.

13

HEWITT NODDED at General Dahl. They'd had a private conversation in the kitchen before Hewitt had brought the Order into session.

"This is Mr. Kohler's confession," Dahl began as he always did, switching on the recording device in front of him. "As documented during meeting forty-eight of the twenty-ninth Order."

Kohler's eyes snapped toward the head of the table. *"What?"*

Hewitt motioned for Laird to get the Scotch from the sideboard. "You will confess tonight, Mr. Kohler."

"What about him?" Kohler asked, pointing down the table. "He missed the last meeting."

"No."

"But I just confessed two meetings ago."

"I wasn't *satisfied* with it." Hewitt let the words hang in the air for a few moments. "And nothing in the bylaws requires me to follow any particular sequence in terms of our confessions. In fact, the bylaws are very clear that I *shouldn't* follow a sequence. That people should wonder whose number is up."

"I understand, but—"

"Bottom line, it's up to the master to decide who goes when, and the bylaws don't say anything about free passes."

Laird placed the Scotch bottle and a glass triumphantly down in front of Kohler.

"Drink," Hewitt demanded.

Kohler hesitated. "This isn't right."

"Drink."

Still Kohler didn't pick up the bottle.

"I'll go, Mr. Hewitt," Fleming volunteered. "I don't mind."

"That's very good of you, Mr. Fleming, but it will be Mr. Kohler."

Finally, Kohler poured. While the other men watched, he drank shot after shot, until he nearly gagged.

"Now. C*onfess.*"

"Give me a second," Kohler gasped, wiping his mouth with a napkin.

"Now," Hewitt ordered. "Don't make me—"

"Jesus," McDonnell cut in. "Give him a break, will you?"

"What's your problem?" Massey demanded.

"I just think we ought to give him a second to catch his breath," McDonnell said, turning quickly in his seat, startled by Massey's voice.

"And I think you ought to keep your mouth shut," Massey snapped. "Mr. Hewitt is master of the Order. He decides what goes on when in these meetings."

"Look, I'm just saying that—"

"It's all right," Kohler broke in. "I'm ready."

Hewitt nodded. "Proceed."

Kohler coughed and pressed his fist to his chest. "Last week I fantasized about a woman I saw in an airport."

"What did she look like?" This question came from Laird.

Kohler glanced at Laird contemptuously, like answering to him was the last thing in the world he felt he should have to do. "Tall and blond with large breasts, *Mr. Laird.* Just like that woman you taped in the bathroom of your office at the Fed." His voice rose through the sentence. "While she was screwing your assistant."

"Hey, I don't have to take that kind of—"

"Careful, Mr. Kohler," Hewitt warned, "or tomorrow I'll turn over your tapes for the press and your wife to see." Kohler looked like he was going to snap but held back. "Keep going," Hewitt ordered.

"Yeah," Massey piped up. "What did you do to her in your fantasy?"

Hewitt smiled to himself. They were going at Kohler hard, just as he'd instructed.

"I convinced her to go to a strip club," Kohler answered, slurring his words as the alcohol set in. "I watched her get lap dances from some of the girls."

"Then what?" Dahl demanded.

"We had sex in one of those back rooms."

"Anything more you want to tell us about strip clubs, Mr. Kohler?" Hewitt asked accusingly.

"What do you mean?"

"You know what I mean."

The other men glanced down the table at Hewitt, then expectantly at Kohler.

Kohler swallowed hard. "Are you having me followed, Samuel?"

"Answer the question," Hewitt ordered. "There's no need to get upset."

"I'm not upset, I just don't want my *entire life* recorded."

"What are you afraid of?"

"Are you kidding me?"

"Answer the question."

Kohler gazed at Hewitt for a few moments. "All right, I admit it, I went to a strip club when I was in Atlanta last week."

"Is that the only time you've been to a strip club lately?"

Kohler held his arms out. "Hey, what is this?"

"Was it *just* last week, or have there been other times?"

"Okay, I've been a few other times in the past couple of months. So what?"

"A *few*?"

"Look, that's all I'm going to—"

"You're having an affair with a stripper in Atlanta, Mr. Kohler!" Hewitt roared. "Isn't that why you go there so often?"

"No!"

Hewitt drew himself up in his chair, giving Kohler a disdainful glare. "Remember, Mr. Kohler, perjury is more of a crime in this room than it is in a court of law. We've all lied in court—that's just beating the system. But this is different. This is about honor among brothers."

"Listen, Hewitt," Kohler went off, "brothers or not, my personal life is my own—"

"No, it isn't!" Hewitt thundered back. "You owe us an explanation when we demand it, that's the oath we take. You tell us *everything*. We all tell each other everything."

Kohler stared hard at Hewitt for a few moments, then slumped in his chair, suddenly out of defiance. "I'm seeing a woman in Atlanta," he admitted. "I met her at a club."

"And she's—"

"And she's a stripper," Kohler finished. "Yes, you're right."

Hewitt raised one eyebrow and looked around the table victoriously. "You'll get us a tape of you and her together. I'll expect it at the next meeting."

Kohler nodded, broken by the onslaught.

Hewitt eased back in his seat. "I need to tell you all why Mr. Benson isn't here," he said to the group, gesturing toward the empty chair. "Our brother has passed on."

The room went silent and all eyes moved to Hewitt's.

"God, what happened?" Laird asked. He and Benson had been initiated into the Order at about the same time.

"He was murdered in Naples, down in Florida. A robbery turned deadly, according to the police."

Fleming shook his head. "That's awful."

"It is," Hewitt agreed. "But when we lose, we shouldn't lose the lesson. Something like this should remind us of how fleeting life can be. How everyone has to be careful in this world, especially men like us, men with a lot to lose. Apparently, Mr. Benson was going to get his car after eating at a restaurant. He was mugged outside a parking garage, then shot."

Dahl sneered. "Probably Puerto Ricans."

"The police don't have any leads," Hewitt said, shaking his head. "I spoke to one of the investigators on the case, and he told me that he doubted they'd ever solve it."

"Maybe *you* could solve it," McDonnell muttered under his breath. "You've probably got the whole thing on tape."

"What did you say?" Hewitt snapped.

"Nothing."

Hewitt gave McDonnell a long look, then cleared his throat. "There are just eight of us now. We need another." He hesitated. "I nominate Mr. Christian Gillette."

Again seven pairs of eyes rose to Hewitt's.

"I met with Mr. Gillette a few days ago," Hewitt continued. "I like him."

"Where did you meet with him?" Fleming asked.

"At Princeton, after that alumni function."

Fleming nodded.

Along with Hewitt, four other members of the Order had gone to

Princeton: Fleming, Massey, Laird, and Dahl. The others were Harvard graduates.

"It's a hell of a coincidence, Samuel," Fleming said, right on cue. "I met Gillette last week, too. He came to Black Brothers to talk to us about a deal he wants us to represent Everest Capital on." Fleming motioned toward Hewitt. "I agree with Mr. Hewitt. Gillette's an impressive man."

"What kind of deal was it?" Hewitt asked.

"It involves one of Everest's portfolio companies, a sell-side thing."

"Oh," Hewitt said with a wave, as though nothing could be less interesting.

Fleming's delivery had been perfect, Hewitt thought to himself. None of the others had any idea that they were working together to get Laurel Energy at a cheap price for U.S. Oil and to get Black Brothers and him a fat fee for doing the transaction. They'd worked together like this before—and they'd do it again. Once the deal was in the bag, Fleming would send Hewitt twenty million dollars to one of the offshore accounts they'd set up. It wasn't like the IRS was ever going to audit Hewitt—he had more dirt on the three top people there than he needed. But you never knew about the press. Sometimes they got creative.

"He's got quite a résumé," Fleming went on. "Good genes, too."

Hewitt nodded. "Mr. Gillette would be a great addition to the Order."

"Wait a minute," Kohler complained, still obviously fighting through the alcohol, "I thought you were concerned because Gillette was meeting with Jesse Wood. I thought you were worried about him being a Wood supporter. Now you want to *initiate* him?"

"Mr. Gillette is meeting with Senator Wood just to cover his ass," Hewitt answered. "Gillette runs the biggest private equity investment firm in the world. It makes sense for him to meet with a presidential candidate. I'm sure Mr. Gillette will end up meeting with several candidates, but he won't be putting any major money in Senator Wood's pocket after my meeting with him. I can tell you that."

"How can you be so sure?"

"I just can."

"What about the doomsday scenario?" Dahl spoke up.

"You mean Wood winning the election in November?" Hewitt asked. Hard to tell for certain, but he thought he'd noticed Kohler and McDonnell exchange a quick glance.

"Yes."

"Right," said Massey. "What *are* we going to do about that?"

"Nothing," Hewitt replied calmly.

"Nothing?"

"That's what I said." Hewitt let the words fall from his mouth smoothly, as if he felt like the topic was trivial and they were wasting time talking about it. "Nothing. Wood doesn't have a snowball's chance in hell of winning the election. There's no reason for us to do anything at all at this point, no reason to take the risk."

Kohler scoffed. "At the last meeting you were sure Wood was going to win. What's going on here, Mr. Hewitt?"

Hewitt took his time answering the question. When he did, he spoke in a low, unwavering voice, glaring fiercely down the table. "Mr. Kohler, you're a man who wants all the facts, who doesn't take anything for granted, and I respect that. But I have more people in my hip pocket than you'll meet in the next ten years. People who tell me things, Mr. Kohler, people who trust me. I know it pains you to do so, but on this one, you'll have to be one of those people. You'll just have to trust me."

A CHILLY RAIN fell as Christian waited in the darkness where the field and the trees met. He'd taken every precaution he could think of. Surgical gloves so there were no prints on the money or the bag, a roundabout route to get here, switching cars at a diner in the next town over to make certain he wasn't being followed. And he'd made the guy demanding the money tell him the location and time of the rendezvous early this morning. Then made the guy call this afternoon supposedly just to confirm everything, and changed the location and the time completely.

The guy had screamed bloody murder, but Christian had paid no attention. Then he'd called back an hour later and changed the location and time *again*. He wasn't worried about being killed. He was wearing a wire so he could yell for help if he needed it, and Quentin was close. More to the point, it didn't make sense for the guy to kill him. What would he gain by doing that? What Christian was worried about was being photographed or taped handing money over to a made man. Of being blackmailed.

He pulled the brim of his Dodger cap further down over his eyes. In the limousine in Vegas the guy had been very specific about *him* being the one to bring the money. That demand had made him think there was another motive behind this whole thing. But, if he didn't do this, he wasn't going to get his casino—a flagship investment of over a billion dollars would be flushed. There'd been a surprise plumbing inspection yesterday. The Dice had failed it miserably. He couldn't have the Dice go down. Full stop.

According to the project manager everything was perfect, installed exactly to spec, and Christian believed him. He was the best plumbing contractor in Las Vegas, but it didn't matter what he said. The only opinion that mattered was the inspector's, and clearly the guy Christian was meeting with and his cronies had gotten to the inspector. If he wanted his casino, Christian was going to have to play ball. Even Quentin had finally admitted that.

Quentin had found Carmine Torino swinging from the rafters of his hideout in a canyon outside Vegas, dead of what looked like a suicide at first. But there were rope marks on his wrists, like he'd been tied up. Quentin was sure it hadn't been a suicide and that Torino hadn't been killed by anyone inside the Mafia. Torino was feeding them money. Why would they kill him? The whole thing made no sense.

Christian glanced down at the brown canvas bag lying at his feet, stuffed full with a million dollars in cash. His *personal* cash. If everything went haywire, at least he'd be able to prove he hadn't used investor money to make the payoff. Of course, if everything went haywire, being able to prove that he hadn't defrauded anyone might be the least of his worries.

He looked up into the gloomy canopy of wet leaves and let out a long breath. If Vivian Davis could only see him now.

Through the mist, Christian spied a figure moving purposefully along the edge of the field—alone, as promised. He picked up the bag and headed back into the woods, more protected back here from a camera with a night lens. As the figure came close, Christian called out softly.

The figure stopped and peered into the gloom.

"Over here," Christian called again, recognizing the man as he got close. It was the guy from the transfer station in Vegas. Same face, same smirk.

"Hello, Mr. Gillette. Got what I want?"

Christian kicked at the bag lying at his feet. "Right there." The man bent down to pick it up, but Christian stepped in front of him. "How do I know this is it? How do I know I won't get another call for another million or more?"

"You don't. But if I don't get the money, you'll definitely know this: The Dice Casino will never open." He smiled. "Now, let me have it."

Christian stepped aside.

The man bent down and snatched the straps of the bag. "You'll get your casino now, Mr. Gillette," he said, rising again, the heavy bag dangling by his side. "Nice doing business with—"

A twig snapped no more than twenty feet away, and Christian's eyes flashed to the right, toward the sound.

The man holding the bag sprinted away instantly, out into the field and back in the direction he'd come.

For a moment Christian was paralyzed. He could hear whoever was in the woods crashing away over the dead leaves and still see the guy with the bag tearing across the field. He could catch the guy lugging the bag, no problem. He was fast and the guy was weighed down by the money. But so what? What was that guy going to tell him? Then again, why was he running?

Christian bolted in the direction the sound had come from, deeper into the woods, straining to hear whoever he was chasing, yelling into the wire for Quentin's help, trying to give him directions. He lost the sound of footsteps crashing over leaves for a moment and stopped short, holding his breath, almost certain he'd heard someone else's shallow breathing not far away. Then there were far-off footsteps, faint thuds definitely growing louder. Quentin. Had to be.

Suddenly, a figure took off from behind a tree only a few feet away, startling Christian. But he recovered quickly, yelling into the wire that they were closing in on whoever had been watching him give up the money. He caught glimpses of the figure through the trees, just flashes of someone dodging the trunks and ducking limbs, changing directions wildly.

Then another figure darted out from nowhere, knocking his quarry to the ground. Christian was on them in a heartbeat, but Quentin already had the guy under control.

They pulled him to his feet together and jacked him up against a tree.

Christian searched the guy quickly and found the camera, then a night lens. He patted Quentin on the back, impressed at his friend's ability to track in total darkness. "I'll tell you something. I'm glad you're on my side."

THE MAN slung the bag full of money into the backseat of a car he'd parked in a grove of pine trees a half mile from where he'd met Christian, then slipped behind the steering wheel. He glanced over at his accomplice in the passenger seat as he turned the key and gunned the engine. "You get the pics?"

"Got 'em, Frank," the other man confirmed, holding up the camera.

Tires spun on the wet leaves and the car fishtailed along the muddy lane as Frank jammed the accelerator to the floor. "He did exactly what he was supposed to do."

"Right," the other man agreed. "He went after Carl. It was perfect, I saw everything through my night lens. Soon as you had the bag, Carl made a little noise and, *boom,* Gillette went right after him. It was beautiful."

"It was beautiful," Frank agreed.

"What do you think'll happen to Carl?"

"What can Gillette do?" Frank scoffed. "Haul Carl's ass to the cops and tell them he was taking pictures of a bribe?"

The other man chuckled. "Ah, no."

"Nope, Gillette got Carl's camera, took the film, let Carl go, and that was that. He'll go to sleep happy tonight, just like we want him to. He'll think he's got his casino license and that there aren't any pictures of him giving me the million bucks."

"He'll be right about the license." The other man held up his camera again. "But wrong about no pictures."

KOHLER AND MCDONNELL stood at one corner of the lodge in the darkness. Hewitt had called for a ten-minute break in the meeting.

"I don't believe Hewitt for a second," Kohler said quietly, glancing around to see if anybody had come out onto the porch.

"What about?" McDonnell asked.

"That he really thinks Wood has no chance of winning the election in November. He doesn't know any more about that than the rest of us."

"Why do you think that?"

"Look, he's connected, sure, but even he doesn't have a crystal ball. The reason he knows Jesse Wood won't win in November is because he's going to have Wood assassinated."

"You're jumping to conclusions."

"No, I'm not," Kohler snapped. "Hewitt'll kill Wood. It's not like Hewitt to sit around and do nothing when it comes to something like this. He's a man of action, a fucking control freak."

"But at least he'll wait until after the general election in November," McDonnell said quietly, taking a long drag on a cigarette. "Don't you think? I mean, from Hewitt's perspective, there's no reason to kill Wood until he's sure the guy's going to the White House, right? If he wins in November, Hewitt still has a few months until Wood's inaugurated."

Kohler watched McDonnell take another puff of his cigarette. He'd always found it ironic that McDonnell smoked. McDonnell was the only member of the Order that did, but he was the CEO of one of the biggest life sciences companies in the world. He ought to know the risks better than any of them.

"You're wrong," Kohler said, checking the porch again. He thought he'd heard a noise. "If Wood wins the election, the security around him will be incredible. Hell, if he wins the Democratic nomination he gets Secret Service. Even Hewitt might not be able to get to him at that point."

"What are you proposing?"

Kohler thought for a moment, then looked directly into McDonnell's eyes. "We take the fight to him."

McDonnell shook his head. "I can't have my tapes get out."

"Don't worry about it."

"Damn it, Mace," McDonnell hissed, "what are you going to do?"

Suddenly Kohler was resolved. He'd been thinking about this for a while, but now he was fully committed. "I'll tell you when we get back to Greenwich," he whispered, turning to go back inside.

"Hey." McDonnell caught Kohler by the shoulder.

"What?"

"Have you noticed that Patty Roth hasn't been around? Just Don."

Kohler hesitated. He hadn't noticed, but now that McDonnell mentioned it . . . He shook his head. God help the woman if she'd pissed off the wrong person on this island.

■ ■ ■

"**COME IN, COME IN,**" Nigel beckoned, closing his apartment door as Christian moved past him into the living room. It was late, almost one in the morning. "Jesus, what happened to you?"

Christian had picked up Nigel's message on his cell phone after he and Quentin made it out of the woods and back to the car. They'd spoken for a few minutes then, but Christian hadn't wanted to go into the details about what Nigel had found out while they were talking on a cell phone. But he didn't want to wait long to hear about it either. So after dropping off Quentin, he'd driven straight to Nigel's Manhattan apartment, not bothering to go back to his place and change first. His clothes were still wet and muddy.

"I was . . . um . . . hell, it doesn't matter," Christian said curtly. He was too tired to make up an excuse. "What's up?"

Nigel gave Christian another quick up and down. "I did what you wanted. Like I told you, I did that quick trip to Chicago and I got close to one of the assistant controllers at CST," he explained. "She's done some digging." Nigel's voice dropped. "The news isn't great."

"Tell me." You couldn't put your head in the sand. He'd learned that long ago.

"It's like the woman at the SEC said. CST's been overstating revenues. And therefore, income," Nigel added quietly. "The earnings-per-share figures they've been releasing to the public are too high. Way too high."

Christian felt his chest cinch. This was it, the nightmare scenario. He tried to stay calm, but it was tough.

"I'm sorry," Nigel said, catching Christian's anger—and disappointment.

"How did she find out so fast?"

"She got into the general ledger software somehow, went into her boss's office late one night and snooped around until she found a couple of passwords or something. Anyway, they worked when she tried them and she saw a subsidiary on the list she'd never heard of before, did some more digging, and figured out it was a total sham. There's nothing to the sub except about three hundred million dollars a year in completely bogus revenues with no associated expenses. Maybe more; she's still checking."

"So basically income's overstated by three hundred million."

Nigel nodded. "Basically."

That hurt. The stock price would dive at least seventy-five percent, maybe more. Maybe to nothing. "How long has the sub been around?"

"Three years, just like the woman at the SEC said."

"How could the accountants miss that?" Christian asked, his blood starting to boil. CST paid their independent auditors almost five million a year. This was ridiculous.

"She's looking into that. Apparently, there's some way she can figure out which one of the accountants' teams was responsible for what. She's going to get back to me in the next couple of days." Nigel hesitated. "Her guess is that this thing involves just a few people. A couple at the company and a couple at the accounting firm." Nigel patted Christian on the shoulder. "It'll be clear that you weren't involved, Chris."

Christian glanced past Nigel, out the glass doors leading to his balcony and the lights of Manhattan beyond. This couldn't be coming at a worse time. More and more he wanted to say yes to Jesse Wood.

HEWITT STOOD in the office of the lighthouse, two men on either side of him—Wayne and one of Wayne's deputies. They'd been the ones who'd flown Jim Benson's body to Naples and made his death look like a mugging turned murder.

Don Roth sat in a wooden chair in front of them, staring at the ground. The men had taken care of Patty Roth, too, when they'd found her in the upstairs room with the Order's door open.

"What happened to Patty?" Roth asked, his voice hoarse, his hands clenched.

"She's gone," Hewitt said simply. He watched Roth's face fall into his hands. "I warned you, Don, but she wouldn't stop. She kept trying."

Roth sobbed quietly.

"I told you if it ever happened again . . ." Hewitt tried another tack. "Look, I'm sorry, I—"

"Fuck you," Roth whispered.

So much for kindness. "I won't hesitate using what I have, Don," Hewitt said firmly, quickly out of patience with Roth's grief. "Everything that happened in Miami." They knew Roth had secretly worked with one of the most violent drug gangs operating in South Florida. Had proof that Roth provided the gang with warnings about police raids and other forms of protection in return for some serious money. "I won't hesitate to contact the authorities in South Florida," Hewitt continued, "and tell them what I know."

Roth's head sank lower.

"And, Don, if you get to the point where you think you don't care anymore and you decide you'll go to somebody and tell them about Champagne Island, the police will find out that Patty's dead. They'll find her body, and they'll suspect you right away. And, believe me, they'll never think for a second that any of us were involved. You can't fight us, Don. Understand that."

"I've done everything you've asked of me," Roth said, his voice shaking. "I met with that reporter to find out what he had. I chased his friend up the coast. I keep people here when you want to hide them."

"And you better keep doing those things, Don. You understand?"

Roth hesitated, then nodded, tears streaming down his face. "I'll never tell anyone what happened to Patty," he whispered. "I promise."

KOHLER'S HEART was in his throat as he moved out of the room on the third floor and into the darkened hallway. He headed quickly for the stairs. Hewitt hadn't been around, and Kohler was going to take advantage of the opportunity. Still, you never knew who was watching.

"Hey!"

Kohler spun around. He'd almost made it to the top of the stairs. He swallowed hard. Samuel Hewitt was moving down the hallway toward him.

Hewitt stopped a few feet away. "What were you doing in there, Mace?"

Kohler remained silent, aware that his hands were shaking badly.

"You better tell me now."

"There's nothing to tell you," Kohler said, turning and heading for the stairs. "Nothing."

14

"HELLO, CHRISTIAN."

"Hello, Jesse." Their initial greeting was informal, not at all as Christian had expected, but he liked it. He hated pomp and circumstance when it wasn't necessary. Sometimes even when it was. "It's a pleasure to meet you."

"The pleasure's all mine."

Jesse Wood was taller than he looked on television, almost Christian's height, and fitter than Christian had imagined. But he recognized that signature smile right away, wide and sincere, full of bright white teeth.

Like Samuel Hewitt, Jesse was blessed with charisma, but they were different. Hewitt's power was darker, not menacing but more reserved. Jesse seemed to wear his heart on his sleeve, like he had at Forest Hills and Wimbledon after a great shot or bad break. But, unlike a lot of people, it worked for Jesse. He made you smile when he smiled, made you feel down when he frowned. You connected with his enthusiasm and his frustration right away—you weren't put off by either one, no, you gravitated to both—which was an incredible gift for a politician. At the same time, you still knew Jesse meant business. Jesse was made for television, Hewitt for the boardroom. They'd both chosen the right careers.

Jesse turned to Osgood and Stephanie. "You're in the presence of greatness, folks. Christian Gillette has probably made more money for investors than any other man alive."

Christian laughed. "I don't know about that." He extended his hand to Osgood. "Hi, Clarence, good to see you again."

"And I'm Stephanie Childress," the woman said, leaning in. "Jesse's PR person."

"Nice to meet you, too." A heavy scent drifted to Christian's nostrils as he took Stephanie's hand, and he had to keep from wincing. The perfume smelled good, but there was too much.

"You'll be spending a lot of time with Clarence and Stephanie over the next few months," Jesse said, the million-dollar smile appearing. "At least, I hope you will." He turned his head to the side and put a hand to one ear. "I'm waiting, Christian. Do I really have to ask?"

Christian hesitated. "Let's talk." He gestured toward the couches in one corner of the Waldorf-Astoria suite. Fortunately they'd been able to keep this meeting quiet. There hadn't been any cameras in the lobby or on Park Avenue when either of them had arrived. "Over here."

"I'm getting nervous, Clarence," Jesse said loudly, elbowing Osgood as they headed for the couches. "I thought I'd get an answer right away."

Osgood chuckled. "Me, too."

Stephanie and Christian sat on one couch, Osgood and Jesse on the other. Christian hadn't asked anyone from his side to join him for the meeting, not even Quentin. He wanted to do this alone.

When they were settled, Christian grinned and looked around innocently. "So, Jesse, what was it you wanted to ask me?"

They all laughed. The ice was broken.

"I heard you were a cool cat," Jesse said, standing up and taking off his suit jacket. "Guess I heard right."

"What else did you hear?" Christian liked these people, mostly because they seemed to like each other.

Jesse folded the jacket and laid it neatly over the arm of the couch, then sat back down. "I heard I couldn't possibly pick a better running mate," he answered. "I heard that no one around works harder, that you finish what you start, and that you're tough but fair."

"You heard a lot."

"All good, too."

"Most of America doesn't know me."

Jesse glanced at Osgood, then Stephanie. "Oh, I think people know who you are. Remember, a few years ago you were in the papers every day."

Christian shook his head. "Jesse, that was—"

Jesse held his hands up. "It's all right, I—"

"We did some digging around Washington," Osgood broke in. "Spoke to some people over at the CIA, in the Directorate of Operations, specifically. We know you're a hero. We know what you did."

Stephanie smiled at Christian. "It was amazing, really."

"Thanks."

"And you've been all over the business mags for a while. Wall Street loves you."

"Now, I do know people on the Street," Christian agreed.

"You've got *star power,*" Jesse said firmly. "You look great in person *and* on camera. Lots of people already know you and lots of people knew your father. Including a lot of important folks on both sides of the aisle in Washington. Clayton was a great man."

Osgood and Stephanie nodded.

"I appreciate that."

"I also heard you were self-made, which, of course, hits home for me." Jesse stared straight into Christian's eyes. "I heard your stepmother didn't treat you very well after your father died in that plane crash."

Christian started to ask Jesse how he'd heard that, but it would have been a stupid question. There were lots of ways Jesse could have found out, and he wasn't going to get a straight answer. Jesse wasn't going to give away his sources any more than Christian would give away his. "No, she didn't."

"I hope you don't mind me saying so," Stephanie spoke up, "but, honey, you'll help us do very well with the female half of the population simply by standing in front of the camera. You'll get votes just by flashing those beautiful gray eyes. Like Bill Clinton did by talking with those beautiful hands of his."

Jesse nodded. "Yup. We know that, we've tested you already."

Christian grinned stiffly. "Let's give women in this country a little more credit than that."

Osgood chuckled. "Already talking like a man who's been in the game for years."

"It's in the genes," Jesse said to Osgood. "He's a natural. Now, you hired Ray Lancaster to be the head coach and GM of your new NFL franchise, the Dice, right?"

"Yes."

"And you brought in a guy named Quentin Stiles to be a managing partner at Everest Capital?"

Christian knew exactly where Jesse was headed, and it didn't feel good. He'd hired Quentin and Lancaster because he sincerely believed they were the best people for the jobs, not because of their skin color. But this was politics, he realized. "Yes."

"Both of them are black, right?"

"Yes, but it's not like I—"

"It's perfect," Jesse interrupted, looking over at Osgood. "Just perfect, Clarence." He leaned forward. "I'm not going to beat around the bush anymore, Christian. I want you to be my vice president. I want you with me in November."

Christian took a deep breath and eased back onto the couch, aware that all three of them were watching him closely. Finally, the official invitation. Christian Gillette, vice president of the United States of America. His father would have been so proud, even if it was the wrong ticket. "Don't you want to ask one of the other candidates if you win? Isn't that usually how it works?"

Jesse shook his head hard. "They're all tired names; they've all said the same crap for years and it hasn't worked. No one's buying it or them. That's why I'm going to win the nomination. I'm fresh, with new ideas, and that's why I want you. You're just like me."

Jesse seemed right about the American public being tired of his opponents. Christian had called Samuel Hewitt yesterday in Dallas to make certain he'd gotten the Laurel Energy book. After promising to get back to him on that quickly, Hewitt had wanted to talk more about Christian being Jesse's running mate. Hewitt had made the same point as Jesse just had: The other Democrats didn't bring anything new to the table, and Christian had far more star power than any of them.

"If you were nominated at the convention, when would you announce me as your running mate?" Christian asked.

"We haven't decided exactly," Osgood replied for Jesse.

"Might even be at the convention," Jesse said. "You said it yourself—you aren't really a household name, so I might want you to get as much camera time as possible right away. If you're standing up there with me on the stage, it might be good."

"But," Stephanie broke in, "as Clarence said, we haven't firmed that up yet."

"I understand."

They were all silent for a few moments.

"So?" Jesse asked, motioning to Christian, "are you in? I mean, I know we have to sit down and have a long discussion about my platform before you could give me a final answer and, candidly, for me to make a final decision on you. I'd want you to completely understand where I intend to go over the next eight years, and I'd need to be comfortable that you were with me on everything. A lot of people will be surprised to see you alongside me, given that your father was a Republican and all."

"I know," Christian agreed. "I've been thinking a lot about that."

"I don't have a problem with it," Jesse said quickly. "That doesn't bother me at all, as long as I know you'd be with me a hundred percent."

"I don't accept any offer unless I'm with it a hundred percent."

"No, I guess you don't." Jesse glanced at Osgood, then back at Christian. "Well, can you at least give me an initial answer now?"

"I have to talk to a few people."

Jesse rolled his eyes and groaned. "How long is that going to take?"

"Not long."

"Okay, fine." Jesse stood up and grabbed his jacket off the couch. "Well, let us know." He started for the door, then stopped and turned around. "I'm sure I don't need to ask you, but there aren't any skeletons in your closet, are there? Anything that could throw the train off the tracks once we really get momentum?"

Christian's mind flashed to CST, to Vivian Davis and the SEC, and to the guy he and Quentin had caught in the woods. They'd gotten the guy's camera, then questioned him, threatening to take him to the cops. But he hadn't told them anything, and they'd been forced to let him go. What else could they do? The cops weren't going to do anything to him. More to the point, Christian didn't want them asking the guy what he was doing in the woods.

What had bothered Christian about that whole incident most was that it proved to him there was another motive to the bribe. Somebody wanted him on film handing money to the Mob. Given that, what made everything even stranger was that yesterday the Dice Casino had passed a second surprise plumbing inspection. Just like that, from failing miserably to passing with flying colors in less than a week. The electrical inspector had called this morning to say he was coming back out, too, and that they might be able to settle everything without ripping all the wiring out of those three floors. The project manager in Las Vegas had told Christian that both inspectors couldn't have been friendlier. It was night and day. It seemed, now that he'd paid the bribe, he was going to get his casino.

"We'll ask you to go through a very intense background scrub if you tell us you're interested in running with Jesse," Osgood explained. "I'm sure you'd expect that, but it would make things a lot easier if you told us now that there was something bad we should know about."

"Look, I know everybody makes enemies in business," Jesse added. "That doesn't bother me at all. You know what we're asking."

"There's nothing like that," Christian said firmly, jaw set. "And I will get back to you quickly."

Jesse motioned for Osgood and Stephanie to leave. "Give me a minute alone with him," he muttered to them as they passed. When they were gone, he moved to where Christian stood. "I want you with me, Christian. We can do great things together. *And*," he said, his tone growing stronger, "remember this. This is the first step toward fulfilling your father's dream of being president. Eight years from now, God willing, you'll finish what he started."

FRANKLIN LAIRD walked out of a high-end jewelry store in northern Virginia and headed across the parking lot toward his car. He'd just ordered his wife a gorgeous diamond ring—four carats—to commemorate the fiftieth wedding anniversary they'd celebrate next month. She was out in California visiting their daughter, so he had a few days to play. He was going to watch some of his favorite movies, then rendezvous with his personal assistant. His wife didn't suspect anything. Life was beautiful.

Laird didn't see the dark blue sedan whip out of a parking space behind him, didn't realize what was happening until he heard the engine roar and turned—directly into the vehicle racing straight at him.

The impact hurled Laird a hundred feet. He was dead even before his body tumbled to a stop against a curb at the far end of the parking lot.

The police would later term the killing a random hit-and-run, and right away determine that the case would be almost impossible to solve. No one had seen the incident, no one had seen anyone acting suspiciously, and whoever was driving was long gone.

WHEN THEY'D all climbed into the limousine waiting outside the Waldorf and the door was shut, Osgood looked over at Jesse. "You okay?"

Jesse rubbed his chin hard. "I don't need Gillette, Clarence. This country's ready for me, with or without that guy. It kills me that I've got to do what Elijah Forte tells me to do. I'm not going to be some kind of puppet," he said angrily. "I'm not."

"Easy, Jesse," Osgood urged, "easy."

"Maybe he'll say no," Stephanie suggested. "He sure didn't jump all over the opportunity back there when you asked."

"No chance," Jesse said. "Gillette'll accept. He's just being careful, that's all. He's doing it right, thinking it through. But he'll say yes. I saw it in his eyes."

Osgood looked out the window glumly. "Then we have to hope his background check turns up something."

"Maybe not, Clarence," Jesse said after a few moments. "Maybe there's another way."

"What do you mean?" Osgood's voice was low.

"Maybe I'm underestimating my own popularity, my own power. Maybe I don't have to listen to Elijah Forte anymore. Maybe I don't need his money and his backing. Maybe I can pick my own man at this point."

"Forte wants Gillette," Stephanie said firmly. "He's made that very clear. He thinks Gillette will play well with blacks and Hispanics, do well with the left, and hook Wall Street. He thinks Gillette will give you that boost with whites you need to win."

"Yeah yeah, I've heard that a hundred times," Jesse said with a roll of his eyes and a groan. "But he's wrong. I think we can do it without Whitey."

"Well . . . there's that thing," Stephanie reminded Jesse. "That thing Forte keeps hinting about."

Forte had never talked about what he claimed he had in front of Stephanie and Osgood, but Jesse had told them about the threats. He trusted them both as though they were family. "Elijah's bluffing. I don't think he has anything on me. But, if by some remote chance he does, he'd have just as much to lose as I would if he used it. His whole plan, what he and the other Shadows have been wanting for so long, *a black man in the White House*. All that would go up in smoke."

"Yeah, but your *whole career* would go up in smoke," Osgood pointed out. "Including your chance to make history, to be the first black president."

Jesse didn't like that Osgood thought there might even be a *possibility* that Forte had something.

"Assume he has something," Osgood said. "What could it be?"

"I don't know. I've thought about it over and over, and I don't know. I've told you that so many times." Jesse looked at Stephanie. "You have any idea?"

She shook her head quickly.

"Do you really want to find out if he's got something?" Osgood asked nervously. "Things are going pretty well right now. Do you really want to push it? Do you really want to find out if he's bluffing?"

Jesse thought about the question for a few moments. "I just might, Clarence, I just might."

TODD HARRISON answered the phone on the first ring. "Hello."

"Harrison?"

The voice at the other end of the line was barely audible. "Who is this?"

"Don Roth."

Harrison's shoulders sagged. "Jesus, I've been waiting for your call. It's been a while. I figured you forgot about me."

"I couldn't call until now."

"Why?"

"I just couldn't."

Roth sounded low, not his usual strong self.

"You okay?"

"Yeah, yeah. Listen, you still want to look around out here?"

"Absolutely," Harrison said.

"You still got that picture?"

"Picture?"

"Of the old man," Roth explained. "The picture you took of the old man who told you the story that night in the bar."

"Yes," Harrison replied hesitantly. "I got it."

"What about that property form? That thing you found in the old courthouse up the coast. Got that, too?"

"Uh-huh."

"All right, well, meet me in town the day after tomorrow. Same time, same place. You can follow me out here. Bring that stuff with you. I want to see it."

"Okay," Harrison agreed, "but I'm going to have a friend along with me." There was dead air for a few moments.

"Sure, sure," Roth finally said. "That's fine."

"See you then."

"Right."

A cold wave coursed through Harrison's body as he put the phone down. For a long time, he'd been hoping he could get out to Champagne Island to look around. Now that he finally had the chance, he wasn't sure it was such a good idea.

STEWART MASSEY clambered down the muddy bank to the lake, checking for rattlesnakes as he negotiated the slope. There were lots of them out here—he'd run into them before—but as long as you were careful, they weren't a problem.

Massey glanced up at the clear blue sky as he reached the water's edge and took a deep breath. He loved it out here—a remote section of a friend's ranch fifty miles outside Oklahoma City. It offered some of the best largemouth bass fishing around, and he'd fished a lot of places. There wasn't much he liked doing more than fishing. He often wished Hewitt liked to fish. They were such good friends, it would have been fun to do together, but Hewitt was a hunter. Hewitt liked blasting the hell out of deer with his grandson, and Massey didn't like hunting. Too messy.

Massey buckled the straps of the hip waders around his belt and moved into the water until he was knee deep, then brought the rod back and hurled the rattle-trap far out into the lake.

As the lure hit the water, two men in scuba suits rose up in front of him, dripping and black. They grabbed Massey and pulled him down. He thrashed about, hurling the fishing rod, fighting them, trying to make it back to his feet, but it was no use. They dragged him into deeper water, forcing his head beneath the surface, forcing him to suck in water.

Massey's body was found floating facedown in the reeds on the far bank the next morning, blown across the lake by a strong westerly breeze. He was the third member of the Order to die in less than a month.

CHRISTIAN DIALED Jesse Wood's private telephone number. He'd just gotten off the line with Samuel Hewitt. He'd told Hewitt that Jesse had officially extended the invitation and Christian and Hewitt had talked it through one last time.

"Hello."

"Jesse?"

"Yes."

"It's Christian Gillette."

"Hello, Christian."

Christian looked out the window of his office at Everest Capital, and asked himself one more time if this was really what he wanted. It was the hundredth time today he'd asked himself the question. The answer kept coming up yes. "I'm calling to accept your offer," he said calmly. "I'll be your vice president."

PART TWO

15

"I REALLY THOUGHT Crenshaw would finally win," Christian murmured, gazing at the television screen, watching Tom Watson put the finishing touches on his victory. "Crenshaw's such a great putter. He should handle Augusta's greens better than anybody. I thought 1981 would be his year."

"You gotta *get* to the green first, son."

Christian glanced over at his father and grinned. "Crenshaw *will* win the Masters, Dad," he said firmly. "He'll win more than one green jacket, too. He'll get at least a couple before he's done."

Clayton Gillette puffed on his pipe for a few moments. "Well, you're the golf pro of the house now. I guess I better listen to you."

Christian and his father had played eighteen holes at the Bel-Air Country Club that morning, then hurried home to Clayton's study to watch the final round of the Masters. It had become a tradition for them—they'd done it six years in a row now. Christian had won their match this morning with a birdie on the last hole. It was the first time he'd ever beaten his father head-to-head at golf.

Clayton shook his head. "That drive you hit on eighteen was incredible," he said proudly. "I've never seen a seventeen-year-old hit a golf ball that far. Heck, other than the pros, I've never seen *anybody* hit a golf ball that far."

"I got lucky."

"You and I both know hitting a golf ball like that has nothing to do with luck." Clayton took another puff off his pipe. "I talked to Jimmy this morning before we teed off."

Jimmy Gray was the Bel-Air club pro.

"He says you're making big strides with your game," Clayton continued. "Says you're one of the best players at the club. Says you need to work more on your sixty-and-in shots, but then, so does everybody. It was fun to watch you today."

"Thanks, Dad."

Christian loved it in here, in this big study where his father spent most of his time when he wasn't in Washington. He loved the high ceiling, dark wood, big desk, leather couches and chairs, pictures of celebrities spread all over the bookcases and tables, the scent of tobacco mixing with leather. The room exuded power, as the study of a United States congressman should. Christian wanted one just like it someday.

"You and I ought to go to the Masters," Clayton suggested, nodding at the TV while he relit his pipe, sucking the flame from the lighter down into the bowl. "We should fly down to Augusta, stay in one of those cabins on the grounds. I know people who could set it up for us. Would you like that, son?"

"Are you kidding?" Christian sat up in his chair. "I'd *love* it."

"You could bring one of your friends," Clayton suggested.

Christian looked away, hoping his father wasn't implying that he intended to take one of his friends, too. "I don't want to go with one of my friends, Dad. I see them all the time. I want to go with you."

Clayton smiled, clutching the pipe with his teeth as he spoke. "Still okay spending time with me, huh? Not ashamed of me like most teenagers are of their dads?"

There wasn't much else in the world Christian liked better than spending time with his father. It didn't happen often because Clayton was in Washington so much, and he was so busy when he was here in California. Christian grinned and shrugged. "Yeah, you're okay."

Clayton laughed. "Well, thanks *a lot.* Hey, I bet we could meet Ben Crenshaw, maybe even play with him in that par-three tournament they have before the real thing starts."

"That would be something."

"Okay, I'll look into it." Clayton took his pipe from his mouth and gestured toward Christian with it. "I know you've still got your senior year of high school left, so there's plenty of time to talk more about this, but have you thought about college yet?"

"I'm pretty sure I'll go," Christian deadpanned.

They both laughed loudly. The question wasn't *if,* it was *where.*

"I like Stanford," Christian volunteered.

"Great school," Clayton agreed, "but you ought to go east, especially if you want to work on Wall Street. That still the plan?" he asked. "To work on the Street?"

Christian nodded.

"Go to Stanford for business school," Clayton suggested, "but go Ivy League for undergraduate. You'll never regret it."

"Which one?"

"Princeton's always an option. I loved my time there."

Originally from a poor mining town in western Pennsylvania, Clayton had gone to the University of Virginia for undergraduate. He'd played football there, starting at quarterback his senior year, but hadn't been good enough to turn pro. He'd married Lana, who he'd met at UVA, then come west, where her father was a Hollywood producer, and gone to work at a little brokerage house—a bucket shop—owned by a friend of Lana's father. A few years later Clayton had opened his own firm, over the next decade growing it into one of the most powerful investment banks on the West Coast.

A few years before selling to one of the New York houses, he'd turned the reins of the firm over to one of his subordinates for a year and gone to Princeton to get a master's in government administration, in anticipation of what he wanted to do after selling up, and to meet the right people in that circle.

"Princeton's a great place," Clayton continued. "You'll never regret going there."

"Can I get in?"

Clayton nodded. "Don't worry about it."

Christian knew what that meant: They had connections. Getting in wouldn't be a problem. "Well, I guess I—"

"Don't get me wrong—you've got to keep your grades up."

"Of course, I—"

There was a knock on the door. Nikki leaned in to Clayton's study. She was Christian's younger sister.

"Come in, kitten," Clayton called.

Nikki burst through the doorway and skipped across the room

toward Clayton and the big leather easy chair he was sitting in. She fell into his lap, giggling.

He groaned as she landed on him. “Oh, God, you’re getting too big to do that to your old dad.”

She sat up on his knee and frowned. “Never tell a girl she’s getting too big, Daddy. You’re a congressman. You should know that.” She smiled down at him. “And you’re not getting old, Daddy, you’re getting *distinguished*.”

Clayton put his head back and gazed up at her. “You’re going to be a congresswoman someday, you know that? *You’re* the one who knows what to say in every situation. Yup, you’re going to be a congresswoman, and”—Clayton gestured over at Christian—“Christian’s going to be president.”

Christian stared at his father. He’d recognized the serious tone. It didn’t surface often, but when it did, you noticed. “Whatever, Dad. *You’ll* be the president. They’re already talking about it.”

“*They* talk a lot, don’t they?”

“You know what I mean. I heard on the radio the other day that Senator McCauley was saying you’re a lock to be—”

“We’ll see, we’ll see,” Clayton interrupted.

“Why can’t I be president?” Nikki demanded. “Why do you and Christian get to be president, but I don’t?”

“The first woman president,” Clayton said, beaming as he stroked her long hair. “I agree. Christian first, then you, kitten. You’re exactly right. You’ll make history as the first woman president, and we’ll make history as a family. It’ll be incredible.”

Nikki smiled and kissed her father’s forehead. “Thanks.”

“Have we heard from Billy?” Clayton asked. “Is he coming over for dinner?”

Billy was the oldest sibling. A junior at the University of Southern California, he’d never made grades or excelled at sports in high school like Christian. The Ivy League had never been an option for him—even with Clayton’s connections. Even USC had been a stretch. Still, Billy was Lana’s favorite son and she didn’t try to hide it.

Nikki shook her head. “No, he’s such a slug.” She snapped her fingers suddenly. “Oh. Chris, I almost forgot.”

Christian looked up. He’d been thinking about what Princeton would be like, about how different the East Coast was from California. He’d wanted to go to Stanford so he could play golf year-round. In the back of his mind he kept thinking maybe he could turn pro, and Stanford would help that. The school had one of the top golf programs in the country. Jimmy Gray was tied into it, too, and he'd told Christian he was sure the Stanford coach would want him. Of course, making the pro tour was a long shot. It was one thing to be a good country club player, even a college star. Quite another to tee it up with Nicklaus and Watson on the weekends. He hated to admit it, but it was probably better to take his father's advice and set his sights on Wall Street. A little disappointing, but he trusted his father's judgment completely.

"What is it?" he asked Nikki.

"Mom wants to see you. I think she wants you to help her with dinner."

His mother didn't need any help. The maids were taking care of dinner, like they always did on Sunday afternoons. It was just that she hated him spending so much time with his father. She was jealous. She was weird that way.

"Go help her, son," Clayton urged. "We'll circle back here after dinner and talk some more, okay?"

"Yes, sir," Christian agreed, standing up.

Lana wasn't in the kitchen when he got there, but one of the maids was peeling potatoes over the sink. "Rita?" he called.

"Sí?"

"Have you seen my mother?"

Rita pointed toward the doorway leading from the kitchen out onto the veranda. "Out there."

"Gracias."

Lana was sitting in a wicker chair, halfway through a glass of white wine. "You wanted to see me?" he asked.

Lana turned slowly toward him. She was a tall, angular woman with sharp facial features. She'd been looking off into the distance, at something on the other side of the big backyard. "Sit down," she said, motioning at a chair next to hers.

Christian could see she was feeling the wine from the way she was blinking slowly and holding her glass at an angle. Since Clayton had won his seat in Congress and been gone so much, Lana had started drinking more and more: pretty much seven days a week now, beginning earlier and earlier in the day, usually by late morning; passed out most nights by eight o'clock.

Lana had begged to go to Washington with Clayton, to live at the sprawling four-story brick town house he'd bought in Georgetown, but he hadn't let her. He'd told her she had to stay in California to take care of the kids. Which was a joke, Christian thought to himself as he sat down. She didn't take care of anyone—including herself.

"What do you want, Mom?"

"Have fun watching golf with your father?"

"Sure. I like spending time with Dad." Lana was gazing at him over the rim of her wineglass. He couldn't help digging it in that he was the one who'd spent the day with Clayton, not her. "You know?"

Her eyes moved deliberately back across the yard, to whatever faraway object she'd been focused on when he'd first come out. "You played golf with him at the club this morning?"

"Yeah."

"I hear you're getting good."

Christian's ears perked up. "Oh?"

Lana smiled coyly from behind her glass. "Jimmy Gray and I have gotten to be good friends."

"What does that mean?" Christian demanded. He'd heard that I've-got-a-secret tone.

Lana brought a hand to her face and gazed at her fingertips. "I need to get my nails done tomorrow, Chris," she said. "A couple of them are chipped. Will you take me?"

She got her nails done every two days. She was so damn spoiled. "What did you mean by the crack about Jimmy—" He stopped himself when he spotted Rita coming out onto the veranda from the kitchen.

"Sorry to interrupt," Rita said. "Did you want another glass of wine, Miss Lana?"

Lana held her glass out. "Yes, and make sure there aren't any pieces of cork floating in it this time, will you?"

"Sorry, ma'am," Rita said quietly, taking the glass and hurrying away.

Lana scoffed. "She's such an idiot."

"No, she's not," Christian said sharply. "She's putting herself through school."

"Probably one of those community colleges. Big deal."

Christian shook his head. Such a bitter woman. "What was that Jimmy Gray crack about?"

Lana drew herself up in her chair. "Your father's in Washington screwing every little piece of ass he can get his hands on," she snapped. "Why shouldn't I have a little fun, too?"

Christian rolled his eyes. "Mom, stop—"

"Your father's been screwing around on me for years," she said, standing up.

"You don't know that," Christian retorted, rising to face her. "You don't have any proof."

"Oh, yes I do."

"What?"

She put her wineglass down on a table near her chair, dangerously close to the edge. "I'm looking at the proof," she whispered. "It's standing right in front of me."

Something inside Christian shattered, and suddenly he realized he had the answer to all those terrible questions and gnawing suspicions that had haunted him for so long. Why Lana seemed to hate him, why she seemed to adore Billy and Nikki, why people always said he looked so much like Clayton and nothing like Lana.

He wanted to shout back that she was lying, just trying to hurt him for whatever reason—because she was drunk, because she was jealous, because she wanted attention. But he didn't. He couldn't. He knew instantly by her cold gaze and matter-of-fact tone that she was being perfectly and brutally honest.

"You aren't mine, Christian," she continued, making everything absolutely clear. "You're someone else's."

"No," he murmured, only because it was all he could think to say at that moment.

"Oh, *yes*. And you aren't the only Clayton mistake running around this city," she said, her voice trembling. "Your father's been busy in Los Angeles, like I'm sure he's busy in Washington now. You're just the first, the only one I agreed to take in."

"Lana!"

Christian's red-rimmed eyes shot to the booming voice. Clayton Gillette was standing by the door to the house, Nikki behind him. An expression on his face Christian had never seen: a helplessness, embarrassment, loss.

"Stop it!" Clayton shouted.

"I won't," Lana muttered. "It's time for Christian to know the truth, time for everyone to know the truth. You screwed a whore and you had *that*," she said, aiming a shaking finger at Christian.

"She wasn't a whore and don't ever talk about my son that way."

"She was a whore!" Lana shouted. "Don't you defend her. She was a little dirty tramp you paid to screw in some fancy hotel and you know it."

"Oh God," Nikki whispered.

"Get inside," Clayton ordered.

"Daddy, I can't believe—"

"Get inside!" he roared.

Clayton moved to where Lana was standing as Nikki melted back in the house. "We agreed never to talk about this in front of anyone," he growled, jaw clenched. "That was our understanding."

"The hell with our understanding."

"Were you just not ever going to tell me, Dad?" Christian asked, his eyes burning. "Were you just going to let me go on believing that this was my mother?"

Clayton turned toward Christian. "I didn't know how to tell you, son. I—I . . ." His voice faltered. "I didn't know how to say it."

Christian gazed at his father. No wonder Lana had treated him differently all these years, no wonder she'd hated him. He was a walking, talking, in-your-face reminder of Clayton's infidelity. Everything was suddenly so clear.

"Christian."

The building across the street from Everest Capital slowly came into focus. God, how long had he been staring out the window?

"Christian!"

He swiveled around in the desk chair. Allison stood in the doorway of his office. She was wearing her hair down today, the way he preferred it, and she had on a pretty knee-length dress that followed the curves of her body perfectly. "Come in."

"What in the world were you thinking about?" she asked, sitting down in front of him.

"Nothing important."

"It must have been *pretty* important. You didn't hear me call you the first couple of times."

"I—I . . ." He didn't finish. "What did you want to see me about?" he asked curtly. He could see she was frustrated because he wouldn't open up.

"I was just trying to be nice. You don't have to bite my head off."

He nodded in a way she could take as an apology. "There's a lot going on."

"I know. That's why I'm here. Talk to me, partner."

He liked the sound of that, someone actually verbalizing their relationship with him. He could see her waiting expectantly for a response, but he said nothing, afraid of the words that might come.

"Okay, okay," she said, her aggravation at his stonewalling obvious. "I want to bring you up to speed on the Aero Systems transaction."

Allison was leading Everest's attempt to buy Aero Systems, a big aircraft and auto parts aftermarket manufacturer based in San Francisco. It was the deal she'd been coming back from working on when she'd met Christian and Quentin in Las Vegas. For the next ten minutes she filled him in: They had the inside track to buy the company from the family that owned it; management was with them and they were offering a fair price. But there was an Atlanta conglomerate named Teldex sniffing around that could ruin everything; Teldex wanted to buy Aero Systems, too.

"Know anyone at Teldex?" Allison asked.

"A couple of people, including their CFO, but I don't know them very well. Not well enough to get them to back off with a phone call. I'll see what I can do," he added, catching the disappointed look on her face. She was used to him being able to solve all the problems she couldn't. "There's something I want to talk to you about."

"Oh?"

"I don't know where to begin," he said, grinning self-consciously.

"Come on," she said, sliding forward on the chair, flipping her long blond hair back over one shoulder, then resting one elbow on the desk, her chin in her hand. "What is it?"

Christian took a deep breath. "Jesse Wood asked me to be his running mate if he wins the nomination at the Democratic convention."

Allison stared at him, eyes unblinking, lips mouthing words that wouldn't come. *"What?"* she finally asked.

"Yeah."

"Are you kidding me?" She shook her head, then broke into a huge smile when she was certain he was serious. "Oh my God, Christian, that's incredible. Did you accept?"

"I took the first step."

"What does that mean?"

"It means I'm going to sit down with Jesse for a day and get to know his platform before I commit, but right now it looks like I'll be his vice president if he wins."

"That's fantastic." She clasped her hands together tightly and put her head back. "And Jesse Wood *is* going to win the Democratic nomination. I don't think there's any doubt."

"You can't tell *anyone* about this."

"The hell I can't. I'm calling *The Wall Street Journal* as soon as I get out of your office."

Christian pointed a warning finger at her. "Allison, you can't do—"

"Oh, keep your boxers on, I'm not going to say anything to anyone. Wow, that's great." She raised one eyebrow. "And as a Democrat. Huh."

"Yeah, I know."

"Wasn't your father a Republican?"

"One of the few from California," Christian confirmed.

"That's what I thought. People will be surprised."

"*Very* surprised, but it doesn't seem to bother Jesse."

"So, who's going to be the new chairman of Everest?"

Christian broke into another grin. Just like her, getting right to the point. But that's why he loved her being his partner. She was as efficient as anyone he'd ever known, even Quentin. Right down to business right away. Now, if he could just figure out her loyalty.

"Are you going to make Nigel chairman?" she asked.

"I'm not sure yet."

She looked up. "Why not?"

"I'm thinking about making you chairman."

Allison sat slowly back in her chair, a stunned expression on her face. "Really?"

As if she hadn't expected it. There was no way she could have faked that reaction. "Well, chair*woman*."

"All the other managing partners except Quentin have been here longer than me."

"I know, but, frankly, they don't have your drive. Or your connections. They're good, very good, all of them, but not like you." He hesitated. "You're something special, Allison. I'd have complete confidence in you, and our investors would love you." He'd never said that to a direct report before. "Would you be interested?" he asked.

She might not. If she went back to Chicago, she'd be running almost as much money as she would here, and there it would be all hers. Of course, it wouldn't be as fun, not nearly. Most of the Wallace money was invested in boring stuff like bond and money market funds or it was with professional equity managers who were the ones who actually decided which stocks to buy. Running the Wallace Trust would be more administrative than anything—checking to make certain the returns on the many different funds they were involved with were in line with industry averages. She wouldn't be chairing outside boards, making major decisions for huge companies, constantly interacting with some of the biggest names on Wall Street and in Washington. "I guess I need to ask you that first."

"I'm definitely interested," she spoke up.

Christian could see she'd just gone through the same analysis. Gordon Meade was doing a fine job overseeing the Wallace Trust. Running Everest Capital was the opportunity of a lifetime, even for her. "Good."

She brought her hand to her chest. "Jesus, me running Everest Capital."

"But I'm not even going to consider you if you're really going back to Chicago when we're through investing this fund," Christian warned. "Like Gordon Meade seems to think you are. I need to know that you're willing to stick around permanently before I take that step, before I could even consider you for chairman. We're going to be revving up soon to raise the next fund, and I can't have you leave in the middle of that."

"Tell me the truth," she said. "Who would you name as chairman, Nigel or me?"

"Honestly, I haven't decided, but it's between the two of you. That's it."

"What if you knew I was a hundred percent committed to Everest Capital?"

"I *don't* know that—you haven't given me your answer yet."

"But what if you did know?"

"I'm not going to operate in a hypothetical—"

"Have dinner with me," Allison interrupted. "Tonight. I'll give you my answer then."

He was supposed to have dinner with Faith tonight. "What about tomorrow night?"

"No. I may have to go to San Francisco. I don't want to wait."

Dinner with Allison was going to be tricky no matter when it was. He'd been thinking a lot about her lately. "How'd you know I wore boxers?"

She cocked her head to the side and gave him a sly look. "I knew the first moment I laid eyes on you that you were a boxers kind of guy. You're too sophisticated to wear jockeys, *and* you'd never do anything that might keep you from being able to carry on the family name."

"What?"

"Jockeys can cause your sperm count to be low."

Christian rolled his eyes and chuckled. "Oh, Jesus."

" 'Oh Jesus' me all you want, but it's true and someday you'll want to have a boy, a little Christian. I know what you're thinking."

He shook his head. "No way."

"*Yes* way. You just haven't hooked up with the right woman yet." She rose from the chair and headed for the door. "See you tonight at Grand Nuit. Eight o'clock. Don't be late."

Christian stared at the door for several moments after Allison was gone. She'd just assumed he'd be there tonight at eight, assumed he'd move anything else he had on his schedule to be able to show up. He put his elbows on the desk and rubbed his eyes. Bad thing about it? She was right.

IT WAS THE FIRST TIME Hewitt had ever met with Dahl anywhere but on Champagne Island. Dahl was an active soldier, a current member of the Joint Chiefs of Staff, and easily recognizable around Washington. Their being spotted together would be a risk. But these were desperate times.

"What is it, Samuel?" Dahl muttered. "What's so damn important?"

They were on the Washington Mall, secluded in a small stand of trees a few hundred yards from the Vietnam Memorial. Dahl was wearing street clothes—as Hewitt had told him to—so he wouldn't stand out.

"Two more of us were murdered."

Dahl's steely dark eyes flashed to Hewitt's. *"What? Who?"*

"Laird and Massey."

"My God. How?"

"Laird was killed coming out of a jewelry store by a hit-and-run driver in northern Virginia. Massey was found dead in a lake outside Oklahoma City. He was fishing."

"Are you sure they were murdered?"

"Both of them dying on the same day?" Hewitt shook his head. "Come on."

"Are the local law enforcement people calling the deaths murders?"

"Well, they're calling Laird's death manslaughter," Hewitt admitted. "They're saying whoever hit him didn't mean to, got scared, and drove off. They're saying they'll probably never find out who did it. As far as Massey goes, the Oklahoma cops haven't closed the book on his death yet. But it's clearly not a simple case of drowning."

"Why not?"

"There was no *cause* for the drowning. Massey didn't have a heart attack or a stroke. The lake bottom wasn't steep, so there's no way he could have fallen off an underwater ledge or anything, and the weather was perfect. *And* it looks like Massey fought with somebody."

"What do you mean?"

"Two fingers on his right hand were broken." Hewitt watched Dahl struggle to accept the truth. Obviously, Dahl wanted the deaths to be accidents. The implications of murder were terrifying, even for a senior military man. "He was defending himself."

"Someone's trying to knock us all off," Dahl whispered.

Hewitt hesitated. "I hate to say it, but I think you're right. There's no proof, but we'd be crazy to stick our heads in the sand and chalk all this up to coincidence." He glanced out through the trees onto the Mall, looking for anything suspicious. "Dick, I asked you to meet with me because I trust your instincts. I thought you might have some ideas about what we could do to protect ourselves." Hewitt motioned toward a man standing by the sidewalk fifty feet away. "I've hired bodyguards, but I'm not stupid. I know that's not enough to protect me from someone who knows what he's doing."

Dahl followed Hewitt's gaze. "Who the hell could it be? How would anyone know who we are?" He snapped his fingers. "Roth," he hissed. "It's gotta be him."

"It's not Roth."

"How can you be sure?"

"I've had my boys watching him. Roth's been on the island or in town, that's it. He hasn't come to D.C., hasn't flown to Oklahoma."

"Maybe he's got friends doing it for him."

"Where would he have friends like that? Miami? I don't think so, Dick. That's why he left Florida. He doesn't have any friends left down there."

"So what do *you* think?" Dahl asked anxiously. "What's going on?"

"I don't know, but . . ." His voice trailed off, like he didn't want to say what he was thinking.

"Come on," Dahl urged. "What is it? What's your gut tell you?"

"It might be one of us." Hewitt's eyes narrowed. "Maybe two of us."

"**DIDN'T YOU SAY** you were going to bring somebody else with you?" Roth asked as Harrison stepped off the boat onto the pier.

"I did bring somebody." Harrison pointed out to sea. "He's out there in another boat. He followed us from town."

Roth looped the bowline of Harrison's boat around a piling. "What's going on here?" he asked suspiciously, standing up and peering out at the ocean. There was nothing in sight, and he hadn't seen anyone follow them out of the harbor. "Why's he waiting out there for you? What, you don't trust me or something?"

"I trust you." Harrison glanced toward the island. "Where's your wife?"

"Not around."

Harrison hesitated. "Look, I'm just being careful. There've been a lot of weird things going on lately."

"Like what?" Roth demanded.

"Like an old man coming up to me in a bar and telling me an effed-up story about a haunted island, then disappearing and nobody in town recognizing his picture." Harrison shaded his eyes against the rays of the afternoon sun glimmering off the water. "Like he's a ghost or something."

"Well, we've—"

"Like one of my friends being pretty sure somebody broke into his apartment the other night."

Roth bit his lower lip. Hewitt must have arranged that. "You got that picture of the old man with you?" he asked.

"Yeah, I got it." Harrison patted the backpack he'd brought with him from the boat. He wasn't going to let it out of his sight. He'd caught Roth taking a long look at the registration number on the bow, and suddenly he was feeling vulnerable.

"Can I see it?" Roth asked.

"Let's take a look around first."

Roth shrugged and exhaled heavily, then gestured back down the pier. "Come on."

First they toured the grounds outside the lodge.

"Pretty secluded here in the middle of the island," Harrison observed as they reached the lodge. It was quiet, too, now that the sounds of the ocean were almost gone.

"What do you mean?"

"It's tough to see the ocean from in here, which means it's hard to see this place *from* the ocean." Harrison made a sweeping gesture with his hand. "The lodge is built in kind of a natural depression, and the trees are really dense around it, denser than in any other spot on the island. You can see that from the ocean when you're coming up on the island. It's almost like the people who built the lodge were trying to hide it."

Roth shook his head. "You got quite an imagination, pal."

"Yeah, *sure* I do."

As they reached the northeast corner of the lodge, Harrison saw instantly what George Bishop had meant about the lack of windows here. There weren't any for twenty feet all the way up this side. He moved back so he could see around the other side. Same thing—no windows for about twenty feet. There were windows all around the rest of the house, close to the other three corners but not close to this one.

"What is it?"

Harrison glanced over at Roth. Roth must have noticed him checking it out. "Nothing. Let's go inside."

For the next fifteen minutes Roth gave Harrison a tour of the inside of the lodge. Finally, they reached the third floor.

When Harrison made it to the last door down the hallway, he tried to turn the knob, but it was locked. And, unlike any of the other doors on the hallway, this one was closed. This was the corner of the lodge where there weren't any windows, he realized. Another odd thing about this spot: a distinct smell of mildew. "What's in here?" he asked, trying to keep his voice light, rapping on the door with his knuckles.

"Don't know. They keep it locked all the time."

"You don't have the key?"

"Nope."

"Never asked them for it?"

"Nope."

"Never asked them what's in there?"

"Nope."

"Aren't you curious about what's in there?"

"Nope."

Harrison ran his fingertips gently down the door. "What really happened in Miami, Don?" He watched Roth's eyes narrow, sensed Roth quickly putting up shields.

"What do you mean?"

"Were you doing something you shouldn't have been doing down there?" Harrison saw Roth glance suspiciously at the backpack. "There's nothing in there you need to worry about," he assured Roth. "No wire, no camera, nothing like that." He tossed the bag back down the hallway toward the steps. "Satisfied?"

Roth said nothing, just eyed the bag now lying in a heap on the long narrow rug that extended the length of the corridor.

"Nothing on me, either," Harrison continued, unbuttoning his shirt to his navel, then spreading his arms. "Go ahead, check me. My cell phone's back in the boat. Wouldn't do me any good if I had it anyway. Lost my reception halfway out here."

Still, Roth remained quiet.

"I know you want to tell me something," Harrison pushed gently, letting his arms fall back to his sides, "otherwise you wouldn't have met me in town. And you almost told me something that day. We both know you did. Come on, maybe I can help."

Nothing.

"What happened in Miami, Don?" Harrison asked directly. "Were you run out of there because you were giving a gang protection? Is that why these guys at this place like you, because they can manipulate you? Do they know something about you that you don't want the rest of the world to know?" He watched Roth swallow hard. He'd hit a nerve, he was positive.

"It doesn't matter what happened in Miami," Roth finally muttered, teeth clenched. "You found the articles on the Internet. Make up your own mind."

"Where's your wife, Don?"

"How do you know I even *have* a wife?" Roth snapped.

"The clerk at the hardware store in Southport told me." Roth seemed ready to open up. Harrison had interviewed lots of people who wanted to talk about something they were hiding—he could read the signs. "Where is she?"

"In town. I dropped her off earlier, then came back out to meet you.

She's spending the night with a girlfriend she met a couple of months ago while she was shopping for linens. I'm picking her up tomorrow."

Too much information, too many details. Roth didn't usually give long answers like that. Harrison shrugged. But you could only push a person so hard before he clammed up for good, especially a guy like Roth. Harrison didn't want that to happen. Well, he'd learned to be patient, too. Maybe at some point Roth would open the spigot and it would all come pouring out. Unfortunately, he wasn't going to have a lot of opportunities. Maybe it was time for the good cop. "That sounds like fun. Probably nice for her to get off the island every once in a while." Harrison realized how that must have sounded. "Not that I meant she needs to—"

"You're right," Roth broke in. "It is good for her to get off the island every once in a while."

Harrison nodded up the hallway, in the direction of the backpack, thankful that Roth hadn't gone ballistic. He seemed like the type that might. "Should we go back downstairs?" Roth seemed relieved at the suggestion.

"Yeah."

When they reached the first floor again, Harrison followed Roth into the kitchen.

"I need to check on something," Roth said, heading toward a door to the outside. "I'll be back in a minute. Do me a favor, stay in here, will you?"

"Yeah, sure."

Through a window over the sink, Harrison watched Roth head across the small yard toward a shed. When he'd disappeared inside, Harrison's eyes flickered to a counter beneath an overhanging cupboard. To a small photograph inside a plain wooden frame sitting on the counter he'd noticed when they first entered the kitchen. He stared at the photograph, thinking about how this day was turning into a complete waste of time, how he should have spent it working on another story he was on a deadline for.

Harrison's eyes focused on the photo and suddenly it occurred to him that there hadn't been any other photographs in the house—not of people, anyway. He moved slowly across the kitchen floor, his eyes zeroing in on the figures inside the frame, noticing how they were standing beside one another but didn't look natural. As if the photo had been touched up to make the people look like they'd been standing together when the picture was taken, but they really hadn't been.

"Jesus," he whispered, the hairs on the back of his neck standing straight up as he leaned down, his face just inches from the print. A chill coursed through his body as he studied the tiny faces, then suddenly he heard the door to the outside opening and he whipped around, putting his hands behind him and gripping the counter, trying to look relaxed, as though he'd been standing like that for a while.

"What's wrong?" Roth asked as he came back inside, stamping his boots on a mat. It had rained last night and his soles were muddy. "You okay?"

"What do you mean?"

"You look sick."

Harrison shook his head. "Nah, I'm fine. What about the lighthouse?" he asked quickly.

Roth stopped stamping his boots. "What about it?"

"I want to see it."

"No you don't."

"Why not?"

"There's no need to see it—there's nothing there. It's a long walk and, besides, I've got stuff to do."

Harrison thought about it for a few seconds. "Yeah, okay."

Roth stared at him hard for a few moments. "I gotta take a leak. When I get back, I'll walk you down to the dock, okay?"

Harrison nodded. "Yeah, okay." He watched Roth go. It was the second time Roth had left him alone in the kitchen. Then it hit him.

IT WAS LATE and Jesse and Stephanie were alone in the office—Osgood had gone home an hour ago. They were reviewing a speech Jesse was going to be making in Houston the day after tomorrow.

"You've done a great job on this," Jesse said, wondering how in the world he could ever fire Stephanie—or Osgood. At times he truly hated Elijah Forte. More often lately. "Really great."

"Thanks," she said softly.

They were sitting close and Jesse could smell her perfume. He smiled at her. The scent was vaguely familiar. "I like your perfume." He knew it was a risky thing to say, but he couldn't help himself. He liked making people feel good about themselves, a natural trait that had served him well over the years.

She reached over and touched his arm. "It's the one you bought me in Vermont that week, when you won that tournament. I don't wear it very often because I don't want to run out of it. You can't get it now. They don't make it anymore."

Jesse closed his eyes. Such a wonderful memory, that weekend in Vermont. His last win, her next to him at night. He felt her hand drop from his arm to his leg, and he caught it halfway up his thigh. He couldn't do this. He wanted to, but he couldn't. Thank God he had some semblance of self-control. "Steph, I—"

"What's wrong?" she snapped, standing up. "Aren't I pretty enough anymore?"

"You're very pretty, but I'm . . ." His voice faded as he watched her stalk from the room. For the first time since he'd known her, he'd seen hatred in her eyes.

16

AS CHRISTIAN made his way through the crowded bar, he caught sight of Faith standing in a far corner, ringed by a crew of beefy security guards wearing dark blue jackets. She was signing autographs, and she looked beautiful in a lacy white top and a short jeans skirt. Blond and petite with captivating green eyes that were shining like two Manhattan spotlights on opening night. He hated to dim those lights, but what had to be said had to be said. As he neared her he saw her tap one of the security guards on the shoulder. The guy glanced at Christian and nodded.

"Hi, sweetheart," she murmured over the noise as he moved inside the ring, her lips pressed to his ear. She handed the paper napkin she'd signed back to a young man in a suit, then slipped her arms around his neck and kissed him. "I missed you."

"Me too."

She let go instantly. "What's wrong?"

He furrowed his eyebrows. "What do you mean?"

"I can always tell when something's wrong. What is it?"

He was beginning to think too many people knew him too well. Or maybe he was just becoming too predictable. "Nothing, it's just that—"

"Just *what*?"

Christian saw it coming. Faith could turn from a kitten to Tasmanian devil in a heartbeat these days. It hadn't been like that when they'd first met, when she was just bursting onto the music scene. She'd been carefree and hard to rile back then. Maybe getting touchy came with the turf, with so many people demanding her time now. He understood that.

"I know we were supposed to have dinner tonight, but—"

"Are you standing me up?" she demanded, pulling back.

Her anger was ratcheting up fast, like the sound of a TV with someone's thumb on the volume button. "I'm sorry, but something came up."

"What?"

"A meeting."

She rolled her eyes. "With who? As if I don't know."

Christian hesitated.

"It's with Allison, isn't it?" She'd barely given him a chance to answer. "You prick! I hate that bitch."

"Faith, it's just business. I've told you that so many times."

"What's so pressing that you *have* to meet with her tonight?"

A wave of guilt surged through him. He hadn't said anything to Faith about Jesse Wood asking him to be vice president. He'd told Nigel, Quentin, Allison, even Samuel Hewitt, but he hadn't said anything to Faith. That ought to tell him something about their relationship right there. He tried to take her hands, but she pulled away. "Allison's going out of town tomorrow to work on a deal on the West Coast and we have to go over a couple of things before she leaves."

"Why can't you do it on the phone?"

Christian shook his head. "The phone doesn't work." He noticed that she was breathing fast, like she was scared or about to say something very important. "You know that."

"That's always your excuse." She ran her hands through her hair, then brought them to her eyes. "Get out of here."

"Faith, we'll get together later." Christian saw the security guards starting to give him hard looks, like they were ready to kick him out of the ring as soon as Faith gave them the high sign. "Come to my apartment around ten. I'll be home by then."

She stuck her chin out and pointed at the door. "I'm not kidding, I want you out of here right now."

This was always her first instinct when she got angry. To lash out, to push him away, not to take a deep breath and talk about what was bothering her. It exhausted him. "If I leave here now and we aren't getting together later, don't bother calling or e-mailing me again. I mean it. I'm sick of this."

"Get out, just get the hell away from me."

He stared into her eyes for a few moments, then turned and walked out. Something told him this was it. No going back.

ROTH MOVED carefully over fallen pine needles covering the faint path leading from the lodge to the lighthouse. It was almost dark on the forest floor, and he had to walk slowly to make certain he didn't run into low-hanging branches. The sun wouldn't set for another thirty minutes, but the trees were dense and they blocked out most of the fading light. He'd waited for several hours to make the trek out here, until he was certain Harrison was gone.

Using a pair of high-powered binoculars, he'd watched Harrison motor away from Champagne Island at the tip of an ever-expanding white wake until the little boat was just a dot on the horizon and the whine of the engine faded into the sounds of the wind and the surf. He shook his head as he moved along the path, pushing a branch out of the way with his forearm. Harrison had claimed that there was someone waiting for him in another boat out on the ocean, a not-so-subtle warning that he was nervous about being on the island alone. That if he didn't come back by an agreed-upon time, someone would know.

Harrison was right to be nervous, Roth thought to himself as he reached the rocky slope leading up to the base of the lighthouse. But the warning about someone waiting out there on the ocean for him was almost certainly a bluff. The only friend Harrison had in Southport was George Bishop, and Bishop was probably dead by now. Hewitt hadn't told him for sure, but it didn't take much to connect the dots.

When Roth reached the base of the lighthouse, he hesitated for a moment and gazed out over the ocean, now covered with whitecaps. Even from the base of the structure he had an excellent view of the ocean in every direction because the lighthouse was built on a ridge. On the western horizon he could see dark clouds building, slashed every few seconds by lightning. The storms the weathermen had been predicting all day on the radio were finally moving in, but he still had an hour or so to get back to the lodge before the fireworks started in earnest.

Roth turned the key, pulled open the metal door, and reached inside, feeling along the rough cinder-block wall for the light switch, flipping it up when his fingers reached it. Instantly the room was bathed in light. The first step of the circular iron stairway leading to the top of the hundred-foot tower was against the far wall. To the right was a small desk where Roth kept maintenance records and to the left a closet where he usually stored cleaning supplies. But he'd moved the supplies over by the desk this morning.

He pulled out a second key, unlocked the closet door, and opened it slightly, peering inside before he pulled it open all the way. The pretty young woman was sitting on the cement floor in the same position he'd left her, wrists and ankles bound with white rope, a gag stuffed in her mouth. She was still dressed in the red tube top and khaki shorts Hewitt's friends had dropped her off in. They were using her for something, to manipulate someone, and they were keeping her here until they needed her. They'd kept girls here before—without Patty's knowledge. Roth hadn't even bothered to ask her name this time. He didn't want to know it.

She looked up at him fearfully and moaned as he knelt down and pulled the gag gently from her mouth. "I'm so thirsty," she murmured, teeth starting to chatter. "Freezing, too."

"Yeah, it still gets cold at night this time of year." He untied the rope from around her ankles. He should have given her one of Patty's sweaters but he'd been too focused on getting her out of the lodge before he had to go into town to get Harrison. "Here." He pressed the mouth of a canteen to her lips, and she gulped the water down. When she was finished drinking, he helped her to her feet.

"Will you please untie my hands?" she begged.

"No," he said brusquely. "Come on." He guided her out of the closet toward the lighthouse door, relocked it when they were back outside, then took her by the arm and helped her down the slope.

"Am I going to be okay?" she asked when they reached the forest floor, tears rimming her lower lids.

He gazed at her for a few moments, then looked away, hoping she hadn't seen the truth in his expression. "You'll be fine."

"**BOY,** you're in a good mood tonight." Allison smiled at Christian from the other side of the candlelit table.

He felt himself smiling back.

"It's nice," she said. "You seem so relaxed."

They were sitting in a back booth of the restaurant. Allison was wearing a low-cut top, but most of the women in the place were wearing outfits that were even more revealing. She didn't stand out, which made Christian happy. More and more he was noticing those lustful stares other men gave Allison, so anything that made her blend in was a good thing.

"Why shouldn't I be in a good mood?" he asked. He could see by the anticipation in her expression that she wanted him to say something like *After all, I'm with you*. Maybe later on, depending on how things went. "Aren't I usually fun to be around?"

"Well, of course you are," she agreed slowly, looking down. "What I meant to say was you aren't as serious as you usually are. I've actually seen that beautiful smile of yours tonight."

"I'm enjoying myself."

"You haven't been checking your e-mails every five minutes like you usually do, either."

She was right: He'd let himself go, even turned off his cell phone. He couldn't remember the last time he'd done that. Maybe he was over the edge—at least a little. "I guess I'm *really* enjoying myself."

And he was. All the same, he wasn't going to jump into anything with her—he couldn't. He was going to give it time, see what happened. Quentin had made a good point out in Chicago about dipping the pen in the company ink. Anything that happened between them had to happen carefully and with as little fanfare as possible. The Everest investors wouldn't be happy if they opened up the *Post* one morning and read about their chairman and one of his managing partners having an affair. But, if he was going to be out of Everest and into the political world soon, maybe it was less of an issue.

Christian gazed at her in the soft light and allowed himself to actually consider the incredible possibilities that lay ahead of him—which he rarely did because he was so superstitious. If you assumed special things were going to happen to you, they usually didn't. Like God was getting you back for having the audacity to think so much of yourself. But for a few moments he let himself believe that Jesse Wood and he were going to win in November and that eight years from now he'd be about to accept the party's nomination for president. Allison Wallace would make an incredible first lady.

Christian put a hand to his mouth to hide a grin and looked down at his plate. Or maybe she wouldn't, now that he thought about it. She probably wouldn't settle for first lady. More likely, she'd be running against him.

"What are you grinning about?" she asked, sipping champagne.

"Nothing."

"Will you *please* have just one glass?" she begged, holding up hers. "It's delicious."

"You know I won't."

She sighed, frustrated. "Well, I guess it's good that you don't drink. If you and Jesse Wood win the election, you won't be able to for at least four years."

"Why not?"

"I thought the president and the vice president weren't supposed to drink. I thought you had to be sober all the time in case you had to set off the nukes and all that."

Christian shrugged. "I don't know. But like you said, it won't matter for me."

Allison glanced at her watch. "What time do you turn into a pumpkin?"

He chuckled. "Excuse me?"

"What time do you have to be home? What time will Faith come stomping in here and drag you out if you aren't back at your apartment?"

"It's not like that anymore," he answered quietly.

Her eyes raced to his.

He folded his napkin and placed it down on the table. "Faith and I broke up."

Allison stared at him for a few more moments, then shook her head and smiled. "And the beat goes on." She raised her glass. "Congratulations, it's been a long time coming." She paused. "Of course . . ." Her voice faded.

"Of course *what*?"

"I know what's going to happen. You'll show up at the office tomorrow morning with this sheepish look on your face, and I'll find out that you two are back together."

"Not this time," Christian vowed.

"Why not? What's different?"

"It doesn't matter, it just is. *Now*," he said loudly when he saw her about to speak up, "I want to know if you're going to stay at Everest after we're through with this fund, or if you're going to run back to Chicago. You told me you'd give me an answer tonight as long as I had dinner with you. Well, here I am."

"I guess you think the fact that you broke up with Faith is a big bonus."

"I don't think one thing has anything to do with the other. I just want your answer. You going to make up your own mind, or is Gordon Meade going to make it up for you?"

"Of course I'm staying here, you dope. You knew that this afternoon." She crossed her arms over her chest, giving him an exaggerated frown. "Now *I* want to know who's going to be chairman of Everest when you leave."

"You willing to sign a contract?"

"Maybe."

"Nope. I want to know right now if you'd sign a multiyear contract to stay at Everest. With noncompete clauses, too."

"Okay."

He pursed his lips. He hadn't been ready for that. "You know . . ."

"Know what?" she asked softly when his voice faded. "Don't start something like that, then not finish. Not right now, anyway."

He nodded. She was right—that wasn't fair. "I hate snobs. My stepmother's a snob, and I hate her for it. I hate her for being a snob even more than I hate her for what she did to me after my dad died."

"I hate snobs, too, but what the hell does that have to do with anything?"

Christian pointed at her. "The first day I met you I thought you were a snob."

Allison put her hand on her chest. *"What?"*

"Yeah, I did."

"Why? We went out to dinner, we had a great time."

"We did have a great time at dinner. But, technically, the first time we met was earlier that day, at Everest, when you and Gordon Meade came into the office to talk."

She moved back slightly from the table. "Oh, that's right."

"You were Miss Prim and Proper, Ally." It was the first time he'd ever called her that. It had come from nowhere, but he liked the way it sounded. "You hardly said a word, but when you did you were pretty condescending."

"That was *business me.* I was acting that way for Gordon. My family's so concerned about appearances, you know?" Allison shook her head. "Most of them are the exact kind of people you hate. Consumed with what other people think of them, who they know, even who they're related to. God, we have a whole huge book locked away in a safe at one of the mansions in Chicago dedicated to our family tree."

"Really?"

"Yeah. I hear it's incredible, but I've never bothered to look at it." She smiled at him and slid her hands across the table, wrapping her slender fingers around his. "This is nice, Chris."

Her fingers were soft and warm. They'd touched before, but it seemed different this time, very different. Everything seemed different this time. "Yeah."

"I'll do whatever you want me to do. You know I will, and you've known it for a while."

It was exactly what he'd wanted her to say, but suddenly the responsibility of the commitment she'd just made came barreling at him. If she agreed to a contract he made her sign, she'd expect a lot in return. Not just what was in the contract. "This has to go slowly."

"Of course."

There was a warmth in her eyes he'd never seen before. "We have to be very careful."

She nodded. *"I know."* She squeezed his fingers. "And I liked the way you called me Ally."

Christian gazed at her over the candles for a few moments, thinking about how right this seemed. "You know, I—" He interrupted himself. He'd spotted Quentin walk in and move directly to the maitre d'—who pointed at their table. Christian could tell right away by Quentin's expression that something was wrong.

"Chris," Quentin called before he even made it to the table. He nodded at Allison.

"Hello," she said.

Strange, Christian thought to himself, he'd heard irritation in her tone. As far as he knew, Allison and Quentin got along fine. She was probably just irritated about being interrupted at this particular moment. "What's up?"

Quentin's eyes flickered to Allison, then back to Christian. "Can I talk to you for a second? Alone."

Christian gestured toward Allison. "It's okay, you can say whatever you want to in front of her."

"It's about that thing, you know?"

Christian raised both eyebrows and pushed back his chair. "Okay." He excused himself and followed Quentin through the restaurant, through the entrance, and out onto the sidewalk. "What *thing*?" he asked loudly. It was almost ten o'clock but Eighth Avenue still swelled with noisy traffic. "I don't know what you're talking about."

"Sorry about the interruption. I tried your cell phone, but it was turned off."

"What's so important it couldn't wait until tomorrow morning or you couldn't leave a message?"

"I've got a lead on who tipped the SEC off about Central States Telecom."

Christian's eyes narrowed. He'd told Quentin about the SEC's pending investigation of CST. Quentin still had all those contacts inside the federal government, so Christian figured maybe he could dig up a clue about what was going on. Who Vivian Davis had gotten her "credible information" from. It was a long shot, but Quentin was a bloodhound. It sounded like he'd sniffed something out.

Quentin motioned toward the restaurant door. "It's all leading to Chicago."

Christian felt his throat go dry. He glanced over his shoulder at the door, then back at Quentin. *"Allison?"*

"I don't know if Allison's involved yet, but I'm pretty sure Gordon Meade is."

Christian's mind flashed back to the dinner in Chicago. How Meade had seemed strangely confrontational. "How sure?"

"Eighty percent, but I'll know more tomorrow."

"Jesus."

"Now you know why I wanted to tell you right away."

Christian nodded.

"Were you and Allison holding hands when I walked in?" Quentin asked. He waited for a few moments, then tried another tack when Christian didn't respond. "Do *you* think she's involved?"

"I don't know." Christian hesitated. "But it wouldn't surprise me."

Quentin glanced down the sidewalk. "Yeah, but nothing ever surprises you."

Maybe not, Christian thought to himself, but when suspicion turned to truth it still disappointed him. He just hoped Allison wouldn't turn out to be one of those disappointments.

▪ ▪ ▪

CHRISTIAN TOSSED his keys on the kitchen counter, then glanced at the answering machine. The red light was blinking, so he picked up the cordless and checked caller ID. Faith's number, four times. The same number of times he'd seen that she'd called his cell phone after he'd turned it back on in the cab after saying good night to Allison.

He reached into his pocket and pulled out his BlackBerry. He purposely hadn't checked it until now. Four e-mails from her, too. He put the BlackBerry down on the counter beside his keys without reading the messages and moved out onto the wide balcony overlooking Central Park.

He took a deep breath as he leaned on the railing and watched the lights move south on Fifth Avenue. A little while ago he'd been thinking about what it would be like to be vice president, maybe even president someday. Now he was thinking about someone in Chicago setting him up on CST—and what it would be like to go to prison.

17

"SO THIS IS WHERE it all happens," said Samuel Hewitt, looking around Christian's office as he took off his black Stetson, laid it on the desk, and ran a hand through his silver hair. "Where the bottom-line decisions at Everest Capital are made." He groaned as he eased into the chair. "Command central."

"You okay?"

"Got arthritis in my knees," Hewitt explained. "My college football days are finally catching up to me."

"What position did you play?"

Hewitt's eyes gleamed. "You don't know?"

According to Quentin, Hewitt had played tight end and linebacker at Princeton, started at both. In those days, the top guys played offense and defense. Christian knew all that, but he didn't want Hewitt to think he was *that* interested, didn't want to scare him off the Laurel Energy deal. He shook his head. "No."

"You mean to tell me Quentin Stiles didn't report that to you, or that you didn't order a yearbook?" Hewitt grinned. "I'm disappointed in you, son. I know you played rugby, and that sure ain't on the Everest Web site." He wagged a finger and used a professor's voice. "Information, Christian, always get information, as much of it as you can."

"Right, Samuel," he said, smiling politely. "I'll remember that."

"Be resourceful, Christian. Be resourceful without going over the line." Hewitt chuckled. "Unless you're sure no one'll find out. Then go flying past the line, go as far past it as you can."

Hewitt's eyes flickered around as he spoke, Christian noticed, checking out the desk, the bookcases, the credenzas. He understood what Hewitt was doing, not looking just to look. He was looking for data, for a shred of something that might give him a window onto the man, something that might give him an advantage. Christian did the same thing when he was in someone else's office. But Hewitt wasn't going to find anything in here. Christian didn't keep things like that around. Except for photos of Faith that he used to have in here.

Hewitt leaned forward and picked a folder off the front of the desk. "What's this?"

God, he should have known. Should have known Hewitt would find something. Never underestimate a man like Samuel Hewitt. How many times had his father hit him over the head with that? "Hey, that's—"

"The Clayton House," Hewitt said, perusing the cover of the folder. "Is this how you spend all that money you make?"

"Some of it."

Hewitt opened the folder. "A home for homeless kids," he read aloud from a brochure inside the folder. "Damn, Christian, this place looks amazing. Nicer than a lot of hotels I've stayed in over the years." He was leafing through the brochure, checking out the pictures. "Where is it?"

"Up in Harlem, near the Apollo."

"Named it for your dad, huh? How many kids do you take care of?"

"Depends. We're always trying to find permanent homes for them, so they come and go. Usually, there's between seventy and eighty at the house."

Hewitt tucked the brochure away and dropped the folder back on Christian's desk. "That's a nice thing you do."

"I just bring the money, Samuel. Some wonderful women up at the home do the real work, a couple of ladies I couldn't keep up with even if I tried. They're angels, really. Wish I could make them executives at a couple of our portfolio companies," he said half seriously. "They'd probably do better than the guys we've got in charge now."

"They couldn't do it without your money."

"Money's money."

"Learn to give yourself credit, son."

Christian's eyes shot to Hewitt's. Exactly what his father had said to him a long time ago, after Christian had won the club golf tournament the summer between his second and third years at Princeton. *Exactly the same thing.* The same words, tone of voice, everything. In his speech at the trophy presentation Christian had given credit to everyone else—his caddie, the club pro, even the grounds crew—then passed off his part of the win as luck. Clayton had gotten on him about that later. Never be cocky, he'd said, but don't tell others you were just lucky if you do something great because they might start to believe you. Learn to give yourself credit, son.

"You miss your dad, Christian?"

Christian glanced up. He'd been looking at Hewitt's Stetson lying beside the Clayton House folder.

"I miss my dad every day," said Hewitt, "and he lived until he was eighty."

Christian nodded. "Yeah, I miss him," he admitted quietly.

He and his father had never gone to the Masters like they'd talked about in the study that afternoon, never spent a night in one of the private cabins at Augusta National, never met Ben Crenshaw. His father had never mentioned the trip again, probably because he wanted to forget that whole day, wanted to forget that Lana had told Christian the awful truth. At least forget about the way in which Christian had found out. Forget that he'd been too afraid to admit to his own son that he'd strayed. It was the only time Christian had ever seen his father at a loss for words or action, the only time he'd ever seen Clayton resort to anger as a response. Which meant Clayton didn't have a response. All he could do was lash out. The way Faith did all the time.

Christian and Nikki had listened to the battle rage for an hour after dinner in the upstairs rooms. Thuds, running footsteps, furniture being thrown about, Clayton's booming voice. So unusual because it was normally Lana's shouts that filled the house. Christian had sent the frightened maids home right away and cleaned up the dinner dishes himself.

The next morning it had been as though nothing had happened. Clayton was his usual enthusiastic self, and Lana started drinking white wine at noon while she watched her soap operas. No one mentioned a thing about the night before. Clayton left in the afternoon for Washington and Lana staggered up to bed at seven thirty, with a little help from Rita. A normal Monday at the Gillette household.

"How are you doing with our Princeton library fund-raising?" Hewitt asked.

Christian hesitated. "I've got fifteen million in commitments for you so far," he answered quietly.

Hewitt didn't hide his surprise or his pleasure. "Wow! Now that's fantastic."

"I made a few calls to some old Tigers who want to do business with Everest. Gave away some mandates I probably shouldn't have, a couple of bond offerings for our portfolio companies we could have done ourselves. But, what the hell, we're not paying that much for them and the guys I hired will do a good job."

"I appreciate that, son. Great work." Hewitt let out a long breath and raised his eyebrows. "I feel bad now."

That sounded ominous. "Why?"

"Aw, I know I was real bullish on buying Laurel Energy from you a few weeks ago, but I've hit a roadblock."

Christian made certain his expression remained impassive, but his heart sank. He'd been sure Hewitt would come through on buying Laurel, especially after hearing about how he'd raised fifteen million bucks for the new Princeton library. Christian had already called some of his biggest investors—including Gordon Meade—to let them know he felt better about the Laurel sale actually happening now. Meade wouldn't benefit financially—the Wallace Family wasn't invested in the fund that had bought Laurel—but Meade seemed so concerned about the whole thing at dinner in Chicago. Meade had given Christian the old it's-not-over-till-it's-over speech on the phone, but Christian had dismissed it. Now he was going to look bad—and he was going to have to call Meade back and eat crow. Worse, it sounded like the deal was dead.

"What happened?" Christian asked. In addition to disappointed investors, he was going to have some very unhappy managing partners.

Hewitt waved a hand angrily. "Our CEO didn't like the idea."

"I thought *you* ran U.S. Oil, Samuel. You're the chairman, aren't you?" It was a brazen thing to say to a legend, but he had to try to keep the deal alive somehow. Quentin had reported to Christian that Hewitt had named the CEO just as a public relations move, just to show Wall Street there was a succession plan in place if anything happened to Hewitt. Supposedly, Hewitt still ran the show with an iron fist. "Doesn't the CEO report to you?"

"Yes," Hewitt answered coldly.

Christian caught Hewitt's look—the same look Meade had given Allison in Chicago when she'd made it clear *she'd* be making the decision about what she'd do after the fund was used up. A look that said no one had spoken to Hewitt like that in a long time.

"Why didn't the CEO like the idea?"

"Said he wasn't convinced the reserves were as big as the engineering reports indicated. Apparently, he had a bad experience in that area of Canada a while back."

"That's ridiculous. The guys who generated those reports are the best engineers in the business. We talked about that."

Hewitt held his hands up. "I know, I know. Don't panic."

Christian eased back in his chair, catching himself. "I'm not." But it sure must have seemed like he was.

"I'm not saying the deal's dead," Hewitt continued. "What I am saying is that you better keep going forward with your sale process as though we weren't talking. I was going to offer you the full five billion and ask you to give me an exclusive for fifteen days to get things in order on my side, but I've got to put that on hold, at least for now."

Christian caught his breath. The full five billion in fifteen days. He tried not to let the disappointment register in his expression, but it was tough. He would have been able to stick that number in front of a lot of doubters, and he would have been able to spread nine hundred and forty million around the firm.

"The CEO called me as I was coming over here." Hewitt shook his head. "Literally as I was walking in the front door."

At this point, Christian only had one card to play. Maybe the prospect of Everest retaining Black Brothers would get Hewitt moving in the right direction again. Black Brothers would gin up more bidders, pushing up the price. Or so Christian hoped. "I guess I'll have to hire Black Brothers after all."

"I understand," Hewitt said gloomily, but his face immediately brightened. "Let's plan a trip for you to come to Dallas, to the ranch. Soon."

"I don't know, I've got a lot going on."

"Oh, come on, Christian, don't be pissed off."

"I'm not."

"Yeah, you are. I can tell. Look, I'm going to talk to my CEO later today. Like I said, the deal's not dead. If I can get him over the hump, and I've got to pay a little more because you hired Trenton 'the Great White Shark' Fleming at Black Brothers"—Hewitt grinned as he said the nickname—"so be it."

"What are the odds you're going to buy Laurel, Samuel?" Christian asked. "Level with me."

"Fifty-fifty."

Of course. The same thing he would have said. Leave room for hope, but don't commit to anything. "When were you thinking about me coming down to Dallas?"

"As soon as possible. I'm headed back there tonight."

It was clear to Christian that if he didn't accept the offer to come to Texas, Hewitt wasn't going to try to persuade anyone at U.S. Oil to buy Laurel. But if he went to the ranch, maybe there might still be a chance. And Hewitt had suggested that if U.S. Oil did decide to move forward, they'd pay full price. That alone made the trip worthwhile. "I'm meeting with Jesse Wood later this week. How about after that?"

"Great. Have Debbie call Rhonda to set it up."

"Okay."

"How's it going with Jesse, by the way?" Hewitt asked.

"Fine. Like I said, I'm meeting with him later this week to go over his platform in detail, so we can make a final decision on each other. But it looks like he's got the nomination locked up."

In the last week Jesse had won two more primaries. He had the delegates he needed.

"Yes, it does," Hewitt agreed. "How's he feeling?"

"Pretty pumped."

"What about November? How's he feeling about the general election?"

"He's confident he's going to win."

Hewitt paused for a few moments, then leaned forward and picked up his Stetson. "Confident, huh? Well, ain't that wonderful."

ALLISON HAD LEFT the office and walked into Central Park to get away from phones and e-mails, so she could concentrate on the Aero Systems deal. She wanted to figure out how to lock up the purchase, to keep the other bidders at bay, but she couldn't stay focused at the office because of the constant interruptions. Now that she was running a couple of companies, she was starting to understand what Christian endured. People constantly clamoring for her time, constantly needing major decisions made. And she was running only two companies at this point. He ran twenty.

So she'd found a lonely bench near a reflecting pool where she hoped no one would find her. She leaned back, watching a couple of young boys sail a remote-control boat on the pool for a few minutes, then pulled out a pad from her bag and started to jot down notes.

"Hello, Allison."

She looked up from the pad, eyes widening. Faith Cassidy stood in front of her. They'd never met, but she recognized Faith from the billboard in Times Square advertising her new album—and the pictures in Christian's office.

"Oh, how I've been looking forward to this."

Allison stood up slowly. She didn't like the look in Faith's eyes. The look of a woman on the brink. "What do you want?"

"Do you know who I am?"

"No, I've been living in a cave for the last few years." Allison saw the boys who'd been playing with the boat stop and point at Faith. She wasn't the only one who recognized her. "What do you want?"

"To let you know that I understand why you're going after Christian so hard. Why you want him to think that you're falling in love with him."

"Really? Why don't you let me in on—"

"It's because you want to run Everest Capital when Christian leaves," Faith interrupted. "You're worried he might make Nigel Faraday chairman instead."

"Oh, please, that's so ridiculous it's—"

"You don't really care about Christian, but you think if you can make him believe you care, then you can manipulate him." Faith smiled. "But I'm going to tell Christian exactly what you're doing . . . and why."

"Tell me something. Who put all this into your little head?"

Faith's smile grew wider. "Like I'd really tell you." She moved close to Allison, until their faces were just inches apart. Her smile faded. "If I were you, I'd start looking over my shoulder. A lot of people want to do me favors."

KOHLER AND MCDONNELL sat in a polished, dark wood pew in a nave of an old midtown Manhattan church. They'd both walked many blocks to get to the church, coming from separate locations, as always worried that Samuel Hewitt might be watching.

"See anything suspicious on your way over here?" Kohler asked, glancing at the altar. It was covered with lighted candles.

McDonnell shook his head. "No."

"Were you at least *looking*?"

"Of course, *damn it*." McDonnell's voice echoed inside the empty church.

McDonnell was getting fed up with the intrigue to the point that he wished he'd never heard of the Order, Samuel Hewitt, Trenton Fleming—any of it. But he had heard of them, joined them, taped himself having sex with women other than his wife for them, and, worst of all, turned those tapes over to them. God, how could he have been so stupid? Okay, so Hewitt was a board member of Jamison & Jamison and had made certain the board voted to elect McDonnell CEO of the corporation four years ago, but he would have won that job even without Hewitt's support at that board meeting. He grimaced, being honest with himself. Maybe he would have won without Hewitt? He thought about it a moment longer. No, probably not. A moment longer. Definitely not. Even though Hewitt wasn't chairman of Jamison & Jamison, he basically ran the board. Just like he ran everything else he was a member of. Without Hewitt's support at that board meeting, he never would have been elected CEO.

"What's the problem, Blanton?" Kohler demanded.

"I'm busy, Mace," McDonnell replied irritably. "I don't have time for all this cloak-and-dagger crap."

"Well, you can thank Samuel Hewitt for that. He's the one who's responsible for it. He's the one who's gone off the deep end."

They were silent for a while.

"Did you see the articles?" Kohler finally asked.

McDonnell looked up from a red prayer book lying on the pew beside him. He'd been staring at it, thinking about how it had been too long since he'd gone to Sunday service. "What articles?"

"About Laird and Massey."

McDonnell sat up, sensing from Kohler's tone that this was big news. "No." He'd been buried at work lately, hadn't had time to answer all his e-mails let alone read a newspaper or browse the Internet. "What happened?"

"They're dead."

"What?"

Kohler nodded. "Both of them. Laird was killed by a hit-and-run driver in northern Virginia, and Massey drowned in a lake in Oklahoma. He was fishing."

McDonnell leaned forward and put his face in his hands. "That's awful."

"Yeah, awful," Kohler repeated sarcastically.

McDonnell looked up. Kohler didn't seem very disturbed about the other men's deaths. It was almost like he was glad they were gone. "Aren't you sorry?"

"Sorry? Why would I be sorry? Why would anyone be sorry about those men being dead?"

"*Jesus Christ*. What's wrong with you?"

"Laird and Massey were insane," Kohler hissed. "Warped men who shouldn't have been allowed to pollute the earth, shouldn't have been allowed to live. Just like Hewitt and the others."

NIGEL AND QUENTIN sat on either side of Christian, overlooking Fifth Avenue and Central Park from the balcony of Christian's two-floor, forty-second-story apartment. Early summer humidity had gripped Manhattan that afternoon, and there were only a few stars visible through the high clouds. In the distance thunder rumbled. Quentin was drinking beer, Nigel Scotch, Christian water.

"We've all been busy," Christian began, "so I figured it might be a good idea to have a catch-up session." He saw Nigel's quick glance at his watch. "I know you want to get out of here." Nigel was still seeing the brunette, still head over heels for her. "We'll be done by ten."

Nigel took a big gulp of Scotch. "I wasn't even thinking about her."

"Sure you weren't, fat man," Quentin piped up, smiling. He was constantly giving Nigel a hard time about his weight. Sometimes Nigel took it well, sometimes he didn't.

Nigel smiled widely, apparently okay with the ribbing tonight. "You just aren't ever going to leave that alone, are you? I could lose forty pounds and you'd still call me fat man. Oh well, have your fun."

"What's gotten into him?" Quentin asked, looking at Christian disappointedly. "Why's he in such a good mood?"

"The love of a good woman," Christian answered, chuckling. "Must be."

"That's no fun."

"Let's get started," Christian urged. What he was about to say wasn't going to go over well. "I met with Samuel Hewitt today. We talked about Laurel Energy." Nigel and Quentin leaned forward in their chairs, suddenly hanging on every word. "Hewitt ran into a problem with his CEO. The guy didn't like the idea of buying Laurel. Selling it to U.S. Oil isn't going to be the slam dunk I thought it was going to be—in fact, it might not happen at all."

"That doesn't make any sense," Quentin spoke up. "My people told me that the CEO never questions Hewitt. Never. He's afraid to."

Christian shrugged. "I don't know what say. The deal isn't dead, but—"

"But we need to hire Black Brothers," Nigel cut in. Christian had told him about the possibility of bringing in Black Brothers to try to get the deal done. "Immediately."

"I think that's right," Christian agreed grudgingly. "It hurts because Trenton Fleming is going to charge an arm and a leg to represent us, but I don't know what else to do. I spoke to the guys at Morgan Stanley today after I met with Hewitt, and they're done. They don't have anyone else to go to."

"What will Black Brothers charge us?" Nigel asked.

"Seven percent of the transaction."

"Damn!"

"I know. It's ridiculous," Christian acknowledged. "But I talked to a couple of people who've worked with Black Brothers in the past, people who've hired the firm to sell companies, and they do get the deal done when other firms can't. They have a knack for that."

"Are they giving you a number?" Nigel asked. "What they think they can get for Laurel?"

"Four and a half billion."

Quentin pushed out his lower lip and nodded. "Well, it isn't five, but it isn't bad, either."

"Especially considering the fact that we only invested three hundred million in the thing a few years ago," Nigel pointed out. "That would still be a grand slam for us. I think we should definitely hire them. Did you give Morgan Stanley any hint today that you were going to go with someone else?"

"Yeah, and they didn't argue. They figured it was coming."

"So do it," Quentin encouraged.

Christian nodded slowly. "I will."

"Did you tell Hewitt you were going to hire Black Brothers when he didn't come through with an offer today?" Nigel wanted to know.

"Yes." Christian smiled. "It didn't faze him a bit."

"Of course not," Quentin grumbled. "It's no biggie for him. He's just on to the next deal."

"Exactly." Christian watched the lights of a commercial jetliner head north up the Hudson River on its way to LaGuardia airport. "One good piece of news. We got the casino license." For a moment he thought about that rainy night in the New Jersey forest handing the guy he and Quentin had met in Las Vegas a million dollars in cash. "Construction's on schedule again, it'll be ready for opening day. By the way, the game's a sellout. And I spoke to Landry."

Kurt Landry was commissioner of the National Football League.

"We're going to be the lead late game on FOX on opening day."

"That's great," Quentin said, patting Christian on the back.

"Yeah, it's all coming together."

"How's the new quarterback from Buffalo doing?" Nigel asked.

"Really well," Christian replied. "Ray Lancaster e-mailed me this afternoon to tell me the guy's really fitting in, really becoming a leader. The rest of the team has responded well, too, even Poe. I guess Poe realized he wasn't the guy."

"Still irritates the hell out of me that we had to pay that guy off to get the license," Nigel said, turning the discussion back to the casino.

"We" wasn't exactly accurate, Christian thought to himself. The million bucks had come directly from his bank account, not Nigel's. Quentin had offered to share the payment—an offer Christian had declined—but Nigel hadn't.

"We ought to go after that Carmine Torino guy. That was supposed to be his job, to keep the Mob happy. We paid him a lot of money."

"You wouldn't get much out of him," Quentin said, glancing at Christian.

"Why not?"

"He's dead," Christian explained.

Nigel gazed at Christian for a few moments. *"Dead?"*

"Yup."

"Jesus. Do you think there's any connection—"

"What about CST?" Christian interrupted, not wanting to go there. "Any news, Nigel?"

Nigel took a few seconds, his eyes flickering back and forth between

Christian and Quentin. "The woman I'm working with at CST is still tracking down information for me. Trying to figure out how high up the fraud goes. But these things take time. She's got to work on this at night and on the weekends, so people don't know she's doing it."

"So, it's real?" Quentin asked. "Was there fraud?"

Nigel nodded. "Apparently."

"What's the woman's name? The one you're working with?"

Nigel hesitated. "Michelle Wan."

"Have you heard anything from Vivian Davis?" Christian asked.

"Nope. All quiet on the SEC front."

The SEC's silence worried Christian, but he didn't want to call over there, either. That made you look like you were worried. "I'm going to get another bottled water," he said, standing up. "Anybody want anything?"

Quentin and Nigel shook their heads.

As Christian moved into the apartment and headed for the kitchen, he pulled out his BlackBerry to check e-mails, leaning against the kitchen counter for a moment while he scrolled south. He took a deep breath when he saw it—another e-mail from Faith. Marked urgent. But he'd kept his promise to her—and himself. Hadn't responded to any of her calls or read any of her e-mails since the day they'd broken up at the bar. It had been a few days since she'd tried to contact him, and she hadn't marked any of her messages urgent before this.

He turned toward the refrigerator to get the bottled water, then stopped. He knew he shouldn't read the message, knew it was a mistake, but the curiosity was killing him. He snatched the BlackBerry off the counter, opened the message, and started to read.

Chris, it's me. You haven't answered anything I've sent you since we broke up so I don't know if you've read or listened to all those other messages, but this one is important. REALLY IMPORTANT. I know this sounds like sour grapes, but Allison's just using you. She wants to run Everest Capital. She isn't interested in a real relationship with you. And this isn't just me spouting off like some madwoman, not me doing anything I can to get you back. I do want you back, but I know what Allison's doing for a FACT, and I'm worried about you. I can't tell you how I know what she's doing, I just know. Please call me. I love you. Faith.

Christian grabbed a bottled water from the fridge, then headed back through the living room toward the balcony. It had to be Faith just trying to do anything she could to come between Allison and him. Had to be.

As Christian passed the couch, he noticed a manila folder poking out of a pocket of Nigel's briefcase. He stopped and peered at it. The tab was marked "Project CES." SEC backward, he realized. He moved closer, then glanced toward the balcony. Nigel and Quentin were talking. He pulled the folder out of Nigel's briefcase and opened it. On top was a copy of an e-mail from a woman named Sylvia Brawn at a CST address. The message was short.

Nigel, I've finished Project CES. What now? Syl.

Below the message were several telephone numbers for Sylvia. Christian checked the date of the e-mail. Two days ago. A different name than Nigel had given him—Michelle Wan, Nigel had said—and this e-mail indicated that the project was complete—again, not ongoing as Nigel had said. Maybe it was a different project, but that possibility seemed remote.

He glanced back at the BlackBerry still lying on the counter, tempted to call Faith. Who to trust? It was a question he'd asked himself over and over today. But there wasn't any answer.

DAHL HAD BEEN working late tonight on an urgent project, classified, top secret: the invasion of another Arab country.

A month ago the National Security Administration had started picking up an immense amount of chatter indicating that there was going to be another massive terrorist attack in the United States—on the scale of 9/11—planned for late summer. The coded messages had ultimately led directly back to the Arab country in question, implicating the country's senior officials of complying with the terrorists, and the president of the United States had made a quick decision—U.S. forces would make a preemptive strike.

But there had to be a rock-solid justification for invading a country that prior to this had been perceived by the American public—wrongly, though—as an ally of the United States. The president couldn't just tell everyone he thought there was going to be a terrorist attack and that he was "pretty sure" the army would find evidence of terrorism and complicity by the Arab government when they invaded, then not find it. They *had* to find it this time. Genuine or planted, it had to be there for the news cameras. That was what Dahl and his team had been working so hard on for the last month. Making *certain* that the evidence would be found when the troops rolled in.

"Driver," Dahl called.

"Yes, General?"

It was almost midnight and they were headed from the Pentagon to Dahl's house in Chevy Chase, Maryland. His wife had some family money, otherwise he wouldn't have been able to afford a home in such an upscale area near Washington, D.C. Even the Joint Chiefs weren't paid that well.

"I want to stop at the Peking Duck." Dahl's favorite Chinese restaurant. He was starving and his wife had told him over the phone before she went to bed that there wasn't anything to eat in the house. So he'd called ahead and placed an order for shrimp fried rice, his favorite. "We've got to hurry," he said loudly, checking his watch. "The place closes at midnight. That only gives us ten minutes."

"Yes, sir."

Dahl flicked on a small light in the backseat, donned his reading glasses, and pulled out a report from his briefcase.

When they reached the restaurant, the parking lot was almost empty.

"Hurry," Dahl urged to the driver as the man wheeled the car up to the front door. "The order is under my name."

The car skidded to a stop, then the driver hopped out and hurried into the restaurant.

Dahl relaxed into the seat, glad the restaurant door hadn't been locked. The man who owned the place was a stickler about closing exactly at midnight. He didn't make exceptions for anyone, not even a five-star general. Dahl smacked his lips. He could already taste the fried rice.

As Dahl glanced back down at the report in his lap, a white Volvo screeched to a stop beside the car and three men jumped out, clutching Uzi machine guns, their faces hidden by plaid scarves. Dahl realized instantly what was happening and reached frantically for the lock button—the car was bulletproof if it was secure—but he was a second late.

The man who'd leapt from the Volvo's front passenger seat wrenched open Dahl's door and opened fire, riddling Dahl's body and head with bullets. Dahl's reading glasses flew from his nose as his body slumped to the right and the lenses shattered against the blood-spattered far window.

Dahl's driver raced out the restaurant door, pistol drawn, but was cut down instantly in a burst of fire from the other two assassins. He tumbled to the asphalt, clutching his stomach and screaming, blood pouring from his body.

"Praise be to Allah!" the assassin who had killed Dahl shouted, raising his weapon above his head in victory. Then he sprinted back to the idling Volvo along with the other two men and raced off.

A few minutes later, the owner of the restaurant opened the front door and peeked out at the carnage. He could hear sirens in the distance, growing closer. He'd called 9-1-1 moments after he'd heard the first shots, but that hadn't been quick enough to save his friend General Dahl. There was no way he could have. The attack had taken less than thirty seconds.

"**WHAT IS IT, BLANTON?**" Hewitt snapped. He sat across from McDonnell in the back of the limousine as it idled in the Newark Airport parking lot, the lights of Manhattan glowing in the distance. He wasn't even trying to hide his irritation. "Hurry up."

"I'm sorry, I—"

"I was supposed to be out of here and headed back to Texas three hours ago," Hewitt complained, checking his watch. "I'd almost be there by now."

"It's important, Samuel. Believe me. Thanks for taking the time."

"Well?"

McDonnell had reached Hewitt by phone just as Hewitt was boarding. Reached him to say that there was an emergency at Jamison & Jamison, an emergency the board of directors needed to know about. He couldn't tell Hewitt the truth on a cell phone.

"Blanton," Hewitt said, exasperated, "out with it."

"This doesn't have anything to do with Jamison and Jamison," McDonnell admitted. "Is the intercom to the front seat off?"

Hewitt checked. "It is now," he said, flipping the switch. "Now *what is it?*"

"It's about the Order."

Hewitt's expression tightened, the wrinkles at the corners of his mouth suddenly more pronounced. "What about the Order?"

"Mace Kohler." McDonnell had almost turned around fifty times on his way to see Hewitt, but now he was resolved. This was the right thing to do—for everybody. "You know Mace doesn't agree with you about Jesse Wood, that's been pretty obvious during the last two meetings. He thinks Wood ought to have a chance to run the country. You don't."

Hewitt nodded. "People can disagree."

"Kohler's convinced you're going to have Senator Wood assassinated if he wins the election in November. Kohler's convinced Wood will never make it to the inauguration."

"*What?* That's absurd!" Hewitt thundered. "I told everyone at the last meeting that we didn't have to do anything, that I'm sure Wood isn't going to win. Even if he did win somehow," Hewitt added, squeezing the armrest, "I wouldn't have him killed. That, Blanton, is insane."

"Of course, it is." McDonnell hesitated. "Kohler told me about Franklin Laird and Stewart Massey, about how they were both dead. He saw the newspaper articles."

Hewitt's expression softened. "Yeah, it's awful," he said hoarsely. "They were both good men."

"Well, Kohler didn't think so."

"What do you mean?"

"He acted like he was glad they were gone."

Hewitt clenched his teeth. "What is Mace's problem?"

McDonnell swallowed hard. He hated ratting out a friend, but he'd be guilty by association if he didn't do something. He'd noticed the way Hewitt was looking at him during the last meeting, like he was Kohler's accomplice or something. He couldn't have his tapes floating around out there for his wife to use in divorce court, couldn't live like a pauper in a one-bedroom Jersey City condominium with nothing but stick furniture, couldn't bear giving up the CEO post at Jamison & Jamison. He couldn't do those things. *Wouldn't* do those things. He loved his life too much. And he was starting to think maybe it was Kohler who was off his rocker, not Hewitt. Even if that was a convenient change of heart to have.

"I think Mace might be the one who killed Laird and Massey," McDonnell said quietly. "Or had them killed."

Hewitt had been looking out the window. His eyes moved slowly to McDonnell's. "What did you say?"

"I think Kohler might have had Laird and Massey killed." McDonnell looked down. "I don't have anything concrete to go on—it's just a feeling—and I feel terrible for saying it. I'm sure I've violated several sections of the Order's code, but I don't want anyone else to get hurt."

"Blanton," Hewitt said comfortingly, "you did the right thing. I'm glad you came to me." He hesitated. "I guess I need to tell you something."

McDonnell looked up. Hewitt's eyes were burning. "What, Samuel?"

"I think you're right," Hewitt said, his voice barely audible. "I told Dahl I thought someone inside the Order was responsible for Laird and Massey's deaths. I didn't say who, but I thought it was Kohler all along. At first I thought maybe it was just me, that I was reading too much into the way he was acting, what he was saying, but now I know I was right."

Both men were quiet for a few moments.

"I'm worried about my safety," McDonnell finally spoke up. "Yours, too. Everybody who's left, really. I was with Mace this afternoon. I think he saw that I was wondering what was wrong with him. You should have seen his face, should have heard his tone of voice. He was so cold. I've never seen anything like it before. It was scary."

Hewitt pulled out his cell phone. "Okay, I'm not going to screw around with this."

Thirty minutes later McDonnell had a bodyguard driving him home to Connecticut—thanks to Hewitt. Someone would be with him twenty-four hours a day from now on. He relaxed into the seat, feeling much safer. Thanking God he'd thrown his loyalty back to Hewitt.

MACE KOHLER had followed McDonnell from Manhattan to Newark Airport, then sat in his car in the parking lot and watched while McDonnell and Hewitt met. Watched McDonnell finally get out of Hewitt's limousine and hop into a dark sedan that pulled up beside it. Now he was following the sedan across the George Washington Bridge as it headed north on I-95, toward Connecticut and McDonnell's home, Kohler assumed.

McDonnell must have turned on him. He'd run to the master and told him everything to save his own ass, to make certain the tapes of him with that woman from the country club didn't get out, to make certain he stayed CEO of Jamison & Jamison, most important to keep himself safe. McDonnell didn't have the stomach for the right thing, didn't understand the sacrifices that had to be made sometimes.

But Kohler did. The most important thing he'd ever learned in the Green Berets. Sometimes men had to die.

CHRISTIAN PEERED through his apartment door's peephole and saw Allison. "Hi," he said, opening the door. It was late for her to be coming by, almost midnight.

She lived in the same building, had ever since she'd moved from Chicago, and it wasn't by coincidence. She'd admitted as much a few weeks after starting at Everest Capital. Claimed she'd chosen his building because that made her search quick. Clearly, Christian wouldn't live in a dump so why not just piggyback off the research he must have done while he was looking for a place. But that explanation had always sounded hollow to Christian. There were plenty of nice buildings in Manhattan, and it wasn't that hard to find them.

"What's up?"

"What's up?" Allison asked, a disdainful look scrunching her face. "What kind of greeting is that? Am I your pal or something now? I thought things had gone a little further than that the other night."

This was what Christian hated about a relationship with a woman becoming more than a friendship—in this case, simply appearing that it *might become* more than a friendship. Everything—words, actions, looks—were suddenly parsed, critiqued, and interpreted so much more intensely. Simple mistakes or slips of the tongue that were quickly forgotten before now turned into ten-alarm blazes. He and Quentin never had that problem, neither had he and Nigel. He'd had frustrations with both men, but they'd always worked things out quickly, and there'd *never* been a problem over something trivial—like a greeting.

Of course, maybe his greeting had been a little formal. Quentin had confirmed that somebody within the Wallace organization had tipped off the SEC about CST, and there were signals that Allison was involved. But he just couldn't believe she had anything to do with it. It had to be Gordon Meade. Of course, the next question was: Why?

"I'm sorry," she said quickly, moving through the doorway into the apartment's foyer. "That was pretty lame."

"What do you mean?"

"For giving you a hard time about the way you said hi."

That was a new one. Someone actually admitting right away that a snipe for something trivial was silly. "You want something to drink?" he asked.

She shook her head.

"Come on, party girl, I've got some champagne in the fridge."

"Would you drink some with me?"

"Ally—"

She held her hands up right away. "I don't want to drink alone tonight. Besides, I'm tired. I really should get to bed. I'm heading out to the West Coast early in the morning."

He gazed at Allison for a few moments. Faith had sent him that e-mail accusing Allison of faking a romantic interest in him so she could take over Everest Capital. Which, as he'd thought more about it, meant someone had told Faith he was leaving, voluntarily or because he was being forced out, though not necessarily because he'd been tapped as a vice presidential candidate. Why else would Faith think there was an opportunity for Allison to take over Everest?

But he still wasn't convinced Allison was dealing from the bottom of the deck. There was something about her that told him she wouldn't do that, something in his gut that told him she would never turn on him. And he'd learned to trust his gut because it was usually right. *Usually.*

"You think you're close with the Aero Systems people?" he asked.

She nodded. "I think the family who owns the company is going to agree to sell it to me this time. I've offered a few more things, and they seem to like the package."

"Make sure we get an exclusive," he reminded her. "Don't let them keep shopping the deal. Put some teeth in your breakup fee."

"Of course, of course. Look, I need to talk to you about something. It's important. That's why I stopped by."

"What's up?"

"Faith Cassidy approached me in Central Park today. Accosted me, really. I went out there at lunchtime to do some thinking, to get away from the phones. I was writing some notes and all of a sudden she was standing in front of me. For a second I thought she was going to attack me or something, but all she wanted to do was talk." Allison paused. "Well, threaten me in a couple of ways, too, but at least she didn't get violent or anything."

Christian had half expected Faith to surprise him sometime—she'd done it before. But her confronting Allison had never even crossed his mind. "How did she *threaten* you?"

"Said she had people who would do her favors. Said someone had told her I was angling to run Everest by trying to get you to fall in love with me," Allison explained. "So that when you left you'd name me chairman."

It was so hard to tell what was really going on here because the stakes were so high. Was Allison truly just reporting back to him on exactly what had happened? Or, figuring Faith would call Christian like she said she would in the park, was Allison telling him everything so it *appeared* she was just reporting back? Was this really just a preemptive strike? "I never told Faith I was leaving Everest."

"Well, she knew." Allison cocked her head. "You don't seem very surprised by all this."

Christian nodded toward the BlackBerry lying on the kitchen counter. "She e-mailed me about it."

Allison's expression soured. "You two still talking?"

"Nope. She's e-mailed and called me a bunch of times, but I haven't responded."

"Uh-huh." Allison made a face like she didn't care one way or the other. "Like I said, she knew you were leaving."

"Did she tell you *why* she thought I was leaving Everest? What I was going to do after I left?"

Allison hesitated, trying to remember. "No, I don't think so."

"The only people I've told about Jesse Wood asking me to be vice president are you, Quentin, and Nigel." He left off Hewitt. There was no need to get into that whole thing right now. Obviously, Allison knew about Black Brothers—she'd gone to the initial meeting with Fleming. But he hadn't told her about Hewitt and U.S. Oil. And he hadn't been specific with Gordon Meade or any of the other Everest investors about *why* he suddenly felt so positive about the Laurel Energy sale.

Allison moved back to the door. "Have you thought about who wants you to leave Everest Capital the least?"

"No."

"Well, *I* have. Quentin Stiles."

"I'll always take care of Quentin," Christian said quickly.

"What do you mean, 'take care of' him?" Allison asked.

Christian shrugged. "He's my best friend. I'll take him with me to Washington."

"Oh, I'm sure he'd *love* that. Making seventy thousand a year again as a government employee."

She had a good point. "Then he'll stay at Everest."

"Christian, let's be honest. Quentin's your special projects guy. Without you here, there isn't nearly as much for him to do."

"You or Nigel would take care of him."

"Speaking of Nigel," she said, raising her voice, "he'd have a lot of incentive to call Faith, too. If Nigel can convince you that I'm not really interested in a romantic relationship with you, that I'm just using you, then he thinks maybe you'll react by giving him the chairman job, not me."

"You've got it all figured out, don't you?"

"I've learned from the best over the last few years." Allison smiled coyly, pointing at Christian. "This I do know," she said, opening the apartment door. "Quentin really wants you to stay." She moved out into the hallway. "And so do I."

"**JUST PULL IN THERE** beside the Escalade," McDonnell directed, leaning over the front seat and pointing at the big white SUV his wife drove. It was parked to the right of the four-car garage. "You're spending the night, right?" he asked nervously. He'd made his play and he didn't want his family to be unprotected—especially tonight. The more he thought about it, the more he didn't trust Mace Kohler. The guy had been a Green Beret. He'd take revenge if he figured out what had happened.

"I'm staying," the bodyguard assured McDonnell. "I'm with you twenty-four seven. Those were Mr. Hewitt's orders."

The bodyguard had shown up at the limousine no more than thirty minutes after Hewitt had placed a call requesting security. McDonnell hadn't bothered to ask how Hewitt could arrange something like that so fast, he'd just been glad Hewitt could. Still was. "Good." As he got out of the car, McDonnell glanced around at the trees surrounding the huge house. It would be so damn easy for someone to sneak up on them.

"Could you go over the house's alarm system?" the bodyguard asked as they moved quickly to the back door. "I'm assuming you have one."

"Yes, yes we do," McDonnell said, glancing over his shoulder one more time before moving inside. He could have sworn he saw something moving in the trees.

18

ELIJAH FORTE made certain he was very careful seeing Jesse Wood. He didn't get together with Jesse often—twice a month, max—but the meetings were meticulously planned so *no one* outside the inner circle knew about them. As the Shadows had told Jesse in the beginning, it wouldn't do him any good to be publicly associated with them, or vice versa. They were all very careful about getting together with him, but none more than Forte. It was for this reason that Forte found himself sitting in Room 14 of a no-name motel on the outskirts of Cleveland, Ohio.

Jesse had been campaigning heavily in Ohio in advance of the Democratic convention—now just a few weeks away. He had the nomination locked up, that was clear. But he hadn't won the Ohio primary back in the spring, and the state was going to be a key to victory in November. One of those three or four swing states the political pundits had already declared would decide the election—as if voters in all the other states across the country didn't really need to bother going to the polls.

"How much longer? When are you guys going to get here?"

Forte glanced over at Heath Johnson, who was talking on his cell phone to one of Jesse's bodyguards. He and Johnson were the only people in the motel room.

"Got it," Johnson said curtly. "Jesse should be here in less than ten minutes," he informed Forte, hanging up. "They just finished the rally at the convention center downtown. Great turnout, too."

"What about Jack Daly?" Daly had won the Ohio primary, then dropped out of the race when it was obvious Jesse would win the nomination. "Was he onstage with Jesse?"

Johnson nodded. "Gave Jesse his full backing. We didn't know if he would until the last minute, but he did. Party headquarters twisted his arm."

"Good." Forte was tired of waiting, tired of sitting in this dingy room that looked like it was rented out by the hour more often than for the night. He'd answered all the e-mails he had the patience for and slashed through several quarterly reports from companies he owned—dashing off terse notes to a couple of the CEOs on how they could improve operations. "How many people does Jesse have with him?"

"Just two."

"Not Osgood and Stephanie, right?"

"No. Just the two security people, like you wanted."

Forte could tell that Johnson didn't like the idea of Jesse having only two bodyguards. "Jesse'll be fine, Heath. Don't worry."

"We've put a lot of time and energy into Jesse Wood, boss, and we're finally on the brink of making history. We should be more careful about protecting him from now on. He'll be a target, you know that. There's plots being hatched out there right now, no doubt, by people who understand that Jesse will probably be the next president of the United States. We shouldn't get careless or cut corners this late in the game."

"I *never* get careless and I *never* cut corners," Forte answered firmly. "You know that."

"Until Jesse is officially the Democratic party's nominee, he doesn't get Secret Service. Until then, it's up to us."

"This has to be *at least* the fiftieth time you've told me that. I understand, believe me. Like I said, he'll be fine." Forte needed to get Johnson thinking about something else. He was starting to obsess about Jesse Wood's personal safety, which could get in the way. "A while back you told me the one big thing you didn't like about Christian Gillette being Jesse's running mate was that we might be handing the Oval Office back to a white man eight years from now." Forte watched Johnson ease back into his chair. "Right?"

"Yeah, I said that." Johnson crossed his arms over his chest defensively. "Christian Gillette has star power. He could easily get elected after Jesse's done. The other thing is, we don't know how Gillette's going to react to the platform yet. He's got a lot of friends on the other side of the fence, in Whiteyville, and he might not like some of the things we want Jesse to do. Gillette might not be wild about Puerto Rico becoming a state, might not want us trying to restructure voting districts so blacks have more power and whites have less, might not like us raising the capital gains tax rate, naming as many black judges as we can, taking away big business deductions in the—"

"Yeah, yeah," Forte said, waving away Johnson's concerns. "Jesse isn't going to tell Christian about any of that at their meeting, and once we're in the White House we'll keep Christian on the road. He'll be nothing but a goodwill ambassador. He'll be in Africa, Asia, Europe, South America. He'll have more miles on him than the space shuttle, and he'll be completely in the dark. He won't know what we're doing until he reads it in the newspaper."

"That doesn't solve the first problem," Johnson pointed out. "Him being elected president when Jesse's done. What about that?"

"I'm gonna do the same thing to Gillette I'm doing to Jesse. Except in Gillette's case, I'll actually use what I find." Forte chuckled. "Or claim I find. The way I see it, we'll feed it to the press halfway through the second term. Gillette will be forced to resign and Jesse will name a black man as Gillette's replacement. That'll give the country two years to get comfortable with whoever we bring in." Forte chuckled. "I told you, Heath, don't worry so much. I've got it all under control."

"What's the *it,* boss?"

"What do you mean?"

"What are you going to find out about Gillette?" Johnson asked.

"Don't know yet, but we'll find something. Maybe him talking bad about blacks *while he's actually in office*. Using the *N* word a few times."

"Gillette would never be stupid enough to do that, not in front of a camera, anyway."

"You probably would have said that about Jesse before you saw the clip."

Johnson nodded grudgingly. "You're right."

"We've got six years," Forte said confidently. "You know me. I'll find something." Forte glanced over at a bureau in one corner of the room. Atop it was a portable combination television/CD player Johnson had brought with them from California. "Everything ready?" he asked, standing up.

"Yeah."

Forte walked to the window, pushed up one of the slats of the closed blind, and peered out at the gloomy day. It had been raining off and on since last night. Through the drizzle he saw a gray sedan approaching. As he watched, it turned into the motel parking lot and rolled quickly toward him. Jesse Wood hopped out of the backseat and sprinted for the door. Forte opened it just as Jesse reached for the knob.

"Hi, guys," Jesse said enthusiastically, brushing water from his jacket as he moved into the room. He pumped Forte's hand, then Johnson's. "God, we just had a great rally, guys. I mean, it was awesome."

Forte pointed to a chair in front of the bureau. "We need to talk."

Jesse's mood soured instantly. "Let's not get into the bad stuff now, Elijah," he pleaded. "I don't want to talk about firing Stephanie and Osgood. I'm on a real high. God, I think we might actually carry Ohio after all. You should have seen the people down there, thousands of them, a lot of them with tears in their eyes. And not just blacks."

"That's fine, Jesse, just fine. But the mark of a truly great politician lies in his ability to handle any situation, moment to moment, good or bad, and stay calm. This is one of those tough situations. This will be good training for when you're actually president."

Jesse shook his head. "*I told you, Elijah,* I'm not firing Stephanie or Osgood, and that's *final.* I'm not getting rid of two people who've been so loyal to me over the last few years. You're just going to have to accept that." He hesitated. "I'm not sure I'm going to accept your choice of vice president, either," he said, his voice strengthening when Forte didn't try to cut him off. "Nothing against Christian Gillette, he seems like a decent guy. But I want someone else, someone I choose. I'm in charge now. I've made decisions, and I'm not going to change them. Not for anything or anyone."

Jesse had become empowered, Forte saw, caught up in the euphoria of the rally downtown, starting to think he could call his own shots now. "Really? Not for *anyone*?"

Jesse stuck his chin out defiantly. "Nope. Not even you."

Forte glanced down, trying to seem discouraged.

"You've been good to me, Elijah," Jesse continued, "and I appreciate everything you've done for me. And of course I'll always listen to your counsel when I'm president. But it's time for me to take over. It's the natural progression."

Forte took a deep, defeated breath, then motioned to Johnson. "Heath."

Johnson moved to the portable television and turned it on.

"What's going on?" Jesse asked, watching Johnson. "What's this?"

Forte sat down beside Jesse and put his hand on Jesse's knee. "This, Jesse," he said in a quiet voice, "is your smoking gun. Your Monica Lewinsky, your Watergate, your Waterloo. The good thing for you is that no one knows about it except me and Heath. Not yet, anyway. And no one else ever *will* know about it, as long as you play ball. As long as you don't get cocky on me ever again."

The screen cleared and images rolled. The same ones Forte and Johnson had watched at Johnson's house. Jesse, Osgood, Stephanie, and Jefferson Roundtree standing in a tight group; Jesse starting his Whitey diatribe; the others chiming in.

When it was over, Forte pulled a handkerchief from his pocket and handed it to Jesse. "Here."

"Thanks," Jesse mumbled, dabbing at the beads of sweat covering his forehead. "Can I have something to drink?" he asked, like a man condemned.

"Heath, could you get Jesse some water please?"

"How did you get that?" Jesse asked, his voice barely audible.

"It doesn't matter *how* I got it, I got it."

Johnson was back quickly from the bathroom with a glass of water. Jesse took it and finished it in several gulps.

"More?"

Jesse wiped his mouth with the back of his hand. "No."

"What we have here is a game of chicken, Jesse," Forte said calmly, nodding at the television. "You might think I'd never show that clip to anyone. You figure I won't, because then I'd lose everything I've worked so hard for: a black president. So you start thinking you can do whatever you want to at this point. That you've got me by the balls." He held his palm out flat, then slowly curled his fingers until he'd made a tight fist. "But what you need to understand, Jesse, is that this isn't just about having a black president for me. It's about more than that, much more. It's about having a black president who does what I want when I want. Frankly, without that control, I don't care much, I really don't." Forte gathered himself up in his chair, then put a hand on Jesse's shoulder, ready to deliver the final, fatal blow. "You disobey me in any way from this moment on, and I release that clip to the press. You know what will happen then? It'll become one of the most-played videos in history, it'll become part of our national lore. You'll be destroyed, you'll become an outcast. I'll go back to being a billionaire, but you'll end up resigning from the Senate and begging your ex-partners to let you practice law again so you can put your kids through college. But your ex-partners won't want you. *No one* will. You'll sell your story to the History Channel for one of those sad biography documentaries, but that'll be the end of the road. After that, you'll be begging on street corners. Or selling some racquet you claim you won the U.S. Open with on eBay just to make a few bucks. It'll be pathetic." Forte leaned back and smiled over at Johnson behind Jesse's back. Jesse had his face in his hands. His defiance had disintegrated. "Just do what I tell you, Jesse," Forte said softly, "and everything will be fine."

Jesse swallowed hard.

Forte smiled thinly. He loved it when a plan came together. He'd waited for just the right moment to go for the throat. When Jesse was on a high, when Jesse could just about taste and smell the Oval Office. Forte checked his watch. Almost four o'clock. "Don't you have a fundraiser back downtown tonight?"

Jesse nodded.

"Well, you better get going." Forte was about to get up but hesitated. "There's something at the end of the clip I want to ask you about."

Jesse looked over. "Huh?"

Forte nodded at Johnson. "Play it back, Heath."

"Sure."

"There," Forte said, pointing at the screen. Pointing at Jesse touching Stephanie's thigh. "What's that all about?"

"Nothing."

"It's not the kind of gesture I'd expect you to make to a coworker." Forte raised one eyebrow. "Or a friend. Anything going on with you and Stephanie I should know about?"

"No."

"Or maybe your wife should know about?"

"No, I swear it, nothing. Please, Elijah."

Forte loved it. Jesse was back on his side, right back where he was supposed to be, as malleable as he'd ever been. Forte pointed at the television again. "What the hell were you thinking about when you said those things?"

Jesse's expression turned glum. "Obviously, I wasn't."

▪ ▪ ▪

TODD HARRISON stared at the photograph he'd taken from the frame in the kitchen of the lodge on Champagne Island. In it were nine men, two of whom he'd recognized immediately from newspaper pictures: ex–United States senator Stewart Massey and former Federal Reserve chairman Franklin Laird. And then there was that third face.

Harrison put the picture down on the desk and began to boot up his computer. George Bishop had disappeared; there'd been no word from him for a while. His boat was moored where it always was, but his car wasn't in the apartment complex parking lot. Harrison had gone to the police, but they wouldn't start looking for Bishop without probable cause—which they said they didn't have. They'd said he was a drifter, in and out of town, and assumed he'd show up again at some point when he needed to make a few bucks. He was on a joy ride somewhere was the explanation they'd given. In the Caribbean getting drunk, like he was known to do every few months.

Now Harrison was worried about himself. He'd quickly moved into a place a few miles away and holed up, putting off deadlines by not answering the phone, then calling back at times when he knew his editors wouldn't be around. But he wasn't sure moving around was going to do him any good. He'd thought about going way far away and starting over, maybe even out of the country. But these people in the photograph were obviously powerful, very powerful, and he was afraid they'd track him down no matter where he went. He wanted to go to the authorities to get help for himself, but he knew he couldn't go to them with just a picture and a ghost story from an old man.

He typed Stewart Massey's name into Google and clicked "search."

FROM THE BACKSEAT of the sedan, Jesse stared out at an endless string of strip malls lining the wide, four-lane road as he headed back downtown for the fund-raiser. It had stopped raining and the sky was clearing in the west. Maybe that was a sign, he hoped. He shook his head. Wishful thinking. He was a puppet and that was that.

How the hell had Forte gotten that damn clip?

Jesse had always worried about that thing being out there somewhere—Osgood had gone after the guy when they realized what was going on, but the cameraman had gotten away. It was his only mistake in hiring Osgood—it took the guy two days to run the hundred-yard dash. Osgood had come back from the chase looking like he was about to have a heart attack. Jesse closed his eyes. He'd almost convinced himself the clip was gone, that it would never be a problem.

"Senator Wood."

Jesse opened his eyes. It was the bodyguard in the passenger seat in front of him.

"Sorry to disturb you, sir."

"It's all right."

"We're going to stop at the next gas station to fill up. It'll only take a few minutes. We'll have you back downtown no later than five thirty, in plenty of time for the dinner."

"Thanks." He sighed. He was going to *have* to let Stephanie and Osgood go now. He didn't have any choice.

THE MAN checked his watch as he stood on the roof of the warehouse, leaning on the cinder-block retaining wall, waiting for the sedan to appear. It was late; it should have been to him by now.

Then he saw it, coming through a light three blocks up, swerving out from behind a furniture delivery truck. He took a quick look through his binoculars to check the license, just to make sure, to confirm that this was what he'd been waiting for. It was.

He picked up the hunting rifle, sighted in the target, and fired.

DON ROTH gazed at the photograph Harrison had left in the frame in the lodge kitchen. Harrison had taken the one Patty had painstakingly put together, the one that had been in the frame when they went to the kitchen after finishing the tour of the lodge's third floor. And Harrison had left this one. Switched them before he left—while Roth left the kitchen the second time. They'd never actually said a word to each other about doing that, but somehow they'd understood what was going to happen. Clearly, Harrison had realized that Roth intentionally left the picture of the nine men who came to Champagne Island for him to find. In return, Harrison had taken the photograph of the old man he'd snapped in the bar that night out of his backpack and left it for Roth. The photo of the old man who'd told Harrison the story about Champagne Island.

Roth shook his head. He'd recognized the old man in the photograph Harrison had left right away. It was one of the men who came to the island, the one he'd overheard the others call Benson. The one who'd committed suicide down by the ocean with the Colt revolver, whose body he'd carried to the freezer in the basement of the lodge that night after Hewitt had roused him. Obviously, Benson had been trying to get Harrison to investigate what was going on at the island. *Why,* he didn't know. Maybe because Benson knew there was something wrong but couldn't be the whistle-blower because he'd put his own life in jeopardy. But then why would he commit suicide?

Patty had thought he didn't know what she was doing the whole time she was sneaking around the woods, taking pictures of the men as they got out of the helicopters or went down to the ocean to fish. She thought he didn't know what the magnifying glass and the tweezers were for. She'd given him the photograph the night before they'd killed her, telling him he might need it someday. Roth felt the lump in his throat growing bigger as he thought about her. He missed her so much—and he owed her.

He put the picture down and glanced over at the young woman lying on the couch, hands and feet bound. She didn't have a chance without him.

"**WHAT! OH MY GOD!**"

Forte glanced over at Johnson, who was on the phone again. Forte had been thinking about Stephanie Childress. How pretty she was, how he hadn't taken much time for romance in his life, how he was getting old. How Stephanie was getting old, too.

"Jesus Christ! I knew it." Johnson ended the call and glared at Forte. "Somebody took a shot at Jesse while he was on his way back downtown to the fund-raiser. Goddamn, it, Elijah, I told you this could happen."

"Was Jesse hit?" Forte asked calmly.

"No, he's okay, but one of the bodyguards took a bullet to the shoulder. He was taken to a hospital. They think he'll be all right, but he's critical."

"Well, the important thing is that Jesse's okay."

Johnson gazed at Forte, awed by his nonchalance. Then his jaw dropped. "You didn't," he whispered.

Forte chuckled. "You kept making the case for me, Heath. You were the one who said Jesse wouldn't get Secret Service protection until he was officially the nominee. I'll bet the Secret Service protects him now. If they don't, the government will look pretty bad, almost like they want him dead. So you know they'll give him Secret Service, probably a bigger force than normal. Which serves two purposes. First, it'll be almost impossible for anyone to get to Jesse now. Second, now he'll look like he's already the president."

"You hired the shooter?" Johnson asked incredulously.

Forte flipped on the car radio. "If that's what you want to believe, Heath, I'm not going to stop you."

"My God, boss, what if the guy had hit—"

"Shh," Forte hissed, holding up his hand as the disc jockey interrupted the song that was playing to make the announcement. Beaming a smile that stretched almost from ear to ear after the DJ announced that there had been an assassination attempt on Senator Jesse Wood's life. That the leading Democratic presidential candidate was apparently unhurt but that one of his bodyguards had been seriously injured. "Fantastic publicity," Forte murmured. "The kind of stuff we dream about when we release a big album at the hip-hop label. I can't wait to see how the cable news stations cover it."

Johnson shook his head in amazement. "Unbelievable."

"Thank you." Forte took out his cell phone and dialed. "Jesse? You all right? Good, I'm glad. What? Really? *No, no, don't change it.* You keep it on, you hear me? And take your jacket off when you give your speech. Let people see it. Right. Good luck tonight."

"What was that all about?" Johnson asked as Forte hung up.

"When the bodyguard was shot, Jesse's shirt got spattered pretty good with blood. I told him not to change it. It'll make for great TV tonight." Forte's smile grew even wider. "We're gonna win this thing in November, Heath. *I know it now.*"

19

"WHERE ARE YOU?"

"Black Brothers Allen," Christian answered, looking around the conference room as he spoke to Quentin by cell phone. "I'm waiting for Trenton Fleming. I'm here to sign the Laurel Energy engagement agreement. They're officially taking over the sale process from Morgan Stanley today."

"That's good, right?"

"I hope so. I don't think we have any other choice. I haven't heard anything more from Samuel Hewitt. He said he was going to talk to his CEO, but that was a few days ago and no word since."

"Aren't you going to see Hewitt in Texas at his ranch? The end of this week, right?"

"That was the plan, but his assistant called this afternoon to put it off. Hewitt had to go to China or something."

"That's too bad. Did you really have to go all the way down to Wall Street just to sign an engagement agreement?" Quentin asked. "Couldn't you have sent them a faxed copy of the signature page?"

"Morgan Stanley sent a bunch of information over here to Black Brothers for them to look at. Engineering reports, financial information, that kind of stuff. The people handling the deal for Black Brothers, the day-to-day people, wanted help going through it."

"Couldn't one of our young people have done that? One of the associates?"

"It won't take long. Besides, I was down here on another transaction anyway."

"Is Allison with you?"

"No." That faint alarm in the back of Christian's brain went off. "Why?"

"I just wondered."

"Need her for something?"

"No. I was just wondering if she was around."

Quentin was probably trying to see how much time they were spending together, probably all there was to that question. "She's in San Francisco, working on the Aero Systems deal." He wouldn't have even have stopped to think about Quentin's motive behind asking the question except that Allison had pointed out why Quentin wouldn't want things to change around Everest Capital. And the more Christian thought about what she'd said, the more he realized she was right. She and Nigel wouldn't use Quentin like he did. They'd try, at least for a while, but it wouldn't be the same. She'd just been honest. It was one of the things Christian respected about her.

"If you need her, call her on her cell phone. You got that number?"

"Yeah, yeah. Well, I hope Black Brothers can bring home the bacon on Laurel Energy because—"

Suddenly Quentin stopped talking and for a few moments there was dead air, then Christian heard garbled voices in the background. "Quentin," he said loudly. "Quentin!"

"Hold on, Chris. Jesus, I— *Wow!*"

"What is it?" Christian demanded. "What's wrong?"

"It's . . . really? Are you *sure*?"

Christian couldn't tell who Quentin was talking to. Him or someone at the other end. "Quentin!"

"Yeah, Chris, I'm back. You gotta turn on CNN."

"Why?" Christian glanced around the conference room, but there wasn't a television in sight. From the sound of Quentin's voice, his first thought was that there had been another major terrorist attack. "What's going on?"

"It's Jesse Wood."

"What about him?"

"Somebody tried to kill him."

"What?" Suddenly the blood was pounding in Christian's brain. "When?"

"A few minutes ago," Quentin answered quickly. "Jesse was on his way to some fund-raiser in Cleveland and somebody took a shot at him while the car he was riding in was stopped at a red light."

Christian knew about the fund-raiser. They'd spoken yesterday and Jesse had told him about it. "Was he hit? Is he all right?"

"Hold on."

Christian heard more muffled voices, then Quentin came back on the line.

"Jesse's fine, at least, according to CNN. One of the men riding in the car with him was hit . . . may have been killed."

"Do they know who the guy was?" It could easily have been Clarence Osgood. "Are they saying?"

"No, they're just reporting it was a bodyguard. No name."

That didn't sound like Osgood. Very few people would mistake him for a bodyguard, but you never knew. There was always so much confusion right after something like this happened.

"Aren't you meeting with Jesse all day tomorrow?" Quentin asked. "To go over his platform?"

"Yeah, here in New York. He's supposed to be flying back from Cleveland tonight after his dinner. I'm meeting with him at ten o'clock."

"Maybe not now."

"Maybe not," Christian agreed grimly. Another call was coming in on his cell phone. "I gotta go, Quentin. I'll call you later." Christian switched lines. "Nigel?"

"Yes."

"Did you hear about Jesse Wood?"

"No. What happened?"

Christian quickly explained what Quentin had relayed.

"My God," Nigel exclaimed. "I'm turning on the television in my office right now. Are you at Black Brothers yet?"

"Yup. Waiting for Fleming. He should be here in a minute."

"Okay, I'll make this quick. Look, the SEC's been calling over to CST a lot. Four times today and the last time it was Vivian Davis. The only time she called before was to set up the meeting you and I had with her. It's been the worker bees since."

Bad news. Christian could feel it. "What did she want?"

"Bob Galloway said she was acting real cagey. No specific questions but a lot of cocky comments. Kinda like she was trying to distract him at the front door while the SWAT team was sneaking in through the back."

"Jesus. What are the attorneys saying?"

"To sit tight. They've called the SEC and demanded that we be kept up-to-date with what's going on. They said that's all they can do."

"What about the woman at CST you're working with?" Christian asked. He hadn't confronted Nigel yet about what he'd found in Nigel's briefcase—the different name—because it was impossible for him to believe that Nigel could be holding back in any way on this, but he wanted to. "Is she finished yet?" Christian could hear the hesitation at the other end of the phone. "Nigel?"

"Almost, almost."

"What's her name again?"

"Who?"

"The woman you're working with at CST."

"Michelle Wan."

"Right, Michelle Wan," Christian repeated, making certain Nigel knew he'd remember the name. The conference door opened and Fleming and Inkster appeared. He'd been about to ask. Now he couldn't. "I gotta go, Nigel."

Christian stood up and shook hands with Fleming and Inkster. "Did you guys hear about Jesse Wood?"

"I did," Fleming spoke up, sliding several copies of the Laurel Energy engagement letter across the table at Christian. "An awful thing. At least the senator wasn't hurt."

"Has that been confirmed?"

"I think so," Inkster spoke up.

"He wasn't hit," Fleming said firmly. "I just saw him on television before I walked in here. They showed him walking into a fund-raiser in Cleveland. He was waving to people." Fleming chuckled. "He's got a lot of security people around him now, I'll tell you that. It's like a swarm."

"Thank God he's all right."

Fleming looked up, keenly interested all of a sudden. "Is he your candidate, Christian?"

"Maybe."

A faint smile appeared on Fleming's lips. "Are you a Democrat?"

"Maybe." Christian watched Fleming's smile turn into a smirk. "Why? Would that be a shock?"

"It would be a surprise," Fleming admitted. "So?"

Fleming was pushing hard. "Why would it surprise you?"

Fleming shrugged. "Your father was a Republican, a very prominent Republican. I wouldn't think you'd turn on . . ." Fleming stopped himself. "Well, I just wouldn't think you'd be a Democrat." His smirk transformed into a polite smile. "It's really none of my business." He glanced at Inkster, then back at Christian. "Can you go ahead and sign the letter? We've already executed it."

Politics and religion. Two subjects you never touched when you didn't know exactly where the other person stood on each, especially in a business situation. It had been odd for Fleming to press the question when he was on the verge of landing such a huge sell-side deal. Odd that he'd risk pushing a client's button in such a way that might sour the deal. Maybe Fleming was confident that Everest Capital needed him so badly he felt like he could ask anything. Christian smiled to himself. The real shocker for Fleming would be seeing Christian standing beside Jesse Wood as the vice presidential candidate.

Christian pulled out a pen and signed the engagement letter, then reached into his jacket pocket, pulled out an envelope, and slid it across the table to Inkster. "Ten million dollars." It was a ton of cash for just a retainer, especially one with a no-refund policy. "I better get my money's worth." He watched Inkster look away and Fleming's face turn to stone.

"You'll get your money's worth," Fleming replied.

After going over a few logistical issues, Fleming bid a curt good-bye and had Inkster lead Christian down a hallway to another, smaller conference room.

"This will be the Laurel Energy war room," Inkster explained, pointing at the stacks of papers already covering the table. "This is Beverly," he said, introducing Christian to a young woman standing near the far wall of the room. "She'll be on the team, managing a lot of the details."

"Hi, Mr. Gillette," she said nervously.

Christian could see that she recognized him, probably from the *Forbes* or *Fortune* covers. "Call me Christian."

She nodded. "Okay."

"I've got to go to my office for a second," Inkster explained. "I'll be back in a minute. You and Bev can get started."

"Sure."

Beverly was short and cute with pretty red hair and freckles. "How long have you been with the firm?" Christian asked.

"About a year," she answered, moving to the table and starting to go through one of the piles. "I've read all about you, Mr., um, Christian. It's a real honor to work with you."

"That's nice," he said, not wanting to make much of it. He gestured at the table. "This looks like some kind of IQ test. Where do we start?"

She laughed. "I'd like to go over the list of companies Morgan Stanley already contacted about Laurel Energy. So Mr. Inkster knows exactly who's already seen the deal."

"Okay." Christian came around to her side of the table.

She pointed down. "This pile has all the comments back from people at the other companies who looked at the deal. It's arranged alphabetically."

Christian ran his finger down the tall pile. Near the bottom was a folder marked U.S. Oil. He pulled it out and opened it, interested to see who had turned it down. As he leafed through the pages, his eye caught something beside one of the gas reserve statistics that instantly sucked the breath out of him. A set of initials. SPH. Samuel Prescott Hewitt. In the exact same looping script Hewitt had used to sign his meal tab at Princeton.

Christian gazed at the initials. Samuel Hewitt had been lying to him all along. He'd seen the Laurel Energy deal months ago. Well before they'd met at Princeton.

FORTE KICKED OFF his shoes and relaxed contentedly onto the plush sofa of his hotel suite. It had been a long but successful night. The ten-thousand-dollar-a-plate fund-raiser had just broken up, and they'd raised almost ten million—a good chunk of change he wouldn't have to fund himself now. More important, the bloodstains on Jesse's white shirt had made a profound effect on the crowd and the throng of cameramen kneeling in front of the stage. Exactly as Forte had hoped.

In his introduction, the emcee had noted the blood before Jesse had taken the dais to make his speech. Senator Jesse Wood was a man on a mission, the emcee shouted, a man who wouldn't be denied the presidency. The crowd had roared its approval as Jesse bounded to the podium, fists raised. Forte had almost fallen for the hype himself.

Stephanie Childress sat in a chair across the room. He'd asked her to come back up here after the dinner to talk about the campaign. It wasn't unusual for them to be alone late like this. "You okay?"

She nodded. "Tired. Worried about Jesse, you know?"

"Of course," said Forte soothingly. "But there might actually be a silver lining to the assassination attempt."

"What?"

"Federal protection from now on. An hour ago Heath Johnson heard that Jesse will have full-time Secret Service starting immediately until the convention. For good, really," he added, "because we all know Jesse's going to win the nomination. And, Lord, the press coverage he's gotten from the shooting? Enormous. You can't begin to put a vote value on that. As his PR person, you've got to agree."

"I'd rather know he's safe."

"He'll be fine from now on, Stephanie." Forte patted the sofa beside where he was sitting. "Come here." He saw her hesitate. "I'm not gonna bite."

She got up slowly from the chair and sat down beside him.

"You're an incredible woman," he said, taking her hand.

"Thank you," she said softly.

"It took a lot of courage to come to me and tell me about Samuel Hewitt." He squeezed her fingers gently. "To tell me about him approaching you and trying to get you to give him information, to be his spy."

"I told you from the start, I want the best for Jesse. I'd do almost anything to get him elected."

Forte felt her squeeze back. She had to be so lonely. She'd carried the torch for Jesse all these years, but she had to see that it wasn't going to happen for them at this point. "Could you love anyone else?"

Her eyes shot to his. "What do you mean?" she snapped, jerking her hand away.

"Could you love someone besides Jesse?"

"There's nothing going on between us, Elijah. I love Jesse as a *person*. For who he is, what he stands for, and what he can do for our country. Not romantically."

"Hey, hey." Forte reached for her fingers again, marveling at her loyalty. "Easy. What's that all about?"

"What did you mean by the question?"

"I know about you and Jesse," he said, caressing the back of her hand lightly. "I know a long time ago for a short while there was a romance. Jesse told me that when I first started to back him. How you were there for him when he wasn't feeling very good about himself, when he realized his tennis days were just about over. He told me you two talked about marriage and children and a lot more, but it never worked out." Forte saw the emotion building in her expression. Tension lines, a tremor here and there on her face. Almost imperceptible but recognizable to the trained eye.

If there was one thing Forte knew how to do, it was get to and pull on people's deepest emotions. And really, it wasn't that hard. Nothing more than having the willingness to go there, to bring it up. Most people weren't willing to do that. They wanted to live on the surface where it was safer. "You must feel something for Jesse on a deeper level. I don't think you care about him just because he's a great man."

Stephanie's head tilted forward and a single tear coursed down her cheek.

"Put your head on my shoulder," Forte urged quietly, slipping his arm around her and pulling her close. "It's all right."

She pressed her face into his shirt. "I really thought he'd leave his wife at some point," she cried.

"I know."

"We were so right for each other."

"He told me that, too."

She sobbed. "But . . . but . . ."

"But he didn't leave his wife," Forte finished the sentence for her. "You can blame me for that."

"What?" Stephanie looked up. "Why?"

"I told him if he did, I wouldn't back him."

Forte hadn't actually said that to Jesse, it was just understood. There couldn't be a divorce in the past of the first black president. He had to be a storybook character, larger than life in a hundred years with no human frailties. A man who didn't yield to temptation or back out of lifetime commitments.

Forte rubbed her shoulder. "So you see, it was my fault."

Stephanie shook her head. "No," she said softly, "you were just protecting him."

"Maybe I had an ulterior motive."

She looked up at him again with a curious expression. "What do you mean?"

"I think you know."

She pivoted on the couch so they were facing each other. "No, I don't."

"I've always admired you, Stephanie. You're smart *and* beautiful.

I've always wondered if the two of us might be good together." Her eyes widened and he watched her search his face for the truth. Jesse must have told her not to trust him, worried that he might make this play someday. Understanding that he couldn't have her for himself but not wanting anyone else to have her either, especially the man who was manipulating him. "No kidding, I've always thought you had so much to offer."

"Why didn't you ever get married?" she asked.

"No time. I've devoted my life to two things. Making as much money as I could and improving the world for our people."

She was quiet for several moments. "Can I ask you a question?"

"Sure."

"Jesse always said you told him you had something on him, something very bad."

Forte suppressed a smile. This couldn't have been going any better. "He told you that, huh?"

"Is there something?"

She'd just answered so many of his questions. Forte nodded.

"What?"

He didn't have any problem telling her at this point. Maybe he could even use telling her to his advantage. "I have a clip of Jesse saying some very nasty things about white people. You're in it, so is Clarence Osgood. So is Jefferson Roundtree."

Stephanie gasped and put her hands to her face. "After that press conference, about a year ago. There was that cameraman."

"Yes."

"Clarence ran after that guy but couldn't catch him." She shook her head and grimaced. "He couldn't catch a lame turtle."

Forte chuckled snidely. "Clarence Osgood is faster than you think."

"Oh, I know, he's very sharp. But how did *you* get the clip?"

"Like I *said*, Osgood is faster than you think."

"Clarence *caught* the guy?" she asked, picking up on what Forte was telegraphing her.

"Caught him and paid him. He told you and Jesse he didn't, but he did. Paid the cameraman ten grand and got the clip."

"Clarence gave the clip to you?"

"There was a price." Half a million. Not enough for Osgood to retire on but enough. "I just showed it to Jesse for the first time this afternoon."

"But why would Clarence want you to have it?"

"He thought Jesse was getting too big a head. He thought I needed some way to hold him back, to control him."

"When did Clarence give it to you?"

"Six months ago."

Stephanie's expression grew grim. "Then why are you firing him?" She looked right into Forte's eyes. *"And me?"*

It took all the self-control Forte had not to give away his guilt. He made certain he didn't blink, made certain his eyebrows furrowed together as sincerely as possible. He was going to make at least one stab at trying to hold on to his innocence. "What in the world are you talking about?"

"Clarence found the e-mail from you to Jesse. Don't lie to me, Elijah."

Forte said nothing for a few moments, then gave in. "When did he find it?"

"At the end of March."

"How did he find it?"

She shrugged. "Like you said, I guess Clarence is faster than he seems. He must have figured out Jesse's password."

"When did he tell you about it?"

"As soon as he found it. He came right into my office."

Which would have been before Stephanie had come to Forte about Samuel Hewitt trying to recruit her. Apparently, they'd found the e-mail in March, but she'd come to him weeks after that. Suddenly he felt bad, which he rarely did. "I did send that e-mail," he admitted. "I've sent several of them to Jesse. One only a little while back. It's not that I don't have a lot of respect for you, Stephanie, you know I do. It's just that Jesse needs a different level of experience now, people who've worked for a president before. Being a senator's one thing; being president is quite another."

"I can do the job, Elijah. I know just as much as—"

Forte held up his hand, silencing her instantly. "I'm not going to discuss it," he said. "I've made up my mind." He took a deep breath. "What there will be for you is a permanent job at Ebony Enterprises. Head of corporate communications. That's a huge position at Ebony. You'll start at five hundred a year, and you'll get a piece of the company. You and Heath Johnson will be my two top officers."

"Five hundred *thousand*?" she asked incredulously.

"Yes." He touched her chin gently. "As long as you promise to have dinner with me once a week."

She sat straight up, pulling herself away from him for the second time. "I'm not going to be your half-a-million-dollar-a-year whore, Elijah," she snapped. "Even if I am getting old and ugly."

Forte laughed loudly. "You're still so beautiful, Stephanie, and I meant what I said. Dinner, just dinner. Hell, I have dinner with Johnson at least twice a week. I figure you can give me at least one night."

She couldn't hide her smile. "Well, I guess."

Forte's eyes narrowed. "Now, let me ask you a question. How upset was Osgood when he found the e-mail I sent Jesse about getting rid of you two?" He knew the answer, but he wanted to see the reaction in Stephanie's eyes so he could judge exactly how pissed off Osgood had been. What the man might do.

She didn't hesitate. "I've never seen him madder."

HEWITT SAT on a leather couch in the living room of Trenton Fleming's spacious Manhattan apartment—tonight he would stay in one of Fleming's guest rooms. It was almost two in the morning, but the first leg of his China trip didn't start until five in the afternoon, so he had time to celebrate. He was spending a few days at U.S. Oil's London office before going on to Shanghai, otherwise he would have gone west from Texas, through Los Angeles, instead of coming to Manhattan.

Fleming returned from the kitchen with a fresh bottle of Scotch and put it down on the coffee table in front of the couch. "Guess I won't be making it into the office until late tomorrow."

"Hey, you only go around once." Hewitt grabbed the Scotch bottle and poured himself another drink—no ice, no water, just Scotch—and a satisfied smile spread across his face. He raised his glass to the elk head above the fireplace on the far wall. It was just like the one on Champagne. Fleming had shot both of them in Wyoming a few years ago, the kills coming just days apart. Hewitt was going to take Three Sticks elk hunting in Wyoming this winter. "Here's to Christian Gillette." His smile grew wider as he thought about his share of the Black Brothers fee. There wasn't any doubt about the firm getting its seven percent on top of the ten million it had collected today. After all, he was the one at U.S.

Oil who'd make the decision to buy Laurel Energy. It was a beautiful world when everything was rigged in your favor. "And here's to another big fat fee."

Fleming matched Hewitt's smile with his own. "You played Christian exactly right, Samuel. Made him think he had Laurel Energy sold, then jerked the deal away. Then made him think there might be a shot again with that invite to your ranch, then left him at the altar again by putting off the ranch trip at the last minute. I bet if your assistant hadn't called this morning to put him off, he wouldn't have given me that check this afternoon."

Hewitt smacked his lips after his first taste of the new bottle. "Oh, yeah, Christian would have waited. He thought he could push me over the edge by coming to the ranch, convince me I had to have Laurel. But he was wrong."

"He thinks he's the master." Fleming chuckled. "Well, let me rephrase that. He *thought* he was the master." He blinked slowly. The alcohol was starting to kick in. "What will you end up offering him for Laurel?"

Hewitt sniffed. "A little over four billion. He'll take it, too. He'll be pissed, but he'll take it. He doesn't have any choice. I'm the only game in town." Hewitt noticed the alcohol getting to Fleming—the bleary-eyed look, his head tilting to one side like a ship with a leak. No one could keep up with him, Hewitt thought to himself proudly. It had been that way since Princeton, and it was a big advantage. "Plus, he told his investors he had a deal. He shouldn't have done that."

"How do you know he did that?"

Hewitt gave Fleming a telling glance.

Fleming smacked himself in the head with his palm. "Of course, of course. I'm an idiot."

"No, you've had too much Scotch."

"Yeah, probably. So, you still want to tap Christian into the Order?"

"Absolutely."

"I don't know. He was pretty shook up about the assassination attempt when he was in our offices today. He seems like a die-hard Democrat to me. I think we've lost him to the dark side."

"He'll come around."

Fleming held his glass up to the light, gazing at the Scotch. It was older than him—seventy-five. "Who do you think tried to kill Wood today?"

Hewitt shook his head. "Damnedest thing. I don't know, I don't even have a clue." And it bothered him to be completely in the dark about anything that important. "I've put out the information traps, but I haven't heard anything yet."

"You think it was just some crackpot?"

"Don't know."

Fleming sneered. "Press sure made a shit storm out of it, didn't they? The blood on his shirt and everything. His picture was everywhere. Probably picked up quite a few votes thanks to the whole thing. Black *and* white."

Hewitt glanced at the elk head again. He couldn't wait to take Three Sticks to Wyoming. "Doesn't matter how many votes he got because of it. Once we get through with him, he won't even have his Senate seat."

Fleming took a long guzzle from his glass. "When do I get to see this infamous clip? This thing that gives you so much power over him."

"Right now." Hewitt pressed the "play" button on the remote. "I queued it up while you were getting the new bottle." The snow on the screen quickly cleared, replaced by Jesse, Stephanie, Osgood, and Jefferson Roundtree. When the clip was finished, Hewitt smiled triumphantly. "What did I tell you?"

Fleming let out a long, low whistle. "Damn." He nodded at the screen. "What's the plan from here?"

Hewitt thought for a second. "I'm going to let Jesse win the nomination and let the public get used to him as the Democratic candidate. Give the country some time to get to know Jesse Wood, to start to like him. And they will because he's a very likable guy. Then I'm going to drop the bomb, after everyone's started to take to him. That way the clip will have maximum effect and people will be as angry as they can be. Whites and blacks. Whites for the obvious reason, blacks because they'll feel like he let 'em down."

Fleming shook his head. "That clip is very powerful."

Hewitt's eyes gleamed. "Jesse's name will evaporate from the political arena faster than an August rain in the West Texas desert. The Democrats will have to scramble for a new candidate. More than likely it'll be whoever ran second to Jesse at the convention. But, remember, that guy will be way behind when the party comes to him, and he'll already have been branded a loser. He'll have no chance. It'll ruin the Democrats for years."

"What about Christian? The clip will ruin him, too." Hewitt had told

Fleming that Jesse Wood was courting Christian as his vice presidential candidate. "Guilt by association, you know?"

"I'm gonna make certain Jesse doesn't announce Christian as his VP candidate before I drop the nuke."

"How?"

"I told you, I got a very important connection in the Jesse Wood camp. I know everything going on there."

"Who is it?"

Hewitt pointed at the television screen. "The same person who gave me that beautiful clip of Jesse bashing every white person in America." Hewitt thought about the night he'd waited at the gate of his ranch for the clip. His man had flown to New York to pick up the disk and to deliver the money. "Clarence Osgood."

"Wood's chief of staff?"

Hewitt's man had met Osgood in Brooklyn beneath the Williamsburg Bridge. Osgood had been petrified that someone was going to see him—but he'd taken the briefcase full of half a million in cash. "Yup."

"How in the hell did you convince Clarence Osgood to give you a clip of Jesse Wood bashing white people? How did you convince him to turn?"

"Osgood found out that once Jesse was elected, he was going to get fired."

A confused expression came to Fleming's face. "Why would Jesse fire Osgood once he was elected? I thought they were tight."

Hewitt rose from the couch with a groan and popped the clip out of the disk player. "I don't think it was Jesse's idea."

"What do you mean?"

"I think somebody else is pulling the strings in the Jesse Wood camp," Hewitt said, ambling back to the couch and stowing the disc in his briefcase.

"Who?"

"Don't know."

"Can't Osgood tell you what's going on?"

"He won't talk about that. He's very scared of whoever it is." Hewitt smiled. "But I'll find out."

"How?"

"I'm working on another connection."

"Infiltrating, huh?"

"I tried with her a while back and she didn't bite. But I got a call from her as I was coming over here. Apparently she found out she's getting fired, too. I think she'll tell me what's going on. She sounded pretty pissed off."

Fleming put his glass down and slumped back on the couch. "Who's killing our brothers, Samuel? Who's after the Order? Goddamn it, I don't like needing bodyguards all the time."

Hewitt felt his jaw clench. "I don't, either."

"But *who's* doing it?"

Hewitt glanced at the elk head one more time. "Well, Benson killed himself, and I'm convinced that Dahl really was killed by a terrorist cell. The information from the witnesses was pretty convincing."

"But what about Laird and Massey?" Fleming asked. "You told me you thought they were murdered, that their deaths weren't accidental."

Hewitt exhaled heavily. "I hate to say it, but I think Mace Kohler's behind those murders."

Fleming gazed at Hewitt glassy-eyed, shaking his head. "*What?*"

"Kohler's off the reservation, Trenton. You've seen him at the last two meetings."

"Yeah, but . . . but off the reservation enough to murder Laird and Massey?"

"We made a mistake with Mace Kohler. He's a bleeding heart. And remember," Hewitt said quickly, "he was Special Forces. He knows how to kill."

"Still, I don't—"

"And Blanton McDonnell came to me," Hewitt continued. He hadn't told anyone else about McDonnell reaching out the other night. "Blanton told me that Kohler's convinced I'm going to have Jesse Wood assassinated if he wins the election in November."

"Well, you were until you got that." Fleming pointed at Hewitt's briefcase. "He probably thinks you were behind the shooting."

"Yeah, probably." Hewitt's expression turned grim. "Now no one can find him."

"Huh?"

Hewitt nodded. "Kohler's gone, completely disappeared. Into the mist."

MCDONNELL KISSED his wife—it was five thirty and dawn was just breaking—then followed the bodyguard to the sedan, looking around before climbing into the backseat. He loved it out here, loved the country. An hour from one of the biggest cities in the world, but you'd never know it. Trees, fields, streams. A gorgeous property, a beautiful life. He was glad he'd gone to Samuel Hewitt and told him about Mace Kohler. He felt like a huge weight had been lifted off his shoulders.

A few hundred yards out of the driveway McDonnell felt the sedan slowing down, and he looked up from his *Wall Street Journal*. Through the gray morning light he could see that there was construction on the bridge. A small team of men in hard hats and orange vests milling around a dark truck with a yellow light flashing on top. One of the men was putting out pylons. "Oh great."

"Looks like they aren't letting anyone past the bridge," the bodyguard said over his shoulder, easing the sedan to a stop.

One of the men on the construction crew jogged toward the car.

"Get out of here!" McDonnell shouted suddenly, the realization hitting him like a freight train: This was a setup. "*Jesus Christ,* get me out of here!"

But the construction worker had already reached them, had already leaned down beside the bodyguard's open window. "Sorry, but you're going to have to turn around," the man informed them. "There's cracks in the bridge. Looks like we're going to have to close it for a couple of weeks."

"Thanks." The driver glanced back at McDonnell, a what-the-hell's-wrong-with-you look on his face. "You okay?"

McDonnell relaxed into the seat, watching the construction worker head back toward the bridge, then let his head fall against the seat. He'd really thought he was a dead man.

BOB GALLOWAY had been the chief financial officer of Central States Telecom for seven years. He'd made over thirty million dollars from the initial public offering the company had completed six months ago. With the proceeds of the stock he'd sold to the public he'd bought a mansion in a ritzy section of north Chicago called Kenilworth; bought a summerhouse on the Upper Peninsula of Michigan, bought a big boat he kept at a marina in downtown Chicago, and put a million dollars in trust for each of his three children. He had the life—except that the SEC was about to indict him for leading a massive accounting fraud. They hadn't actually taken any action yet, but he knew it was coming. He was guilty as sin, too.

Galloway had known this day would come sooner or later, but he'd been planning for it. Still, that didn't make it any easier.

In the divorce he'd given everything to his wife and made certain that no one could pierce the agreement. Made certain no one could go after her for the money and the property for any reason once the state of Illinois finalized and made official their split.

He looked out over the lake from the second floor deck of the Michigan summerhouse. He still loved his wife dearly, but this was the only way. It had taken her a while to see that, but she'd finally come around. His lawyer had called him at the office yesterday to tell him the divorce had come through. He'd left right after hanging up and driven straight here.

Galloway picked up the vial of pills. They'd kept the Alzheimer's at bay for the last two years. He'd had bad days when his memory went in and out—more so lately—but, miraculously, he'd been able to keep up his job and perpetrate the fraud without anyone finding out. With a little help from the outside, of course. He didn't know what their motives were—he'd never asked, didn't care. Just accepted their cash so he could keep the company afloat until the IPO went through. Now his wife and their children would never want for anything again. They were set for the rest of their lives.

If he hadn't committed the fraud, Everest Capital wouldn't have been able to take CST public so quickly and for such a huge profit. And, if Everest hadn't been able to do that, he wouldn't have been able to cash out. The Alzheimer's would have caught up with him before the company was ready for the IPO, and he would have been replaced by someone else who would have ended up getting his options, getting what he deserved after toiling at the company for so many years. But it had all worked out, apparently for everyone—for the people from the outside who'd helped him, too. They wouldn't tell him why, but they were satisfied.

Galloway leaned back in his chair and reread the note. The answer to why those people were so happy was probably here. In the note he admitted to the CST fraud and said that he'd done it specifically at the direction of Christian Gillette, chairman of CST and Everest Capital. He picked up a pen and slowly signed the bottom. Christian had been nothing but supportive ever since they'd first met, when Everest had bought CST three and a half years ago. Galloway felt bad for him—but not that bad. Life was hard. You did what you had to do to take care of the people you loved most. And you didn't need to worry about being accused of accounting fraud from the grave.

He put the note down, drained what was left of his bourbon and soda, picked up the pistol, pressed it to his temple, and fired.

20

"QUENTIN, I need something on Samuel Hewitt and I need it fast."

"What do you mean by *something*?"

"Some way to manipulate him. I know that's a lot to ask, but I've gotta have it."

Christian was on his way into Manhattan from LaGuardia airport after taking the red-eye back from San Francisco. He'd been there with Allison and Quentin working on the Aero Systems deal. The family had finally agreed to sell last night after dinner when, in a lighthearted moment around the negotiating table, he'd thrown in five years' worth of free skybox season tickets to Dice games along with a free stay in one of the casino's suites the night before any game. The sixty-year-old matriarch who controlled Aero's stock had slammed her fist on the table and accepted right away. Turned out she spent most of her time in Los Angeles and had been a huge Rams fan until the team moved to St. Louis and she'd desperately wanted a new one to root for. So often it was the little things that made the world go around.

"The grandson," Quentin answered after a few moments. "That's the only way I can think of. From what I keep hearing, Hewitt adores the kid. Really doesn't care much about anybody else. Remember I told you he was close to ex-senator Stewart Massey?"

"The guy who drowned in Oklahoma?"

"Yeah."

"So?"

"Hewitt didn't even show up at the funeral. They asked him to say a few words, and he didn't even show up, didn't even respond."

"Jesus."

Christian was going to drop off Quentin at Everest Capital and pick up Nigel. Then Nigel and he were going to review a couple of company reports together during the drive from Everest to Jesse Wood's headquarters in Brooklyn, where Christian was going to spend the day with Jesse going over the platform. They were supposed to have met last week, but Jesse had put off the meeting for a few days, making the rounds of the news shows instead, to take advantage of the free publicity from the assassination attempt. Christian glanced out the window. They were almost at Everest.

"By the way," Quentin spoke up, checking his BlackBerry, "Allison's been talking to Chicago a lot lately, a lot more than usual. I had our internal network guy track her chatter for me," he explained, anticipating Christian's question. "Phone and e-mail."

Christian rubbed his eyes. He was tired, hadn't slept well on the plane, and he was going to have to be on his game all day. Obviously, there was a tremendous amount to cover with Jesse. "Do you really think Allison and Gordon Meade are setting me up at CST?"

"Maybe."

"But why? What's the endgame?"

"So the Wallaces can control Everest. Maybe they think if you're indicted because of CST, they can kick you out and put her in as chairman. You told me how Meade knows a lot of your other investors, and they are twenty-five percent of the fund. He buddies up with them to force you out and makes Allison chairman."

"Why go through the trouble?" Christian asked, trying to see the benefit.

"They control that much more money."

"Five billion of it's already theirs."

"Yeah, but then they get the other fifteen."

Christian shook his head. It didn't seem right. Besides, at dinner it had sure as hell seemed like Gordon Meade wanted Allison back in Chicago after the fund was fully invested. Not staying in New York to run Everest. Of course, maybe that was all an act, all part of a carefully conceived plan to throw him off. He hated always wondering about people's motivations. It made you unable to completely trust anyone. "Is this the calm, cool, analytical Quentin Stiles I've come to know or somebody else? Somebody with another agenda? Somebody who doesn't want me to be a vice presidential candidate?"

Quentin glanced down. "Well, what *are* you going to do with me if you and Jesse win the election?"

"You're jumping the gun, pal. I haven't even committed to Jesse yet."

"You will."

"How do you know?"

"I just know." Quentin looked up. "What are you going to do with me, Chris? Seriously."

"What do you want to do?"

"Exactly what I'm doing now."

"Okay, fine."

Quentin went back to scrolling through messages. "That'll be tough if you're not around. It wouldn't be the same with Allison or Nigel running Everest."

Even if it was true, he couldn't let Quentin think that. "I don't understand that because—"

"Uh-oh."

"What?"

Quentin handed his BlackBerry to Christian. "One of our associates just sent me this. Better read it."

Christian scanned the small screen quickly, reading the news article the young woman had downloaded off the Internet, then sent to Quentin. Bob Galloway, the chief financial officer of CST, had been found dead at his summer home in northern Michigan. The cause of death was a single gunshot wound to the head—self-inflicted, the police had determined. Christian took a deep breath. So, one of CST's most senior executives—the man in charge of all the numbers—had committed suicide. He felt sorry for the man, but it sure hung a guilty sign around the necks of everyone in charge at CST who was left. Merry Christmas, Vivian Davis.

"That's not good," said Quentin quietly.

"No, it's not," Christian agreed, handing the BlackBerry back to him as the limousine came to a stop in front of the Everest Capital building. Maybe he needed to tell Jesse to forget everything. He could feel the walls closing in, and he didn't want to put Jesse in a bad position. That wasn't fair. Of course, the SEC coming after him wasn't fair, either, but the public wasn't going to have much sympathy for the chairman of Everest Capital. "See you."

Christian watched Quentin clamber out of the car and Nigel get in.

"Hi, chap," said Nigel, putting his briefcase down on the seat. "How are you?"

"All right."

Nigel looked up. "What's wrong?" he asked as the limousine moved back into Park Avenue traffic. "I've known you long enough to recognize that tone."

"Bob Galloway committed suicide."

Nigel's face went white. "Oh no."

"Shot himself in the head. I just found out."

Nigel glanced out the window. "Bob was a good man. You didn't know him very well. You only saw him at the quarterly board meetings. But he really was a good man."

"Was he married?" Christian asked, his voice dropping. "Did he have kids?"

"Yes on both counts. Three kids, I think."

"That's awful. Make sure he had life insurance, will you, Nigel? If he didn't, we'll have to do something for them."

"Galloway made thirty million bucks on the CST public offering. He's fine."

"The SEC could grab that from his wife in a heartbeat. They won't give a damn that he's gone."

"It'll take them forever to prove—"

"Just do it!" Christian snapped, fatigue and pressure suddenly combining forces. He took a deep breath. "Will you please just do it?"

Nigel nodded. "Yeah."

Christian put his hand on Nigel's knee. "Sorry, I'm just tired."

"Did you guys land the deal in San Francisco?"

"Yeah." Christian chuckled. "I offered them a skybox at Dice games and a suite at the casino. The woman who runs the family took it right away."

"Guess Allison needed you after all."

Christian reached into his jacket for his BlackBerry. "What's that? What did you say?"

"Allison kept telling me how she was going to land the Aero Systems deal all by herself. Turns out she needed you in the end. Which is what I'm worried about, Christian. You name her chairman, and it turns out she can't do anything all by herself. Turns out she's not a closer. One of those people who can get everyone to the altar but can't get the ring on the finger. We'll go from the most powerful private equity firm in the world to a wounded duck so fast. The word will get out that Allison can't handle the job, and the house of Everest will come tumbling down like it got hit by a category five hurricane. Everything you and I worked so hard to build will be destroyed."

"You're blowing this out of proportion, Nigel. I haven't even committed to Jesse Wood yet."

"You will."

Everyone just assumed he was going to make the jump into politics, and he wondered if there was a message in that. If maybe they thought he *needed* a change. "And I haven't made a decision on you or Allison yet."

"Yes, you have," he retorted angrily. "Did you sleep with her while you were in San Francisco? She get you to commit to naming her chairman while she was humping your willy?"

Christian felt his anger flash. *"Nigel, you better—"*

"She's been asking me a lot about CST lately."

Christian felt the air rush from his lungs, like he'd been punched in the stomach. *"What?"*

"I thought that might interest you."

"What's she been asking?"

"How much you personally made on the CST public offering. How involved you were with the company day to day. How well you knew Bob Galloway." Nigel shrugged. "I didn't think anything of it at first, but she kept asking."

And Quentin had mentioned that Allison was talking to Chicago a lot lately. To Gordon Meade, no doubt.

"Where is Allison?" Nigel asked.

"She stayed in San Francisco to go over a few details of our letter of intent to purchase Aero Systems with the sellers. She's coming back this afternoon." God, he was tired. News like this was the last thing he needed. "Has your contact at CST finished her investigation yet?"

"Today," Nigel promised. "Late today. Realistically, probably tonight."

"Michelle, right?"

"Huh?"

"Michelle Wan. That's your contact at CST, right?"

A curious expression crossed Nigel's face. "Yeah, that's right, but why do you keep asking?"

Christian couldn't hold back any longer. He'd known Nigel a long time, but he had to confront him about the memo in the briefcase. "Who's Sylvia Brawn?"

Nigel gazed at Christian hard for a few moments. "Sylvia Brawn is another woman at CST who has no idea what's going on. Michelle is using Sylvia's CST e-mail late at night so nobody finds out it's her who's helping me. Sylvia's an administrative assistant in the marketing department. No one would ever believe she was involved in the fraud or believe that she could help me figure out who's behind the fraud or how it was done. Sylvia doesn't have the training. She wouldn't know the first thing about how to track down accounting fraud. Like I said, Michelle uses her e-mail to communicate, then erases the correspondences. You want to tell me why you asked?" Nigel asked, his voice rising.

Not really, Christian thought to himself, feeling a wave of guilt coming on. "How is CST staying afloat?" he asked, looking away from Nigel's withering glare. "Where is the cash coming from?"

"Michelle thinks she's close to figuring that out. She's followed the money trail to a couple of banks and it looks like there's been help from somebody outside. An entity that isn't associated with any of the company's current lenders. Michelle thinks she's almost got the answer. She's working a couple of friends of hers at two of the big clearinghouses. She's meeting with them later this afternoon. That's why I said it'll probably be tonight."

"Uh-huh." Nigel seemed to have calmed down a little. God, he hated himself for thinking an old friend might be a Judas. What pressure like this did to people. He'd never felt anything to match it. "I need that answer." If Nigel could find out where the cash was coming from, Christian could take that information to the SEC. It would prove that he and Everest weren't involved and that he was doing all he could to take care of the problem—short of refunding money to the public. Which he was prepared to do, too. "That's probably the most important thing you could tell me."

"I know, and I'm working my ass off to find the answer." He cocked his head. "You look rough, Chris. Want some coffee?"

Christian glanced out the window. They were almost to the Brooklyn Battery Tunnel. Coffee sounded good. "Yeah."

"Driver," Nigel called, "pull over at that corner, will you?"

A moment later the limousine was idling in front of a coffee shop and Nigel had headed inside.

Christian put his head back on the seat for a few moments. Finally, he looked out the window. Nigel was still waiting in line. Then his eyes fell to the leather seat and the object lying on it. He focused on it. Nigel's cell phone. It must have fallen from his pocket. He gazed at it for several moments, wishing the thought hadn't raced right through his mind. Wishing he didn't want to pick up the phone to see what calls Nigel had received and what calls he'd made. He tried to resist the temptation, but it was too much.

He leaned over and grabbed the phone off the seat, first checking the calls Nigel had received. The fifth call was from a 312 area code—Chicago. He checked the shop again and saw Nigel coming out. His eyes flashed back to the screen and he stared at the digits hard, trying to memorize the number, then dropped the phone on the seat just as Nigel opened the door. He wasn't absolutely positive, but he was pretty sure the number he'd been staring at was Gordon Meade's cell number. Nigel would have been calling CST a lot and CST was in Chicago, so there was a chance it wasn't Meade's. He'd call Debbie as soon as he was alone and get her to check the number.

FROM HIS VANTAGE POINT behind the tree line at the back of the yard, Kohler watched McDonnell and his wife get into the sedan, and the bodyguard close the door and head to the driver's seat. McDonnell had ignored all of Kohler's attempts to try to contact him. Or maybe McDonnell had checked, found the messages in the soup section of the grocery store, but decided not to come to the graveyard because he was petrified that the messages would lead to an ambush. McDonnell had good reason to fear that, Kohler thought. Members of the Order were falling like flies—Benson, Laird, Massey, Dahl. Four dead, five left.

Kohler leaned against a tree as the sedan headed down the driveway. McDonnell had told Hewitt everything that night at Newark Airport, ratted him out like some common street snitch so his tapes would stay put. He was sure that was what had happened now.

JESSE RELAXED in his big desk chair and took a break from the speech he was drafting—the one he would use to accept the nomination.

It would be the most important speech of his life, the most important night of his life. One of the most important nights in all of black history.

It was almost eleven and Jesse still hadn't heard back from Christian. They'd finished up an hour ago, after an all-day skull session. He'd expected Christian to officially accept the vice presidential spot on the ticket at that point, as they were headed to the door of the office. He'd expected a shake of the hand, a big smile, and words like, *I couldn't be prouder, Jesse, I accept your kind offer. We're going to make history together.* Something like that.

Instead, Christian had claimed he still needed a little more time to think about it—the guy was harder to land than a five-hundred-pound marlin on ten-pound test. It was almost as if there was something bothering Christian, or he was actually thinking about not accepting. Which seemed unimaginable to Jesse. Turning down the chance to be the vice president of the United States, maybe the president in eight years. But different things drove different people. Maybe making money was more important than anything else to Christian Gillette. Jesse hoped it was. Then maybe he'd get to pick the candidate he wanted. At least have some input.

Jesse glanced at the phone. He hadn't heard from Stephanie in a couple of days. She'd gone on a sudden vacation, hadn't even bothered to tell him where she was headed or how long she'd be gone. He'd tried to call her a couple of times today on her cell phone, but nothing. No answer, no return call. He didn't even know if she was going to be back in time for the convention.

THE NUMBER on Nigel Faraday's cell phone had turned out to be Gordon Meade's—Debbie had confirmed that. As far as Christian knew, Nigel had never spoken to Meade before—never had a reason to. Christian had always handled the Wallace investment directly. Besides, Meade was constantly talking to Allison. As far as Christian knew, Meade had never even met Nigel, thought Meade was probably barely aware Nigel even existed. Obviously, he was wrong. He'd thought about calling Nigel to confront him, but Nigel would have had some smooth explanation—it seemed he always did these days. Nigel was supposed to have called tonight with Michelle Wan's update about CST, too, but he never had.

Allison moved into the living room and sat down beside Christian on the couch. She'd gotten a glass of champagne from the fridge. "I feel like celebrating," she said, smiling. "We finally landed Aero Systems. One of the associates called me from the office a little while ago. We got the signed letter."

Christian tried to smile back. She'd taken a leisurely flight from the West Coast this afternoon. Slept most of the way, she'd said, so she was wide awake. He could barely keep his eyes open. "I'm afraid you're going to have to celebrate by yourself."

"Tired?"

"Yeah."

"Well, thanks for helping me with the deal," Allison said. "That old woman who controls the company really likes you. She was telling everybody after you left what a great guy you are." She sighed. "Seems like you can charm anyone . . . including me." She leaned around and kissed him on the cheek. "So, what are you going to do about Jesse?" she asked.

He'd felt his face flush at the touch of her lips. "I don't know."

"What's your problem?" she asked. "Why wouldn't you want to be vice president? Why wouldn't anybody want to be vice president?"

Christian still hadn't told Allison about CST and what was going on with the SEC. He glanced up at her, wishing that just once he could be a mind reader. The problem was: Maybe she already knew what the SEC was about to do at CST. Maybe she'd known for a while. "You want to do it?"

"*Sure.* But I doubt Jesse would be very happy about that. He's expecting you to show up for that one."

"There's a lot to think about."

"Look, if it's that you're struggling with whether to name me or Nigel chairman, I'll make it easy for you. Name him."

"It's not that."

"Then what is it?"

Christian gazed at her for a few moments, then picked up his phone and dialed. Sometimes you just had to assume things would work out. "Jesse? Yeah, it's me. I've decided. I'm with you. Officially."

PART THREE

21

THERE WASN'T TIME for McDonnell. The situation had reached a critical stage and Kohler had to prioritize. Christian Gillette had to be his sole focus at this point. Kohler pressed his right arm against his torso as he leaned against the wall just outside a security checkpoint of the Dallas/Fort Worth Airport, feeling the pistol wedged deeply into the shoulder holster strapped tightly to his body beneath his jacket. He glanced back over his shoulder. Outside the checkpoint in the main terminal there wasn't an obvious police presence, but he'd only have a few precious seconds. They were there—you just couldn't see them. They'd be all over him if they recognized him.

Every few moments Kohler scanned the long corridor past the checkpoint, searching for Gillette. He wasn't going to execute here, but he wanted to identify the target. He chuckled wryly. He was talking to himself like he was back in Special Forces. Amazing how training kicked in during times of intense pressure.

Gillette was on his cell phone when Kohler spotted him, fifty yards away. Kohler moved back into the airport, away from security, checking behind every few paces to make certain Gillette was still coming. He stopped outside a newsstand and pretended to read a newspaper, casing the area, making certain he wasn't going to be surprised by anyone. Gillette was almost to security. Kohler could feel his hands shaking slightly, his blood pulsing. But his mind was perfectly clear. Thank God for all that training.

"**ALLISON KEEPS** asking me about CST, Chris. She came into my office *again* this morning."

"What did she want this time?" Christian demanded, looking ahead at the security checkpoint as he spoke to Nigel on his cell phone.

"She wanted to talk about Bob Galloway's suicide. Asked me if I knew why he'd done it."

"What did you say?"

"I told her I had no idea why Bob did what he did. Told her it must have been just one of those awful things nobody sees coming."

Christian could hear Nigel munching on something at the other end of the line. "Anything else?"

"Yeah, she asked me if the SEC had contacted CST."

Christian stopped dead in his tracks. *"She asked what?"* He still hadn't told Allison anything about CST's problems with the SEC. Christ, this thing was getting nuts.

"Yeah, she asked about it," Nigel confirmed. "I don't know what's going on with that woman, but something's definitely up. She acted real squirrelly about it, too. She wanted me to swear I wasn't going to say anything to you about her asking me all these questions. I told her I wouldn't, but . . . well . . . I always tell you everything."

Christian's phone beeped, indicating another call. "I'll buzz you back in a few minutes." It was Quentin. "Yeah, pal?"

"I got a line on who killed Torino."

Christian held his breath. "Who?"

"You're not going to believe it."

"Who?"

"Chicago again."

Christian glanced around. "The Wallaces?" he whispered.

"That's where everything's pointing. CST *and* Torino."

Christian's mind was spinning, and he staggered toward the wall to support himself. He'd asked Quentin to do whatever was necessary—call in favors from his contacts, make payoffs to them, whatever—to find out who had killed Carmine Torino. If he was going to be a vice presidential candidate, he had to have *all* the answers. In this case he had to know who wanted pictures of him giving the Mob money, and it seemed to him it was the same people who wanted Carmine Torino dead.

Jesse was going to officially accept the presidential nomination tonight at the Democratic convention, but they'd decided to wait a few days before announcing Christian as his running mate. To give Jesse time alone on the national stage and to give themselves a second bite at the apple. So Jesse could make a big announcement after the initial hype about his nomination had settled down, and they could grab a few more headlines.

Christian had to have as many loose ends as possible tied up before he and Jesse made the announcement, before they passed the point of no return. Which was why he was having the lawyers call the SEC again, too, to demand an update on CST. If they didn't get an acceptable answer, Christian had given the attorneys orders to go over Vivian Davis's head, to go to the senior people they knew at the agency. It was a risky strategy because it was sure to piss Vivian off, but Christian saw no alternative. He couldn't accept Jesse's invitation to be the vice president, then have the SEC announce an investigation of CST, Everest, and him. That was the nightmare scenario—for everyone.

"Where are you?" Christian asked.

"Vegas. I had to come out here for a face-to-face to get the answer on Torino."

Christian started moving again, passing the security checkpoint. "Who from Everest knew you were going to Las Vegas?" He noticed a man standing against the wall ahead and to his right. The guy seemed to be staring directly at him over his newspaper.

"Nobody. Uh, well, that's not exactly true. I stopped by Allison's office yesterday to congratulate her on the Aero Systems deal, I'd been meaning to do that for a while. She asked me if I wanted to get a drink after work. I told her I couldn't because I was coming out here." Quentin hesitated. "And I always tell Nigel where I'm going per your instructions. As the chief admin officer at Everest, you told me he's supposed to know all our schedules. I e-mailed his assistant about my trip yesterday, like I always do the day before I'm going out of town."

Christian stared back at the man who'd been leaning against the wall. He'd folded the newspaper up and was walking this way. "Don't tell Allison where you're going from now on." The guy was moving faster with each step, still staring at him, still coming right at him. "Got it?"

"Yeah, but what's the deal? What's wrong?"

"Just don't say anything to her about where you're—Jesus!" Christian whipped around quickly. He'd been staring at the guy walking toward him and had backed into someone. "God, I'm sorry, I wasn't looking—"

"Hello, Christian," the person he'd run into said loudly. "Welcome to Texas."

Christian recognized the face beneath the snazzy black Stetson. "Hello, Samuel."

"Glad you made it down here okay," Hewitt said after Christian muttered a quick good-bye to Quentin. "We're gonna have some fun. Hope you're ready for a good time."

Christian's eyes snapped back toward the spot where he'd last seen the man coming at him. "Yeah, sure, I'm ready." He glanced around the area as they shook hands, but the guy was gone. "What are you doing here, Samuel? I thought you were sending a chopper for me, I thought I was meeting you at the ranch."

Hewitt grinned. "I couldn't wait to give you the good news, Chris, and I wanted to do it in person."

"Oh?"

"Yep. I got my CEO over the hump on Laurel Energy this morning. We're ready to buy it. Wish you hadn't hired Black Brothers, but what's done is done."

Christian gazed at Hewitt, wondering why they were going through the charade. Hewitt was still acting like he hadn't known Laurel Energy was for sale until they'd met at Princeton. "What are you offering? Still five billion?"

"We'll talk about that later," Hewitt said, gesturing to his right at the young man standing beside him. "I want you to meet someone. This is my grandson, Samuel Prescott Hewitt the third. He's the best kid in all Texas."

"Jeez, Granddad, I wish you wouldn't—"

"Meet Christian Gillette, Three Sticks," Hewitt interrupted. "He's about the best investor you'll ever meet. We got all kinds of bests going on here. Just like I like it."

Christian shook the young man's hand. "How you doing?"

"Hello, sir," the young man said respectfully.

Christian grinned. "Don't call me sir, you make me feel old. Christian's fine, okay?"

"Okay."

"I hope you don't mind," Hewitt spoke up, starting to walk, "I've asked my boy here to join us at the ranch. I don't get to see him often," he said, patting the young man's shoulder, "so I jump at every chance I get."

"I don't mind at all," Christian answered, checking the area one more time. But the guy had vanished. "Like you said, we'll have fun."

ROTH GAZED at the young woman's bare legs as she lay bound on the bed. Hewitt had always made it clear that he was welcome to do anything he wanted with the women who were temporarily under his care on Champagne Island. *Anything at all,* Hewitt had said with a smug grin.

"What are you doing?" she asked, struggling against the ropes securing her wrists and ankles as she came to.

"Stop it," Roth ordered loudly. He'd been watching her sleep. "You can't get free," he muttered, sitting down on the bed. "I'm too good with knots. You'll only make them tighter."

"Please don't do anything to me," she begged, trying desperately to move away from him. "Please!"

Roth felt his breath run shallow as he gazed at her, thinking about how he'd watched her in the shower last night. He couldn't trust her in there by herself.

Suddenly there was a wild banging downstairs, loud and hard on the front door of the lodge.

NIGEL SLIPPED INTO the back of a long blue limousine idling on the South Bronx street corner and quickly closed the door. He'd ridden the subway up here from midtown, then hoofed it from the stop to this corner. The neighborhood was rough, so he'd walked the two blocks quickly, and now he was hot as hell. Summer was in full swing in New York.

Trenton Fleming sat in the limo.

"Hello," Nigel said, easing back on the seat.

"Thanks for being on time." Fleming tapped his watch. "I know it's a pain in the ass to do it like this, but we can't use phones or e-mail, especially now."

"I understand."

"Have some water," Fleming suggested, tossing a plastic bottle at Nigel. "So where are we?"

Nigel twisted off the bottle's cap and guzzled some down. "I think you're right, Trenton. I think Christian suspects he's being set up on CST. He hasn't said anything to me specifically, but I've gotten that feeling."

"We've confirmed that Christian got some information," Fleming explained. "At least we now know that Quentin Stiles was nosing around before we could get to people and shut them up. If Quentin got the information we think he got, at this point Christian probably believes Gordon Meade is involved."

Nigel took another swig. "Well, whatever happens, I did what you told me. I made sure he thinks Allison's involved, too."

Fleming nodded. "Good, because we don't want him thinking you're involved. Is Christian still pushing you on your investigation at CST?"

"Yeah, and I can't put him off any longer. I keep telling him it's almost finished, but he's getting impatient. I'm worried he's going to call CST himself looking for Michelle Wan. That wouldn't be good."

"It's all right," Fleming said confidently. "You've done a fine job. We have what we need now anyway. Everything fell into place when Bob Galloway did his part."

"What do you mean?"

"He wrote a suicide note, just like we told him to. He claimed in the note that the entire accounting fraud at CST had been done at the personal direction of Christian Gillette."

Nigel's mouth fell slowly open.

"Galloway got what he wanted: thirty million for his wife free and clear. And we got what we wanted: Christian in the crosshairs."

Nigel shook his head. "Just to keep him off the ticket."

Fleming's expression hardened. "Yes," he said quietly.

"How much has Black Brothers put into CST so far?" Christian was one sharp cat, Nigel thought to himself. He'd known all along that CST was getting cash from somewhere. Yeah, Christian was smart all right. His downfall lay in trusting those close to him too much. "In total?"

"About a hundred million."

Nigel whistled. "Wow. You won't get that back, either. That's a lot of money to throw away."

Fleming waved. "It's an investment. We'll make three hundred million on our Laurel Energy fee. Lose a hundred on CST, make *three* hundred on Laurel. I think that's a pretty good trade."

"That's right. I forgot about the Laurel fee." Nigel frowned. "But you never know, you might not get Laurel sold. Morgan Stanley couldn't find anyone to buy it, and they're one of the best investment banks around."

Fleming smiled thinly. "I'll take my chances."

Nigel grimaced. "Is Christian going to jail?"

"Not if he plays ball."

"But I get the chairmanship. Allison goes back to Chicago and I get the chairmanship. No matter what."

Fleming nodded slowly. "No matter what."

ROTH FLUNG the front door of the lodge open. Todd Harrison stood on the porch in front of him. "What do you want?" he growled angrily. "What are you doing coming out here like this? You could get us both in a lot of trouble."

"How?" Harrison demanded, stepping inside without being asked. "How could I get us in a lot of trouble?"

Roth said nothing, just glared at Harrison.

"What's going on?"

Still Roth said nothing.

"Do you know who these men are?" Harrison asked, his voice shaking as he gestured around the lodge. "They're incredibly powerful. And three of them are dead."

Roth's gaze snapped up from the floor. "What?"

"Yeah. Franklin Laird, Stewart Massey, and Richard Dahl. I recognized them from the photo I took out of the kitchen. Laird was chairman of the Federal Reserve, Massey was an ex–U.S. senator from Texas, and Dahl was a five-star Army general. Laird was killed in a hit-and-run incident in northern Virginia, Massey drowned in a lake in Oklahoma, and Dahl was killed in a terrorist attack a few weeks ago."

"Jesus." Roth never had any idea who they were. He'd never let him-

self think on it, just wanted to live a quiet life on an island for a while and forget. "Who are the others?"

"I don't know yet, but I'm working on it." Harrison paused. "Except for the old man, the one who came to me in the bar that night."

"Are you sure it was him?" Roth asked.

"Positive. You saw that picture I left here. It's the same guy in the picture you had on the counter in the kitchen. The one I took."

Roth let out a long breath. So actually four of them were dead. He'd carried Benson's cold body himself. Four dead that he knew of anyway.

"So, Don, what are we going to do?"

FLEMING SMILED as he watched Faraday trudge toward the subway. Nigel actually thought there was a chance Black Brothers might not sell Laurel Energy. He had no idea how it all fit together. When it came down to it, Nigel only cared that he was going to be chairman of Everest Capital—which was perfect. His greed made him malleable, and that was what the Order needed him to be.

Nigel thought this whole thing was about keeping Christian Gillette off Jesse Wood's presidential ticket. Part of it was, but only a small part of it. The bigger part had to do with honor and loyalty, with doing the right thing, with protecting a son of the Order when the man of the Order couldn't do it himself, with protecting a country from itself. Clayton Gillette had been a man of the Order when he died in that plane crash twenty years ago, a man Samuel Hewitt had admired, even before Hewitt was initiated into the society. So, Hewitt had taken it upon himself to help Clayton as he lay in his grave. To keep his son, Christian, from making a huge mistake, to keep Christian from helping destroy what the Order stood for. Preserving the status quo. Preserving control of the nation by whites.

And Christian could have done it, too, Fleming thought to himself. Could have wrested control from the Order. Christian had that charisma. He could have pulled enough whites to Jesse's side to get the man elected. Thank God Hewitt had figured that out long ago—and taken the appropriate action. Christian Gillette wouldn't be running with Jesse Wood. Hell, in a few weeks, Jesse wouldn't be running at all.

Fleming chuckled as he watched Nigel disappear down the subway stairs. He could have given Nigel a ride back to Manhattan, could have dropped him off somewhere out of the way on the West Side. But it was too much fun to think about him riding in a subway car, sitting next to some half-drunk stinking Mexican headed somewhere deep into Brooklyn, headed to some hovel he called home.

"Driver," he called, "take me back to Wall Street."

22

"I'VE GOT A FEW FOLKS coming out from Dallas tomorrow night for poker. I hope you can stay, Christian."

Hewitt, Three Sticks, and Christian were sitting on the porch of the huge house, gazing up at the vast night sky glittering over Texas. The sun had been down for almost an hour, but the stars were brilliant, casting a glow on the fields sweeping down from the ridge the house was built on. Horses and cows were visible in the distance, dotting the field like gray ghosts. Christian had kept to water while Hewitt and Three Sticks had worked on a bottle of Scotch together, but he'd allowed himself the pleasure of a good Cuban cigar from the humidor just inside the double doors. It had been a long time since he'd done that and it tasted good.

"We think the stakes are pretty high," Hewitt continued, "but you won't."

Christian glanced at Three Sticks. The kid was bleary-eyed, staring straight ahead, his glass balanced precariously on one leg. Hewitt was breaking the kid in young, getting him ready to drink his mates under the table. Hopefully, he wouldn't kill the kid in the process. "What's the ante?"

"Hundred bucks a hand."

"Any limits?"

"Nope."

That was rougher than the game back in Manhattan. At least those guys had a ten-grand limit per hand. Good thing he didn't drink. You always had a better chance in poker if you didn't drink. In anything, really. "Yeah, I can stay." Christian felt a relaxing buzz from the cigar coming on. "That'd be fun."

"Nice out here," Hewitt murmured, "don't you think?"

"Yeah."

"Nice way of life. Wouldn't want to ever see it change."

Christian could feel Hewitt trying to draw him into a political discussion. Of course, that was going to happen more often now. He shut his eyes tightly. Unless the SEC came after him. Damn it. He'd almost been able to put it out of his mind. The lawyers hadn't heard back from Vivian Davis today. If they didn't by noon tomorrow, they were going over her head. Then it was anybody's guess what would happen. "Can we talk about Laurel Energy for a minute?"

"What about it?"

Hewitt had swallowed his share of Scotch, too. Christian could hear it in his voice, a trace of meanness creeping in. "Price."

Hewitt groaned. "Everything's always gotta be about price, doesn't it?"

"Of course. So what's yours?"

"Well, let me tell you what happened. I got my CEO over the hump as far as *buying* Laurel but not over it as far as paying five billion. He agreed to four point three billion, but not—"

"Let's not screw around," Christian said calmly, glancing at Three Sticks. The boy's eyes were slits. "The last thing I want to do is be rude, Samuel. You've let me enjoy this wonderful place, fed me a big meal, and I'm smoking a great cigar. But we both know your CEO is just a guy taking up a desk and an office in downtown Dallas. He wouldn't argue with you if you told him the sun rose in the west and set in the east, let alone if you told him you wanted to pay five billion for Laurel Energy. Let me be as polite as possible. You're bullshitting me, Samuel."

Hewitt laughed. "That was *very* polite, Christian. I appreciate the way you put it." His smile disappeared. "Now get the hell out of here."

Christian's eyes raced to Hewitt's.

"Just kidding, son." Hewitt put his glass down on the arm of the chair and slid his feet into a pair of slippers lined with rabbit fur. "Obviously, you've done your homework. Unfortunately for you, so have I. Trenton Fleming can brag all he wants about ginning up a bunch of other buyers for Laurel, but he won't."

"What's wrong with Laurel that I don't know about?" It was a brutally honest question and it made Christian look very vulnerable, but he had to ask. "How do you know Fleming won't be able to get me any other buyers?"

"There's nothing wrong with Laurel, it's just that I put out the word."

"Put out the word?"

"I made sure people in the industry who mattered wouldn't make you an offer."

It seemed inconceivable for Hewitt to think he could keep an entire industry away from Laurel. Christian had run into people who had a lot of power, but this sounded over the top. "And how exactly can you do that?"

"I just can."

"Sorry, but I don't believe—"

"How long have you had Laurel on the block?" Hewitt cut in.

"A while," Christian admitted.

"Any offers?"

"A few."

"Any *real* offers?"

Christian shook his head.

"Anything wrong with Laurel that *you* know of? Be honest with me."

"No, I told you that. It's clean."

"Had all the best engineers in the world confirm your reserves, right?"

"Yes."

"Had Morgan Stanley give it the seal of approval, too?"

"Right."

"They couldn't figure out what was wrong, either?"

"No," Christian agreed impatiently, "they couldn't."

"I rest my case." Hewitt rose from his chair. "Come on, let's go inside."

"What about your grandson?" The boy was snoring softly.

"He'll come inside when he gets cold. He's a smart boy," Hewitt said with a laugh.

They moved through the double doors into a comfortable living room. Hewitt picked up the television remote and switched it on to the Democratic convention. "Just about time for your boy to accept the nomination." Hewitt eased onto a couch and put his slippers up on the coffee table. "Why aren't you there?"

"They didn't want any rumors starting." Christian sat in a chair beside the couch.

"When is Jesse going to announce you as his running mate?"

"They're not sure yet, probably a week or so."

"Wanted him to have solo time in the spotlight, huh?"

Christian nodded. "Why did you tell me you didn't know Laurel Energy was for sale when we met in Princeton?" he asked. "Obviously you did if you put out the word on it."

Hewitt stared at the television, watching the governor of New York take the stage. The governor was a close friend of Jesse's and was going to officially nominate him as the party's candidate for president. "It's complicated, Christian," he finally answered, "very complicated."

"I've got time."

"Tell you what, I'll give you your five billion for Laurel. Full price. Which means nine hundred some odd million for you guys at Everest. Let's leave it at that."

"That's great, but I still want to know why you didn't tell me."

Hewitt grimaced, then the phone on the table beside him rang. He snatched it quickly. "Hello." A few moments later he hung up, then stood. "Sorry, Christian, but I've got to get to Dallas for a meeting. U.S. Oil has a situation in the North Sea."

FORTE COULD barely control himself as he watched Jesse take the stage on the hotel room television. The dream was actually coming true. "I can't believe it, Heath." He heard his voice shaking, felt his heart pounding, his throat going dry. He hated showing emotion, but right now he didn't care. This was history, and he'd made it happen. "Jesse Wood is going to be the next president of the United States. It's incredible."

"Sure looks like it," Johnson agreed quietly.

"It's amazing," Osgood spoke up.

Forte, Johnson, and Osgood were watching the nomination together in Forte's hotel room. When the convention was over for the night, Osgood was heading downstairs to the ballroom for an after party, but Forte and Johnson were staying up here. Forte still didn't want to be seen anywhere near Jesse. They were so close to making it all happen, he couldn't take the risk.

"A tribute to you, Elijah," Osgood continued. "You've made this all possible."

Forte glanced from Johnson to Osgood. Osgood was the traitor, the one who'd turned on him. Forte was sure of that now. Stephanie had tried to get in touch with Samuel Hewitt several times, but Hewitt had turned her down. Because Hewitt didn't need Stephanie anymore, he had Osgood. That was why he'd declined her offer. There wasn't any hard proof Osgood was the rat, but Forte could feel it. Osgood was being too much of a kiss ass, too deferential for a man who knew he was going to be out on his ass after Jesse won the election. For a man who was going to fall one tiny step short of his own dream.

"Thanks, Clarence," Forte said calmly.

Forte never thought he could hate anyone as much as he did the man who'd done those awful things to his mother, but he was wrong. He hated Clarence Osgood more. He'd take care of Osgood when the time was right, but the more immediate problem was Samuel Hewitt. Hewitt almost certainly had the clip of Jesse—thanks to Osgood.

Forte's expression turned to steel. He'd done his homework on Hewitt ever since Stephanie had told him she'd been approached. Hewitt was a powerful man—and a racist. It had taken Forte a while to dig that up, but there was no doubt about it. Obviously, Hewitt had approached Stephanie for information in an effort to derail Jesse Wood's campaign. Probably had a blood pact with his racist buddies in Texas to keep Jesse out of the White House at any cost and now that he had Clarence Osgood in his hip pocket, figured he had everything under control. Well, Hewitt had a surprise coming to him. A *Texas-sized* surprise.

THE HELICOPTER had taken off from the lawn in front of the house fifteen minutes earlier, heading for Dallas. Hewitt had bid a quick goodbye, promising to be back in the morning at the latest, in time for the poker game tomorrow night. Christian just hoped Hewitt would remember that he'd agreed to pay the full five billion for Laurel when he got back.

Christian moved into Hewitt's darkened den, toward the desk. That was where he was going to start. He didn't like digging through another man's personal files, but this was a chance he wasn't going to pass up. Three Sticks was still here—other than that, the house was empty. The help lived in another place a few miles away, and they were gone for the night.

For fifteen minutes Christian carefully searched the den, but he found nothing out of the ordinary—until he looked in a lower drawer of a credenza against a far wall. The folder was marked simply "CG." He opened it and in the dim light gazed at the paper on the top of the file, the blood beginning to pound so hard in his head he could barely focus on the hand-scrawled words. It was a suicide note from Bob Galloway, the CFO of CST, clearly a copy of an original. His eyes raced to a name he recognized instantly in the body of the letter—his own. Galloway was blaming everything on him.

Beneath Galloway's suicide note were pictures, dark pictures of him in the New Jersey woods handing over the bag to the guy he'd first met at the transfer station in Las Vegas. He picked one of the pictures up and felt himself beginning to sweat as he studied it. Obviously him, obviously the mobster.

Christian shook his head, feeling an awful panic he'd never felt before. What the hell was Hewitt—

"What are you doing?"

Christian's eyes flashed from the picture to the den doorway. Three Sticks.

MCDONNELL UNDID the knot of his black bow tie as the sedan approached the country road's last curve before his driveway. It was late and he was tired. Fortunately, he'd convinced his wife not to come into Manhattan tonight for the formal dinner Jamison & Jamison had held celebrating the company's one hundredth anniversary. Otherwise, they'd still be there. God, she could gab.

McDonnell put his head back on the seat and thought about the soft mattress he was only minutes away from, thought about how he was getting used to having a bodyguard all the time. He liked being driven everywhere, liked feeling protected. Jamison & Jamison had never allowed its senior executives to enjoy perks like these. He smiled. When Samuel Hewitt decided he wasn't going to pay for it anymore, he'd pay for it himself. He couldn't give it up now that he had it.

As the sedan came out of the sharp curve, it was suddenly face-to-face with two huge headlights. The bodyguard shouted and twisted the steering wheel hard to the right, toward a ditch, but not in time. The eighteen wheeler hit the sedan almost head-on, crushing the car.

A hundred yards down the road, the truck driver brought the rig to a screeching stop, hopped out of the cab, and sprinted back toward what little was left of the sedan. McDonnell's mangled body lay beside the wreckage.

CHRISTIAN HAD TAKEN the first vehicle he could commandeer from Hewitt's ranch. An old Jeep parked in one of the barns near the house that sounded like it didn't have many more miles left in it—but hopefully enough to get to the Dallas Airport. Three Sticks had helped him find the keys in a kitchen drawer, somehow able to function despite the alcohol still coursing through his system. Tomorrow morning the kid probably wouldn't even remember that he'd surprised Christian in Hewitt's den. Christian had made up a quick story about looking for papers on a deal he and Hewitt were working on. Fortunately, Three Sticks hadn't asked to look at the file Christian had taken from the credenza. If he had, he might have questioned the pictures.

Christian's cell phone rang. It was surprising to have cell phone reception still ninety miles from Dallas. Not much out here but grassland.

"Yeah?" he shouted over the din of the engine.

"Where are you?" It was Quentin.

"Don't worry about it." Christian didn't want to say anything over a cell phone right now. Too risky. "What do you want?"

"To tell you that it's definitely the Wallace Family pulling the strings. All confirmed."

Which didn't surprise Christian at all. The question was whether or not Allison was involved. And if Hewitt was working with them—or alone. Hewitt had photos of Christian handing the bag of money to the mobster in the New Jersey woods, so he was obviously somehow involved in the delay of the casino license—or at least knew about it. Christian glanced out over the darkened Texas grassland. Hewitt knew about the CST fraud too, given the copy of Galloway's suicide note that was in the file. They all had to be working together. He muttered to himself. He should have known he had a problem, a big problem, when he saw Hewitt's initials on that paper at Black Brothers. He shook his head. God, if Jesse Wood only knew what was going on.

Christian's cell phone beeped, indicating another call. He pulled it away from his ear and gazed at the number as it flashed, wondering whether or not to answer. It was Allison. According to Quentin, the odds were now a hundred percent that somebody inside the Wallace clan had alerted the SEC to the fraud at CST. Which meant that—

"You gonna answer that?" Quentin asked.

"No." But the phone started beeping a second time right away. Allison again. He made a snap decision. "I'll call you right back." Christian switched lines. "Yeah?"

"Christian! My God, I'm so glad I got you! Where are you?"

Allison was upset, at least she was acting like it, but he wasn't going to tell her anything at this point. "Why have you been asking Nigel about CST so much lately?" he demanded.

"Is that what Nigel told you? That I was asking about CST?"

"Yup."

"Figures."

"What do you mean, 'figures'?"

"I *never* talked to Nigel about CST. Listen, I know there's trouble at the company. I know about the accounting issues, and I know you and Nigel were on it. But I didn't find out from Nigel."

"Then how do you know?"

"Because I know that Gordon Meade is the one who put the SEC onto CST. I don't know why Gordon did it, but I know he did."

Not what Christian had expected to hear. "How did you find out?" he yelled over the whine of the Jeep's engine.

"A young guy at our family office found something Gordon had faxed over to a man named Samuel Hewitt at U.S. Oil and asked me what to do with it," Allison explained quickly. "I was talking to the kid on the phone a couple of weeks ago, I guess Gordon had gone home for the night already. Anyway, Hewitt's the CEO of U.S. Oil. Why the hell Gordon sent something to Hewitt, I don't know. Apparently, he must have sent it over himself and somehow hit the 'copy' button on the fax machine. I'm sure Gordon doesn't fax too many things himself, so he probably didn't realize what he'd done. Anyway, I had the kid at our office scan it into his computer and e-mail it to me. Told him I was working on the deal with Gordon when he asked. The note Gordon sent to Hewitt was handwritten and it mentioned somebody named Bob Galloway at CST who was working with them. Given that you're chairman of CST, I'm sure you know that Galloway's the CFO. I wasn't very familiar with CST, I just knew that we'd taken them public last winter, so I went through our internal files and found Galloway's name.

"The fax Gordon sent also mentioned someone named Vivian Davis at the SEC," Allison continued. "I know a lawyer at the SEC, so I called him. He told me Davis was taking a real hard look at CST because they thought there were accounting irregularities. That it was a big deal, that there was heavy pressure coming down from the top for her to press on it, and that he could get fired for talking to me, maybe worse. He told me that the person who had put them onto CST was Gordon Meade." Allison paused. "My friend also told me that you and Nigel had already met with this Davis woman."

Christian thought about why Meade would use the fax machine to communicate. E-mails could be tracked so easily in so many different places, and phones could be bugged. Not that faxes couldn't be intercepted, too, but people would be so much less likely to think of that these days. "Why didn't you tell me you knew?"

"Because you didn't tell me, and because I wasn't sure until just this minute. My friend from the SEC just called me back. He was calling from a pay phone, too. It's wild stuff. He was scared. He said he couldn't talk to me again."

"I don't blame him," Christian said quietly, almost to himself.

"There's one more thing."

"What?"

"The fax said that CST needed more cash. That Black Brothers was going to have to make one more deposit."

Christian's mind was racing. At least he had a place to start now. "I'm going to Chicago, Ally. I need you to meet me there, okay?"

"Fine, but tell me what's—"

"Just do it!" he shouted, thinking about why Nigel had tried so hard to make Allison seem suspicious lately. He shook his head. It was so hard to think that Nigel might be a traitor. "Okay?" he repeated. "At O'Hare, at that place we met a couple of months ago when I came out. Don't tell anyone you're going to Chicago and don't take the Everest jet. Fly commercial, back of the bus. I'll call you as soon as I know when I'm going to be there."

23

"MY GOD. It's incestuous."

"What do you mean?"

Christian had met Allison at O'Hare just before nine o'clock. He'd caught a couple of hours of sleep on the plane from Dallas to Chicago, then gotten a few more at a motel near the airport so he was ready to go. They'd needed to wait until later to get into the Wallace Family office anyway, couldn't risk going in until everyone had gone home.

Christian pointed at a diagram he'd mapped out on a piece of paper based on the information they'd uncovered in Gordon Meade's office. Based on faxes from Meade to Hewitt, and from Meade to Trenton Fleming, and from those men back to Meade. All of them catalogued with cover sheets neatly arranged in a locked drawer of Meade's desk. Fortunately, they hadn't been forced to break into anything. Allison had the keys to every lock in the place.

"I think Meade is working directly with Samuel Hewitt to frame me for the accounting fraud at CST."

"Can you prove it?"

Christian pulled out the copy of Bob Galloway's suicide note from his pocket and handed it to her. "I found this at Hewitt's ranch," he explained, watching her scan the page.

She winced as she reached the incriminating words. "Jesus."

"And Meade's working with Trenton Fleming at Black Brothers to secretly put money into CST to keep it going until they bankrupt the company and lay the blame for that on my doorstep, too." He shook his head. "And I hired Black Brothers to sell Laurel Energy and now Hewitt's going to buy Laurel."

Fleming and Hewitt had played that game neatly, Christian realized. Committing to buy Laurel, then backing off, then committing again, then backing off again. They'd left him thinking he had no choice but Black Brothers.

"Hewitt'll probably get a kickback from Fleming on the fee for selling Laurel." He shook his head again, harder. He'd been set up from the get-go. "No wonder Hewitt's willing to pay five billion for Laurel. The more he pays, the bigger Black Brothers' fee is, the more he gets kicked back. It isn't good for his U.S. Oil shareholders for him to pay that much, but I bet it works out great for him personally. And Black Brothers more than makes up for the money they'll lose in the CST bankruptcy with the fee they charge on the Laurel Energy sale. According to what we've found here," he said, pointing at the paper, "Black Brothers has put a hundred million into CST. But a five-billion-dollar price tag for Laurel will shag them a three-hundred-million fee."

He'd always heard rumors about a Wall Street inside crew, a tight cartel of moneymen and their blue-blood families who had controlled the flow of funds for hundreds of years. But he'd passed the rumors off as hearsay, as nothing but one of those wild conspiracy theories concocted by people who had no idea what they were talking about. Maybe the theory wasn't so wild after all. "And they've done it all with Nigel Faraday's help," Christian observed quietly. Nigel's name was all over the faxes. Nigel had given Meade and Hewitt a ton of highly confidential information on CST, the casino, the football team, Laurel Energy. He glanced at Allison. "I'm sorry I ever even—" He didn't finish. "It's just that I could never imagine Nigel turning on me. He's been a friend for a long time. I guess you never really know."

"And you told him you were thinking about naming me chairman, too," she pointed out.

Christian nodded at the paper. "Yeah, but that was just fuel for the fire, just confirmation for him that he was doing the right thing. Nigel's been working with these guys for a while, but you're probably right. Me telling him I was thinking about you as chairman probably got him to go to Faith." That thought had just struck him.

Allison pulled Christian's diagram in front of her and gazed at it. "But why did they do all this? Just to make money on Laurel? I can't believe that," she said quickly. "There has to be something else."

"I don't know. Maybe it's got something to do with me being Jesse Wood's vice president." He pointed at the page. "Them framing me for CST or them having the pictures of me paying off the Mob to get the casino license could force me out of the race. I don't know."

"But it wasn't that long ago that Jesse asked you to be his running mate," she argued, "and this thing with CST has been going on for a while. How could they have known?"

Suddenly nothing about these men could surprise Christian. They seemed to know everything, to be able to get to anyone. "Jesse told me the other day when we were going over his platform that his camp had decided a while ago that I was the person they wanted." Probably since that whole episode when he'd been in the news, when he'd figured out that a couple of senior feds were trying to profit off the nanotechnology breakthrough they'd developed. "Hewitt's probably had somebody inside Jesse's camp for a long time."

"But why would Hewitt care so much?"

Christian's expression turned grim. "I think he's worried that if Jesse's elected president, it's the beginning of the end for his way of life."

"Are you serious?"

"Absolutely. I think he really believes that." Christian gazed at Allison for a few moments, then touched her chin gently. "Thanks for your help."

She nodded wearily.

"I never should have— Jesus!" He snapped his fingers.

"What?"

The thought had flashed to him. "Didn't you say there was a book that detailed your family tree?"

She nodded. "Yes, it's out at the estate."

"I want to see it. Now."

ROTH LED HARRISON down the steps of the lodge's basement, toward the freezer where he'd stored the old man's body after carrying it back from the woods for the group's leader. For the man he and Patty had nicknamed Stetson for the black cowboy hat he always wore.

"What are we doing?" Harrison asked, smelling mildew.

"I want to check something," Roth said curtly. He moved to a small bureau near the freezer door, opened one of the drawers, and pulled out a pearl-handled Colt revolver.

"Jesus." Harrison stopped in his tracks and held up his hands. "Hey, I—"

"Shut up." Roth opened the gun and spun the chamber. Then he froze.

"What is it?" Harrison asked, edging closer.

Roth gazed at the gun. "The old guy? The one who sat down at the bar that night and started telling you the story of Champagne Island?"

"What about him?"

Roth flipped the chamber of the Colt back into place. "This was his gun." He'd already told Harrison that the old guy had committed suicide on the island, that he'd carried the body back to the lodge. "The one he was supposed to have shot himself with, the gun I found in his hand when the guy who runs this place—the one I told you wears the black Stetson all the time—came to me and told me there'd been an accident."

"So?"

"So I picked up the body, and Stetson picked up the gun. I saw him stick it in that bureau when he thought I wasn't looking."

"So what?"

Roth took a deep breath. "It's fully loaded. Six bullets."

Harrison took the gun from Roth and checked it himself. "The old man didn't kill himself." He glanced around the basement, sniffing. The smell of mildew was strong. "What's in that room on the third floor?" he asked. "The one that was locked the day I came out here to look around."

"I don't know, just boxes."

"Damn it, Don, you've got to open up to me. We're both screwed if we don't help each other."

"Another door, made of steel, but I don't know what's behind it. It's padlocked and Stetson told me never to try to open it, told me I'd regret it if I did. I don't have keys to it."

"We'll bust the locks. You got a sledgehammer?"

"They'll know what we did. We don't want that, believe me."

"Maybe we can take what we find behind the door to the cops. They'll give us protection."

"No." Roth shook his head. "Too big a risk."

Harrison let out a frustrated breath. "Where's your wife, Don?"

Roth stared back at Harrison for a few moments, then his eyes fell to the cement floor.

CHRISTIAN FOLLOWED ALLISON into a large second-floor room in one of the five mansions on the Wallace estate. He watched her move to a far wall and pull a large painting back—it was on hinges. Behind the painting was a wall safe.

"Thank God Aunt Sadie always loved me," Allison murmured.

Christian had stayed in the car listening to the radio while Allison disappeared into another of the mansions before they'd come here. She'd come back twenty minutes later clutching a piece of paper—the safe's combination written on it.

Allison laughed as she spun the lock left, then right, then left again. "Sadie was so happy I was finally taking an interest in the family history she couldn't wait to give me the combination." She stepped back and reached for the small handle. "Here goes nothing." She turned it and it clicked. "Bingo."

Christian's heart began to pound. He watched Allison reach inside and pull out a huge book that she carried to a table in the middle of the room.

"Here you go," she said triumphantly, putting it down. "Have fun."

For the next few minutes Christian studied the book, page by page, tracing the family's history from the beginning.

"We're Scots," Allison explained as he gazed at the different branches. "Came over right after the Revolution. Settled in New England for a while, then moved here." She smiled. "Actually, I heard we got kicked out—of *both* places. England *and* New England. Not sure why. Nobody talks much about that."

Christian nodded, still tracing. Flipping pages back and forth. "There!" he shouted suddenly, pointing. "The Hewitts."

Allison put her hands to her mouth. "My God."

He flipped forward. "And here, the Flemings."

She grabbed his arm. "Down there, look."

Christian's eyes flashed to where she was pointing. "The Meades," he muttered. "Gordon's actually family, not outside at all. Your grandfather and uncle didn't bring in an outsider to run the money, they kept it in the family." He was tracing a branch down. "Damn."

"What?"

"The Lairds. Franklin Laird."

"The ex-chairman of the Federal Reserve?"

"Gotta be."

Christian eased into a chair, his mouth falling open in awe as he connected the web in his mind. "It's unbelievable," he whispered.

She looked at him and shook her head. "I had no idea. No one ever talks about this."

Christian's phone rang. He glanced up at Allison after checking the number. "It's Nigel. He's been calling me all day, but he hasn't left a single message."

ROTH HELPED the young woman into Harrison's boat. "Keep going that way," he told her, nodding into the pitch dark, toward the mainland. "Keep the arrow on this mark once you get a couple of hundred yards out from the island." He pointed at the compass. "You'll see lights pretty soon. It'll be Southport. Head toward them."

"I don't know how to drive a boat," she whispered. "I can't do this."

"Would you rather stay here with me?"

She shook her head.

"When you get to town, get away from it. Don't go to the authorities, don't try to get help, just get out. Go somewhere, anywhere, but forget you've ever heard of this place and me. Don't ever tell anyone you were here."

"**SO WHAT** do we do now?" Allison asked. She and Christian were standing outside the house, beside the car he'd rented at the airport. "Now that we know all this."

Christian was about to answer when he spotted a figure moving up the driveway toward them through the darkness. "Come on," he urged when the man suddenly broke into a sprint. "Get in the car."

"What?"

But Christian realized there wasn't time to get in the car. The man would be on them too fast. If the guy had a gun, it wouldn't be a fair fight and now didn't seem like the time to assume the guy was a Girl Scout's dad working overtime to sell the most cookies. He grabbed Allison's hand. "Come on!"

They raced across the lawn toward the woods surrounding the house.

"What's happening?" she shrieked, trying to keep up as they sprinted into the woods.

"Just run!" he yelled.

But then she went down hard, screaming as she hit the dried leaves covering the forest floor.

"Get up, get up!" he hissed. "Come on." Then he knelt down and covered her mouth with his hand, trying to hear anything. Listening for any sound that might—

"Christian Gillette."

Christian stood up and whipped around. "What the—" He brought his fists up as a man moved toward him from the shadows.

"**WHERE WE GOING, BOSS?**" Johnson looked at the men who were climbing on the private plane. Five of them, all big, all armed. "What is this?"

"Don't worry about it," said Forte. "Just get on the damn plane."

Johnson swallowed hard, wondering if this was the last flight he'd ever take.

"**PUT YOUR FISTS DOWN,**" the man ordered calmly, stopping a few feet away. "I'm not gonna hurt you."

"Who are you?" Christian asked loudly.

The man smiled thinly. "Mace Kohler," he answered, reaching into his jacket pocket. He pulled out an envelope and handed it to Christian. "I'm going to tell you an incredible story, but I took the time to write a lot of it down, too, just in case you need help remembering the details later."

Christian peered through the gloom as he took the envelope. Kohler looked so familiar.

"I'm a member of a group called the Order."

Christian felt his face twist with doubt. *"The Order?"*

"You've had some strange things going on in your life lately, haven't you?" Kohler asked.

Christian felt the doubt drain away. "You could say that."

"Well, you can thank the Order, specifically Samuel Hewitt." Kohler pointed at the envelope. "It's all in there."

"I know who Samuel Hewitt is," Christian said. "U.S. Oil is buying a company we own."

"That son of a bitch," Kohler blurted out. "Is Trenton Fleming involved?"

Christian nodded.

Kohler shook his head grimly. "The crew inside the crew."

"What are you doing here?" Christian wanted to know. "How did you find me like this?"

"I've been following you for days. You saw me in the Dallas Airport right before you ran into Hewitt. I was over by the newsstand past security."

Christian snapped his finger. "*That's* where I saw you."

"Yeah, I was going to make contact with you right after you passed through security, but then Hewitt showed up out of nowhere. I couldn't believe it."

"Why are you giving me this?" Christian asked, holding up the envelope.

"They want you. You need to understand what's going on."

"What do you mean 'they—' "

A gunshot rang out and Kohler pitched forward, tumbling onto the ground beside Allison.

"Oh Jesus!" Allison screamed, scrambling away.

Kohler lay on his stomach, moaning pitifully, a quickly growing pool of blood staining the ground around him. "Champagne Island," he gasped as Christian yanked Allison to her feet. "Off Maine, near Acadia. Everything's there. The tapes," he moaned, "get the tapes on Champagne." Then his eyes rolled back.

There was nothing they could do for Kohler. "Come on," Christian urged, teeth gritted as his eyes raced around the shadows looking for the shooter. "We gotta get out of here."

ROTH HUNG the phone up in the lodge's kitchen and glanced at Harrison. "That was Stetson. He says I need to get ready for a visitor."

CHRISTIAN DIALED Quentin's cell phone number. He had just dropped Allison off at a hotel downtown. Now he was headed to Maine.

She'd begged to go with him, but that was out of the question. He had to do this alone. He couldn't put her in danger again.

"Hello."

"Quentin, it's me. Get to Southport, Maine—fast! It's on the coast near Acadia."

"*What?* Why?"

"Just do it. There's a place right on the waterfront called the Southport Harbor Diner." He'd called an operator in town and asked for a landmark. She'd given him the diner. "Meet me there no later than six o'clock this evening." It was still before midnight here in Chicago, but not where Quentin was. "Got it?"

"Yeah, but—"

"I don't want to stay on this line. It's a cell phone."

"All right, all right. See you then."

"Quentin!"

"Yeah?"

"Don't tell anyone where you're going."

QUENTIN BOUNDED down the steps of his apartment building on the Upper West Side, headed for his parking garage. He was going to drive from New York to Maine. There was plenty of time and this way he didn't have to risk a plane being delayed. He wasn't putting control in anyone else's hands.

He jogged down 85th Street through the darkness, bag slung over his shoulder. Christian needed him. He'd recognized that tone of voice on the call. He'd heard it before.

Two men darted out from behind a parked SUV as Quentin jogged past—he never saw them until they were right on him. One hit him low and one high, and as he went down the world went black.

24

IT WAS EIGHT O'CLOCK and Quentin was still a no-show at the Southport Harbor Diner. Quentin was never two hours late for anything. Something had happened to him. Somebody was listening to their calls. Christian had turned off his cell phone before getting on the plane in Chicago so no one could track him down, and he didn't dare turn it on now, not even for a second. The network's closest antenna would give him away. But somebody must have picked up his communication with Quentin, the last call he'd made before turning off the phone.

Christian paid his tab—he'd ordered a cheeseburger and a Coke and eaten it at the counter—then headed out of the diner and walked around the harbor, wondering how he was going to get to Champagne Island. He'd thought about chartering a chopper in Portland after landing from Chicago, but if there was anyone on the island who didn't want him there, they'd sure as hell know he'd arrived. And there was no guarantee any of the chopper pilots in Portland would have ever heard of Champagne anyway—unless that was how Kohler and the rest of them got out there. Kohler's nine pages of notes inside the envelope hadn't indicated. There were lots of little islands off the Maine coast, and Christian didn't want to end up marooned on the wrong one if the pilot got confused.

As he moved down a long wooden pier lined with pleasure crafts, he saw a kid hosing down a boat, a sleek-looking twenty-foot outboard.

"Excuse me."

The kid looked up. He had dirty-blond hair, crooked front teeth, and a sleepy-eyed expression. He didn't look a day over sixteen. "Yeah?"

"You ever heard of Champagne Island?"

The kid stopped spraying the deck and looked up. "Yeah."

"I gotta get out there. Is this your boat?"

"My father's."

"Will you take me?" Christian could see it was the last thing the kid wanted to do. "I'll pay you." The kid still didn't seem interested. "Five hundred bucks." Now the kid seemed suspicious. "Look, I—"

"He's really got to get out there."

Christian whipped around. Allison stood behind him.

"What's your name?" she asked the boy, moving beside Christian.

The boy straightened up, instantly entranced. "Danny."

"Well, Danny, you'd be doing us a huge favor if you took us out there. It's very important that—"

"No way, Ally. I can't let you do that."

She looked over her shoulder. "You don't have a choice, Chris."

"It's too dangerous," he muttered, low so Danny couldn't hear.

"So, will you take us?" she asked the kid.

"Yeah, okay. For five hundred bucks. But I need to fill up first. You gotta pay for that, too," he called to Christian. "On top of the five hundred."

Christian pursed his lips. "Fine."

"Let me have the money."

Christian pulled out his wallet and opened it so the kid could see the cash, a row of hundred-dollar bills. "I'll give it to you when we're on our way." The kid wasn't happy about that, but screw him, he'd accept the terms. "How long will it take us to get out there?"

"About an hour."

"Well, let's get going."

They filled up at a pump a few piers away, then headed out. When they reached the edge of the harbor, they hit waves and spray started flying over the gunnels.

"Is it always like this?" Christian yelled as he and Allison crouched down behind the windshield, holding tightly to the bulkhead as the small boat bounced up and down in the swells.

"No, we got weather coming in tonight. A front with some big thunderstorms." The kid grabbed Christian's arm. "Hey, give me my money."

Christian took three hundred dollars out and pressed it in the kid's palm. "I'll give you the rest on the way back."

"Bullshit, man! The storms are gonna be here in a few hours. I ain't staying out there for that."

"I'll give you a thousand bucks." The kid's eyes flashed open, big as fifty-cent pieces. "Five hundred now, five hundred when we get back to Southport."

The kid nodded, grabbing the two additional hundred-dollar bills Christian pulled out of his wallet. "Okay, but how long you gonna be?" he asked, flipping on the boat's red and green running lights. It was almost dark.

"Not long." Christian reached over and turned the lights back off. He noticed a flash on the horizon. "What's that?"

"The lighthouse on Champagne."

Mace Kohler hadn't mentioned a lighthouse on the island, but he'd mentioned a lot of other things—amazing, terrifying things. He'd described the Order in detail, its history, its reason to be, what Samuel Hewitt was trying to do—keep Jesse Wood out of the White House and the minority population down. The hatred and the lengths to which the Order's "inside crew," as Kohler described them—Hewitt, Trenton Fleming, Gordon Meade, and Franklin Laird—would go to accomplish their objectives. Most important, Kohler had described what Christian needed to do once he got to Champagne Island.

Christian glanced back over his shoulder to the west. Huge storm clouds were building over the mainland and lightning was ripping the sky. "Have you ever been to Champagne Island?" he yelled.

The kid shook his head. "Why no lights?"

"I don't want anyone to know I'm coming," Christian said. The flash from the lighthouse was growing brighter. "So whatever you can do to help me be invisible, I'd appreciate."

"What are you doing out there?"

"Don't ask, just steer."

The kid eased off the throttle when the island loomed in front of them, cutting the engine's noise. "I can't get you all the way into shore, the surf's too rough. I'd bottom out. You're gonna have to swim for it."

"Don't you leave me here," Christian warned again.

"I won't."

Christian checked the western horizon once more. The sky was completely dark now, except for the lightning cutting jagged streaks behind them.

"This is as far as I can go," the kid said, checking the depth finder. They were still a hundred feet from shore. "The waves aren't too bad. You should be able to touch bottom pretty quick."

Christian checked the shoreline. No beach, just an immediate steep climb of about ten feet to the tree line. In the dark it was impossible to see if anyone was waiting in there for him. He glanced at Allison. "I'll be back as fast as I can. Make sure the kid stays here."

"The kid'll stay here. I'm going with you."

He'd been afraid of this. "No." But it was clear from her expression that she wasn't going to listen. "I can't be responsible."

She shook her head. "Get your butt overboard."

He moved carefully to the side of the boat, threw his legs over, and dropped down slowly into the water up to his chest. "Jesus!" he muttered as he treaded water. It was freezing, and it seemed to suck the breath from his lungs. He turned back just as Allison dove over him into the water. He started swimming quickly when her head and shoulders popped to the surface, following her into shore, keeping his head out of the water, trying to time his approach so he didn't get caught in the roll of a wave. But they both got caught in the same swell and tumbled along the bottom until they finally grabbed hold of the slippery rocks and managed to drag themselves into shallow water.

A few moments later they were climbing up the bank side by side, gasping for air, freezing. When they'd made it into the trees, Christian glanced back, barely able to see the outline of the boat rocking with the waves. Hopefully, the kid would wait, but right now he had to focus on moving ahead. According to Kohler's notes, there was a huge lodge in the middle of the island and that was where they were going. That was where the tapes were, the tapes he could use to destroy the Order. Kohler had asked at the end of his notes that Christian not let his tapes get out, and Christian was going to do all he could to honor that request.

They stole through the woods, teeth chattering. Kohler had said it wouldn't be hard to find the lodge, but it was pitch-black on the forest floor and he was becoming disoriented.

Christian stopped and listened, keeping his hand on Allison's cold arm to make certain they didn't get separated. He tried to hear if they were being followed, but there was nothing. Nothing but the wind moving through the trees.

"Come on," he whispered.

A few moments later they made it to the edge of a clearing. He peered around a tree and saw a flat cement slab—the helipad Kohler had drawn in his notes. They weren't far from the lodge now.

They started moving again, but there was a sudden blaze of lightning and a crash of thunder from nowhere. He threw Allison to the ground and covered her head with his arms, assuming one of the trees right above them had been hit. But when he looked up he couldn't see any damage. The wind had picked up suddenly, causing the treetops to sway violently, but they were still intact.

When they reached the lodge, he hesitated at the perimeter of the lawn. Kohler's notes had mentioned a caretaker and his wife—Don and Patty Roth—but the huge house was completely dark. He took a deep breath, then motioned to Allison. When she nodded back, they sprinted across the grass to the kitchen door. According to Kohler there was no alarm, so he pushed the door open and they slipped inside.

Upstairs was where he had to go, but he stayed in the kitchen for a few moments, listening again. Still nothing. They moved out of the kitchen and stole up the staircase to the second floor, then up to the third floor and down the hall to the last door on the left—to the door to which Kohler had directed him. There was supposed to be a sledgehammer hidden behind some boxes in the room—what Christian would need to break the locks on the steel door inside. Kohler had hidden the sledgehammer there during his last trip to Champagne. In his notes, Kohler had warned Christian that it might not be there. Hewitt had caught him coming out of the room after he'd hidden it and might have searched the room and found the tool. If it wasn't there, he was to go back outside to a shed near the lodge. There he'd find another sledgehammer.

Christian reached the door at the end of the hall and tried to turn the knob—but it was locked. He stood in the darkened hallway for a moment, thinking. If the caretakers were here, he'd wake them up instantly by breaking the door down, but Kohler had given him information to use. Roth had run into trouble as a Miami cop. Christian was to tell

Roth he knew about the trouble, that he knew some very specific details of the trouble that the Miami force didn't know, and that he'd told a friend. That if Roth didn't let him keep going, one way or another the cops in Miami would find out something they'd wanted to find out for a long time. Either from Christian or Christian's friend if Christian didn't make it back. They'd also find out where Roth had been hiding out the last three years. He backed up a step and got ready to kick open the door. The hell with it—he was going to wake up anybody in the house when he started smashing the locks on the inside door.

The door popped open on his second try. He quickly flipped on the light and starting searching for the sledgehammer. He was committed now, no going back. He found the hammer right away and moved to the steel door. Two swings and the top lock flew off. He took aim at the bottom one and swung hard. It popped off instantly and he pulled the door back, then listened again. No sounds. He turned the room light off, then moved back to the steel door and flipped the switch inside—the one Kohler had told him would be there—the heavy smell of mildew reaching his nostrils as the area was bathed in light. In front of him was a steep, narrow stairway.

He turned around. "Stay here, Ally."

"Christian, I—"

"It'll be faster. I'll be right back."

She hesitated, then nodded. "Okay."

Three windowless flights down Christian came to another door—this time made of a darkly stained wood—also with a large padlock on it. As best he could tell, he was underground now—three flights down versus the two he'd climbed. Standing on the last step he wound up and slammed the hammer down on the lock. This time it took four tries, but this one finally popped off, too. He pulled the door back and reached into the room, feeling along the wall for the switch. When his fingertips reached it, he flipped it up and the room was illuminated by a faint blue light.

The room reminded him of a tiny chapel. There was a large, wooden chair at the front of the room—thronelike in that it was raised several feet above the maroon-colored carpet and there were steps leading up to it. It was built into the wall and was ornate with beautiful carvings and moldings on the sides of the wide arms. In front of the chair was an altar covered by an azure cloth. On the altar were two candles, a skull, a saber, a Bible, and a rolled-up parchment tied with a red ribbon. In front of the altar were two pews each with four individual seats, made of dark wood like the door.

Incredible. This was the Order room, as Kohler had described. Where they met for formal ceremonies, initiated new members, and kept their most secret archives—including the tapes.

Christian hurried to a closet on the far wall and yanked open the door. On the shelves were rows and rows of videotapes, audio cassettes, and DVDs all clearly marked with names. "Jesus." The infidelity requirement. He reached for one of the DVDs. It was marked "Gordon Meade."

"Hello, Mr. Gillette."

Christian whipped around. Standing in the doorway was Samuel Hewitt. Beside him was another man Christian didn't recognize. He was holding Allison, one hand over her mouth.

"I see Mr. Kohler gave you excellent directions," Hewitt said calmly. "Last thing he ever did, poor man. Mr. Kohler didn't approve of me," he continued, walking past the altar to the chair at the front of the room, ascending the steps, and sitting down. "Mr. Kohler didn't approve of what I'm trying to do." He nodded toward the doorway. "What *we're* trying to do. What we stand for."

Christian's gaze flashed to the doorway, following Hewitt's nod. His heart was pounding as Trenton Fleming and Gordon Meade appeared at the bottom of the steps. They moved into the Order room, past the man holding Allison, and sat down in the pews, one on either side of the short aisle leading to the altar and the chair.

Hewitt motioned to the man holding Allison. "Take her upstairs, then back to the main floor. Wait for us there."

"Yes, sir."

"You wanted me to look in your study at the ranch," Christian uttered, realizing suddenly that he'd been played the whole time.

"Figured you might. I left that file for you to find. I wanted you to know what I had. That I could take you down whenever I wanted to with the CST fraud or with the bribe you paid to get the casino license."

"Why did Bob Galloway blame me in his suicide note? What did you do for him?"

Hewitt pointed at Fleming. "We kept CST going by putting money into it from Black Brothers. Not directly, of course. Through a series of dummy corporations to keep the origin of the money secret. That gave

Mr. Galloway time to pump up the numbers and get that nice valuation in the initial public offering. The one you took twenty million bucks out of, Mr. Gillette."

"Why would Galloway do all that, then commit suicide?"

"Mr. Galloway had Alzheimer's. He wanted his wife and children to be set for life before he couldn't take care of them anymore. His deal with me was that he had to commit suicide once he had everything permanently in his wife's name. Then blame you in his suicide note for the fraud that would be discovered. That way he wouldn't be around to recant. In return, his wife's now worth thirty million dollars and there's no way the government can take it from her. I understand she's going to open an adoption agency with part of that money, a lifelong dream of hers. I'm sure you can relate to that. Maybe she and the Clayton House can work together someday." Hewitt smiled, pleased with himself. "I convinced Mr. Galloway that he didn't want to put his family through Alzheimer's, especially without enough money to take care of him. He saw the light very quickly."

"Did you kill Carmine Torino?"

"A friend of the Wallace Family did," Hewitt answered. "But don't worry about that. Mr. Torino was scum. He tried to hide in that canyon outside Vegas when he heard about what we did to Mr. Agee, the chairman of the Gaming Commission, but it didn't work. We found him, the same way we found Mr. Stiles this morning." Hewitt chuckled. "But don't worry, Mr. Stiles is resting comfortably. I'm surprised you even hired Mr. Torino," Hewitt continued. "Actually, I was surprised you got into the casino business in the first place, but I guess we all make mistakes. I really don't like that business. I'll want you to sell the casino as soon as possible."

"What have you done to Quentin?"

"We didn't want Mr. Stiles interfering in our discussions with you, so we've taken him into custody for now. He's fine, and he'll stay that way as long as you cooperate."

Hewitt was talking like the world was his, like he was the law, like he decided who went into custody and who didn't. "What did you mean when you said you wanted me to sell the casino?"

Hewitt took off his black Stetson and placed it in his lap. "You won't be running as Jesse Wood's vice president this fall."

"You going to give the SEC that suicide note of Bob Galloway's?"

Christian asked. "Show them the pictures you have of me handing the bag of money to the Mob guy? Let the press go wild?"

"If I have to," Hewitt replied, "but it won't be because I don't want you to run with Jesse Wood."

"What do you mean?"

"Senator Wood won't be a presidential candidate by this time next week, so *you* won't *have him* to run with. But I do have some things I want you to do for me, which include selling the casino. If you don't want to work with me, I'll do as you suggested. I'll contact the SEC and the authorities in New Jersey and Nevada, let them know about the proof of your involvement in CST and the bribe you paid to get the license."

"Why won't Jesse be running for president by this time next week?"

"I'll show you in a few minutes."

"What else do you want me to do?"

Hewitt stroked his chin for a few moments. "I want you to join me, Mr. Gillette. I want you to join us. I want you to be a member of the Order." He paused. "Just like your father was."

Christian's eyes narrowed. The news about his father was no surprise. Kohler had mentioned that in his notes.

"Obviously Mr. Kohler ruined my surprise. You can't be that good a poker player."

"I guess not."

Hewitt stood up and moved down the steps to the altar. "You made a terrible mistake joining Senator Wood's team. You need to join *this* team, Mr. Gillette," he said, gesturing around the room. "In the end, you'll be very glad you did. So will your father. Make him proud, don't embarrass him. Don't ruin his good name as he lies cold in his grave." Hewitt smiled. "Look at us, Mr. Gillette, we're old. We need new blood. You can end up being one of the most powerful men in the world without ever having to be elected, without ever having to answer to anyone. You're already powerful but nothing compared to what you could be. Nothing compared to how powerful I can make you."

Christian stared at Hewitt for several moments. "Show me what you have on Jesse Wood."

"Gladly."

The four men climbed back up the narrow stairway to the third floor, then headed for the main staircase.

As they neared the first floor, Christian could hear Allison yelling. He spotted her as they all moved into the great room, sitting in a chair, now guarded by two men.

"You piece of slime!" she shouted at Meade. "The family's going to find out all about you."

"The ones that matter already know, sweetie pie," he shot back.

"Then the authorities will—"

"Shut her up," Hewitt ordered.

Instantly, one of the men guarding her grabbed her hair and pulled her head back, choking off her cries.

"Now," Hewitt said calmly, picking up the television remote. "Watch."

The clip of Wood, Stephanie, Osgood, and Roundtree began to play. Christian watched it all the way through, more shocked as each moment passed, amazed and disappointed that Jesse could ever be so stupid.

"I'll be sending that to Jesse sometime next week with instructions for him to drop out of the race immediately," Hewitt explained when the screen went dark. "I'm pretty sure he'll do so for unspecified personal reasons the very next day. I doubt he'll fight this."

Jesse would definitely drop out of the race the next day. There was no way he'd fight it, no way he *could* fight it. It would be political suicide to even try, to prolong it in the media. It would be much better for him just to pack his bags and go home.

"I haven't decided whether I'll release the clip anyway," Hewitt added. "Even after Jesse drops out. I might want him out of the Senate, too."

Christian rubbed his eyes for a moment. "So if I join the Order, then you don't send Galloway's suicide note to the SEC, and you don't send those pictures of me handing the bag to the mobster to New Jersey, Nevada, or the feds? Is that the deal?"

"Better than that. I'll fix it so the SEC stands down, so Vivian Davis gets off her high horse and goes away completely. I'll fix it so you never even have to worry about the accounting scandal coming out. And don't forget the carrots, Christian," Hewitt added quickly. "Me buying Laurel Energy from you and Everest Capital for five billion dollars, you continuing to get good players for the Dice. You'll be in the Super Bowl before you know it." He gestured at Fleming and Meade. "We'll all watch a few games from your skybox."

So that was why the trade with Buffalo had suddenly changed so drastically in the Dice's favor. "The Bills' quarterback. Did you—"

Hewitt shrugged. "Don't worry about it."

Incredible. Christian looked over at Meade. He was staring back with a satisfied smile.

"Don't fight us, Christian," Meade said quietly. "You won't win."

As he started to say something, five men burst into the room, guns drawn. Three of them raced to the two men holding Allison, reached inside their jackets, and pulled out pistols. The other two moved smartly to where Christian, Hewitt, Fleming, and Meade sat, then forced each man to stand and searched each of them for weapons.

"All clear!" one of them yelled.

"What the hell's going on here?" Hewitt roared.

Elijah Forte strode into the room, Heath Johnson behind him. Christian recognized Forte instantly from pictures he'd seen in business magazines.

"Hello, Samuel," Forte said calmly, moving to where Hewitt stood. "You can sit down now."

"How in God's name did you—"

"All in good time," Forte interrupted, "all in good time." He moved to where Christian stood. "Hello, Christian, it's nice to finally meet you. I assume you know who I am."

Christian nodded.

Forte smiled, then walked to the television, popped the CD out of the DVD player, and put it down on top of the set.

"That's not the only one of those I have, Mr. Forte," Hewitt snapped.

"I'm sure it's not, but I know you'll tell me where the rest of them are by the time we're through here tonight." Forte waved at the men with the guns. "These guys are very good at what they do. Just ask your spy, Samuel. Ask Clarence Osgood."

Christian glanced up at the mention of Osgood's name.

Forte snapped his fingers. "Oh, that's right, you can't ask Clarence anything. We pulled his brain out through his nose last night while we were getting the last few pieces of information from him. I don't think I've ever seen anyone in so much pain."

Christian glanced over at Fleming, who looked as if *he* was about to pass out.

"How did you find this place?" Meade asked angrily.

"I'm the man behind the man," Forte answered. "Jesse being president is my dream come true. I've been working on getting him into the White House for years, and I'm very close to his staff, including Stephanie Childress and Clarence. So I was able to figure out that Clarence was working with Samuel. After that, it was pretty easy. I had Samuel followed. One of the places he kept coming to was here. We've been all over this place for a while." He chuckled. "I think we surprised poor little Patty Roth a couple of times. Of course, no one's going to surprise her anymore. Are they, Samuel?"

"What do you want?" Hewitt demanded. "Other than my copies of the clip."

Forte pointed at Fleming and Meade. "I thought it might be interesting for these two men to hear about what you did to their friend Jim Benson."

Christian watched Hewitt's face for some sign of pressure. In his notes, Kohler had accused Hewitt of murdering five members of the Order, the last, Blanton McDonnell, CEO of Jamison & Jamison. But Hewitt's face remained impassive.

"Jim Benson committed suicide," Hewitt said calmly.

"Did he now?" Forte asked sarcastically. He snapped his fingers loudly, and a moment later Todd Harrison and Don Roth entered the room. Forte pointed at Harrison. "Mr. Harrison is an investigative reporter. He works for me now. Tell them, Todd."

Harrison held up Benson's pearl-handled revolver. "This was the gun Benson was supposed to have killed himself with, but it was never fired. Still has six bullets in it." Harrison pointed at Hewitt. "You had him killed, Mr. Hewitt. You had him killed because he came to me and told me there was something bad going on here at Champagne Island. You suspected that he'd turned on you, so you had him followed. Your men probably saw him come up to me in the bar that night."

"You killed them all," Christian said, "didn't you, Samuel? Benson, Massey, Dahl, McDonnell, Kohler, and Laird."

Hewitt laughed bitterly. "Me? No, no. Kohler killed them."

"Kohler didn't kill himself. I know that."

Harrison pointed at Hewitt. "I know you killed Jim Benson. I know beyond a shadow of a doubt." He turned and looked at Roth. "Right, Don?"

Roth nodded as he stared at the floor.

"You piece of shit!" Hewitt yelled. "The Miami cops will—"

"Shut up, Samuel!" Fleming shouted, standing up. "Did you have Laird killed?" he demanded, his voice shaking. "Did you?" Fleming's voice rose even higher. "He's *blood,* Samuel. Our blood."

"I didn't, I—"

"Goddamn it!"

Fleming lunged at Hewitt, but one of Forte's men grabbed Fleming and wrestled them apart.

"All right," Forte said loudly, "that's enough." He pointed at two of his men. "Take Mr. Hewitt upstairs," he ordered. "Find out where all his copies of the Jesse clip are. Do whatever you have to do, I don't care."

"There's another way," Christian spoke up.

Forte peered keenly at Christian. "What do you mean?"

"Give me five minutes."

Forte shook his head. "No, I—"

"If you're the man behind the man, then you must want me to be Jesse's vice president," Christian said. "Right?"

Forte nodded. "Yes."

"If you trust me that much with your dream, then give me five minutes."

"Why do you want to save Samuel Hewitt?"

"I don't, believe me."

"What is it, then?"

"Just give me the time."

Forte chewed on it for a second. "All right. But make it fast."

Christian raced to the main stairway and to the second floor, checking in bedroom closets, finally finding two canvas bags. Then he headed up again, taking two steps at a time, sprinting down the hallway to the far door on the left when he reached the third floor, racing down the three flights of narrow steps back to the Order room. He moved to the closet and rifled through the tapes and DVDs, gathering up all the ones marked "Hewitt," "Fleming," "Meade," and "Kohler," and stuffed them into the two bags. Then he retraced his steps, back down to the great room.

"Time's up, Christian," Forte announced loudly as Christian jogged back into the room. "What do you have?"

"Clips *you* want," Christian answered, breathing hard. He bent over and grabbed his knees, catching his breath. Catching Allison's eye, too. Then he tossed one of the canvas bags at Forte, the heavier one. "Check it out." He nodded at the television, then at Hewitt, Fleming, and Meade. "You can destroy these men with what's in that bag." In the bag Christian was still holding were one each of Hewitt's, Fleming's, and Meade's clips, and all of Kohler's. The one he'd tossed at Forte contained the rest. "Go on, Elijah, take a look."

Forte unzipped the bag, pulled out one of the CDs marked "Hewitt," slid it into the DVD player, and turned it on. Moments later Samuel Hewitt appeared on the screen. He was naked, as was the young boy in front of him.

Hewitt howled and bolted for the television. But one of Forte's men stepped in front of him, grabbed him, and tossed him backward like a rag doll.

Forte turned toward Christian. "So what we have here is a stand off. Mutually assured destruction. Mutually assured inaction. I'm impressed."

"Even if you tortured Hewitt, you'd never know for sure if you got all the copies of the Jesse clip. This way Hewitt has the clips of Jesse, but you have this clip of him—and more. If you ever released it, he'd lose his job as CEO of U.S. Oil, his family, everything." Christian pointed at Fleming and Meade. "You have clips of them, too, Elijah, as insurance."

Forte thought about it for a few moments. "Yeah, I'm okay with—"

A burst of gunfire erupted and two of Forte's men collapsed. Christian hit the floor, spotting a shooter in the kitchen doorway, then another in the dining room. Hewitt hadn't come alone.

Then all hell broke loose, guns spitting and bullets flying as Forte's men returned fire. Christian saw Harrison hit in the arm and Johnson take one to the leg. Meade went down clutching his stomach, followed by Forte.

Christian jumped to his feet and grabbed his bag of tapes, then Forte's and raced ahead, snatching the Jesse clip off the top of the television. As he did, he came face-to-face with Hewitt—who was aiming a pistol straight at him.

Hewitt smiled even amid the chaos, as the bullets flew, cool as always under pressure, then lifted the gun and squeezed the trigger.

Christian recoiled, certain Hewitt had gotten off a shot. But when he looked up, Hewitt was on his knees, the gun on the floor in front of him.

Hewitt was gazing at him, through him, really. And then Christian realized. Hewitt had taken a bullet.

"Come on," Allison shouted, tossing the pistol she'd scooped up off the floor to shoot Hewitt with and grabbing Christian by the arm. "Let's get the hell out of here!"

He dashed after her. God, he hoped the kid had waited.

EPILOGUE

CHRISTIAN PICKED UP *The National Enquirer* that Debbie had dropped on his desk a few minutes earlier and glanced at the headline: "Shootout at the Champagne Corral." Then his eyes flickered down and he began to read.

> Early on the morning of July 19th, state law enforcement officers descended on Champagne Island—a tiny island located a few miles off Southport, Maine—and discovered a stunning scene. Nine men killed in a shootout one of the first officers on the island likened to the famous gun battle at the OK Corral which took place more than a century ago in Tombstone, Arizona. Among the dead were: Samuel Hewitt, CEO of U.S. Oil, the largest industrial company in the world; Elijah Forte, one of the nation's wealthiest African Americans; and Gordon Meade, a prominent member of Chicago's Wallace Family, rumored to be worth around thirty billion.

As Christian finished the article, his office door opened and Allison appeared. He motioned for her to come in. He'd been expecting her.

"The National Enquirer?" she asked when she saw what he was reading. "I never thought I'd see the day you'd pick up that."

He held it up so she could see the headline, then slid it across the desk at her as she sat down. "Todd Harrison wrote a little piece in there you might be interested in." He chuckled, watching her eyes bug out as she started the first paragraph.

"My God, what are we going to do? Are you mentioned in here?"

Christian shook his head. "No. How would Harrison prove I was ever there?"

After crashing through the window and tumbling to the ground, they'd picked themselves up and sprinted back to where they'd swam ashore. Thankfully, the kid had waited.

"I guess that's why Trenton Fleming isn't mentioned, either," Christian continued. "He must have gotten out, too. Besides, it wouldn't matter if I was mentioned. Harrison admits near the end of the article that he basically doesn't have any hard evidence. And none of the other big newspapers have reported anything about this. The only thing that corroborates Harrison's story at all right now is that no one can find Hewitt, Forte, or Meade. But so what? I'm sure U.S. Oil and Ebony Enterprises will put out statements saying the guy's off his rocker. I'm sure your family will, too."

She shrugged. "I don't know. I haven't talked to anyone in the family. I don't know who to trust anymore."

Christian could see she was scared. She'd always known wealth, tremendous wealth. Now she didn't know if she could count on that anymore. Maybe the family would disown her after what had happened on Champagne. "Look, Ally, you'll always have a place here at—"

"What about this police officer?" Allison interrupted. "The one Harrison claims he interviewed."

She was scared but proud. She didn't want to talk about it right now. Well, he could understand that. "A lie, I'm sure. We called the feds as soon as we got back to the mainland, not the local guys. I'm sure the local guys weren't even allowed on the island for a few days."

Allison dropped the paper on the desk. "There was that one tape of Hewitt with the boy. We didn't get that."

Christian shrugged. "All that proves is that Hewitt was a pervert. It doesn't do anything to back up Harrison's claim that Hewitt was the leader of some secret society that 'influenced events around the world.' " He put his fingers up and made quotation signs.

"Is that what Harrison says in here?"

Christian nodded.

"You think he got Hewitt's tape?"

"Probably, but I don't think he'll release it. Candidly, I don't think anyone would care that much if he did. I'm sure U.S. Oil will come out with a statement sometime today explaining how Hewitt has stepped down. They'll say all the right things. They'll basically end their association with him somehow. They'll claim he had a stroke or something and in a couple of weeks he'll be a distant memory."

"I guess you're right," Allison agreed. "What did you do with all the tapes we got off the island?"

"Burned them."

"But you could have used them against Trenton Fleming. I mean, the SEC's still going to come after—"

"It's all taken care of, Ally," Christian interrupted. "Fleming doesn't know I burned them. Black Brothers agreed to pay all damages associated with the class action suit the CST investors have filed. And I gave Bob Galloway's wife a nice check for her adoption agency."

There was a knock on the door.

"Yes?" Christian called. Quentin appeared at the door and Christian motioned for him to come in and sit down beside Allison. "I was just bringing Ally up to speed on everything." He'd talked to Quentin at length by phone an hour ago.

"You tell her about our great friend Nigel Faraday?" Quentin asked.

Christian shook his head slowly. "Nigel went back to London to one of the big buyout shops over there," he explained.

"Aren't you going after him?" she asked.

Christian shook his head again. "It's done," he said quietly.

"Sorry about Jesse," Quentin spoke up.

"Jeez," Allison said loudly. "Guess I'm in the dark about everything. What happened with Jesse?"

Christian smiled sadly. "He's going with someone else as his VP. Turns out Forte was the one pushing me, not Jesse."

"I'm sorry. That's too bad."

Christian nodded slowly. "Yeah." It was too bad. He'd wanted that—a lot. Almost as much for his dad as himself.

"I've got an idea," Allison spoke up, her expression brightening. "Let's all three go to Vegas."

Christian laughed. "I'm one step ahead of you, Ally. The plane's already waiting for us at LaGuardia. Sunday's opening day for the Dice." He glanced at Quentin. "First step on the road to the Super Bowl. We're all going to watch from the box."

"Awesome."

As they headed for the door, Christian caught Allison by the wrist and pulled her toward him. "I'll take you on one condition, Ms. Wallace," he said, grinning.

"And what's that, Mr. Gillette?"

"I'll take you as long as you agree that whatever happens in Vegas, *stays* in Vegas. Okay?"

She gazed into his eyes for a few moments, then nodded. "Oh, yeah. I'm fine with that."

ABOUT THE AUTHOR

STEPHEN FREY is a managing director at a private equity firm. He previously worked in mergers and acquisitions at JP Morgan and as a vice president of corporate finance at an international bank in Manhattan. Frey is the bestselling author of *The Protégé, The Chairman, Shadow Account, Silent Partner, The Day Trader, Trust Fund, The Insider, The Legacy, The Inner Sanctum, The Vulture Fund,* and *The Takeover.* He lives in Florida.

ABOUT THE TYPE

This book was set in Galliard, a typeface designed by Matthew Carter for the Merganthaler Linotype Company in 1978. Galliard is based on the sixteenth-century typefaces of Robert Granjon.